RID ENGLAND
OF THIS PLAGUE

**Published in Great Britain by
Paradise Press
BM Box 5700
London WC1N 3XX**

British Library Cataloguing in Publication Data.
A catalogue record of this book
is available from the British Library

ISBN 1-904585-08-6

DEDICATION

This book is dedicated to my partner
John
without whose inspiration and dedication
this account of the 1950s Purge would not have
been written.

It is also dedicated
to the many gay men who suffered at
the hands of the law and a homophobic media
because of their sexuality.

My thanks to the
Gay Authors Workshop
for their support and encouragement.

The freedom we have today was bought at a high
price by gay men who asked nothing more than to
live their lives as nature intended.
Why it took our learnéd Law Makers so many
centuries to see the obvious is a question
yet to be fully answered.

RID ENGLAND OF THIS PLAGUE

Rex Batten

Gay and Living through the 1950s Purge

This novel is based on the society the author experienced as a young man and adolescent. It spans the latter war years through to 1955.

When the free world was fighting tyranny it meant, ironically, that in the best British traditions the telescope of the Establishment could be put to the blind eye but when victory had established universal freedom the magnifying glass was put to the other eye. What it saw shocked right thinking society and the purge of unnatural sex had to be pursued with righteous fervour.

AUTHOR'S NOTES

The high profile cases of the mid 1950s have been well catalogued. In this book I have set out to give a picture of the society my late partner and I experienced. A society where there was no place for two young men wanting to live as partners.

The New Elizabethan Age had begun. The young Queen had been crowned. The highest mountain, Everest, had been climbed. The future was bright and the Establishment had set out to 'Rid England of the Plague'. The plague of homosexuality. Propaganda and indoctrination had convinced the bulk of the population that shirt lifters, bum boys, pansies and nancy boys were a threat to society.

Headlines proclaimed:- UNNATURAL PRACTICES, CORRUPTING INFLUENCE, and IMPROPER & INDECENT BEHAVIOUR.

It is a story that needs to be told. It was from, and because of, the purge of the 50s that the more liberal world we know today emerged.

Tom and Michael are the low profile gay couple whose importance has taken half a century to be recognised. They were not unique.

For those in the homosexual fraternity, the world was divided into two, queer and TBH. If you were queer you recognised your sexuality. TBH or the 'To Be Had' included all who played, but would not admit to being queer. Married men and a large number of ambitious males who for career, family, or religious reasons dared not admit any 'inverted' sexual behaviour fell into that group. Straights were termed 'normal' which, paradoxically, should have implied abnormality but in Tom and Michael's world such definitions did not apply. They asked for nothing more than to be allowed to live free from nametags and prejudice.

The society that tried to break them was, eventually, crushed by the weight of its intolerance and prejudice, exposed by those who dared to stand up and be counted.

RID ENGLAND OF THIS PLAGUE

Chapter 1

That May morning in 1954 promised a beautiful early summer's day. The rising sun lit the hilltops but had yet to reach the deep valley floor. The wife of the dairyman, in the little Dorset village of Lower Budleigh, was about to make herself a cup of tea. The kettle was almost boiling on the paraffin primus stove. The cottage had electric light but an electric kettle, or cooker, was way beyond the income of a farm worker and there was still years of wear in the old appliance. The kettle whistled. She ignored it. Two large cars had passed the kitchen window.

"That don't seem right. It baint even seven o'clock yet," she said to herself.

The main road that ran along the valley, in the folds of the chalk hills of central Dorset, bypasses the village. It is almost as if history considered Lower Budleigh to be of so little interest it could be ignored. A half made up road did branch off into the handful of cottages, a farmhouse, and a church but even that petered out into a cart track.

Common sense and, or, curiosity told the dairyman's wife the two big cars had either lost their way or there was something up. It wasn't even milking time! Nothing ever happened before the cows were got in from the meadow. The cars didn't turn and go back so there had to be something up and she had to find out what. There were only two cottages further up the lane and the occupants of one were away. So what was going on? Wearing only her nightdress, the dairyman's wife went into the lane to find out. The cars had pulled up outside the end cottage but, without making it too obvious, she couldn't see what was happening.

"He wouldn't have nobody calling at this time. If that blasted bush weren't there I could see, and that damned kettle, whistling like that it'll wake the dead." In her frustration she caught her nightdress on the rose bush. "Damn and blast!" she swore as she went back into the cottage.

It couldn't have been much more than ten minutes later, she hadn't had time to drink her tea, that one of the cars backed down the lane. Peeping round the door she watched. The car screeched as it turned, scattering the cows her husband was driving into the farmyard for milking. Then it drove off at speed out of the village.

The dairyman cursed the driver of the car but when he saw his wife running towards him still in her nightgown he was totally lost for words.

"What the. . .?" he yelled.

His wife almost screamed at him, "The police. That were the police! They've got Ashley-Jones. He were in the back. I saw him."

"Ashley. . . . You sure? Help me get these bloody cows in. Stupid sods frightening the animals."

When the cows were safely in the yard and the gate shut, he turned to his wife, "And you'd better get home afore you get your nightie covered in cow shit."

Tom Adamson's parents lived in a village over the hill from Lower Budleigh. As the crow flies they were only a few miles apart but the villages lying in the deep valleys of central Dorset were, largely, isolated from each other. News of the events of the previous morning would not have travelled fast enough to reach the Adamson's.

Tom had moved away from the village several years earlier to seek pastures new and escape the unreal tweeness so beloved of painters of the rural scene of yesteryear. Tom had worked on a farm and knew, only too well, how in that world of romanticism the discomforts of reality are lost under the distorting mirror of the artists' colour loaded brush strokes.

Tom's parents had finished their tea and were waiting for the *Dorset Daily Echo* to be delivered, as it was every weekday. The evening paper carried articles of local interest, whist drives, local politics and a sprinkling of court cases. It was always a comfortable, cosy, read at the end of the day. They had a wireless but apart from the news there was never much they wanted to listen to; often sitting in contented silence. Tom's mother pushed her plate back and thought it time she went down the garden to get her husband's white coats in off the clothes line. Thankfully it had been a good drying day. Tom's father was the village butcher and keeping him in clean white coats, for some reason called 'slops', was the bane of her life. She had a secret dream that Tom would become famous and make enough money for them to be able to move out of the cottage and build a modern bungalow. She had even selected the site, a field just outside the village overlooking a meadow and across to the church. She wanted a bungalow exactly like those on the road leading out of the market town. They had been built in 1938, just before the war, and had nice big bay windows where you could watch people go past. The cottage in which Mr and Mrs Adamson lived had no windows facing the road, but more than the bay window she would like a few mod cons, a proper sink and a lavatory. Their lavatory was a corrugated iron cubicle at the bottom of the garden, and it was her husband's job to deal with the contents of the bucket under the seat. That was important because it ensured a good supply of fertiliser producing flavoursome organic peas and runner beans in summer. Mrs Adamson led too busy a social life to ever think of leaving the village, but it would be nice to have a living room where the wallpaper wasn't stained by rising damp, where the doors fitted, and you didn't have to sit, in winter, with a draught that chilled the backs of your legs.

The *Echo* was thrown through the open door of the Adamson's cottage. In summer, the front door was left open; as it did not face the road there was no fear of intruders. Mr

Adamson had bent an old meat skewer to hold the door open allowing Vic, the Adamson's dog, to wander in and out at will. Tom's mother heard the paper flop on the stone floor.

"*Echo's* come," Mrs Adamson said as she did every night.

Her husband stopped listening to the news. It was something about solving the housing crisis. He had heard it all before so he got up, switched the wireless off - you didn't waste electricity, and went to the cottage door, picked up the paper and sat in the window seat to read it as he did every summer's evening. There was little of interest on the front page but something on page three made him stop. He closed the paper.

"Anything in the paper?" Tom's mother asked.

There was no answer. The paper was passed to her. She read the article on page three in silence as Tom's father had done, then put the paper down and began to clear the tea things off the table.

Mr Adamson shook his head, looked out of the cottage window across his wife's flower knot to the vegetable garden beyond and then up over the downs, in the direction of Lower Budleigh, and said almost silently, "Oh dear."

They did not speak about what they had read, but the following morning, when her husband had gone to work in the village butcher's shop, Tom's mother wrote a letter.

Less than twenty-four hours later the letter was pushed through the heavy ornamental cast-iron letterbox of 13, South Villas. The black letter box snapped shut nipping the postman's finger. He swore, as he swore every morning. It was the only flap in the street where the spring still worked.

"Bugger it!" he muttered to himself as he looked at the house, and went back down the half dozen steps from the door to the pavement.

The letter was addressed to Tom Adamson, 13, South Villas, Camden Square, London NW1. The postmark was Tom's home village in Dorset, and the handwriting was his mother's. The clear perfectly formed letters were the result of careful teaching in the village school during the first decade of the twentieth century.

Tom was working; he would not see the letter until he got home and he wouldn't be expecting it. Tom and his mother wrote on alternate weeks. This was not her week. It was 1954. Letter writing was the main means of communication. Telephoning from Dorset to London meant a half-mile walk to the nearest public phone from the Adamson's cottage and an expensive trunk call through a telephone operator. Tom's mother had never used a telephone. His father thought it best to wait. He was unable to grasp the full implications of that short item in the paper. It said simply that Mr Ashley-Jones of Lower Budleigh had been charged with gross indecency and remanded on bail for two weeks.

The article in the *Echo* was not mentioned in the village butcher's shop the following day. As he sliced the chops and weighed the sausages Tom's father wondered why. It was possible his customers had not bothered to read the piece. The headline did say *Lower Budleigh man arrested* and the significance might not have registered. The village was over the hill, and even if they had read it they may not have made the connection between his son and Ashley-Jones. But, and he thought this a dozen times, the silence was to spare his feelings.

At the same time as his wife's letter dropped through the letterbox of 13, South Villas Mr Adamson shook his head, not for the first time since passing the paper to his wife. What did it mean? Gross indecency, what did it mean? What did it mean for his son? Tom had lived, for several years, in the cottage at Lower Budleigh with Ashley Ashley-Jones, so what did it mean?

Tom would have been labelled a pervert or, at best, an invert though he would have accepted neither nomenclature. He had heard a nutty religious orator at Speakers Corner, Marble Arch, repeat what he claimed the Home Secretary had said, "I will rid England of this plague," meaning that by the end of his tenure in office the word homosexuality would be known only to scholars of antiquity. Whether the illustrious minister actually made the statement, or whether he believed he could do it, is beside the point.

Tom heard a man standing behind him in the crowd, listening to the speaker, say to his companion, "I reckon if a Martian landed in this demi-paradise, I think that's how Shakespeare described our land, just standing here or glancing at any newspaper the Martian would be convinced our new young Queen, and she was only crowned last year, is sitting on the throne of a nation on the brink of disaster from the exposure to indecency - gross or otherwise!"

His companion replied with, "You are so right. Penicillin has cured the clap and our upholders of morality hope to be applauded for finding the cure for non-standard sex. What more is there to say?"

Tom turned. The two men realising they had been overheard quickly left the scene. The idea of a plague or what the two men standing behind had said did not really register with Tom. As far as he was concerned all the speakers were merely letting off steam on their pet obsessions and his reason for being there had nothing to do with freedom of speech. Marble Arch was the only outdoor cruising spot in central London. The words that floated over the crowds had little, or no connection, with what hands were doing below the waist.

London gave both Tom and Michael what they wanted. They had friends and the freedom to live their lives, and there were lots of worse places to live than Camden Town.

13, South Villas where the letter from Dorset, that was to change Tom's thinking, had been delivered was divided into bedsits. A bedsitter was exactly what the name implied, a bed in a sitting or living room. The 1950s was the era of bedsitters. The large Victorian house just off Camden Square, in London, where Tom now lived with his boyfriend, had once been the home of a prosperous family with the servants housed in the semi basement. The imposing flight of steps up to the front door had, originally, clearly defined the social status of the building, but now it was very much part of a classless bedsitter land. What had been the drawing room was home to Tom and Michael. They were both in their mid twenties. Tom, who'd had a rural upbringing, surprised his parents by winning a scholarship to the Royal Academy of Dramatic Art (R.A.D.A.) and then coming to London with Michael, but Mr and Mrs Adamson had learned their youngest son was a law to himself. Unlike his elder brother who had been the archetypal schoolboy, an athlete and rugby player, good at science and maths, and now married and reproducing, Tom fitted none of those categories. He was queer, though to his parents, the word would have meant either peculiar or not very well and their son was neither odd nor sick. They had also accepted Michael as one of the family.

Tom and Michael were just part of the eclectic mix of the upper four floors of 13, South Villas. The semi-basement had been converted into a flat where the landlady and her husband lived. He was a handsome, thirty something, Italian waiter at the Berkeley Hotel. She had a regular male caller; possibly because her husband had so much serving to do in his line of duty, at the prestigious hotel, there was little inclination for more when he got home.

Mrs Urbano was a good landlady. South Villas, Camden Town was fairly up-market. There was a sink and a gas cooker plus a kitchen table in the corner of each room. The single bathroom in the house had to be shared with the dozen other occupants and the only toilet was in the bathroom. Patience and considerable self-control was needed if nature called when one of the other tenants was in the bath, but such an inconvenience was part of the world in which they lived and no one thought of complaining. It was the way things were in most rooming houses, and hotels for that matter. Mrs Urbano's bedsits were well furnished. Cutlery and crockery were supplied and the bed linen changed every Tuesday when the room was thoroughly cleaned. Tom and Michael got on well with her and she had said to Michael, "I don't mind what you do as long as you don't mark the sheets!"

Tom and Michael were lovers. Though they lived together their love had to be a secret. They knew, only too

11

well, that love between two males manifesting itself in sex was illegal. Exposure meant not only the heavy hand of the law - fines or imprisonment - it also meant being ostracised from, what was considered, decent society. Your family, friends and your job were at stake. Confirmed bachelors living together were O.K., though who did the confirmation was never defined. An important male personage having a live-in male secretary was also acceptable, but jail was the place for those who practised perverted love. Michael's working/lower middle-class upbringing had told him, only too well, that 'Pests to Society' had to be put well out of the way of decent folk, and all right thinking people knew that homosexuality was contagious. The effect of a touch on a penis could be incurable! Generations of theologians and lawgivers had told the populace so. No one bothered to discuss it. Such truth was unquestionable.

However, Tom, Michael and their entire circle were aware that the heavy hand of the law was no deterrent. There were enough other gentler hands available in the thousands of Gentlemen's Conveniences throughout the Sceptred Isle to bring relief from the hard facts of life, and it would have been the height of bad manners to ask if he who held your dick was married. Though there are no figures to prove it, many a family man, after making such contact, went on his way contented and better able to handle the rigours of connubial bliss. A fact conveniently ignored by the devotees of family life.

The threat of arrest was ever present. Tom and Michael knew it. Their friends knew it. What was the point of talking about it? Heavy fines, prison or public disgrace were realities. Realities they had learned to live with.

Whatever the law might do, it did not deter the two young men who loved with all the assurance of youth. They met in 1950 and had been together for four years. They were queer, so were their friends. For men who liked men, queer was the only word.

They were aware of the high-profile cases that had hit the national headlines, where perverts were charged with gross indecency.

But media reports are media reports. Tom and Michael lived their lives as they had always done, and felt safe provided they took reasonable precautions.

There was no need to spell out how fragile their world was. It was like crossing the road you instinctively knew you had to look both ways. If you didn't then there could be trouble. The queer world was pretty discreet. The camp queens, who, with the courage of their erections, flaunted their defiance of the status quo, were regarded by Tom and Michael's circle as being beyond the pale. As with so much in their lives they had never thought deeply about it.

Simply being in a queer bar carried a risk. The law had raided such places frequented by effeminate men. Police activity was a reality. The law was administered like a three card game. Turn over the man. Turn up the evidence. Turn in the man. The cards were marked. The police held the pack. They played the hand and won the trick.

Using the queer haunts (bars, Turkish baths etc.) was not seen by Tom or Michael as making any political statement. Had they been asked they would not have understood the concept. There was never a question of congregating in a particular place to establish a right to meet. By definition, such men had no rights to politicise. The United Nations might well have established Human Rights but that did not cover something as unmentionable as sex between two males. The Establishment gave only tacit permission for such places to exist. Overstep the mark and in stepped the law.

Tom and Michael were lovers not just in the sense that they had sex together. They were in love in the true sense of the word but the relationship was not monogamous which in their world was, paradoxically, a source of strength. They never tried to define or make rules. As with any human relationship there were disagreements and jealousies but neither had any doubt they were together for life and they did what they felt was right.

To their families, particularly Michael's, they were just great friends or chums. Brotherly love or comradeship might have been other words, providing, of course, it was all set on a high aesthetic plain, and all above the belt.

Tom and Michael had been in London for three years. They had not been back to Ashley-Jones' period cottage where they lived together for a year. They saw no reason to. They had started a new life in the capital. The Dorset village of Lower Budleigh was in the past.

Tom clanged the heavy door of 13, South Villas shut. He was home from work. The door always clanged. It was designed to be imposing. Their high-ceilinged room with two large windows overlooked the garden. The room was carpeted, and comfortably furnished with two single beds, a couple of arm chairs, a polished dining table and had a gas fire that seemed to eat up pennies in an almost hopeless attempt, in winter, to heat the large room. There was, also, a wireless that could get the three BBC programmes, named simply the Home, Light and Third. The one commercial station, Radio Luxembourg, was not available on their set.

The room did cost two pounds ten shillings a week. A fair rent and as their combined income was about seven pounds they were not badly off. It was within easy reach of the West End. They had, on occasions, even walked home. The tube station at Camden Town combined with the trolley bus service from the nearby Camden Road, that would take you all the way to Warren Street, made travelling reliable and easy. In a world with few cars the roads were comparatively clear. Traffic congestion had yet to be invented.

Out of habit Tom looked on the table just inside the door on which Mrs Urbano laid out the letters that had arrived for the various tenants. He was surprised to see the one from his mother. It wasn't her turn to write. It was Thursday, and he felt a twinge of conscience. He should have written home but there was nothing much to tell. Neither the Imperial Turkish Baths in Russell Square nor the White Bear Pub in Piccadilly were suitable subjects for a Dorset village Women's Institute gossip. Had such things been reported it would have shocked the Sunday paper readers' fresh home from church or chapel. It should be pointed out that both

Tom and Michael's parents took *The People,* a much less scurrilous paper than the *News of the World.*

He picked up the letter and took it along the passage to their room. Tom was 'resting', a theatrical euphemism for an out-of-work actor. He had taken a job with a leather firm in Kentish Town, within walking distance of Camden Square. In the innocent world of 1954 leather goods meant attaché cases, ladies handbags and soles for boots and shoes. Leather and sex had yet to become wedded.

Leather trousers were the preserve of Her Majesty's Horse Guards to be viewed in Whitehall whenever the urge demanded - it was the only place to see men in leather. Tom fantasised more than once as to what happened when those resplendent men got off their horses. The helmets and breast plates were mere historical campery but thoughts of those white buckskin breeches and high black boots held the plot of more than one porno masturbation.

Tom had been through drama school and it was on his future that his mother hung her hopes of a suburban bungalow, but there were numerous reasons why he was not now looking for any acting work. Michael had followed Tom to London from Dorset and had got himself a job on the headquarters staff of a major food retailing company where he had settled with a promising future.

Tom dropped the letter on his bed. He would read it after he had prepared the evening meal. It was pretty certain to be full of village gossip, interesting and amusing, but not a priority. That world was over a hundred miles away. London was, for both of them, an escape. Tom's family had accepted Michael as another son, but a gay relationship in a small community did create problems, and the big city offered anonymity with like-minded friends. As an aspiring actor with dreams of a great future Tom had to get away.

He was half way through preparing the meal when the thought struck him that there might be a reason why his mother had written when it was not her turn. He heard the front door clang as he was about to pick up the letter. It was Michael. Tom was holding the half opened letter when

15

Michael came into the room. They kissed.

"Letter from mother," Tom took the letter out of the envelope.

"What does she say?" Michael asked.

"Give us half a chance. I haven't read it yet."

"You had a letter last week?" Michael said questioningly.

"I know," Tom snapped impatiently, "I should have written. She's probably wondering why."

"Your mother is not like that, and you know it." Michael was always very direct. There had to be some reason why she had written. Tom read the letter.

Dear Tom and Michael (Michael was always included. To Tom's mother it seemed the natural thing to do.)

They tell me that Ash is in some sort of trouble. I don't know what it's all about but I thought you might like to know.

The weather has been nice and sunny. Vic (Vic their Golden Cocker Spaniel dog) *was bitten by a snake but we think he's going to be all right.*

Love
Your Mum and Dad.

"Let me see," Michael took the letter. He read it again. "Trouble?"

"That's what she says."

"What trouble?"

"I only know what I've read."

"Why should she write?"

"Could be anything."

Their automatic unspoken reaction was; 'Trouble with the police'.

Ash had been Tom's first great love affair. He was thirteen years older than Tom and it was through him that Tom and Michael met. Was this to be another of the high profile, meat for the media, sodomy cases? The police would have discovered that Tom had lived with Ash in Lower Budleigh for three years before Michael joined him there and

16

there was no escaping the conclusion they would have arrived at.

Ash's full name was Ashley Ashley-Jones but he preferred to be known as Ash. Tom was nineteen, still legally a minor, when they met; Ash was attracted to healthy country lads in their late teens and early twenties - a very dangerous attraction. He was then in his early thirties, handsome, virile, confident with enough charm for two, and a man compelled to keep a high profile.

Tom could hear the gossip the arrest engendered in the local pub, and he was certain the police listened to every detail including his involvement.

The couple said little that evening. They had no plans to go out. The wireless was on but they weren't listening. Their attention was focused on the letter. In turn they would look at it, trying to decipher whatever coding Tom's mother may have used. Had Ash done something silly and got himself into financial trouble? Since he wanted a life style to match his upper class hyphenated name, he had always been short of money. Whatever reasoning they applied they went to bed more than half afraid of the future.

In the morning Michael used a logic that Tom was only too willing to accept. He pointed out that they held their breath, the previous year, when Michael Pitt-Rivers was arrested with Lord Montagu and Peter Wildeblood in a case that became known as the 'Montagu Scandal' and was front-page news. Those three were sent to jail, incriminated by two airmen who had been 'persuaded' to turn Queen's evidence.

Tom and Michael had known Michael Pitt-Rivers. Tom had met him in Weymouth. There was never any sex between them but they became good friends. In fact, when Tom and Michael came to London he took them on a tour of all the bars, clubs and other haunts where no respectable young man would dream of putting a foot through the door! But their names and addresses were in his address book and an address book was the first thing the police went for in these cases. Their names were amongst the booty the police acquired. When that case broke they waited expecting to be incriminated but nothing happened. There were no visits from the law and the fear of being victims of the plague passed. Such was the optimism of youth that the pattern of life in the West End of London appeared unchanged.

In an attempt to find some peace of mind the two young lovers tried to convince themselves the same scenario would be repeated with Ashley, and whatever had happened in Dorset would not affect them. Like a litany, through their heads ran the words, 'It can't affect us. We've been away long enough to be in the clear'.

Tom tried a kind of logic by saying, "Mother would have told us if it had been really serious".

Michael tacitly agreed but in their hearts they both knew they were fooling themselves.

They were trying to see the Home Secretary's boast; 'I will Rid England of this Plague' as a joke, but no one was laughing. The church, state and media had been on a thorough homophobic mind bending course.

RID ENGLAND OF THIS PLAGUE

Chapter 2

Over two weeks had passed since the Police banged on the door of Ashley's cottage in Lower Budleigh when he was still asleep. He jumped out of bed and looked through the bedroom window. In the lane outside were two police cars, three uniformed officers and two in plain clothes. Barely dressed he went downstairs and opened the door.

"Mr Ashley Ashley-Jones?" the police officer sounded over polite.

"Yes?" Ashley answered. He tried to make it sound a question but fear had robbed his voice of any intonation.

A warrant for his arrest and a search warrant were produced. He was ordered to get fully dressed and collect anything he might need. The uniformed policemen watched his every move. Handcuffed, he was led out to the leading car and driven away. Three hours later, after being questioned and a statement taken, he stood before the local magistrate where he was charged with a heinous crime.

The second car did not follow. The two plain-clothes men began a thorough search of the cottage. They carefully combed it for any evidence; letters with addresses, telephone numbers and photographs that would provide proof of a life of homosexual depravity. Armed with such information the net could be cast and the catch selected for the fish the law wished to devour. They found a full frontal photograph of Ashley nude! What further evidence would the upholders of the law need? The fact that he had more to offer than either of the detectives did elicit some coarse envious comments.

The regular exchange of letters between Tom and his mother made no further mention of Lower Budleigh, and no news had to be good news. If anything was going to happen it would have happened by now was the logic both Tom and Michael applied. Tom's mother would have been well aware of any news or gossip. The fear engendered by the 'Ash is in some sort of trouble' letter was dissipating; after all they had been away from Dorset for three years and when Tom went down to Dorset to visit his parents he had made no contact with Lower Budleigh. Ashley Ashley-Jones was in the past. Tom and Michael had begun to breathe again.

It was Thursday. Michael was working but Tom was free so he decided to go into the West End and see what was doing and meet Michael later. The West End had the feel of a small town and you were pretty certain to meet someone you knew in or around Piccadilly. By the standards of the fifties it was a busy lunchtime, but elbowing your way through a crowd was a rare event. Eros was still a traffic island in the centre of the circus. Tourists had not begun to breed and to get a queer foreigner was really a catch. Social life revolved around the few pubs and coffee bars that were becoming the place to meet.

Penicillin had liberated sex. Sexually transmitted diseases, diagnosed in time, interrupted one's activities for a few weeks but they were not life threatening. AIDS was years away. As far as the clinic was concerned, if you did land yourself with a dose of the clap, you caught it from a female. To admit it was a male would have been unthinkable, even if the doctor knew better. Though one lab technician told Tom a bloke claimed he got the clap, gonorrhoea, on a railway station. How or where on a railway station? The patient would not admit it was in the GENTS.

That Thursday was the first time Tom had been out on his own since the 'trouble' letter, and he made straight for the White Bear, a basement bar, next door to the Criterion Theatre on the south side of Piccadilly. The White Bear was a Mecca for queers in the fifties, the word gay simply meant bright and happy. It was the place for meeting old friends or making new ones but it did have the ambience of a gentleman's club. There was no music. You shook hands with someone you knew or made eye contact with someone you wished to know. An embrace was out of the question. Tom wearing a suit and tie - standard dress of the period - was standing holding his half pint of bitter and for the first time for over a week felt relaxed when he was approached with the question, "How did the wedding go?"

He surprised himself with his reply.

What wedding Tom did not attempt to find out. He simply replied, "It went off very well." He had made contact and that was all that mattered.

An hour later, lying on the questioner's bed, smoking the obligatory cigarette, he was asked, "Have you been to a wedding?"

"No," was Tom's honest answer, "Thought asking about a wedding was an original pick up line."

"Damn!" said the naked man next to him. "I'd promised to meet this chap who was going to a wedding this morning. Oh well! Perhaps he didn't turn up. And who knows, it was meant to be. Thanks for lying. I'm sure I got the best of the bargain."

But things did not always work out that way. A couple of months earlier Tom had been down to Dorset for one of his regular visits to his parents. There was bad news waiting when he got back to London. Michael's gold watch had been stolen. His family had given the watch to him for his twenty-first birthday, and there was no way he could go home without it. It wasn't insured and a new watch would cost at least £20. A crippling sum as far as they were concerned.

Michael did not try to hide any of the facts of what happened. He told Tom everything. The previous Saturday he had been in the White Bear and had met a very attractive guy about the same age as himself. They had a couple of drinks together. Michael decided this guy who said his name was Rod, short for Roderick, was O.K. It sounded convincing, and the name had a sexy classy ring to it. Rod had come up from Brighton to see his sister and had made an excuse to leave her early to have a drink in the West End. Michael could see no reason to disbelieve him. By this time it was too late to get back to Brighton, so Michael invited him to stay in Camden Square for the night. There the first thing Rod did was to offer Michael a cigarette. Two hours later Michael regained consciousness. His wallet was empty and his gold watch was gone.

The cigarette was drugged. Michael could have been killed but neither Tom nor Michael dared contemplate such an outcome.

"We'll have to go without, save, and get a new watch," was Tom's reaction, "Can you get one that is exactly the same?"

"Yes. There's a jewellers in Hatton Garden 'Watches of Switzerland' and it's £20, I've got £12 in my Post Office book." Michael was obviously very angry with himself.

"We'll manage." Tom gave his partner a hug. There was little else he could do. Recrimination would have been pointless and unfair. Reporting to the police could not even be considered. Michael had broken the law and his crime would have been seen as being greater than using drugs to commit a robbery. The powers that be would have put the blame totally on Michael. Had he not been soliciting for an immoral purpose the watch would not have been stolen. He was guilty of inciting a crime and got what he deserved. A few weeks later Michael saw Rod again in Leicester Square, tried to catch him, but the guy got away. A new watch was purchased and Rod was consigned to the past though Michael never again took a cigarette from a stranger.

It was just after six o'clock on the Saturday, two days after Tom felt free to resume his old habits in the West End haunts that the tenant of the front ground floor bedsitter at 13, South Villas, Camden Square put the telephone down. The caller wanted to speak to Tom Adamson but his thick West Country accent, almost dialect, made it difficult to understand what he was saying. By the telephone was a list of names of the various tenants with their room numbers. The single communal payphone served all the bedsits and it was an unwritten rule that messages would be taken for the other tenants in the building. Knocking on Tom and Michael's door produced no response. They were, obviously, out for the evening.

The front room tenant put the phone down. His girlfriend, with whom he was living, came out into the hallway to find out what was going on. He shook his head and said, "I have no idea what message to leave. It sounded like some real country yokel. I could barely understand what he was talking about. There's no

22

point in writing a note. It will have to wait until they are back in their room. We will hear them come in."

"What did the caller want?" his girlfriend asked.

"I don't know. That's what I am trying to say. It sounded something like ash or ashes. Whether he was trying to say there had been a fire, I have no idea."

"Ashes?"

"All I could understand was Ashes at a station and real trouble. Tom must be warned. It sounded to me as if he was taking the Mickey out of the Archers. He kept saying 'tell him it be important'. Well, there is nothing I can do but wait till they are back. I must remember to tell him when he gets in."

His girlfriend then reminded him that they were going away and wouldn't be back until tomorrow evening.

"It will have to wait, then. I'll tell him when I can. There's nothing else I can do."

And the couple went into the front room bedsit and closed the door.

It was just before they were going out that the girl friend said, "I think we ought to leave a note. You know what your memory is like. Explain the difficulty with the accent. Say about the ashes and Tom will probably understand. We'll push the note under their door."

Tom and Michael were spending the evening with Denzil, one of their close friends. Denzil had done an audition and had got a small part in a revue going into rehearsal and that was something to celebrate. The three met at the same time as the note was pushed under the door of room 2. It was too early to start drinking and as they hadn't eaten they decided to go to Lyon's Corner House on the corner of Oxford Street and Tottenham Court Road. It was one of the very few restaurants the young men could afford. There, at the Salad Bowl Help Yourself, for half a crown (2/6) you could take as much as you could devour.

Denzil had arranged that they should join four others for a drink later. The meeting with his friends wasn't to be in one of the queer bars, they would be too busy and crowded on a Saturday night. Tom and Michael readily agreed. Denzil had an interesting mix of friends and it should be the evening the couple wanted, a chance to relax and forget their fears. They all met in the saloon bar of the pub not far from Charing Cross Road. After the introductions – names a nod and an hello – one of the four came forward and offered to buy a round of drinks. Denzil explained his friend had played a small, but well paid, part in the film Doctor in the House and could afford the round of drinks. This seemed to set the tone for the conversation after the introductions. The bar was not crowded and the seven young men were able to stand in a corner well away from the dozen or so other customers.

Though he was not actively looking for film or theatre work Tom was still very interested in the entertainment world. There were the usual bits of gossip about the actual making of the film but the main focus was on the star Dirk Bogarde and whether he was . . . . . The word queer was not mentioned. The reactions varied from a maybe shrug of the shoulders to "He's got to be. But use a bit of sense. A star like that has got to be careful." and "I never fancied him myself." to "I think he's gorgeous."

One of the group lived with an older man in a flat in Hanover Square, (a fact Denzil explained to Tom and Michael as an aside) and in the flat was a radiogram. He was, obviously, setting out to impress when he casually mentioned he had bought two records that afternoon, Doris Day singing 'Secret Love' and Eddie Calvert's 'Oh my papa' but that piece of information was only a cover for tit bit he wanted to say.

That lunchtime he was in Wards Irish House, a basement bar by the side of the Pavilion Cinema on the north side of Piccadilly Circus. The bar counter was an oval in the centre of a large room and, if you positioned yourself correctly, it was possible to size up any newcomer walking down the curved stairs from the street. That was exactly what he was doing and he did it to an American airman in uniform. (Even though the war had been over nine years there were still service men around, including Americans, in uniform.) The bar was used by queers, though not predominately so, and was never very crowded. He watched the airman who looked around the bar

24

without appearing to take particular notice of anyone. The Yank went to the opposite side of the bar and ordered a drink, took a mouthful then looked across the bar and casually strolled round to where Denzil's friend was standing. He placed his glass on the counter and said, "Hell, you look bored and tired."

"Do I?" Was the only thing the young Englishman could think of saying. He would have thought he looked anything but tired and looking at this beautiful creature in uniform he was not in the least bit bored – anything but.

"I know where there's a very comfortable bed. You could get laid," the Yank said.

To that, there was only one possible reply, "I didn't realise how tired I was."

The American pushed his glass across the bar. "I hate this warm English beer. Say, I'm from Alabama, do you think you can make it to a room I have in the Edgware Road and try some Southern Comfort?"

"Try me."

There was nothing more to say. Two glasses of beer were left unfinished. The exchange of names had to wait until they were climbing the stairs out of the bar. Oh and the records! They were bought in Oxford Street on the way back to Hanover Square.

In that sort of company each story had to be capped but Tom decided to stay silent about being the misidentified wedding guest two days previously. It was the film extra who chipped in.

A couple of weeks ago he was in Holloway and wanted a pee and there was a 'Gents' nearby. There were four stalls. Numbers two and four were occupied. The occupant of number two looked the most interesting so he opted for number one, unbuttoned and began to spray the glazed curved slab in front of him. Sadly, old habits die hard and he glanced to his right. He closed his eyes. What he saw was gorgeous. Unable to resist he took a surreptitious peep. He glanced down, and then a quick look up and finally a slow long lingering look down. The inspiration for wet dreams leaned toward the bemused, "If you don't get out, I'll have to arrest you."

He did exactly that. He got out, pinching his foreskin as he frantically tried to do up his flies. Later he thought it was very rude not to have said, "Thank you."

It had to be a policeman in plain clothes - an agent provocateur. Handsome young coppers were used to entrap the unwary. What his reason was for warning Denzil's friend off is anybody's guess. Cool logic should have said he was out to get the guy in stall four.

After the laugher died away Denzil made the comment, "Why go all the way to Holloway? There are enough cottages in central London to spend a whole evening going from one to another of these edifices without retracing one's steps. I've spent many an evening doing the rounds and knowing full well the risks involved."

"That adds to the excitement," was the observant throw away line.

Denzil did not, however, add that it was in the cast iron cottage off Long Acre that he met Michael. He did add, "I don't suppose there will ever be another time like last year, Coronation Year, with all the temporary conveniences erected for the relief of men coming to see the young queen, as she rode by in her golden carriage, or any other queen for that matter!"

"We were all there ducky," was the quick riposte from more than one of the group.

Michael commented that he had asked a friend what he thought of the splendid Coronation Procession and got the reply, "I was far too busy attending to the needs of her majesty's male subjects. But, don't worry, I'll be able to watch it in the comfort of the cinema."

The fifth member of the group, whose name was Terry and who had said little other than acknowledge the introductions, did intervene with the comment that the police were getting more and more active and that cottaging could be dangerous. He ended with, "Never forget every time you go into one of those places you are sticking your neck out."

Who added the obvious pun, "It's not your neck you stick out," is irrelevant. Terry started to say something about the

26

Home Secretary but one of the others, who had heard it all before, stopped that line of conversation with, "Not tonight."

After that it was time for another half pint all round followed by a general buzz of conversation including references to the Coronation, the firework display on the Thames and inevitably some comment had to be made about the huge number of servicemen looking for diversion in the Capital the previous summer, but none of the group noticed a man holding a pint of beer standing close enough to hear every word that was said.

After he had half emptied his glass Tom thought it time he said something and camped it up to make it all a bit theatrical, or maybe just to show off his R.A.D.A. training.

"Talking of the Coronation, though this has nothing directly to do with it, I was walking along Park Lane with a well-dressed man, I had only just met him in one of those temporary Coronation erections, when an obvious gentleman, obvious because of his well-tailored suit and the fact that he came out of the Dorchester Hotel, hailed my companion. The two knew each other. They passed the expected pleasantries, and then I was introduced and asked which barracks I was at. He thought I was a guardsman. Me a guardsman! I was insulted. It was not until later I realised, by pointing out the error, I'd missed earning myself at least a fiver. As you must know five pounds is the going rate for a bit from a member of the Brigade of Guards."

Out of the laughter came the comments, "He obviously reckoned you had all the physical attributes of a guardsman." and, "It did mean you don't look in the least bit like a queer or a pansy!" then, "You should have been flattered. I bet Michael never realised he had such a butch number for a boyfriend."

"O.K. O.K." Terry was determined to get into the conversation, "I am going to say my piece. I have a couple of friends who are in the know and it isn't all fun and games."

The collector of records groaned. Terry ignored him.

"Sir David Maxwell Fyffe, our respected Home Secretary, is deadly serious. Getting rid of us is almost a crusade. The number of arrests and convictions is going up year after year.

Since before the war they have gone up six or seven times, I can't remember the exact number, but they are out to get us."

That wasn't what the others, except for Denzil, wanted to hear. Remarks that punctuated Terry's words showed just how carefully the others were listening.

"I don't know if any of you have seen them but I've bought, from Selfridges, a shirt made of nylon. It's wonderful. You wash it in the sink then hang it up and it drips dry and you don't have to iron it. Perfect for living in a bedsitter."

Terry did not give up. "At the end of last year. When all the Coronation stuff had been taken down a chap came over from Australia. He's living in Kangaroo Valley, Earls Court, and he has shown me a piece from the Sydney Daily Telegraph. It's a report covering plans to make the Home Secretary's claim to Rid England a reality. The United States has given the Met advice on how to weed out homosexuals from government posts, such people are hopeless security risks. One of Scotland Yard's top men, Commander E. A. Cole, has spent three months in America consulting with FBI officials about the plan."

Michael took a sip of his beer and shook his head in disbelief.

The fourth member of the group who had made only brief remarks gave his opinion, "You can forget that lot. They can do what they like but they are not going to change anything."

"He works for one of our leading fashion houses I am not sure which." Denzil whispered to Tom and Michael.

"I've been to Paris, my dears, there is nowhere else to go for fashion. I was there for the launch of the Chanel collection. As you may, or may not know, my dears, Chanel has been out of the scene for absolute ages. Now she has turned the fashion world over. The 'New Look' is very definitely old hat. It had to happen. Chanel had taken the fashion world by storm. Slim almost sculptured and beautifully designed. I was told Chanel has come back into the fashion scene simply because she hates those flared skirts and tight corseted waists Dior brought in after the war. Why does she hate them? You might well ask. They were designed by queers, homosexuals, call the 'New

Look' designers what you will, she hates them - so I'm told. Watch out fashion will follow her!" and he felt he had said it all.

Terry raised his voice. "An American working in the United States Embassy claims service chiefs in the United States have been systematically trying to purge the armed forces to the extent of putting known homosexuals in a virtual concentration camp watched by psychiatrists whose job it is to make a definitive catalogue of identifiable homosexual characteristics. No matter what his service record, a queer is given a dishonourable discharge and thrown into Civvy Street labelled 'Pervert', and a high-ranking FBI McCarthy man with experience of hunting out Commies and Queers has been brought over to advise Scotland Yard."

The group were far too involved in their chatter to notice that the man who had been listening had moved away. In fact, the group had virtually split up leaving Denzil and Terry trying to make their point about the Home Secretary and his crusade to rid our land of this sodomic plague. It wasn't that the others weren't interested; it was, simply, that they did not believe what was being said. They moved in the world of ordinary, non-political homosexuals, who wanted to live their lives in peace and who, in their various ways, made a real contribution to society. But what Denzil heard from Terry was to have a profound effect on his thinking.

Terry was determined to have the last word. "Simply reading the popular press should make it obvious that ridding England of the Plague is no idle threat. Scotland Yard has sworn it will rip the cover off all London's filth spots."

Years later Terry, who voiced those radical views, was to clash with the Establishment and the law, but like so many others who made such a contribution to gay liberty he is unrecognised and almost forgotten.

It was time for another round of drinks. Michael offered to pay.

"Seven halves of bitter, please."

The barman turned to the landlord. Then he looked at Michael and shook his head and indicated he should go to the end of the bar where the landlord was now standing well away from the other customers.

Denzil came up to Michael and asked, "What's up?"

"No idea. The barman's pointing to the landlord."

They both moved down to the end of the bar to be greeted with, "I'm afraid I must ask you all to leave."

"Leave?" Denzil was indignant.

"I said leave. All of you. Now."

"Why? What have we done?"

"I am the boss here and I do not have to give any reasons."

"We have done nothing."

"Please go and take your queer friends with you. There's a place over in St. Martin's Lane you can go to. I run a decent pub. Do I make myself clear?"

The man listening to their conversation must have gone to the landlord and told him what he had heard. A pub, described in the press as being frequented by effeminate types, had been raided only a month or two before and the landlord was taking no chances. The seven young men had no choice but to leave. Outside Denzil exploded. Terry had told him what he needed to know and now the landlord had confirmed his thinking. Like sheep they had been driven out of the pub. It was time to turn and face the dogs that barked to the shepherd's orders. There had to be many queer men who think they are the only person in the world with such feelings. Terry had freed his thinking. Now he realised there were others with the same views. The anti-queer pub owner had done him a favour but, the present reality was, they were powerless. The landlord was acting within the law and they were outside it. Their conversation was unacceptable in a 'decent' pub. Denzil had read some of Gore Vidal's writing and he had said, "Those acts are entirely natural; if not, no one would be able to perform them." That made sense.

The group split up. Denzil walked away knowing his thinking was out of step with most of his friends, but what of that?

By ten o'clock Tom and Michael were back at 13, South Villas. It wasn't until they were half undressed getting ready for bed that they noticed the piece of paper on the floor. It was the message about the strange phone call the occupants of the other bedsitter had pushed under the door. Michael picked up the note and read it. He frowned, "What the. . .?" He read it again and then passed it to Tom, who took it, read the words and closed his eyes. Their reaction was almost a repeat of Tom's parents reading the arrest of Ash in the local paper.

"Oh my god!" was all he could say.

The note was put on the table. They said nothing. There was nothing they could say. Something very serious had happened. The 'Rid England' jokes had turned sour. They were afraid to ask questions. But there was no one to ask. Neither had the courage to even consider finding out more. There was nothing to indicate who had made the call. Could it have been Tom's father? There was no way of knowing. Tom could not contact his parents - they had no telephone. The two youngsters were beginning to realise how the law was working. To have asked too many questions would have aroused interest and the interest of the law was likely to be aroused soon enough. There was no way out. Tom's name was too closely linked with Ash. They may have left Dorset three years ago, but he realised three years was nothing. Not knowing what had happened, or what had been said, was the most frightening thing. Tom's imagination ran riot. He knew Ash's taste for nineteen year olds - he had been one of them. The recent high profile court cases screamed what the guardians of morality thought and Tom himself had picked up a soldier from the local army camp and taken him back to the cottage in Lower Budleigh. If the police discovered that, Tom could be in real trouble. What had the police uncovered?

This was all very different from being mistaken for a Guardsman or claiming to have been to a wedding. This was not funny or erotic. Being thrown out of the bar took on a new frightening aspect. Tom and Michael went to their separate beds hoping sleep would ease the numbing pain. Tom lay trying not to think. After a while he did not even hope to sleep. Pictures and sounds swirled, filling the endless space above him with neither sense nor logic. He closed his eyes and was totally alone. He was not imagining. The black space was limitless. If he opened his eyes scrapbook pictures from the past flashed in the darkness. Voices spoke but made no sense. Ashley had been arrested. The deep-toned phrase repeated itself lulling him into a distorted peace.

Scenes, disjointed, passed in meaningless slow motion. Scenes from the countryside. The countryside of Thomas Hardy but now there was no romance. No invented literature. No Tess seduced. Only a mess. He could see no bodies, though some of them had been beautiful. There was only a heap and over it all, like a storm cloud, was the face of Ash.

Tom must have dozed off. He was a kid again. He had travelled with his father out of their village and over the hill to Cerne Abbas and there he gazed for the first time on the Giant. But it wasn't a real giant. He had expected to see a huge man standing over the village; this was only a great big drawing cut out of the chalk on the green turf. As he looked the boy realised that the giant holding a huge club above its head was naked - penis erect. The boy had never seen anything like it.

Tom was to see the ancient form often, and familiarity bred a kind of contempt. In the chapel Sunday school it was never mentioned. Why should it be? Its origins were lost in the mists of time. It was said that a bride to be should climb the hillside the night before her wedding to find fertility. Whether unrealistic expectations were ever raised as to the groom's equipment was never discussed. The giant's gigantic phallus stood straight up. Tom and Ashley had looked at it together the first day they met. The thirty-foot erect penis was a fact of life to the villagers round about but to the boy Tom it was a thing of wonder.

Tom forced himself awake, to stop imagining. He lay still on his bed in South Villas, Camden Square and looked up to the ceiling above his head. He must not close his eyes. He stared. The shadows moved. They cleared and he could again see the Giant. Tom found he was no longer lying on his bed. He was standing, with Ash, by the side of the road looking over the valley at the huge maleness. The 180 foot high chalk figure stirred as if to stand. Tom put his hand out but there was no one beside him. Ash was no longer there. He was alone. The emptiness frightened him. His gaze moved up past the colossal cock and balls, past the huge round nipples to the face that had looked out over the West Country hills for a thousand years. The lines blurred and the featureless face slowly came back into focus. It was Ashley. The face smiled as it gazed back at him. The head turned and looked down the valley to where it had all happened, where they had lived together. But now the giant was no longer on the hillside. He was crouching. Prison bars closed over him. The clanging of the metal made Tom jump. He lay with his eyes wide open, but there was no escaping the reality of his dream.

RID ENGLAND OF THIS PLAGUE

Chapter 3

It was a Wednesday in early July 1947, midway between haymaking and harvest. At that time Tom Adamson was working on a farm and had been given the whole day off to travel the eight miles from his home village into the local market town. Wednesdays and Saturdays were market days. They were the days to go to town when farmers and their wives converged to buy and sell. For two days a week the streets were busy and some of the rural males might have intentions not directly linked to agriculture. Tom had expectations. At worst he could go to the pictures since market days were also matinee days. On other days the two cinemas did not open until the evening

The bus could no longer be said to trundle along the picturesque roads as buses had done through the 1930s and the war years. A new company had bought up the one-man operators and replaced the ancient vehicles with what seemed modern luxury coaches. The first part of the journey followed the river, through another village, before turning off and climbing the hill out of the valley. On a clear day, from the top of the hill there was a superb view of the rolling downlands, but most of the passengers had seen it so many times they paid it little or no attention, though they may glance above the hills to see what the weather was going to do.

On 'Market Day' there was a more frequent service than on other days of the week, and it was even possible to get a bus home from town as late as 9.00 pm! It gave you time to go to the first house of the pictures. Films were shown at 'two houses' not a continuous performance. The nine o'clock bus meant you were back in the village just before the pubs closed. A perfectly reasonable time for why would anyone want to be out later?

After arriving in the town and getting off the bus Tom went for a pee, which was natural since the eight-mile journey took almost half an hour. There was no one in the GENTS. Tom checked that the penny-in-the-slot cubicles registered vacant before doing up his fly buttons. He decided to count up to thirty before leaving just in case, but no one came to keep him company. That particular GENTS was the smallest of the conveniences in the town but the most frequented. None of them had an attendant. The establishments were far too small, but they were always clean with the brass coin boxes on the cubicle doors together with the brass and copper pipes, supplying the stand up piss places, all polished to parade ground standard. Who applied the Brasso, or when that work was done, was not given a second thought by the regulars. They had other things on their minds or in their hands, but whoever was responsible for cleaning obviously took a pride in his work. Tom often wondered if there was some message intended since each curved glazed division, or stall, was stamped with the words TWYFORD ADAMANT. The words seemed to have a far too mystic symbolism to be simply the maker's name.

It was mid morning, possibly too early in the day for what he had in mind. He reckoned patrons were too busy with trade in the market, but anything could happen so he counted to fifty before climbing the stone steps up out of the half-dark convenience.

Tom was nineteen. Six foot one and a half inches, tall for that era. He was not an athlete, and was not interested in the village football team but he did enjoying playing tennis on the village vicarage lawn. It had to be hard physical farm work and clean clear air that did more for his figure than any number of hours spent in a gym. The lithe sinewy bodies of farm labourers would not have won a Mr Universe Competition but they were fit with a very definite animal attractiveness.

Tom's clear blue eyes, set in an oval face toned to a healthy bronze by the seasons, were framed by dark hair that sat in natural, fashionable, waves across his forehead. His appearance was not a matter of great concern to him, though he had once grown a pencil line moustache, but when one of the village women asked him if he was trying to look like a film star he shaved the moustache off. He was once told he was bloomin' good looking, by a soldier who must have been well over thirty, but since Tom was only too well aware what the man wanted, the observation was taken as flattery.

Though he'd had a good education and passed his matriculation exam (the equivalent of A levels) his vocabulary did not extend to 'homosexual': another year was to pass before he even heard the word.

Had you asked anyone in the village, in the 1940s, what homosexuality was the reply would have been "Never heard of it," or "Isn't it having it off at home?" Sex was not a word in common usage. That particular activity was usually referred as 'it'. That was not false modesty. Everybody knew what doing it, or having it, meant. A female animal was served or mated. In humans it was something that happened. It was not a question of prudery. It was a matter of accepting that men were men and men did what men do. After all they had been doing it since time began.

There were plenty of dirty jokes, but the technicalities of sex were not a matter for discussion. Men enjoyed sex, whether women did was not up for consideration. They produced babies.

In a pause from pulling turnips on the farm, one of the older hands, known by the nickname Sodger, asked the group of three late teenagers working with him if they had ever had a 'gammeroosh'. The youngsters were mystified.

"Gammeroosh?"

"Dunno what you mean."

"It be when you get somebody," then he added quickly, "a woman, to suck your thing."

"You be jokin'. Nobody 'ud do that."

"Don't you believe it, boy. If you get half a chance, have it. You'll like it."

"Have you had it done to thee?"

"Mor'n once."

"Who by?"

"Now that would be tellin'."

Tom said nothing. He had not heard the word 'gammeroosh', in fact, he had never heard that particular act being given a name. Whether Sodger implied a male performed the gamerooshing was not queried. Tom decided not to join in the crude jokes and fake invitations that followed. Discretion had to be the better part of valour.

Such rustic philosophy worked on the farm and in the wider world also. Throughout World War Two morale was a priority. ENSA (Entertainments National Services Association) or as was colloquially know 'Every Night Something Awful' did a great job putting on shows where female impersonators figured prominently. Separated from their wives, girl friends and sweethearts the boys needed something. It was considered too hazardous for women to be put in the danger zones so most shows included a drag act to provide that something. 'Soldiers in Skirts' were a great laugh and applauded by the military hierarchy. These were real men who had dressed up for entertainment. They were brilliant female impersonators, but it must be remembered that there was a vast difference between what was great fun on the stage and what was acceptable on the parade ground. There was always the get out clause 'one expects theatrical types to be a bit bohemian' and more than one blind eye was turned.

Nobody would deny a bit of 'dressing up' did a lot for morale. Morals didn't come into it. They weren't an issue. The boys' spirits, or whatever, had to be kept up. The nation was fighting for survival, for freedom, for the rights of the individual! Chin up even if the hands were busy below the waist. There was a war to be won, and with thousands upon thousands of men with loaded weapons somebody had to shoot.

Service personnel were always known as boys. Our boys in blue, or in Khaki, but everyone knew they were men, and fighting men at that, even though a large proportion were legally defined as minors i.e. under the age of twenty one. When conscription was first introduced in 1939 the call-up age was   twenty-one but was soon reduced to eighteen. Tom's brother enlisted in the air force soon after the outbreak of war. In the 1940s the term servicemen meant exactly what is said; men in the service of their king and country and the word 'man' had only one definition and so, by definition, all our gallant boys were heterosexual. It needs to be pointed out that though bum boys and shirt lifters were said to exist, the simple fact was 'men were men' and classification was irrelevant. The accepted logic was that any male who fancied his own sex was not a man, which common sense should have shown to be illogical.

Watch any film, or listen to any of the popular songs, of the period and the one great truth emerges - boy met girl - boy got girl. The fact that, at least, half the romantic actors were homosexual was irrelevant. Their fame, success and pay depended on perpetuating the myth. Any other thought would have been unthinkable. Boy walked out with girl but only with the purest of intentions. They may walk together down an English lane but with never a thought of getting laid under a haystack. It was as if the whole structure of society would collapse if it was even hinted that Little Boy Blue wore pink. For the bulk of the population it was an immutable fact that marriage was the ultimate goal. No one will ever know how many men married only to find themselves, on the nuptial bed, unable to rise to the occasion.

As for sodomy that was almost as serious a crime as murder. Though it has to be remembered that, statistically, such a crime was extremely rare, even if 'Well I'll be buggered.' was a common and acceptable exclamation of surprise.

In later life, Tom Adamson felt that though he had never worn a uniform, or marched carrying a gun, he did do his bit for the war effort. Though official recognition will never be given, he is certain his visits to the various GENTS did help to keep up morale. It must have been much easier for quite a number of serving men to face the macho barrack room after a, not bad looking, country lad had lightened the load in their underpants.

If, at that time, most people had been asked, they would have told you it was a well-known fact that scandalous behaviour between two males was so rare as to be well beyond the experience of ordinary folk. Very few could, or more accurately would, claim to know, personally, one of those! For the very good reason that if you wanted that sort of life then you kept your sexual preferences out of the public view and any activity would be practised with the utmost discretion. Outside London, and a few other large conurbations, if you were to be accepted in the pub you had to be seen as normal. Minds were buttoned up as it was assumed trousers were.

Church and State thought they had done a good job. Ironically vicars could be dragged across the front page of the *News of the World* but, then, they were vicars. One headline said it all:-

What the organist saw the vicar do in the garden.
Disgusting, said the judge.'

It was against that background Tom grew up. Superficially it was the heterosexual romantic world of the novelist and their cultured readers but harness the horses to the plough and turn the sod and there, beneath the daisies, was a much earthier Wessex than the great writers dared record. Could it be that literary insight was unable to see that world, and if they had seen it what publisher would have even touched the paper on which such a disgusting tale was written?

Whether the war and immediate post war years were halcyon days or the calm before the storm is a matter of opinion. In the wartime blackout, the law enforcement line was 'if it is too dark to see then it isn't happening' but far more practical advice was 'if it is pitch dark then grope'. Modern 'anything goes' back rooms are a poor recreation.

By 1947 the lights were on again even in the loos, which was a mixed blessing. The dark days were over. Freedom was assured. A bright future was dawning. Few noticed the tiny black specks barely visible in the bright euphoric sunlight.

Within a decade the virus of bigotry would spread from government down to those who charged themselves with the guardianship of the public good and on down, down to the upholders of the law to whom entrapment became a game.

But all that was in the future for Tom. He had grown up in a village, but he'd been to London to stay with relations whilst most villagers travelled no further than the nearest market town. He was now a farm hand, something he never intended. Farm labourers left the village school at fourteen. Any education beyond that age was considered a waste of time. In fact, it would not have even been considered unless your father farmed a reasonably large amount of land.

Two years' military service was compulsory for all eighteen year olds and Tom assumed he would be conscripted into one of the three services. However, there were two categories of men who were not called up; one being the medically unfit and, the other, those working in a reserved occupation i.e. doing work of national importance. Farm work was a reserved occupation.

Tom stayed on at school until he was seventeen, and then filled in the year between leaving school and his eighteenth birthday working on a local farm. He had no intention of making it a career. He wanted to go into the services - it was the chance, at eighteen, to get away into the great big world. The War was over and the chances of any real fighting were slim. He registered, as did all seventeen year olds, but was never called up. He found himself trapped as the result of bureaucratic muddle. Part of his papers labelled him 'Reserved', part 'Not Reserved' and part 'Don't Know'. So against this background he had to till the soil until His Majesty's government decided otherwise, which in hindsight was probably no bad thing. It was not until the ripe old age of twenty he was to discover, through the help of his Member of Parliament, he didn't officially exist. Eventually the Civil Service decided he would not be called upon to serve his country, unless there was a national emergency, and he could, therefore, change his job.

Tom had been born in the cottage in which he lived with

his parents. Until the outbreak of World War Two the village had changed little, in essence, since the nineteenth century. There were ten telephones, and about the same number of cars - a modest recognition of change. A blacksmith still nailed shoes to the hooves of working shire horses but tractors were replacing the horses. Steam traction engines worked threshing machines, but at harvest time the sheaves of corn were still stooked by men walking behind the corn cutter known simply as a binder since it cut and bound the sheaves with string. A major advance on cutting by hand, though combine harvesters were working on some farms.

The wireless brought the news and sounds of the outer world while the occasional visit to the cinema showed moving images of that world too remote to be real. The First World War was labelled the war to end all wars but its aftermath spawned the Second World War and so it was that the war born of the war to end all wars brought changes undreamed of by his grandparents. Soldiers in khaki were not surprising but Land Girls in breeches were. Girls had to do war work. They could opt for the services or work on farms, hence the name Land Girls. However, it was the influx of American troops in the nearby army camp that wrought the biggest change to village life.

In the market town things were different. Marks and Spencers, Woolworths and two departmental stores proclaimed the advance of the twentieth century. In addition to the market and shops there were two cinemas and three public toilets.

A warning Tom had received several years earlier eventually made sense. He'd been helping a farmer's wife pick apples which meant there would be a basket full to take home and since they were russets it was all the more worth doing. He was standing under the tree eating one of the forbidden fruits when the farmer's wife, whose name was Maud, warned him that when he went into the nearby town not to go into public lavatories. She had read about what could happen to young men and she knew. . . . What she knew was not fully explained. But it appeared that men who went into those places were the kind of men who often did not get married.

Tom did say, "I don't know what you mean."

To which Maud replied, "And it's as well you don't."

She also told him that boys were lured into those places by strange men, what they did to the boys it was better he did not know. Her warning went unheeded. The men Tom met in those places were not in the least bit strange. Quite the reverse. He could have been considered street wise, but since there was only one road through the village any wisdom had, of necessity, to be limited.

Tom was still at school when he learned that the information scrawled on the lavatory walls often meant exactly what it said:-

'I tossed a solder off be here on Saturday and I will toss you to',

That was a fair example. Grammar and spelling may not have been of the highest standard but the message was clear. The exact Saturday, or time, was not specified but experience had taught the teenager that any day or time of the day was worth a try. Only those interested were importuned, and nothing that took place could in any way be described as anti-social. The truth was that the underground sanctuary was the only place in which to socialise. The local habitués all knew each other, and were usually sufficiently well mannered not to queer another's pitch.

Dominating the road going west out of the town stood the castle-like military barracks, and there was always a good chance of meeting a lonely member of His Majesty's armed forces down there in the GENTS looking for a bit of relief. In barracks they lived and slept together. In the dormitories a bit of macho wrestling was O.K. even if it did have strong homoerotic undertones, but there could be nothing more in that mans' world. Those eighteen to twenty year old conscripts were to be in their seventies before the defenders of our freedoms were forced, in 1998, to admit it was safe to turn your back on a gay whilst working gel into one's privates under the shower.

A notice by the exit of one establishment requested, in

black and white lettering, 'PLEASE ADJUST YOUR DRESS BEFORE LEAVING'. The teenager always did as requested. He once joked about the word 'dress' to a soldier, which led to the serviceman servicing, and the young civilian getting his cum uppence.

The twentieth century had not reached the half way mark when Tom walked from the underground GENTS that once burrowed its way half under the back of the Town Hall. In the years immediately following the Second World War the West Country Market Town served the needs of a farming community. The fabric of the buildings has been preserved but the whole atmosphere has changed since those days. Then the accent would have been unmistakably West Country. Now a multitude of tourist languages and accents fill the air of the once quaint quiet streets of the town. The GENTS has been sealed and forgotten. One small piece of damaged brickwork shows where the iron handrail was fixed.

It also belonged to another age now municipally forgotten. What part the convenience played in the cultural life of the community is a question historians have yet to ponder. That it served its purpose as a convenient place for relief and as a Mecca for the eighteen-year-old Tom is beyond dispute. The term 'cottage' may have been used in sophisticated places like London when referring to cruisy toilets, but for Tom the word 'GENTS' said it all. For him a 'cottage', meant quite simply his home. The place where he was born. He didn't know he was queer either. He just liked doing what a lot of other men also liked doing, and the only place to meet was in the GENTS. (Some being more productive than others.)

That particular convenience had only three stalls and two penny in the slot cubicles (with carefully carved holes, at the right height in the doors). It was a question of tactics whether one stood in the middle stall or the one on the left. There were advantages in both. The centre stall was obvious - you had a 180 degree field of vision. The far one was in direct sight line with the hole in one of the cubical doors. The fear that there might be any danger from being so clearly visible, never occurred to anyone using the cubicles for the purpose for which they were intended.

Tom climbed the steps out of the bowels of the convenience. He crossed the road.

They passed each other where the wall of the church, facing the GENTS, curves into the High Street - the youngster and the handsome debonair man. They paused, and in unison glanced back. The youth walked on a couple of steps, stopped, looked innocently around as if unsure which direction to take while the older man walked purposefully in the direction from which Tom had just come.

Tom hesitated.

RID ENGLAND OF THIS PLAGUE

Chapter 4

The older man walked on toward the sign bearing the single word GENTLEMEN. The sign was chipped and rusting. It had seen better days. It clung to the wall as if to say the great days of 'gentlemen' had passed. The streets of the town were laid out in Roman times but the convenience dated, only, from the era of Victorian morality. Time enough for numberless such encounters. It was the only route a man in need of relief could take.

Tom waited on the corner. The man looked back as he crossed the road and gave an almost imperceptible jerk of his head. Tom did not doubt where the man was heading, but he was not the usual type. He was very handsome. Dark hair combed into perfect waves and clothes that only a gentleman would wear. He was no farmer. His photograph could well have been on the front of a knitting pattern. This was something new. Something beyond Tom's, not inconsiderable, experience.

The teenager turned, hesitated for a few moments until he was certain of the invitation. The man paused at the top of the steps. He was in his early thirties and. dressed in hacking jacket, waistcoat, cavalry twill trousers, check shirt and hand-woven tie he looked the country gentleman. His Brylcreamed hair, the height of fashion in 1947, gleamed in the weak summer sunlight.

Then, as soon as the prey started to descend the stone steps into the bowels of the convenience, Tom's eyes lit up in expectation of fun. He followed. He had slight doubts, but the magnetism was too strong. It pulled him across the street.

This meeting wasn't coincidence. It was inevitable, what queer life the town could boast was centred on the GENTS or the pub a little further up the High Street. You would go to the Volunteer for a pint and you might, even, meet someone but everything had to be done with the utmost discretion.

From the first glance Tom felt, instinctively, this man was different. His clothes and his manner marked him out. The backward glance, the half closing of the eye, not a wink, not an invitation was almost a dare, as he paused at the top of the steps. The smile as he turned left Tom no choice. Then with quick steps the man disappeared into the underground sanctuary.

Tom followed. He could hear his heart beating in his ears as he neared the steps that led down to the man. With each step he took downwards his cock hardened. He unbuttoned his flies. All he expected was anonymous sex. A wank in the stand ups or maybe more in the cubicle. It wouldn't be the first time.

He knew there would be no one else in the GENTS. It had been empty when he left, and so he was a little surprised to see his quarry standing at the far end well away from the entrance. The teenager had unbuttoned and pulled out his hard cock and held it in his hand. The man looked and invited the lad to stand next to him. He was of average height, five feet ten. Some three inches shorter than Tom. Stocky build. He turned to the youngster. What Tom saw made the lad's eyes light up. This was more, much more, than he had expected. A two second glance was all he needed, and then he gripped the well-proportioned, clean circumcised tool.

Footsteps on the stone stairs. They froze momentarily, then both faced front, and the youngster with one deft practised step moved from the centre stall. The newcomer was in town for the market. That was clear. He went straight to the centre vacant stall, looked directly at the polished copper pipe coming down from the cistern, undid his flies without flicking an eye downwards; then with the tips of his thumb and forefinger of his right hand held his penis whilst the rest of his palm served the dual purpose of forming a protective umbrella over that organ as well as directing a forceful jet straight ahead. He gave no indication that he was aware of the glances coming from either side. The handsome man buttoned up. As he passed he pinched the youngster's arse, and motioned for the teenager to follow.

When he had gone, the occupant of the centre stall raised

the outside of his hand sufficiently to invite a preview of what might be on offer. Tom hesitated. The choice was simple, a foreskin that might or might not be clean, or the well-shaped circumcised manliness he had held a minute or so earlier. Experience had taught him that rustic hygiene often went no lower than the armpits. There was no choice.

When Tom reached the top of the steps he assumed his potential sex would be heading for the town centre. He was wrong. He looked left and saw no one; and was about to run that way thinking his quarry had turned the corner when he saw the back of the well-tailored hacking jacket sauntering away in the other direction. The man looked back, smiled and with the faintest movement of the head invited the youngster to follow.

Tom had his hand on the iron handrail of the steps. He tightened his grip and looked. He had no idea what he felt. He knew he had to follow. This man epitomised his dreams. The expensive tweed jacket with a suede leather shoulder patch on which to rest a gun, the soft, sensual, cavalry twill trousers, were clothes Tom had only been able to admire in the window of the town's one classy men's outfitter. He wanted to feel the soft, sensual crotch; to slowly undo the fly buttons. Then to stop and feel the strong legs that filled the tailored trousers as if they had grown into them. How long did it take to think this? Such infinite time is timeless. Fascinated, spellbound, mesmerised, he watched the man stroll carelessly along. His assurance made Tom gasp.

When he went down into the GENTS, Tom was only after a quick bit of sex. How could he know that with each step he was climbing out of his past and into an unknown future? It was to be several years before he realised that the instantaneous choice he had made between a cut and an uncut was to change the course of his life. In reality it wasn't that simple. What he saw was the choice between a farmer and a gentleman. The mundane against the glamorous. Tom did not hurry. He watched the walk and closed his eyes in anticipation. He eventually caught up.

"Hello."

"Hello."

"Let's walk."

Together they strolled on.

"I'm Ash," said the man and held out his hand.

"Ash," Tom repeated. It was a name he had never heard before.

"That's right. It's really Ashley; it's derived from an old family name. I prefer Ash. It's less pretentious. And you are?"

"Tom."

"Hello Tom," and they shook hands, "A good straight-forward name."

"As a kid was I was called Little Tommy and I hated it. Then when I was about nine, a man lodged with us. He was felling trees up in the wood. Big Tom they called him and he called me 'Tom' and ever since then I've only ever answered to Tom."

Tom was doing his best to appear relaxed, but the ease and charm of this man was making it difficult to even think. Tom knew the town and could see no reason for walking in this particular direction. He could only think that Ash had to be a stranger in town. There was, certainly, nowhere in the direction they were heading for what he had in mind. The footpath was very quiet, hardly anyone used it, and it was mid morning. But there was no privacy. On one side was a high wall and on the other a six-foot drop into a road that wound its way down and out of the town. It would be silly to try anything there.

"Were you interested in that chap - the one who came into the GENTS?"

Tom sensed this was more than a simple question. It was almost an accusation. In spite of the charm the question was really; "How could you have looked at anyone else when there was me?"

"No, no. Did you think I was?" This again was made to sound like a joke. Ash was satisfied. The look in the young man's eyes told him he had scored again.

Then Ash asked, "What's behind this wall?"

He was referring to the high featureless hard red brick wall that looked totally out of place with the older buildings of the town.

"It's the prison," said Tom, "Don't you know the town?"

"Yah, fairly well."

"When you come in, on the Lynscombe road, you can see the prison building. It dominates the skyline. I see it every time I come into town."

"I drive in from the opposite direction and have to keep my eyes on the road," he said with a half laugh, characteristic of Ash's manner of speech, "I know how to steer clear of trouble," said with absolute self-assurance.

Then Ash added, "I could teach you a lot," as he looked the youngster up and down.

Tom's brain stopped working. Here was a film star, but the screen had gone blank. Instead of being drawn on, he felt like walking away. He was out of his depth, in the shallow stream that ran through the garden of his parents' cottage.

"Shall we walk on?" brought him back to a kind of reality. The pair strolled on to where they could look out over water meadows, and where they were not overlooked. An ancient rusting iron seat, set against the prison wall proved a good stopping place. Ash sat, unbuttoned his jacket, and spread his legs. It seemed a deliberate invitation. Tom looked at the crotch and started to move his hand towards the bulging prize. Ash shook his head. Tom stopped.

"I think you're worth more than a grope," was Ash's comment and he added, "What do you do?"

Tom naïvely thought the question referred to his social or working life. Being asked one's sexual predilection was not part of his experience. For this country boy, sex was still a matter of continuous experiment. He had yet to learn the intricacies of role-play.

"Do? All sorts," was the reply. His intention was to impress, and he started to explain that he helped run a social club in the village. They had put on a pantomime.

Ash, realising what the youngster thought, cut in, and again with his half laugh said, "Are you in the army?"

The youngster shook his head. "Never been called up."

"So what work do you do, then?"

"On a farm."

"A farm labourer!" Ash's eyes lit up. Tom was too unsophisticated to hear the bells, in Ash's head, ringing *'rough trade'*. "You have a very charming accent," he wasn't being condescending, and when he added "Earthy" it was meant as a sexual tribute, "Working on the land will probably do you more good that marching up and down on a parade ground."

The fact that there could be anything glamorous in hard physical work was something Tom could not understand. He had done backbreaking work in the wet and the cold and reckoned there were better ways to spend your life. Two years in the Navy was what he'd wanted. Now, in his late teens he was feeling the urge to move. He was outgrowing the constraints of village life. There was a world beyond the hills that ringed his village and he wanted to see some of it. Ash had, obviously, been part of that world. Tom wanted both the man and his world.

"You were in the services?"

"A rather lowly lieutenant. I've been demobbed eighteen months." Those two sentences were almost thrown away, but the next was an order. "Take off your coat."

Unquestioningly, the teenager did as he was told though he had no idea why. "Turn round, with your back to me."

Tom turned and stood still, thinking he might have split his trousers he put his hand on his arse and felt the seam running down between his checks. This was exactly the turn-on Ash wanted. He opened his mouth, took a deep slow breath, as his eyes measured the tight, round, firm arse.

"Your trousers are too tight."

Tom turned back and he saw that Ash was standing with his hands in his pockets rubbing his crotch.

"Clothes are rationed," was all Tom could say. He was unsure what to do. Clothes were rationed and with his non-conformist background he knew there had to be a good reason before anything was discarded. He had grown into and out of the trousers he was wearing. His waist was still fine and slim but his thighs and arse had developed until now there was a real danger of splitting seams.

50

"You leave nothing to the imagination," Ash's charm defused Tom's embarrassment. What he said was far from true; unwittingly the teenager was firing the older man's imagination.

"Put your coat back on, quickly." It was a quick, half whispered, order, from Ash.

A prison warder said, "Excuse me," as he tried to pass Tom.

"This is a view of the town I don't think many people see," Ash said deliberately loud enough for the warder to hear, but the man had gone. He was a warder, not a policeman, and was more interested in getting home than worrying what two men were doing chattering on a quiet footpath.

"I think we'll get back into town. I have an appointment and being late is bad form."

They walked in silence until they were away from the prison wall. Then Tom asked, "What do you do?"

"I hope you'll find out." Ash answered and gave his characteristic laugh. Then he added with calculated carelessness, "I dabble in antiques, valuations. That sort of thing."

They were now walking past the GENTS. Ash looked down the steps and said, "I had no intention of going down there until I saw you. Why did you turn back?"

"I saw you," was the only reply Tom could give, "You looked back too," he added. That was a challenge. Tom was really saying, "Why did you look back."

"I liked what I saw. What are you doing for the rest of the day?"

"Nothing much. My last bus home isn't till nine," Tom was making himself available for the next ten hours. He had thought of going to the pictures but in view of what this man might suggest the silver screen didn't stand a chance.

By now they had reached the High Street. Ash stopped and indicated, "I go this way." He took a gold pocket watch from his waistcoat. "Are you prepared to hang around until this afternoon?" Tom nodded. His brain was numb. He couldn't speak. "Right," Ash gave his half smile half wink, "Then I'll pick you up at the top of the town at two. You are very good looking," he said as an almost throwaway line. Tom didn't answer. Flattery was something he couldn't

51

handle. "I have a cottage." Ash continued, "I've done a lot of work on it. Would you like to see it?"

"Yes, yes I would."

"We'll go," Ash said as he plunged his hands into his trouser pockets anchoring them firmly on the future. Tom got the message.

"Where is it, the cottage?" Tom knew most of the villages.

"Lower Budleigh. You know it?"

Tom shook his head. "I know of it. Never been there."

"That's something else new for you to take in today." Ash took his right hand from his pocket and held it out for the teenager to take. "Till two o'clock. To this afternoon." and added, "If you hitch your wagon to my star you will go places!"

Chapter 5

The late teenage, Tom Adamson's, eyes followed the handsome figure as it walked away. The name Ashley, alone, had a ring of class about it. He would wait. What did a few hours matter? It did not cross his mind that this Ashley (he kept repeating the name to himself) would not be at the top of the town at the time he said. The idea he might be let down did not occur.

Having grown up in a simple rural setting without the pressures to conform to an artificial set of standards, Tom had reached his late teens with far fewer hang-ups than many from more, so-called, privileged backgrounds. Neither his family life in the village, nor his education, had been plagued by any set of rules designed to force him to become some kind of male automaton. The only parental expectation had been that he should always do the best he could. A simple uncomplicated world, maybe, but there was another world beyond, of which he knew nothing. How, then, could he have had any idea when he followed Ash down into that underground convenience he was taking the first of a flight of steps that were to completely change and reshape his life, leading him to Camden Town, the letter from his mother ' They tell me that Ashley is in some sort of trouble.' and the garbled phone call?

It was only now, several years later, when faced with the harsh realities of the world, he realised how fateful that day had been. Ashley Ashley-Jones was directly responsible for Tom and Michael meeting and, indirectly, for them being in London.

Tom's original intention, that day in 1947, of going to the cinema wasn't given a second thought. In competition with Ash neither Elstree nor Hollywood had a chance. Film and film stars belonged to an unreal unattainable world. The well-dressed man and his outstanding manhood was real and attainable. It was that vision which completely clouded the

53

youngster's thinking. He walked slap into a lamppost in the High Street because all he could see was that man. Ashley Ashley-Jones: the name alone set the man apart. That, coupled with his clothes, looks, and his other assets were as much as Tom could handle. But he had never been one to shrink away from a challenge. It was a question of precopulation or preoccupation; the word hardly matters, the effect was the same.

It was only a few weeks before that fateful day he had told a lad on the farm he felt like a square peg in a round hole. Whether one can ever change one's shape or the shape of the hole into which fate has put you is a problem that has faced mankind since time began. Because of the government orders he could not change his job. He was stuck on the farm. He was not unhappy, but he felt unsatisfied. He did not despise farm work, far from it. He admired the knowledge and skill of the other men, but he knew it wasn't for him. His sexuality was a major factor. Having sex was not a problem. There was never any shortage of partners. That was not the issue. At nineteen he was already well aware that marriage was not for him, and he knew he didn't belong to the world of farming and village life. There had to be something else. Instinctively he felt this man offered that something, and the same instinct made it certain nothing would stop him being at the top of town at two o'clock.

When he followed Ash down those steps he went into more than the bargain basement.

'It was just an ordinary morning that became extra-ordinary day'.

The title of a Joyce Grenfell song and a cliché. But then that's life. The difference being that popular romantic songs end with a kiss in a perfect sunset but never include the final verse i.e. what happened next day. They, possibly, would not be as romantic nor as popular if they did. This time the extraordinary day's sunset would eventually be obscured as thunderclouds darkened the sky.

Tom knew the word pansy. There was one barman in a pub in the market town who did waddle a bit as he walked and was described as a bit of a pansy, but Tom would not have applied the word to himself. The barman was just plain camp but Tom's vocabulary did not include such concepts as camp, butch or macho.

He wasn't interested in having sex with girls. Why should he? There had been no problem with the boys in the village or with servicemen later. That his sexual activities would have been considered both immoral and illegal never gave him cause for concern.

'Your mates on the farm do it,
Soldiers in the nearby camp do it,
Even sailors in their skin-tight pants do it.
Let's do it. Let's have it off.'

Popular songs can be the source of infinite wisdom!

The young man wandered down the main shopping street. Woolworth's was of little interest and Marks and Spencer even less. He thought of wandering up to the Municipal Gardens but decided against it. There was a 'GENTS' in a quiet corner of the gardens and he might be tempted. No use taking a risk. Not that cumming twice in the same day would have been a problem; it was that Ash was something different. That word would not leave him. Tom did not try to define what he meant by different, he just knew.

He wandered not caring much where. It was simply a question of spending an hour or so until they met again. If meeting Ash was a coincidence then most meetings are. That they would have met sometime was certain. Whatever views are held about men seeking out like-minded men in public lavatories is irrelevant. Where else could they have met? No pub would have dared to be openly poof-friendly and no club allowed to exist in a 1940's country market town and it is doubtful if over half a century later such a club would have a chance in most small towns. Since both Ash and Tom lived in the same district it had to be only a matter of time before they stood side by side facing the brass water piping on the same tiled wall.

It is the reasons why the young man was in that place and

doing what he did that matters. It wasn't simply a case of a highly sexed farm worker getting on the village bus that morning. Tom's journey into town, for that encounter, started many years before.

In spite of going to the village Methodist chapel twice most Sundays, and listening to a wide range of lay and collar preachers, the idea that sex could be sinful was never a major part of Tom's upbringing. That sex and sin were synonymous was a quasi religious/middle class concept that had not filtered down to the rustics. Much of Tom's thinking was due to the attitude of his father who, though a Chapel Steward, was very pragmatic.

Years later Tom was to ask his father, "Dad one thing has always bothered me."

"What's that son?"

"How have you squared your Guinness with your chapel going?" (Alcohol was a devil's snare to a nonconformist.)

"Well, it's like this. I be happy, but you look at some of the other buggers."

And a few slip-ups were not so terrible. Tom's elder brother was born just five months after his parents' marriage! Tom's religious hang-ups were to come later.

When he was still in primary school he heard two women gossiping in the village street. They must have known he was passing but made no attempt to lower their voices. One, whose husband was known to be visiting a certain lady living in another village not too far away, was saying, "What she has to put up with I don't."

To which the other replied: "You be lucky," and she pointed to the baby in the pram she was pushing; "I had to produce him on a pint of piss on a Saturday night."

Whether that was a crude, or simply an earthy, statement of fact depends on the reaction of the listener, but it was an obvious reference to the reality of marriage. It was nothing more than a contract where she was expected to lie back and be shagged when her old man got back from the pub with enough beer in him to fan the embers of desire into producing a spark, and enough blood pressure to pump up an erection to last a few minutes. Hardly the stuff of great romance!

There was, too, the conversation in the village smithy (blacksmith's). The smith said to a carter who was watching his horse being shod, "Hear your wife's had another little 'un."

"Arr," was the snort of agreement.

"How many's that?" the smith asked.

"Six," and the family man added, "Doctor said I should keep me prick in me pocket."

Tom remembered the exact words but whether the carter had quoted the medic verbatim is another matter. What's important is that it was not considered wrong to discuss family planning in front of a ten year old.

Again a little too earthy for even the fertile world of Victorian art, and a little too hardy for great literature!

Living in the depth of the country there was so much shagging going on around that it had to be all part of the wonderful world God created. Dogs, sheep and cattle did it publicly. Cats were much more discreet. Tom could never remember seeing a tomcat on the job.

With so many examples to follow it was only natural that boys should experiment, and since animals had four legs it invited a particular form of experimentation. In the corner of a field high above the village, one summer's day, three schoolboys did take their clothes off and took turns at being a bull with two cows. Corruption didn't come into it.

West Country rural morality often gave a deceptive appearance of rigid Puritanism. The truth was much more complex. Any community that had lived with itself for centuries must have developed a mechanism for coping with, and absorbing, the oddball in whatever form he, or she, appeared. Certainly, human frailty could not be lost in the village but it could be accommodated. People erring and straying like lost sheep was a simple fact of life and as long as they did not stray too far, and not where they could be seen, then there was no great problem.

The erring started by scrumping apples in Eden. The straying followed the covering up of that unmentionable bit of the anatomy which has provided the human race with a great deal of pleasure ever since. But in a tightly knit community there had to be boundaries beyond which the sheep, and in particular the ewes (rams had more leeway) did not stray. If they went too far the dogs, dog-collared, would round them up, but if it was simply a case of finding some tasty nibble away from the flock that could be accommodated.

In a predominately non-conformist community a puritan sex ethic would have been expected. That wasn't the case in Tom's upbringing. Historical factors, undoubtedly, had a bearing on attitudes. Unlike some of the surrounding villages, where the Lord of the Manor could exert real influence, the houses and land of Tom's village belonged to an absentee landlord whose only interest was income from rents. There wasn't even a resident agent.

This had a strong liberating effect on Tom's father, and may well have shaped his thinking, since he grew up in a village where the landowner's family was, virtually, all powerful. The squire owned most of the village including the farms. The inhabitants worked on his land and lived in his houses. He was, also, the local magistrate. His brother was the vicar. Temporal and spiritual dominance. A Nonconformist chapel was built on one of the very few bits of land that did not belong to the squire's family. A row of trees was very quickly planted to screen the offending edifice from, even, the servant quarters in the manor house. Tom's grandfather nearly lost his job as village blacksmith when he foolishly claimed to have voted Liberal in blatant defiance of the Tory candidate who happened to be a member of ruling family.

None of that applied to Tom's village of Lynscombe. Over the years the village had become a refuge for dissenters, both political and religious. There was no single person or family who could dominate politically or morally. Even the manor house was rented and so, in common with rural communities world wide, the villagers had learned to handle the whole range of human behaviour providing it was done within the accepted rules. This was simply being realistic. Centuries of experience had evolved a system that made life bearable. The first and greatest rule being that any unusual activities did not upset the family, or frighten the horses. In fact, rules that worked.

Early in his life, before he had grasped the facts of sexuality, Tom did experience some confusion. By the time he was seven he was able to read fairly fluently, and since his mother regularly contributed items of news, weddings, funerals, whist drives etc. for the *County Chronicle*. He often tried to read the paper. The problem arose with a report of a court case involving a local vicar accused of immorality, which Tom read as immortality - only a matter of having T in the wrong place! To the boy's logic becoming immortal was what it was all about. His questions yielded one important truth; 'Little boys do not ask questions'.

This advice stood him in good stead. His naturally curious nature drove him to find answers for himself, and on reaching puberty he decided he could work out his own sexuality.

Guided by instinct, and a few helping hands, he was able to take a firm hold of the problem, free from adult misinformation and spurious morality. Even the constant battering from the establishment, including newspapers and the wireless, telling him what a real boy was, did not deflect him from running on his genetically engineered track. By his late teens he had collected enough information to explode more than a few of the myths about our red-blooded servicemen.

Not long after the question regarding the immortal vicar another problem arose, which he knew would fall into the 'don't ask' category, so he didn't ask. This was the question of 'Adult Trees'. A particular lay preacher would regularly exhort the chapel congregation to heed the Ten Commandments, one of which must not be broken. The other nine paled into insignificance compared with the five uncompromising words THOU SHALT NOT COMMIT ADULTERY which Tom misheard as ADULT TREE. The boy knew what adults were; and he knew what trees were but why it should be such a crime to bring the two together was beyond him. Though he did have a sneaking feeling it had something to do with the Garden of Eden.

Regular members of the congregation had their own pews. No one would have dreamt of sitting in the wrong one. In front of the Adamson family sat an elderly farm worker who had misspent his youth in riotous pursuits. The demon drink had got him. Then one night, whilst weaving his unsteady way home, he found himself on the road to Damascus. Since then no drop of any intoxicant had ever passed his lips. His conversion was complete. Young Tom would watch him, and if sinning trees figured during a fiery sermon the reformed sinner would turn to a particular male member of the congregation and nod as if to say; ' That one fits you. So watch it!'

Another mystery Tom was sure he would unravel as he grew older concerned Adam whom God had told to cover his nakedness. He studied the picture in the chapel vestry but could not work out how Adam managed to keep that bit of rag, with no obvious means of support, over the only part of his body Tom wanted to see. One question was answered. Tom's surname was Adamson. 'My child, we are all sons of Adam.'

He also spent time during chapel services pondering a similar problem. The chapel had been built around 1900. Adjacent to it was an older building now used for Sunday school and the village scouts. Above the door and facing the road had been an inscribed tablet, now plastered over, but the plasterer had not done a good job and it was still possible to read some of the words. 'Primitive Methodist' were the two key words still partly visible. In Tom's encyclopaedia were graphic pictures of primitive tribes in Africa. The young boy would look around at the assembled congregation and wonder if the village matrons exposed the same amount of their upper anatomy when they were Primitive Methodists in the building next door.

The pictures of the African men were frustrating. Like Adam, the interesting bits were always covered. Was it possible that 'man' had, since time began, something to hide? Apart from fascinating detailed illustration of how a moving staircase on the London Underground worked, his encyclopaedia had very revealing photographs of classical statues. One or two were free of the bit of rag or fig leaves. Several nights a week his mother was out, Women's Institute, Whist Drives or the Social Club and his father would sit by the fire reading. Night after

60

night the young Tom would pore over his well of knowledge. His proud father would warm himself in front of the log fire certain his son was learning when, in fact, the pubescent boy was trying to pluck up courage to ask his father if he looked like the statues with his clothes off. He never did.

In a rural community, it was never felt necessary to explain the facts of life to anyone, including children. Nature explained itself. As far as the birds and the bees were concerned their sex lives were an irrelevancy. Birds hardly give themselves time to experience any pleasure and those wretched tail feathers must get in the way, but more to the point is the fact that they only did it in the spring, while the bees, on the other hand, are secretive. They have to find a queen in all that sticky honey. Some kind of moral maze?

Examples hardly likely to help anyone climb into the marriage bed.

RID ENGLAND OF THIS PLAGUE

Chapter 6

Tom was not yet ten years old when the lad learned more of the pain and hazards of procreation one Sunday morning at chapel than ever he could in the most enlightened classroom.

The setting for the Methodist Chapel was a pastoral painting. The structure, with its pointed windows, was unmistakably turn of the twentieth century and never likely to become a listed building, though the part it played in the social history of the village was immense.

The original site was too narrow to build anything bigger than a cottage, and so the hillside had to be dug away and a high retaining wall built to provide sufficient level space. From the field above the wall it was possible to look down onto the chapel's roof. The restrained mellow brick building feels as though it has grown out of the hillside and is a living part of the downland from which it emerges.

The village straddles either side of the stream that makes its way, lazily, along the floor of the deep valley in the folds of the chalk hills. This Nonconformist Chapel was at the southern end of the village. The Anglican Church was a mile or more away at the northern end. The two religious establishments were as far apart as it was possible to put them. The Anglican Church set on rising ground, dominated what would have been the original settlement, but through the centuries the village had spread along the valley and the site of the Methodist Chapel may have been, simply, the necessity of finding somewhere to put it, but the physical distance between the two religious establishments had great symbolic significance. The two denominations worshipped the same God with the same hymns but were a whole community apart. Tom knew that the headmistress of the Church of England village school could not bring herself to give the nonconformist edifice a name; rather she called it,

"That place at the other end of the village."

Even on the dullest day the chapel's simple interior was given a warm glow by the light that would stream or filter, depending on the whim of the sun, through the multicoloured diamond paned tall pointed windows. In those far off days there was little traffic noise. There was nothing to compete with the rich melodies that gushed from the organ. Across the road, in front of the chapel, water meadows filled the valley floor with lush grazing. God was in his heaven and all was - well almost - right with the world.

On the day of Tom's introduction to birth pangs, Sunday morning service was proceeding as a thousand others had done before. The collection had been taken and the Almighty duly thanked for such bounty. The average combined collection for both morning and evening services was one pound made up of pennies, sixpences and one or two shillings. Such a sum represented the equivalent of approximately a half a week's wages for a farm worker.

The congregation closed their hymnbooks and sat down after '*All people that on earth do dwell.*' had soared heavenward. The preacher rose to his feet and stood in the pulpit waiting for the shuffle of feet to subside when a farmer came in, indicated with his hand an apology to the preacher, hurried down the aisle to where Tom's father was sitting and whispered something. Tom's father nodded, got up and beckoned the boy to follow. The trio left the service.

Outside the farmer picked up a rope he had left hanging on the gate and the three made their way up the hill and into the field overlooking the chapel. The men were so engrossed in the crisis they had no time to explain to the lad what was wrong. As they entered the field the moaning of a cow in pain competed for attention with the speaker in the building below. The wretched animal was lying almost on her back with a baby calf was half way out of her body.

The farmer pointed to the calf. "It's dead and she can't deliver. You and the boy get the rope round the calf, then pull, and I'll try and help her."

The three worked, and the dead calf came free. The low

moaning became a scream as the sermon in the chapel below came to its climax. The calf was hauled away from its mother, and the stillborn offspring hurriedly buried under the hedge above the chapel. The hymn of praise for the beauty of creation, '*All things bright and beautiful*', closed the morning service, but the words and the organ accompaniment could be barely heard above the bellowing of the mother in pain. The irony of the hymn and the birth did not register on the boy, but he did think having babies all rather nasty.

In this pastoral idyll of rampant copulation someone was bound to take the boy in hand. In Tom's case it was a village lad some two years his senior.

The manor house is too late to be Georgian, and too early to be Victorian. It will not be found listed among the county's houses of interest, and though the village street runs within fifty yards of the front door, the building is discreetly hidden behind a high wall topped with a yew hedge. Villagers who regularly pass hardly bother to give a second glance through the pair of gates that gave carriage access to the front door. The building faces the rising sun and a shallow valley curving away into the distant folds of the downland.

A stream once ran, as nature intended, down the centre of the valley, but here nature was at odds with the ideal English landscape. The situation had to be remedied and the remedy, to create a perfect vista for those privileged to understand and appreciate the beauties of nature from the drawing room windows, was to move the offending waterway. Though to be fair, the re-sited stream becomes a babbling brook as it tumbles among rocks placed with great skill, through the trees, just out of sight of the manor gates. Then a hint of magic, the stream is lost in a pile of rocks and disappears into underground pipe work.

The inner, northern, curve of the valley is crowned with a beech wood. The trees, in their turn, are crowned with rooks' nests visible only in winter when the dark glistening branches of the trees claw against the cold sky. In spring the delicate green provides the perfect background to the one or two specimen copper beech trees planted to prove the skill of the landscape designer.

All this is nothing more than a foil, to guide the eye down the hillside and across the valley to the focal point of the composition. Facing the manor a ribbon of horse chestnuts chart the seasons. Spring is heralded by the flamboyant pink flames of the chestnut flowers that sweep the eye along the crescent and away up the valley and round into the depths of whatever primeval mysteries lie hidden in the rolling chalk hills. The chestnut flowers fade in the summer sun and the deep green band of leaves seem to glisten in the evening light at the end of the long summer's day. In autumn the green turns a rich flaming red before falling, telling rich and poor alike that summer is done, and also telling schoolboys that it is conker time. As so often in nature some seed will give pleasure but most will fall and almost all will never reproduce.

The chestnuts are the showpiece of this designer English landscape and are given centre stage but do not cover all the southern edge of the valley. There, a strip of woodland comprising mainly beech trees, balancing that on the northern side and acting as wings, complete this living theatre set. There is nothing in that vista to jar the sensibilities of those privileged to view it from the box - the balcony above the entrance to the manor.

In that small wood, stage right, is Arcadia. To enter, you pass between two square stone pillars that once supported a gate. The path curves as it rises. Here, the babble of the diverted stream, as it falls back to its original course, is almost lost in the overhanging bushes. The path rises so gently that it is not until it levels off one realises you are now above the valley floor. The stream borders the path and is almost silent as it flows along this level course. What other name could be given to such a path in such a place than 'Lovers Walk'? Here one can imagine the wooing of a bashful Victorian maid or the rustic swain enticing a milkmaid into the bushes, but as with all Lovers Walks the path leads nowhere. At the far end of the wood a gate opens onto a patch of mud churned up by cows going to the stream to drink.

It was in this idyllic, quintessential English setting that

Tom's sex education began. A village lad, Derrick, a couple years older and physically more developed than Tom, suggested they went up through Lovers Walk to get conkers. Knocking two chestnuts together had never interested Tom but he guessed that wasn't what Derrick had in mind who, at the ripe old age of twelve, thought it time to pass on, for the want of a better expression, a useful tip. Not for the first time a path that went nowhere led to sex. There on the soft mossy bank of the stream, where if the lovers were so romantically or poetically inclined, they could hear the stream murmuring its assent to the gurgles of pleasure and the rhythmic pounding of a pair of over charged balls.

"Do you know what men do to women?" Derrick asked.

Tom knew it had something to do with their 'things'. He knew that boys had diddlers but girls were different. It looked as though theirs were tucked in. He knew why he was a boy and his sister a girl. He knew what dogs did, but they were animals.

"I will show you." Derrick said.

By now they were well into the wood to where the path levelled out and the stream was barely audible though neither boy was interested in such sights or sounds.

"This is about the right place," Derrick said. Tom stopped anxious to know what would happen next. "We're goin' to lie down, 'cause that's what men and girls do."

Had this been a boy and a girl taking their first innocent steps into the adult world of love making in this romantic spot then this episode would be endowed with a timeless poetic beauty; but since they were two boys everything changes. Or does it?

"Take down your trousers." Tom did as he was told. "You've got to pretend you're a girl."

"What do I do now?" Innocence, excitement and anticipation made the ten year old look at his instructor's flies.

"You undo my buttons and take out my cock."

Cock! That had to be a grown up word. Tom was a good pupil and did as instructed. Derrick's cock was hard. Hard like a piece of wood, and it was different to Tom's. Tom had skin

66

that covered the top of his. The skin on the one he was holding was tight and did not cover the top. The pink top was free just as he had seen on horses when they peed, only Derrick's was much much smaller than any horse's.

"Lie down on your back." Dutifully Tom lay down.

Derrick stood over him. "If you was a girl you would have a slit between your legs. Close your legs." Tom closed his legs. Derrick knelt with one knee on either side. "The slit would be just there." and Derrick worked his fingers down into Tom's crotch.

"What do 'ee do then?" Tom feigned ignorance. He had seen enough animals copulate to have a good idea what would happen next, but even at his tender age he knew how some games should be played.

"I be goin' to show 'ee." Derrick leaned forward and pushed his cock down between Tom's legs, ignoring Tom's own hard cock.

"What have I got to do?" Tom asked.

"You just lie there. That's all a girl's got to do." Derrick pumped away. "I be fucking you. If you were a girl I would be giving you a baby."

Tom looked up, "There's somebody coming." Derrick jumped, "Pull up your trousers." Again Tom did as he was told. He was still trying to make himself look respectable when the man approached. They both recognised him. He was not a villager though he lived in the village. He and his wife had moved in from somewhere away; some said London. He didn't seem to work, but they did hear he wrote books, and didn't mix in the village a lot. He walked straight past, absorbed in his thoughts. He had not seen the boys.

"Hope he don't tell," said Tom. Instilled guilt made him afraid.

"We'll be alright," Derrick assured him. "He never speaks to my mum. We'll go home, any way."

The boys put their clothes straight and started on their way home. Just before they got to the stone gateposts at the entrance to the wood Tom asked, "What would have happened?"

"When?"

"If he hadn't come along."

"I'd have spunked. I'll show 'ee another time when we be somewhere safer."

A week or so later a safe spot was found in a half-ruined dovecote and it was there that Tom learned what made babies. Over the years as Derrick and Tom grew into men the lesson had to be repeated. A classroom was not hard to find. A barn, a quiet lane or a haystack all served in turn.

In due course Derrick joined the army and claimed when on leave in London his cock was sucked, in a rowing boat, on the Serpentine in Hyde Park, implying he was with a girl who did the sucking.

"Lucky you!" said Tom, colluding in a macho lie.

Tom first witnessed sex on a grand scale while still at the village primary school. It was high summer and school was over for the day. In those far off days there was no danger. Children could play in the village street or in the woods and fields. There were few cars and they travelled at a rate that made any speed limit irrelevant. And, in any case, they made so much noise they could be heard far enough away for even the slowest child to get out of the way. Tom was on his way home from school. There was no need to hurry home. Television was unknown. There was more to be learned out of doors. The world around them held the children's interest and that is exactly what happened on this particular day. A boy shouted across the road. He was excited and told Tom to follow. He wouldn't say why.

He just repeated, "Come on, come on."

Tom wasn't at all sure. This lad did get into trouble, but he was insistent and almost dragged Tom along. The two boys followed a narrow path between the stream and the back of a row of cottages, then crossed a bridge and along a lane to a walled yard. On one side of the yard was a large thatched barn used for storage and adjacent to the barn was a single storied stable. Though it had stalls for four horses only one mare was kept.

The boys arrived at the gate in time to see the mare being

led out of the stable into the centre of the yard. There she stood quite still patiently allowing the men to tie her legs so that she couldn't move. She stood still waiting to be serviced. The young boys did wonder if being tied up was all part of it, but decided it couldn't be.

The stallion was stamping in the lorry that had brought him to perform the function for which he existed. He possessed the finest characteristics of a Shire Horse; strength and docility. Because he was such a superb animal he had been selected for breeding. Had he not matched up to those high standards, he would have been neutered when still a young colt, and spent his life pulling wagons and ploughs with no interest in procreation. Instead, he devoted his life to being taken around the countryside ready to pass on his genes at his owner's command. The two boys watched the stallion being led down the ramp from the lorry. The animal raised his nostrils. He could smell sex. Tom put his hand to his mouth when he saw the enormous penis. He could not believe it. As the stallion mounted the mare two men, one on either side, held and directed the mega-sized tool into the mare. The stallion raised his upper lip as if smiling but the boys weren't allowed to stay for the climax.

The lorry driver, who wasn't a local, told them to get off home. But they had seen enough to know.

Tom was mesmerised by the size and shape of the twitching male appendage. His primary school friend intrigued with the mechanics of the operation wondered, as other country boys had done before, did your wife have to be on all fours and where did your thing go? Could it go up her bum?

Tom remembered his lesson in Lovers Walk; "No. That be only for animals. Girls have got to lie on their backs."

"How do you know?" demanded his friend.

"There's a picture in my encyclopaedia." Tom lied. Even at that tender age he knew truth had to be edited to protect identities.

But innocence has to end and by his early teens Tom had lost his. Such a statement has to imply that innocence can be equated with an umbrella left, inadvertently, on a bus and never recovered. If losing innocence is deflowering then, as night follows day, one has to go to seed, added to which is the fact that the only replacement for innocence is guilt, then Tom Adamson should have had problems, but he did not. Guiltless youth was blooming. He was now nineteen and, in spite of considerable experience, was comparatively innocent. His sexual knowledge would have horrified right thinking folk but he knew practically nothing of the great big world. It was instinct, curiosity and anticipation that took him up the High Street to the appointed meeting place at the top of the town. When Tom reached the junction there was no one waiting. He did not possess a watch but it was no matter. A 'given time' meant the time give-or-take however long it took. He would wait. He did not doubt Ashley would come.

From where he stood he could see the barracks. It still housed soldiers (conscripts) since the experienced fighting men were being demobilised and sent back to their wives. The war had ended a couple of years ago. Things were changing. Those permissive years were, rapidly, being consigned to history.

RID ENGLAND OF THIS PLAGUE

Chapter 7

An ancient motorcar came into view. It couldn't be Ash. Tom knew Ash would drive a much smarter newer vehicle. The car pulled up. It had to be someone wanting to know which road to take. He was wrong. The car was the first of many wrong assumptions. Ash was at the wheel of a dark blue Model A Ford; the distinctive 1930's car with its dickey seat and folding hood. The vehicle, nearly as old as Tom, was beginning to show its age, but it was still road worthy having spent the war years, half-forgotten, in a barn. The side windscreens had long since disappeared and riding in Betsy, as the vehicle was affectionately known, meant almost total exposure to the elements.

Ashley opened the car door and beamed a welcome. "Hop in," he said as he leaned over and opened the door. The young Tom, instantly, became bright-eyed and smiling as he jumped in beside the man who was to shape much of his life.

"I knew you'd be here." Tom nodded. He was tongue-tied. "You said you knew where Lower Budleigh is but you don't know it. I promise you by the end of the day you will," Ash added, with a knowing glance, as he pushed the gear handle forward into first gear. Betsy made a grinding noise when Ash's foot came off the clutch and the old lady jerked forward.

There was very little traffic on the road and Betsy was able to wend her way sedately toward Lower Budleigh. Tom paid little attention to the road as it meandered along by the stream through the valley. His attention was centred on the driver whose hacking jacket was open showing the cut of his expertly tailored cavalry twill trousers. The magnetic bulge formed in the crotch drew the youngster's eyes and would have drawn his hands with the slightest encouragement.

In reply to a question from Tom, Ash explained his reasons for choosing to live out in an obscure little village. He couldn't consider living on the outskirts of any town. The only place to live was in the country. Taking a semi-derelict cottage gave him the perfect opportunity to create a place of his own and, after all, it was only a few miles into town for old Betsy. Ash was proud of the old car and always called her by name. She had a top speed of just over thirty miles an hour on the level.

They passed a farm worker who waved a salute. Ash was, obviously, well known and liked.

"Would you have any way of getting over to Lower Budleigh without going into town?" Ash asked. Tom was sure there was a way. If an invitation were made nothing would stop him taking it.

"I've got a bike," Tom said without hesitation. Cycling was the only means of transport except for the bus into town. Owning a car? Forget it! But whichever way you went out of his village there was a steep hill to climb. The idea of cycling for pleasure was totally alien. Though cycling and walking were strictly means of moving from A to B, cycling over the hill to Ash's cottage would be a pleasure and no problem to the fit teenager.

Tom was not familiar with the first part of the road to Lower Budleigh but when Old Betsy slowed he knew where, and why, Ash was stopping.

"You've seen it?" Ash asked as the car pulled into the side of the road.

"It's always been here." Tom gave the obvious answer. They got out of the car and looked over the hedge to the hill across the valley, there, cut in the chalk on the hillside facing them was a one hundred and eighty foot outline of a naked male holding a club. 'The Cerne Giant'. The chalk whiteness made the figure stand out against the green of the downland. His nudity was there for all to see. A thirty-foot erect penis, surmounting two huge balls, had for centuries provided the world with the opportunity to gaze on ultimate masculinity.

It is worth a thought that had any village male stood next to the Giant striking the same pose he would have either been put in jail, or more likely into the lunatic asylum a few miles down the road. Tom had no idea of the origins of the figure. It could have appeared out of the swirling mists of time one primeval dawn. He had seen it before, but it then had been only what it was, the outline of a man. Its sexuality was less erotic than a drawing on a lavatory wall. Now, standing next to Ash, its masculinity throbbed with life.

Tom had no intention of wasting time climbing the hill. What he wanted was standing next to him.

"Could you handle that?" Ash asked.

Instead of replying Tom gripped Ash's crotch. "Not here. Wait till we get to the cottage," Ash said as he turned to get back into the car.

Since the main road did not run through the village of Lower Budleigh a passing motorist would only get a brief glimpse of the church and the farm house through a clump of beech trees, which is why Tom had been virtually unaware of its existence. There was a small wooden sign pointing off the road Budleigh-wards but that, too, could be easily missed negotiating the rolling English road laid out by the rolling English drunk, as a poet claimed. The road into the village curved off the main highway and turned sharply when it reached the stream. There was only a narrow footbridge. Vehicles had to drive through the shallow water and once past the stream the road was unmade. Ash's cottage, nestling under the hillside, was the last in the village. The road beyond the cottage became a cart track as it wound its way up over the downs.

The origin of the name, Lower Budleigh, mattered nothing to the inhabitants. There was no Upper or even Middle Budleigh so why a lower one? But who cared?

Tom linked the name with a soldier who whispered in the darkness of the wartime black-out at the back of the village hall whilst the locals were waltzing to a quickstep inside: "What I do to you do to me. That's budley for budley."

The phrase 'budley for budley', not in common use, may have its origins in the word buddie.

There were only a dozen cottages making Lower Budleigh a perfect retreat. It had no pub. A pint in the local meant, for the locals, a mile walk though Ash always used Betsy. Lower Budleigh may not have had a pub but it could boast a church thus giving it the status of a village. Without a church it would have been, merely, a hamlet.

In the church the chesty harmonium wheezed out annually *'All is safely gathered in ere the winter storms begin'*, but since only three of the cottages were let to people who worked on the land, the hymn had a cosy rusticity rather than a thanksgiving for the successful outcome of yet another year's work. In fact, several of the dwellings were, even then, weekend cottages. A trend well in advance of its time.

Ash did put forward the idea, in the nearby pub, that the whole village of Lower Budleigh be turned into a rural holiday retreat. This was greeted with disbelief.

The farmhouse, rebuilt over the centuries, was now largely rustic Victorian. It sat happily with its neighbour the church looking out over meadows. The perfect symbol of church and state.

Ash's cottage, in common with all the other dwellings, had neither running water nor mains drainage, though it did have electricity and could boast a telephone. When they arrived Ash seemed far more interested in showing Tom his house than getting him into bed. Tom knew only too well what cottages were really like to live in. He had known nothing else. A rural slum was an apt description. Lying in bed and listening to rats, from the stream, running above the ceiling was part of rural life; as were damp patches on wallpaper. Here in Lower Budleigh was another world. Tom was impressed. There was work still to be done. A post held up a beam where a partition had been taken out. Coconut matting covered some of the uneven flagstones, but the overall effect was class. The transformation Ash had worked moved the man into a realm way beyond simple sex. He had created a showpiece. A two hundred year old gate-legged table stood in the middle of the room and against one wall was a Welsh Dresser of solid oak. The best Tom's parents could boast was cheap painted pine.

The cottage known as 'Tuckers' is shown on at least one old map as 'Tuckers Bottom' but Ash felt that might be taking historical accuracy far too far. Since he paid a nominal rent of a few shillings a week it was not a bad bargain; and as the farmer, from whom it was rented, allowed him to make whatever alterations he wanted Ash had all he could wish for.

Thatched and built of napped flint, panelled with rough stone slabs, the cottage had weathered into the landscape. It was probably not much more than a century and a half old but in such a timeless setting dates count for little. The cottage was built into the hillside, and Ashley described how he planned to build a terrace in front of the house where the beech trees would give shade from the midday sun but as the sun moved round, you would be able to lounge, on a warm summer's afternoon and evening, and gaze out over the valley across the meadows and the stream to the hills beyond. This would more than repay such inconveniences as no sewerage and having to go to the well for water.

Inside, after two years' work, was the perfect recreation of the archetypal cottage that never existed. The original interior had been ripped out. Wooden partitions, erected to create snug little rooms, had all been removed. The ground floor was now one large, stone flagged, room. All the plaster had been stripped from the walls exposing a mixture of handmade brick and chalk blocks painstakingly cleaned and polished making a perfect, almost theatrical, setting for the quality period furniture Ash had been able to acquire.

Working for a local auctioneer had given him first choice when desirable pieces of furniture came onto the market, often at a bargain price. Coffin stools were at home by the side of a pair of winged-armchairs. Against a half-timbered wall stood a Victorian reproduction of an Elizabethan Court Cupboard, originally created for one of the Victorian/Elizabethan manor houses scattered around the countryside. Horse brasses, some old, lined the oak beams. And, as was very much the fashion in those post war days, lampshades made from old handwritten legal documents gave a touch of class to the wall lights and standard lamps. The inglenook had been bricked up with a small modern fireplace and the heavy wooden door of the old bakers oven served as a fire screen.

The centrepiece of the room was the genuine Cromwellian gate-legged table. The rich dark surface of the folding leaves, slightly bowed by time, were a memorial to the wax of countless bees and innumerable hours of elbow grease.

A small kitchen had been added to the back of the building. A Baby Belling cooker augmented with an electric boiling ring provided all the cooking facilities needed. Under the sink was a bucket that had to be watched carefully, in case it overflowed.

The cottage undeniably had flair and style, as did the man who lived there. Whilst explaining how the work on the cottage had been carried out, Ash gave enough clues for Tom to learn his new found lover had been a young man about town, in London in the late thirties, when one's name helped create one's persona. In addition to his name he had the looks and the equipment to please the most discerning. To complete the person, Ash, quickly cultivated the voice and manners of a gentleman thus creating an aura necessary to reach the desired social status.

The first thing Ash told Tom about himself was that he was married but waiting for a divorce. The marriage could not have lasted more than a year or two at most. What had gone wrong was never fully explained, nor did Ash explain his reasons for getting married in the first place. Even if he had tried, it is doubtful if Tom would have understood. The young man's experience of the world was far too limited. In spite of his education and his sexual activity, Tom was still essentially a late teenage village lad with little or no understanding of the complexities of sexuality. Being straight or 'bent' carried virtually no meaning. The concept had never occurred to him. He knew the sex he liked and avoided that which he didn't. What he did was as natural as breathing. He had yet to learn the crass stupidity of categorization.

He had been driven to what, he was certain, would be the most exciting sex he had ever known and it was neither the time nor the place to ask questions.

Ash's marriage had to end in failure, but he was not the first nor would he be the last homosexual to believe he could, for whatever reason, make a marriage work. The war was coming to an end. The world was looking to the future and he knew he had to look for a future. He was just thirty and too old to resume his role of playboy or bachelor gay. Tom's knowledge of the pre-war smart world was virtually nonexistent and nothing would have even hinted at a male orientated sexual enclave hidden beneath the higher, frightfully decent, society. How Ashley obtained membership to that exclusive club was never fully explained. He had, certainly, not been a rent boy. Patronage, maybe, but not hard cash. It was going to take a long time for Tom to even begin to understand the world Ash had inhabited in the heady days before the outbreak of war when his looks, charm and equipment could get him an infinitely better living than working in his father's Estate Agency.

It is not possible to place human beings in defined categories. Ash was an active homosexual but he'd had convincing sex with women. The war was coming to an end and he had to think of the future.

When he returned to civilian life he planned to be the country gentleman, albeit one with a profession since he could not be described as having independent means. To be acceptable he needed a wife, preferably one with access to a reasonable bank balance. His preference was for young men but he had no doubt he could keep a wife happy. He met a W.R.A.C. (Women's Royal Army Corps) Officer and gradually became convinced she held the key to his future. She was good company and sex had been successful. She came of a '*good*' West Country family with the right connections. Though he adored his mother, going back to North Wales to be near his parents was, therefore, not an option. The fact that his wife's family held the purse strings may have persuaded him to settle in Dorset. It is doubtful if he even questioned whether he could make a go of marriage. He would provide the handsome husband with flair and her father would provide the cash. It needs to be restated he was neither the first nor the last to embark on such a course. Many a family tree is decorated with such baubles.

The picture Ash drew was that he had married into a family of snobs. His invective was directed at her father rather than at the woman he chose to marry. It seems they took and restored this quaint charming country cottage to either set, or be ahead of, fashion. But Mrs Ashley-Jones concept of rustic fashion did not embrace a lavatory where the bucket was emptied to help fertilise the garden. Whether she discovered her husband's sexuality was never mentioned. The divorce was far from amicable. Ash arranged with the local farmer to hide some of the better pieces of furniture in a barn to prevent her family getting their hands on it. How it was all settled Tom never knew.

There must have been wedding photographs but Tom never saw them. The only thing he ever knew about that event was that the bride went to church in a Bentley. Her father considered a Rolls vulgar! What the bride wore was never mentioned, but Tom did see a photograph of Ash in the uniform he wore on that auspicious occasion. Nothing vulgar about that. Riding boots, cord breeches, tailored uniform jacket and peaked cap. Tom masturbated more than once whilst looking at the photograph and holding the breeches. He was too much in love, or too besotted, with the charisma of the man and overwhelmed with expectation to question the past.

Thomas Adamson had a lot to learn.

It was a full half hour before Ash led the way upstairs. The bed was bigger than anything Tom had seen. It had been built to special order, and because of the shortage of suitable cloth the mattress was black for it was covered with redundant blackout material, light-proof curtaining, manufactured during the war to ensure that all windows were totally blacked out. Tom could lie full length across it and did as soon as he had taken off his clothes.

This man and his house were in a class of their own and that was true of his sex. They did nothing that the young man had not already experienced, but this was different. Tom submitted to everything Ash wanted. Though he had never been totally passive, with this man he had no choice. He lay flat on his face and meteors flashed across the heavens of his tightly shut eyes. The contradictions of excitement beyond expectation, pain, pleasure, fulfilment and the power to move mountains were his as he submitted totally.

Tom had known that morning, when he first held Ash, that

this was the tool he had been searching for. The tool that was to prise open the door to a new world. What he did not, and could not, realise was that he had surrendered to a personality more complex and overwhelming than anything he could imagine or handle.

When he eventually got home that night Tom wanted to tell his parents everything, but since they never enquired where he had been or what he had been doing there was no reason why that day should be different.

His father was listening to the wireless. A very cultured voice was explaining it was the day on which the Bastille fell. The irony was lost on Tom who went off to bed, masturbated, and went to sleep.

Though Tom was to be with Ash for three years he never really knew him. It was long after they parted that he was asked, "What was this man, who had such an influence on you, really like?"

It was a straightforward question. It was easy to describe him physically but attempting to go beyond that Tom found impossible. It was like flicking through a photograph album where all the pictures are of the same man, but whether it was a trick of the light, the position of the camera, the pose or the setting, each photograph showed a different person and, remember, photographs cannot lie.

The lasting impression was that of a gentleman when the word is defined as a member of a caste where the semblance of good manners and breeding set you above the common herd. Hanging in the cottage was a pewter beer mug and on it was engraved the motto of one of our illustrious families: - *'Manners maketh man.'* Ash had learned well. No one could have ever accused him of being rough trade. He had chosen to be one of the traders. Tom was never to know the details of how the son of a provincial estate agent came to be accepted in a world where trade in all its various definitions was not discussed. But Ash had a disarming ease of manner that simply made him acceptable in almost any company. He had the easy sophistication of a nineteen thirties man of the world who could mingle and work easily with a squire or a farm hand.

If charisma is the result of genes Ash had inherited a warehouse full of Levis.

Though the photographs in the album labelled Ashley Ashley-Jones were all taken before the days of colour, none were black and white. Shades of sepia blurred each exposure. The analogy carried through to the man himself. There was nothing about him that could be simply defined as black or white, good or bad.

Ash did make a few references to his hey-day. The days when the skies were blue and the sun always shone and he was able to make hay. He would casually mention country house parties in the days before the Second World War. Photographs proved each claim. One was to fall into the wrong hands and be used to try and trap Tom. It showed Ash by an outdoor swimming pool set in the garden of a large and identifiable house. He would have been in his early twenties. A very fit athletic body with hair carefully groomed, but the focus was on neither the body nor the hair. It was on his hands. One was cupped under his cock and the other out stretched invitingly. The genetic over supply had not stopped with charisma. To say he was loaded would be an understatement. Over loaded would be nearer the truth. Who had taken and who had processed the picture in those puritanical days was never disclosed. To Ash that was a mere detail. The photographer would have been paid to work and keep his mouth shut. It was exactly the sort of picture the police would and did find very interesting. At that period the genitals of either sex were indecent except, of course, in works of art.

In another grand country house Ash, told Tom, he was present when the footmen served dinner nude with their cocks and balls painted gold. There was no picture to back this claim and taken on face value could be thought to be gilding the lily.

One incident that Tom did not doubt also concerned a footman, this time gorgeously apparelled in livery supplied by Gorringes of Pimlico. The Adonis captured the attention and imagination of the male guests, which was most probably the major reason why he was taken on in the first place, though the fact that one did not need to ask which side he dressed might

80

also have been a factor. Try as the gentlemen guests might, he kept himself to himself and all hands well away. Ash did not join the pack in pursuit of this quarry. He bided his time. In fact he waited until turning in time for the staff. Then he crept along to the servant's quarter, having first ascertained the bed in which the Greek God slept. The imperceptible rustle of bedclothes as he slipped his hand under caused no disturbance. The hand had no difficulty in finding its way. It was so successful that it was met with a firing that would have done the Royal Horse Artillery proud as a royal salute. The problem came when Ashley-Jones' hand proved too slippery to open the door for his getaway.

A few months later he saw the young footman trolling for rent at Speaker's Corner in London's Hyde Park. Whether this was liberation from domestic servitude is debatable. In less than six months the young man would be serving his King and Country for a few shillings a week. Tom often wondered what happened to him. Was his name to be honoured on some village War Memorial? If not where would he fit into the egalitarian world he had fought for?

Much of the world Ash described was way beyond Tom's experience. It was the world of a young man on the town at the time when Tom was in the infant class of the village school. The two worlds were whole flights of social steps apart. What Tom knew of Ash's world he would have gleaned from the Daily Express, the ultra respectable voice of the BBC or films, but none would have given the village boy even a hint that such 'goings on' went on. All Tom's parents would have known, or guessed, was that it was a world where smart men chased fast women. Men chasing men would have been as improbable as putting a man on the moon!

In Tom's experience sex had always been between two people but Ash was talking of three or even more. He would talk of men and places with such an assured familiarity that Tom never felt able to ask for an explanation. He would hint at events but they were always in the past tense. What Tom did not realise was that this man, whom he idolised, had qualified for entrée into that glamorous erotic world simply on his youth.

His ticket was date stamped. The ticket was useless anyway since the war had blown the smart world of the thirties into the past. The hints Ash gave did create erotic fantasies. He spoke of a senior lawyer who was rich and lived in Mayfair. This wasn't the Mayfair of the cinema or women's magazines. This was one where older men could pay, and pay well, to watch younger men perform. This shocked Tom, the young country youth. He had once been given a bar of chocolate for a wank and had parted with one and sixpence (7 ½p) to pay the bus fare of a bloke who claimed to be broke, but that was a different world. He was not too sure, either, how to handle the idea of a Horse Guardsman being hailed as a celebrity because of his ability to cum twice without uncocking. Given another half-century such pleasures would not be confined to the wealthy few. Videos would make them commonplace.

Ashley now wanted to be accepted as a country gentleman, but one who needed to work. He could not afford to mix with the real landed gentry so he lived as someone, so much at ease with himself, where pretensions were irrelevant. His ease of manner and courtesy made him acceptable and liked wherever he went. Though not a big spender he was always welcome in the village pub. He caused a sensation one night. From somewhere he had acquired a pair of flesh coloured theatrical tights and wore them to the pub under his trousers. In the middle of a darts match he dropped his trousers. When the raucous rustic laughter died down and Ash's glass was refilled, on the house, the darts match restarted. The home team won. The visitors claimed underhand tactics.

"Bollocks!" scoffed the winning team. And they all agreed.

RID ENGLAND OF THIS PLAGUE

Chapter 8

A well-constructed play, at that period, had to have a beginning, middle and an end. Great drama, Tom's studies at R.A.D.A had told him, reflected the human condition but he could never see his relationship with Ashley fitting that model. There was a beginning (the meeting in the GENTS) and an end (when he and Michael came to London), other than that Tom could only recall a series of episodes. His memory of the intervening years followed no logical sequence.

There was never any doubt in his mind that the time spent living in Lower Budleigh influenced his thinking for years to come. Through the days and nights that followed the arrival of his mother's letter, Tom relived many of those episodes but not necessarily in chronological order. Though he was now away from Lower Budleigh, and living a new life with Michael, there was no escaping the man who had taken him out of the simple world of adolescent sex.

Sex played a major role in the three years he spent with Ash but, even from the short distance of the time with Michael, Tom was only able to recall clearly a few of those scenes that once were so important. One thing he could not forget: Ash was the dominant partner. That was established from the very beginning.

A few scenes he did replay from that era. One had nothing to do with sex. It was a memory of peace that helped him face the fear of the future. He lay in warm midday sunlight on the downs above the village. Peace. No human sound. His head rested on soft grass. Above? Nothing save the great blue dome of the heavens where a few clouds hung, too lazy to move, in the windless air. A bird ran across the sheep cropped grass, jumped and fluttered skywards sweeping away the silence. A skylark. The lark sang its inimitable song. Tom watched the bouncing flight rise higher and higher. The bird, half the size of a man's hand, the source of the magic, was lost to view. The dome filled with its song. The young man lay listening until the sound itself dissolved into the depths of the universe. He slept for a while recording forever those moments of peace. Then it was time to move. As Tom got to his feet the bird, the source of the song, dropped to earth and disappeared; its plumage perfect camouflage as it scuttled through the grass to its hidden nest. The singer and the song were gone from view.

The one event that was indelibly imprinted in Tom's memory occurred only a few weeks after he and Ashley met. They were standing naked in the bedroom of the cottage. Farm work had given Tom a firm lithe, sinewy, but not over muscular body. A body typical of his generation. Throughout the war years there had been rationing but few of the youngsters growing up in the country went short of food. They had a healthy diet. Fat and sugar were in very short supply but fresh vegetables, which you grew, were seasonal and plentiful, there was always enough to share with anyone elderly or infirm. Butcher's meat was scarce but rabbits were there for the taking. Farmers were only too pleased to have the pests controlled.

On one occasion Tom was cycling home along the road that ran between fields when he heard a squeal. It was a squeal of terror from a rabbit. Tom knew the creature had been caught by a stoat. In a couple of movements he was off his bike and over the hedge. There the rabbit sat, hypnotised with fear, waiting for the stoat to attack. The stoat didn't get its dinner. Tom kicked it out of the way and his mother was able to put stewed rabbit on the next day's menu.

The range of fruit was limited to what was grown locally but bottling and other forms of storage ensured availability out of season. Such a diet combined with plenty of physical outdoor work in an unpolluted atmosphere had, with any reasonable material, to produce some presentable results, and Tom had to come into the category of reasonable material. It wasn't false modesty. Though he knew he wasn't bad looking he never saw himself as handsome.

Ash looked at his youthful lover. "You are the nearest thing to perfection I've ever seen."

Tom was flattered. Ash was not piss taking. His voice was too sincere. No one had ever said anything like it to the young man before. That anyone so sophisticated, handsome and debonair could say such a thing was unbelievable. Ash stroked the teenager's body, repeating and emphasising his words, "The nearest thing to perfection. . . ."

Later lying side-by-side on the bed and staring up at the ceiling Ash asked, "Do you know the story of Pygmalion?"

"The ancient Greek tale or the Bernard Shaw play?"

Ash ignored Tom's question. He carried on with his own train of thought, "A professor takes a flower-seller from Covent Garden and passes her off as a lady," he said and was obviously talking about Bernard Shaw's play.

"I have read the play but never seen it performed," was Tom's comment.

"I could do a Pygmalion on you. I could change you from a farm hand into a gentleman. You have all the potential. I could teach you. I could train you and introduce you to people I know."

Tom lay quite still trying to visualise, not only the world Ash could open up, but why Ash should see him as a farm hand. He worked on a farm, that was true, but he had no intention of spending his life there. All he did was labouring; the skilled work was beyond him. But he did see the analogy. Eliza Doolittle was taken from the lowest almost to the very top. Could Ash do the same? Such was the youngster's infatuation that he was ready to believe anything.

Ash did not wait for his young lover to confirm his willingness to abandon his pitch on the steps of St Paul's, Covent Garden. With the phrase, "Nearest thing to perfection," still in his ears Tom could not have said 'No'. His adoration for this man was total. Tears welled up in his eyes as he thought, again, he could not tell anyone how he felt.

"The first thing we must change is your clothes."

Tom still said nothing. He had a grey flannel suit. The one he was wearing the day he met Ash. He got it second hand. It had been advertised in the local paper.

"Clothes are rationed." Tom said.

"I expect we can get together enough clothing coupons." Ash sounded certain he would get the necessary bits of paper. It was not a simple question of being able to buy, say, one pair of trousers a year. Each garment required a specific number of coupons. It was a matter of balancing need against dockets. As if to prove his argument Ash went on to say, "Appearance is everything. A man is judged on two points, his clothes and his manners. A duke dressed as a dustman wouldn't get past the doorman. The Duke of Northumberland, I've been told, on good account, dressed as a dustman to prove the point. He was turned away by the doorman from his own exclusive club."

Ash paused for some response from Tom but when there was none he added, "You will have to accept what I say."

Tom could not face the prospect of losing this man, so he accepted that his idol becomes lover and mentor; and by his tacit agreement to play the Eliza role Tom showed he lacked the experience to understand the consequences of casting himself as the submissive partner. Infatuation was blinding him. He could not, or did not want to, see he was taking on a role he would, eventually, be unable to play.

Misgivings, quickly suppressed, did lurk at the back of his mind. In his various social activities in the village he had usually done his own thing. There had never been any problem but, of course, he had never tried to pass himself off as anyone other than who he was, and no one saw him as a gentleman. His misgivings came from the way he knew the world was shaping. The war had swept away the old order. The foundations were being laid for a new planned society of opportunity, yet in spite of this he was attracted to the man lying next to him. Ash embodied the timeless fascination of self-assurance, class and glamour. It would have been useless to tell young Tom, he was far too immature to be able to divorce sexual attraction and fantasy from the harsh realities of living.

Tom was prepared to agree to whatever Ash suggested. From then on, Tom was to be corrected on points of behaviour but the thorough overhaul of his wardrobe was the priority.

Ash used a bespoke tailor in a town some twenty miles distant. A ready-made suit would not have been acceptable. To get a suit that was really a suit one needed to be measured and given a minimum of two fittings. But getting to the tailor presented a problem. Petrol was rationed. The journey was more than the petrol permitted for Ash's use would cover. Getting fuel, possibly from a farmer, was strictly illegal but would not have been considered, by anyone, a crime. Tom knew a farmer and a can of petrol was put into Betsy's tank. A couple of chops from his dad's butchers' shop may have helped the bargain.

In addition to getting there and finding clothing coupons, a suit from a bespoke tailor did not come cheap. Tom had saved thirty-five pounds (His weekly wage was £2 9/9 (almost £2 50p). The suit would cost 20 guineas (£21), which represented more than two months wages.

But such was Ash's Svengali like influence that Tom agreed and parted with his money. The suit, material and style were chosen by Ash. A month later the rest of Tom's savings were handed over to the same tailor for a hacking jacket (a sports coat worn by countrymen) and flannels. Now he looked the gentleman and since he had nothing in the bank, was a gentleman!

Ash, in common with many ex-servicemen, often recounted his war years. One episode he recalled, with relish, which Tom knew to be wrong. Dispatch riders, in training, were ordered to chase each other over heath land destroying vegetation and wrecking the wildlife habitat. This seemed to Tom to have no purpose other than enjoying the sense of power and pleasure derived from the ability to destroy. When Tom voiced his reservations the riposte from Ash said everything. "They were training for war."

He had to be right. That was the only reason needed. War can be enjoyed.

Ash went to France but he was not involved in the D Day Landings and never, as far as Tom could remember, ever spoke of being involved in combat. Ash's recollections of service life that stuck in Tom's mind, not surprisingly, concerned sex. In the blackout, in a GENTS, it was absolutely necessary to have some idea of the rank of the person standing next to you. Ash was not interested in fellow officers. He wanted other ranks i.e. men. The blackout was total. There was little difficulty finding the intentions of your neighbour but ascertaining rank required a little effort. Everyone would have been in uniform but the wartime battle dress presented a problem. Running your fingers along the shoulder and feeling pips told you if it was an officer standing next you. If that proved negative then feeling the upper arm for stripes would tell you if he who required attention was one of the non-commission variety. Neither pips nor stripes meant you could hold a private's privates.

There was also the matter of practical mechanics. Lubrication was a problem easily solved by an over supply of Brylcream on the head. It only required wiping ones hands over your carefully combed glistening waves and applying the lubricant, thus acquired, over the plunger to facilitate the smoothest of passages. For Tom the odour of Brylcream always recalled sex. KY, smelling of nothing, lacked glamour.

There was no definite date when Tom left home and moved over to Lower Budleigh. At first it was weekends, then a night midweek but that meant rising early and cycling over the hill to start work at seven; it was not until he left farm work that he lived there permanently.

Ash kept his promise to open up Tom's world. Tom had been to London staying with relatives, but his first time in a London hotel was to accompany Ash to a regimental reunion. He was also taken to the City of Quebec, a pub in the same block as the hotel, off Oxford Street. The hotel was not half as impressive as the youngster expected. A large pre-war brick building with no real foyer or grand staircase. Meeting Ash's fellow service men was reminiscent of a badly edited film. The gathering, like the hotel, failed to come up to expectations. Stripped of their uniforms these men were nothing special. In fact, some were distinctly unattractive.

Tom was shown off, almost as a possession.

"He'd have been very popular in the regiment, don't you think?" asked ex-lieutenant Ashley-Jones.

"With certain sections, I agree," said the ex-major as he smiled knowingly before he moved on to socialise with the diverse body of men who had gathered to relive edited memories of those years.

The next day Ash visited some old friends. This time Tom was not invited. It did not bother the youngster who was picked up by a very presentable theatrical person with a rather grand flat in Chelsea. A mink coat thrown across the bed was an extra! Tom thought the Pygmalion effect was working. He decided to be rather grand and have his shoes polished by a shoeshine boy not far from Marble Arch. The boy remarked on the quality of the Tom's trousers and felt the material. He was rewarded with a tip which Tom thought generous, but probably wasn't, since it was greeted with a very arch, "Fanks sir." It did not occur to the 'would-be gentleman' that there might be more in the feel of the trousers than mere flattery.

On an afternoon in early summer, a month later, it was a different story. Again it was like watching scenes from a film where the linking shots had been edited out. Tom had cycled over the hill to Lower Budleigh. The track down the hill into the village was through a field of barley that Tom saw as a sea of silken wind-blown waves in the soft sunlight. He walked into the cottage wearing old working clothes. A man, whom Tom did not know, was lounging in one of the winged armchairs. Ash sat in the other. Both were smoking.

"Edward, Tom. Tom, Edward." Ash introduced them without getting up.

"Hello, Tom, we've been talking about you." Edward, striped-tie'd, white-shirted and cord-trousered, greeted him.

"Edward is an old friend. He'll be staying overnight."

When the arrangements for the visit were made and whether they were made by letter or telephone Tom was never told.

Tom nodded, "I'll go and change," was all he could think of saying. He was at the top of the stairs when he heard, "Your beautiful farm labourer."

Ash made some reply that Tom didn't hear.

Edward? Details sketchy. Handsome. Younger than Ash. Lived in Hanover Square in London. Met Ash at a country house weekend the summer war broke out. Was down from

Oxford at the time. Some relation to the host. Details of the weekend weren't specified. Edward had served in a Guards Regiment.

Tom's clothes had been moved to the small back bedroom. He realised that was where he would be sleeping.

Much of Edward's conversation was about people Tom had never heard of, but he didn't feel particularly left out.

Ash had been given some home made wine – wheat and potato. The vintage country tipple was tasted and rated, "Quite admirable!"

Tom told of his father's experience with homemade wine given him by a farmer's wife. One sip was more than enough. Not wishing to offend the lady he poured it into her prize aspidistra. After a few days the poor intoxicated plant keeled over and died. "Something must have poisoned it but I cannot, for the life of me, think what," bemoaned the farmer's wife.

"Your father could have met the same dreadful fate as the biggest aspidistra in the world," sang Edward to Gracie Field's song. He sipped the wine and asked, "Is there an aspidistra here?" Laughter all round.

Ash had to excuse himself to prepare a meal.

"He can turn his hand to anything," quipped Edward. "I think he is quite remarkable." He looked around the room. "Ash has done most of this work here himself. It's absolutely charming. Now about yourself."

Tom, thinking to amuse and entertain the visitor, related an incident that had happened on the farm a couple of days before.

A patch of fresh succulent clover had been fenced off for the newly shorn sheep. Modern methods were being employed. In the old days the shepherd would have laboriously portioned out each new patch of feed with hurdles. These were woven hazel fencing that are now the expensive preserves of cottage gardens, but then they were the traditional method of making folds in which the sheep could graze. The modern method being used here was electric fencing. A single strand of wire set at the correct height carrying a twelve-volt current did the job. The shock was enough to deter any would be stray. Four farm hands were looking at the fencing. Two were older men, plus Tom and another seventeen year old, Ron. The inspection over, the quartet prepared to move on to the next field where their work lay.

"Hang on a bit," said Ron and he turned to have pee.

"Bet you can't piss over that fence," was the challenge thrown down by one of the men.

"Want to bet?" Young men have ever been ready to take up a challenge.

"Sixpence you don't."

"Sixpence from both of 'ee." Ron was going to make it worthwhile.

"Done." The betting was agreed.

Tom knew the current had been switched on and wanted to warn Ron of the danger but one of the men motioned to him to be quiet. Young Ron turned round. He was holding his cock, squeezing it to hold back the flow of water and walked to the fence, then released his fingers. The valve opened and a powerful jet of hot piss shot into the air, arched over the fence, and landed on the far side. His youthful muscles were able to maintain this golden fountain clearing the electric wire by a good foot.

"Let's see the colour of your money," said the triumphant still pissing youngster.

"Thee hasn't finished," argued the challenger.

"What do 'ee mean?" Ron was contemptuous.

The young man turned to collect his winnings, but by now the bladder muscles of the healthy young farm worker were beginning to lose their pressure. The golden arch was drooping. It hit the electrified wire; instead of the expected twelve pence he got twelve volts straight up his cock. Not sufficient to do any damage but enough to make him jump. There was an almost instant erection, a yell accompanied by roars of rustic laughter and two silver sixpences (twelve pence) were handed over.

Ash and Edward spent the evening in the nearby village pub. Tom tagged along. Ash was in his element with a handsome, obviously upper class friend to show off. By closing time Tom was ready to get to bed. He slept well and heard nothing from the other room. After Edward had returned to London, almost as a throw away line, Ash told Tom Edward got what he came for - twice. Tom asked if they would be seeing him again.

"No," was the short reply from Ash as he walked into the kitchen. He paused, turned and added, "He won't be coming here again."

"I thought you two enjoyed yourself. That's the way it looked to me."

For a few moments Ash was silent. He stood with his hands in his trouser pockets and said, "Edward thought you were gauche."

Tom wasn't sure what the word meant so he repeated it. "Gauche am I?"

"You lack social graces. As a bit of rough trade he could see why I find you attractive."

"When did he tell you this?" Tom thought it was a sort of joke.

"On the way to the station. Your humour was a little too earthy." Ash again walked toward the kitchen.

"Oh yes. I laughed when he said he'd gone into a GENTS for a perfectly legitimate reason. And the joke about the electric wire?"

"He pretended to find that funny," Ash called from the kitchen.

"I suppose it was too earthy. That's where the electric current went - straight to earth."

Ash came back. He went over to Tom, held him by the shoulders and looked him straight in the face, "You have a lot to learn, but it's not for him, or anyone else, to put you down." Silently they looked at each other. Ash turned away. "I'll have to empty the lavatory bucket. Its full."

"You are too late," said Tom. "I've already done it."

Ash turned, "Being earthy has its uses." and took Tom upstairs.

A very different partner from the War Years turned up at the cottage one Sunday. A very good-looking Londoner in his mid twenties arrived on a motorbike. He had been a private in

Ash's regiment. Contact had been made at the Regimental Reunion. Ash took him on a tour of the farm buildings, presumably with the intention of having sex. Tom learned, later, it was a fumbling failure. The ex-private was sitting on his motorbike, putting on his old army helmet, ready to leave, when he held Ash's arm and whispered, but Tom overheard, "Treat Tom well. He's in love with you." He kick-started the bike and rode away.

When Ashley inherited some money on his mother's death he gave up work to live as a man of independent means, but the inheritance was far from sufficient to fulfil his aspirations so, when the cash was running out, he took any job to provide enough money to give, at least, the appearance of affluence.

The Pygmalion experiment died as it had to. The Regimental Reunion was as near to an Embassy Ball as Tom was likely to get. There was no chance of mixing with the local gentry. If any of them had similar interests to Ash they most certainly were not going to let it be known.

Ash was a mixer and finding remote country pubs was the smart thing to do. There were no drink-driving laws and as Ash had an eye for handsome young men the village pubs were good hunting ground. He sought the world of Greek male beauty which translated into art would cost you a fortune to buy and, paradoxically, cost you your freedom if you touched it in real life.

Tom played second fiddle, but that was the relationship

RID ENGLAND OF THIS PLAGUE

Chapter 9

The letter from Tom's mother lay for a week on the table. Mrs Urbano had moved it to dust when she cleaned the room but neither Tom nor Michael touched it. It was as if they were ignoring its existence.

Michael had left for work. Tom was alone. He looked at the letter. No matter how he tried to rationalise, he knew when his mother used the word trouble she meant trouble. Real trouble. The letter had to be destroyed. He put a match to it but couldn't hold it still long enough for the flame to catch. He burnt his fingers. He threw the match away. The letter stuck to his hand. Tom swore. Ashley Ashley-Jones belonged to the past, and he was more than a hundred miles away.

Tom tried to tear up the letter, but again his hands weren't steady enough. There had been practically no contact with Lower Budleigh since they left Dorset three years ago. London, Camden Square, was a new life. He'd outlived Ashley and his restored period cottage but Thomas Adamson was learning that the past lurks just over your shoulder no matter how intently you set your gaze on the future. In desperation he hid the letter in his back trouser pocket.

Ash was in some kind of trouble. He could hide the letter but the words hung in the air. What trouble? Why had his mother not said more? And who made the telephone call? Who would have known the number? Why did they ring? A trunk call cost money. What? Who? Why? The words spun. Tom lit his pipe hoping the smoke would clear his head. He sat down to calm himself. He would probably be late for work but that didn't matter. He knew his mother was no gossip but he also knew very little of what was done, or said, in the village escaped her notice and things must have been said. Too many people knew his connection with Ash.

The half-awake dream of the Cerne Giant left him with only one kind of trouble - the police. He wished desperately to forget the Giant but the huge male nakedness stayed in the back of his mind just as his mother's letter stayed at the back of his trousers. The dream was a creation of his fears and imaginings. He knew that. He knew his overheated brain had engineered the face, the look along the valley and the bars that closed over it, but it was Ashley. The big erect penis was real and he knew his first love's appetite for sex. He knew Ash's taste: young men in their late teens and early twenties and he knew how dangerous that could be.

He knew, too, that the climate had changed. The heady years of his teens when anything went, or for that matter came, had given way to something very different. It was called normality, and that was returning with a vengeance. Ashley's late teens as a thirties society stud, and war service with unlimited randy twenty year olds was a thing of the past. His ilk had no place in the new planned economy racing headlong to Utopia. When that goal was reached all young men would walk proudly to the altar without a second glance at the best man.

Ash was in some kind of trouble. Ash was in some kind of trouble. Ash was in some kind of trouble. The sentence repeated itself like an old 78 r.p.m. gramophone record stuck in a groove.

The morning passed. He made a couple of fairly serious mistakes at work. He wasn't thinking. Lunchtime came. He was in the chip shop in Kentish Town. 1/3d was the top limit he could go for lunch. He was sitting at a table eating his cod and chips watching other customers buying their fish or pie and chips - about the limit of fast food available then. Hardly the place to be philosophising, but these were ordinary people who would have no hesitation in spewing out the horror with which the press had gorged them had they known he was one of *those*. They would have shunned him like the plague and suggested he had his chips elsewhere!

He finished his meal, took his plate back to the counter

where he got the usual cheery, "Alright, mate?"

"As always."

The world was going on as if nothing had happened. A customer was being served with fish and chips to take away. They were being wrapped in newspaper, as they always were. It was an old newspaper and no one bothered to notice the article about the Nazi Concentration Camps. Had they done so they would have found no reference to the thousands of homosexuals who were sent to the gas chambers or that the ones who survived were sent, by the victorious Allies, to civilian prisons to complete their sentences.

Tom left the fish and chip shop and walked down the road. He didn't go into the 'cottage'. He crossed the road rather than pass near it, thus avoiding temptation. He realised it was a knee jerk reaction, but he couldn't take any risks; simply watching could be misconstrued. There was still half an hour before he was due back at work. He sat on a low wall in the sun to let the world go by. His eyes followed a young sailor, in all probability home on leave, go into the 'cottage'. He may well have gone in for a legitimate reason but the half dozen words in his mother's letter pounded through his head, and told him to stay clear.

The Rupert Croft-Cooke case had hit the headlines just the previous autumn. Two men, Croft-Cooke and Joseph Alexander had been in a pub off Oxford Street. It had to be the City of Quebec, not far from Marble Arch. There they met two sailors and invited them to spend the weekend at their Sussex home. The sailors had difficulty in getting back to their Base at Chatham on the Sunday evening and tried to steal a bike. They were arrested and questioned and claimed to have committed indecencies over the weekend. Rupert Croft-Cooke's house was searched without a warrant. The two men were convicted on virtually uncorroborated evidence. How could that be seen other than as corruption of young service men by well-heeled perverts? The fact that the sailors knew what they were doing did not come into the reckoning.

Tom shook his head in disbelief.

That case was in October; the following New Year's Eve, 1953, Tom and Michael were in Piccadilly Circus, then the centre of celebrations. All very peaceful. All great fun. The pubs were even open until midnight, a very special concession. Traffic was stopped. The circus was crowded.   Tom and Michael were standing on the pavement at the end of Regent Street not far from the entrance to the Underground. There was about ten minutes to go before midnight. It was a perfect evening, dry and not too cold. Everybody was friendly. Strangers were chatting. The couple were trying to decide if they should speak to a sailor who was standing alone near them when Tom realised he was not the only one eyeing the form-hugging bell-bottoms. A rather camp number elbowed his way through the crowd and said something to the sailor. What he said Tom could not hear, but the sailor's reply was perfectly audible, "Fuck off. I'm looking for a man!"

A few years later the sailor would have been dismissed the service for upholding such a basic naval tradition but in 1953 another naval tradition, Nelson putting the telescope to his blind eye, was also upheld.

It was the Drag Queen, Mrs Shufflewick, who would be certain to get the biggest laugh with, "And I said to him; get thee behind me Satan. [pause] Believe you me, I couldn't have said a worse thing to a sailor!"

Then walking back to work, past the Kentish Town shops that held no interest for him, for the first time in his life Tom asked himself the question. Had he been corrupted, and if so by whom? It was a non-question. He had followed instinct. Corruption didn't come into it. He knew exactly what he was doing when he picked up Ashley Ashley-Jones, but did that change anything?

Incidents from the past leapt into his consciousness at odd intervals. The first time he fucked a guy, a villager, a little older than himself, who later married and had a family. Tom never forgot the exquisite pleasure of that moment. Was that corruption? It was a response to an invitation. Was he guilty of corrupting? He had made suggestions to other men. Some had been taken up and others rejected.

It was time to stop thinking and get back to work. He stood up and realised that on more than one occasion since the

97

arrival of the letter he was not paying attention to his work. When he got back the two men with whom he worked were talking. The older appeared embarrassed. The younger, a thick set thirty year old, who had often talked about his daughter, was saying how he had once posed for porno photographs, "I haven't got any of them now." he explained. "I wouldn't want my daughter to get hold of them."

Ernie, the older man, stopped the conversation with, "I think it's time we got back to work."

As they started the afternoon's work Tom was asked if he'd ever thought of having a go, meaning posing for pictures with women. The answer had to be no. He couldn't say he wasn't interested in women. It was the wrong day to even joke. Any pornography was illegal, but he did think that claiming to have been photographed screwing a woman put you in the category of a real man.

Tom had only ever seen one pornographic photograph and that didn't strike him as erotic. There were ten or so men in a circle making a '*daisy chain*' i.e. all screwing each other. But it was all so indistinct as to be meaningless.

As he walked home after work, he wondered why he only wanted sex with men. No one had forced him into it. Films and books had told him that the natural and inevitable end of adolescence was to marry. Nothing he had ever seen or read suggested otherwise.

Why was it then he knew he wanted nothing more than to spend his life with Michael? He was unhappy when they were apart. When he was in the theatre, on tour, or in weekly rep, half his mind was with the man he loved.

Why was their love despised? If not despise it was, at best, a joke.

He stepped off the pavement to cross the road. He felt a blow, staggered and fell backwards. A man helped him up.

"Sorry mate. Had to hit you. You were going straight out in front of a bleedin' trolley bus. You were miles away."

Tom thanked him. The man went off shaking his head. "Bloody daydreaming."

There was no post when Tom got back to South Villas. He

wasn't sure what he felt. Not knowing was becoming an almost unbearable strain. He did think of finding Mrs Urbano and asking if anyone had called but there was very little time. He was meeting Michael and an old friend of Michael's. They had tickets for *The Boy Friend* at Wyndhams Theatre.

By coincidence they were to spend part of the evening with the two people who were in very different ways, and quite unknowingly, to be very much part of their lives as Ashley-Jones' bit of trouble unfolded.

Michael was waiting in the foyer of the theatre.

"No James?" asked Tom.

"No, but he'll be here."

James and Michael had known each other since they were in the Services, Michael in the R.A.F and James in the Royal Navy. They met in the Union Jack Club across the Waterloo Road from the railway station. To young men, from all three services, the club was a haven. For a matter of shillings these lads far from home could have a small cubicle for the night or others, like Michael and James, who wanted a base for a forty-eight hour leave in London. There friendships were made; some transitory others long lasting. In the post war world the outdated Edwardian building was replaced with the modern structure with its entrance round the corner in Sandell Street.

James was in his final year at the Royal College of Art. Almost six feet tall and in common with most young men of that generation very slim. The post war diet gave little scope for obesity; James prided himself on a twenty-four inch waist. His regular, usually impassive, features gave him an almost sculptured appearance beneath soft, fine, light brown hair that in bright sunlight was almost blonde. From his school days he intended to become a photographer and so after leaving the services he took advantage of the grants available and enrolled as a student at the Royal College of Art. His father thought it a waste of time. James had chosen his career so why go to college to learn to take photographs. He could have trained at reputable photographers in his hometown of Norwich, but as his mother pointed out, James was over twenty-one and able to decide his own future. She knew her son. He would have decided his own

99

future no matter what parental pressure was applied. He had inherited streaks of stubbornness and determination that were to stand him in good stead. The limited constricted world of the provinces was not for James. London offered the two things he was determined to get. Firstly, the freedom to live his life as he would want, and secondly the scope to pursue his chosen career as a fashion photographer.

When James did arrive he was seething. Tom and Michael were aware he had been doing some work for an agency but knew no details.

"My dears, I am so angry, I cannot tell you. I do not know how to contain myself. That old queen Penrose, the agent, you know, who promised to help me. I showed talent, he said. He would handle my work. Handle my work! Forget the word work, he was after a grope. I didn't fancy him but thought what the hell? The man's revolting. He assumes because you want a job he has the right to your cock. I ask you. I'm no prude and I'm not that fussy but there are limits. It was a disaster; I cannot tell you! The size of his belly was revolting. And to crown it all, the bastard is using one of my pictures. He swears it wasn't mine. Gave me back all my photographs, he said! He didn't. He kept one and the negative. What can I do? I can't prove anything."

Michael looked at his watch. "It's time to go in."

"Of course." and James added as an apology, "I promise I won't spoil the evening. And after hearing my trouble how are you two?"

"We're fine." There was no other reply Tom and Michael could give.

The show had only been running for a couple of months. It was still fresh and camp and playing to an audience that adored every minute. The twenties pastiche hit just the right note.

It is a point worth recording that though both Michael and James were sexually very active whilst they were in the services neither did anything either on board ship or on the Air Force base. Wrestling and horseplay was acceptable but the real stuff had to wait until they were safely away. Shitting on one's own doorstep did not even enter into their service life.

After the show the only possible place to go was the Salisbury in St. Martin's Lane. It was the venue if you were queer. The interior of the pub would have changed little since it was built in the late 19th century. Its atmosphere was right; solid mahogany counter, polished brass, plush seats curved around cast iron tables. The deep reds and browns were friendly and certainly not camp. There was space to sit, to stand or move nearer whoever you might feel needed, or wanted, your company.

The Salisbury is mentioned in the Orton Diary. The incident referred to by Joe (Tom knew him as John) Orton in 'Prick up your Ears' had taken place a year earlier. Later the pub was to be used as a setting for the film 'Victim' starring Dirk Bogarde, the first film to address the fact that being homosexual made one easy prey to blackmail; but at the time of this visit a pervert could only be the victim of his own depravity, meriting no sympathy.

James insisted on getting the drinks, half pints of bitter - the standard for all young queers. It was while he was at the bar Tom and Michael agreed nothing should be said about Ashley. As Michael said, "He doesn't know Ashley existed. He doesn't know how we met. I've never mentioned him. I don't know about you, have you ever said anything?"

"No, never," was Tom's reply. James letting off steam about his picture was one thing, but instinct told them that Ashley's trouble was different.

The three stood chatting for a while about the show. At that period the twenties were high fashion and high camp. The song 'All I want is a room in Bloomsbury', was particularly poignant for Tom and Michael. When they first came to London they had taken a room in Handel Street, Bloomsbury, where the landlady had to be called either Mrs Browning or Mrs Lee depending on which 'husband' was in favour. The room was furnished with two rickety bamboo chairs, a table to match, and a brass bedstead. They swapped sides of the bed each night. One side was O.K. On the other the mattress was so worn that one of the bedsprings dug into your arse. There was a danger of

101

instant circumcision if you lay face down. They had, therefore, to practise a variation of safe sex.

James, Tom and Michael all agreed the young men in the show were gorgeous. The magic of '*The Boy Friend*' had worked; it lifted the fear and depression from Tom and Michael. Ashley was in the past. They had made a life together in London, a new world with new friends.

James was passing on the juicy bit of gossip that a friend of his, working in the exciting new medium of television, had had a one-night stand with one of the chorus boys in the show when Michael heard a voice he recognised. It was Denzil. Denzil and James were their closest friends. The agreement that James should not be told about Ash was applied to all their friends. It was instinctive self-preservation. Carelessness on Tom's part allowed Denzil, sometime later, to learn what had happened. Denzil was rather more thickset than Michael or James though by later standards he would be considered lean. Dark brown hair set with just the faintest hint of a fashionable wave. He envied Tom his abundant natural waves. His firmer jaw line and features contrasted with the angular high cheekbones that gave James such a distinctive appearance.

Unlike Tom, Denzil had not been to drama school although he had spent his life, except for two years National Service, in the theatre and was for a couple of years a boy in the chorus of a West End show. Now he'd landed a small part in a revue due to open in a couple of weeks; in addition he was always able to find work as a film extra, and at three or four pounds a day, a couple of days work a week was enough. Michael was often able to help him out if there was a bit part as a detective. Plain-clothes detectives in films always wore a trilby hat. It was, paradoxically, almost a uniform and the actor was expected to provide the appropriate headgear, and Michael had one. His bluish grey trilby appeared in more than a dozen 'Cops and Robbers' pictures.

Denzil's father had been killed in the war. His mother had been a showgirl in the thirties but had never made the big time. From the day he was born she knew he was to be the star she never was. To say she guided him on to the stage would not be entirely accurate, forced would be nearer the truth. His chosen career was chosen for him. The name 'Denzil' was intended to set him apart. From early childhood he was taught to sing and dance. On any and every occasion Denzil had to perform. The stars in his mother's eyes blinded her to reality. Denzil was competent and able to get work; chorus or walk on parts. He was still having singing lessons more to please her than to satisfy any burning ambition to become a singer. He realised this when he and a friend went to an audition for a part in a musical. His friend went on stage and everybody stopped to watch. Denzil followed and got the 'don't call us we'll call you'. There was no bitterness, no resentment.

Denzil loved the theatre but knew he was never going to be a great performer. Clothes were his particular interest and wardrobe work was his aim. He was prepared to do anything to further that aim. It is an overworked cliché to talk of finding one's self at a crossroad. But in Denzil's case it was true. He did his two years National Service and in the army was forced to obey orders that he knew were often nonsense. It started when he got seven days C.B. (confined to barracks) for not having his kit laid out correctly for an inspection. The sergeant made no secret of what he thought of 'theatrical types'. Two years of his life were wasted and left him with a sense of grievance. But National Service had taken him away from his mother's direct influence. He had even spent one leave with a boy friend instead of with his mother; a defiant act of rebellion. The fact that he could do such a thing instilled itself in his thinking. He was no longer prepared to accept the role into which she had cast him. However, the last thing he wanted was to hurt her, but the mixture of freeing himself from domination and theatrical unconventionality had made him more than a bit of a rebel. He needed to be himself. To take charge of his own life rather than let others decide for him. Fate intervened and helped. His mother married again. Tactfully Denzil took a basement bedsitter in Pimlico and fed his mother sufficient half-truths to perpetuate the belief that stardom was just around the corner.

When Michael and Denzil indulged in a bit of a fling Tom

103

was on tour with a production of Terence Rattigan's *'The Deep Blue Sea'*. There was never any jealousy or bad feeling after the tour was over and the three became firm friends.

Tom did have a violent disagreement with Denzil after going to see *'Hamlet'*. An American girl sitting next to Tom in the Gallery added her own comment when she said, "Either these seats are hard or this play been going on a hell of a long time but my ass is sure sore!"

It was the first time Denzil had seen the play. Tom had studied it in depth as part of his drama course. Denzil argued that the ending is nonsense. Nothing is sorted out. Far from being a hero Hamlet was a disaster for Denmark. There was nothing to applaud except the acting. Tom explained in detail the cultural value of the finest work of our greatest dramatist.

Denzil was scathing, "We spent four hours listening to a prince who analysed everything, finishing up in a blood bath, leaving somebody else to sort out the mess he'd created."

But that was Denzil. He'd challenge anything and everything, and Tom thought no more about it. He could be relied on to give gratuitous, if not always helpful, advice and this was exactly what was happening in the bar. Something had, obviously, been said about the high profile cases that had hit the headlines and Denzil was propounding a very simple final solution.

"Men in their position must know dozens of prominent queers. We all know a few. I would bet half of 'Who's Who' has gone trolling sometime in their lives. There's has to be lawyers and politicians who are queer. What these people in high positions have got to say straight out is, "You bring charges against me and I will give you such a list of names that will clog the courts for years," and they would have to build special jails up to the standard of the Ritz to hold them. The Establishment wouldn't dare. But then, who do we know would dare challenge the Establishment?"

Neither Tom nor Michael bothered to argue or question the logic of his thinking. Neither wanted advice. Neither wanted to think. They knew the days were going to be long and the sleepless nights even longer.

An older chap, who had to be in his mid thirties, was listening. He leaned over and added his comment, "Why can't they just leave us alone. They did during the war. What's so different now? We won the war, I think. Or have I got that wrong?"

The irony was lost on most of the group.

Then he added, "My boyfriend was killed on D. Day, and now the bastards hunt me." That was said as he walked out of the bar. It was half directed at Tom who was probably the only person to hear it.

James added a story to end the evening. He could put on a camp manner that was always very amusing. He had just moved into a studio flat in Earls Court. It was one step up from a bedsit.

"Now you don't need to tell me. I am only too well aware that a studio flat is just a pretentious name for a glorified bedsit, but it is nice to be able to call your loo your own. If you know what I mean and I am sure you do. Well my dears, and this, I assure you, was purely fortuitous, from the window of my room I can keep a watchful eye on the 'cottage' in the side road opposite. This afternoon I strolled across to the aforesaid convenience. I felt it my duty to reconnoitre the neighbourhood. The only other person in there happened to be an ex-student friend from the Royal College of Art. He wanted a coffee; I think that is how you pronounce it: so I invited him back to the flat. Would you believe it! We had barely got inside the door of the flat when a black van full of police pulled up outside the afore mentioned erection. There is an entrance at either end and six of the most gorgeous men charged in, three at each end. Now there are only four stalls so what the six of them did defies imagination. My dears, they did look so sheepish when they came out empty handed. Whether they were empty-handed in there is an entirely different matter. The mind boggles. My friend said, "To hell with the coffee. This calls for a stiff whisky," and I assure you nothing else was stiff."

Only days before Tom and Michael would have found the story highly amusing but the letter, the non-specific letter with the phone call, changed their thinking.

Tom remembered something very similar had happened to him near St.Pancras Station, but said nothing. He had just crossed the road, after leaving a very well known, or one could say notorious, old-fashioned cast-iron Urinal that stood in the middle of the road, when a police van drew up. This time Tom knew the place was not empty, but there was no time to warn the four men inside. He walked off. He was safe. There was nothing he could do. He felt a twinge of guilt. He'd been lucky. Had the police arrived two minutes earlier it would have been a very different story. There was no hiding the fact that he and most of his queer friends had, at some time or other, sailed very close to the wind.

RID ENGLAND OF THIS PLAGUE

Chapter 10

"Today is the anniversary of our meeting," Michael said as he turned the key in the lock of the front door at 13, South Villas

Tom had forgotten. "Why didn't you say? We could have celebrated it with James and Denzil."

Michael opened the door. The door clanged shut behind them as it always did. Neither spoke as they went to their room. '*The Boy Friend*' had been the only topic of conversation on the way home from the Salisbury. Neither James nor Denzil were mentioned.

"Today didn't seem the day for a celebration, and it might have meant telling them too much."

As a silent apology Tom embraced Michael and kissed him.

"Don't worry," Michael said very gently. "An anniversary is only a date. We didn't bother last year. It's only because of what's happened I thought of it now."

They undressed in silence. Michael got into bed. Tom bent over and 'kissed him again and whispered, "Good night, my love. We don't know what has happened to Ash. It could be anything. If it had been something . . . . something. . . . You know what I mean, I'm sure mother would have said. We may be worrying for nothing."

Michael said nothing. He had spent the day trying to convince himself Tom's mother was not warning them, but without success. The fact that the letter existed was proof enough. Tom went to his own bed. They lay in silence for a few minutes then Michael said in a half whisper, "Sleep well. Whatever happens we must never forget it was Ash who brought us together."

That was true. Ash arranged their meeting not with the

intention they should live together. He had a rather different scenario in mind. Ashley's original proposal involved doing an old friend a favour and he expected one in return. What are friends for? But 'the best laid schemes of mice and men' is an old adage Ashley should have heeded.

When he arranged the meeting the relationship between Tom and himself had lost its early intensity. Tom was no longer happy to play the Eliza Doolittle to the Shavian Professor Higgins. Such a relationship couldn't have worked. Tom was sexually far from totally passive and he had been so socially proactive in village life that a relationship where he was totally dominated had to break down. The original infatuation could not have lasted. Sooner or later Tom was to realise his mentor had feet of clay.

Nine months before the Tom and Michael meeting Ash had gone back to North Wales to take care of his ailing widower father, and run the family business, a small estate agency. Tom had been left to look after the cottage, something he was more than happy to do. It meant he could run his own life. It did mean doing the domestic chores but that was a small price to pay for the freedom he now enjoyed. He had now come of age in more senses than one. His twenty first birthday was the non-event of non-events. No cards. No presents. He celebrated by buying himself a pint of local brew in the village pub. Birthdays, other than for children, were not celebrated.

Ashley had missed the point of Shaw's *Pygmalion*. Clothes and behaviour were an adjunct to speech. In polite society people were classified by their accent. Listen to any recording of the period and anything other than Standard English is at best comic. Ash had imitated his 'Betters' so successfully it was not possible to put him into any particular strata. Though Tom still spoke with a pronounced West Country accent Ash had made significant changes to his personality; giving him the ability to mix in almost any company and an ease of manner similar to that of his instructor.

Tom was now out of Ashley's shadow. He was able to entertain at Tuckers and indulge himself in his great passion -

acting. As a young schoolboy he built his own marionette theatre, made the dolls, the scenery and wrote the plays. Now he gathered a group of friends in his home village to enter the County Shakespeare Festival with a thirty-minute *'Hamlet'*, adapted by Tom Adamson who also played the name part. Making the costumes was a group effort.

Presumption of mammoth proportions, but it worked.

A special performance for the village was given on the lawns of the Manor. Yew hedges, all neatly clipped with arches, provided a near perfect setting. A minor discomfort Tom, bitten by the acting bug, failed to anticipate was that his audience would be bitten by gnats!

It was after the festival that a Mrs Boyer-Foulkes, who had inspired Tom to build the marionette theatre and who had guided him through producing a pantomime and several one act plays, said, "Well, Thomas, I think it is high time you looked beyond a village Hamlet. Stay here and you will have no experience of life. Are you planning to marry?" Tom shook his head. "I thought not. Then think very carefully about the future. I believe you have a talent. Waste it and you will regret it. Believe me, I know what I am talking about."

It was a meeting with her a year and a half later that set Tom on the road to the Royal Academy of Dramatic Art and a life beyond Lower Budleigh.

Tom was now in his early twenties and had long since realised Ash had neither the connections nor the money to even pretend to be part of the country gentry set. In the post war world the country house scene of Ashley's youth had been consigned to nostalgic Noel Coward. The thirties, the years immediately prior to the Second World War, had little to recommend them to the planners busily engaged on creating the 1951 Festival of Britain and its aftermath. Modernism belonged to the past. Something new was needed and so *'contemporary'* became the buzzword.

Ash, too, was making a life for himself in north Wales. Being the gregarious man he was, and with his liking for country pubs, he soon struck a friendship with the landlord of a pub several miles from Chester and offered to look after it while the landlord and his wife had a couple of weeks' holiday. Tom was also due for two weeks holiday. The logical thing was to use his holiday to help Ash with the pub. The plan suited Tom admirably. This was 1950. He had very little money and the idea of going away on his own did not cross his mind. Where would he go? He had been to London and in any case that meant staying with relations, and foreign holidays were rare and expensive. The fact that he would be spending his holiday working didn't bother him. He had never done any bar work but he was certain it wouldn't take long to learn.

Ash had renewed his relationship with an old friend, Gareth, whom he had known since his adolescence. Together they had discovered their sexual identity. Unlike Ash, Gareth had remained at home working in the family bookshop he was to inherit. They did have one thing in common and that was an attraction to good-looking young men in their late teens or early twenties.

Gareth had a near miss with the law when a police car happened to spot his car parked off the road in a wood. Fortunately, he and his companion were well buttoned up and smoking 'Craven A' when the blue uniformed arm tapped on the car window. Nothing could be proved but they were warned. Gareth undeterred carried on hunting and eventually met, in a regular haunt on the banks of the river Dee, a beautiful ex-airman.

This prize was shown off to Ashley who decided in the name of comradeship the two old schoolmates could enhance their experience by indulging in a little boyfriend swapping. Gareth to have Tom. Ashley the ex-airman. Nothing could be simpler. Ashley came down to Lower Budleigh to arrange Tom's holiday. Tom was shown a photograph of the young ex-airman whose name was Michael and was not impressed. He was, also, to meet Ash's friend Gareth. Tom had heard numerous tales of their exploits, but there was no hint of the proposed swap.

Tom travelled up by train. At Chester station Ash and Gareth were waiting. Tom was polite, but did not find Gareth

110

at all physically attractive. Willowy and gushing were the words that came into Tom's mind. He was tall, very slim and moved as if his body were made from a single flexible willow stem.

"So lovely to meet you," gushed out like water from a hand pump.

Had Ash been able to read Tom's mind he would have known the swap was doomed from the start.

Gareth couldn't get to the pub that day; he was needed in the bookshop, but would be over as soon as he could. Tom and Ash climbed into old Betsy, who was still clocking up the miles in spite of the fact that the old lady should have been retired years before. Gareth said something, which Tom didn't understand, when he waved as they drove away to the pub.

The pub stood alone on a main road. It dated from about the early nineteenth century, had one bar and was built to cater for travellers. Now the interior had been Tudorised to give it a rustic ambience designed to attract car-owning customers in search of '*Ye Olde English Pub*' bent on escaping middle classness and mixing on unequal terms with 'Honest-to-God-Yokels'. Mine host in such a pub was the perfect role for Ashley. A woman from the near-by village came in to do the cleaning and a bit of cooking for the landlord's family. This was all long before pubs did pub grub. A barman's or maid's job was simply one of serving alcohol. Tom arrived on Friday. The pub wasn't busy and Ash was well able to cope on his own.

It wasn't until the next day, Saturday, that Tom learned a little more was expected of him than pulling up pints of beer.

"Gareth fancies you." Ash said in the most calculating throw away manner. To which Tom said a noncommittal "Oh!" and carried on unloading a crate of Guinness.

Ash tried again and was met with the same response, so he decided to hold the planned boyfriend swapping in abeyance. There was plenty of time for Tom to come round to the idea and his less than enthusiastic reaction to the photograph of this Michael was all to the good.

It was mid afternoon. The pub was closed, as all pubs were by law. The sale of alcohol outside permitted hours could lose a landlord his licence. Serving alcohol in the afternoon was definitely not within permitted hours. Ash was in the bar having a drink with a customer making certain they were well out of sight of a window. Tom went into the sitting room and fell half asleep pretending to read the paper. A knocking on the door failed to produce a reaction. Tom reasoned it was someone wanting a drink out-of-hours.

Ash yelled from the bar, "See who it is, Tom."

Tom roused himself sufficiently to call back, "Alright, I'll go."

He went not knowing what he would say. When he opened the door, two pairs of eyes faced each other. Like the door they opened wider and wider.

"You are Tom!"

"You are Michael!"

"Yes." They said in unison.

Tom looked. This was not the face or the figure in the photograph. That was a picture of an overgrown boy. This was. . . . He looked. He felt his eyes staring until they would burst. His mind tried to register the warm glowing dark brown eyes, the soft silk-like, near black-thinning hair, and lips shaped for kissing that faced him. Poor Tom! He couldn't think. He stood back to let the visitor through and from the back he measured the slim waist and the firm round arse that winked an invitation with every step he took.

Tom led the visitor into the sitting room. They sat and looked at each other.

"How did you get here?" Tom asked for the want of something to say.

"I walked."

"From Chester?" Tom couldn't believe it. "Chester is five miles away."

"There wasn't a bus at the time I wanted, so I had no choice. In any case I enjoy walking." Michael sounded so matter of fact.

"I hope it will be worth the walk." That was more than a hint from Tom.

"I didn't want to meet you," Michael said. "I knew a

Tommy who was short and fat and I thought you had to be the same. Illogical, I know."

"Tom, please," Tom cut in. "I finished with Tommy years ago. I hated the name."

And they both laughed. They both knew what they wanted to say but neither knew how to begin.

"I didn't go a lot on your photograph," Tom said eventually.

"I thought it was quite a good one."

"The real thing is much better."

Again they laughed together not knowing what else to do. Then Michael asked where the toilet was.

"I'll show you." This was obviously the invite Tom was waiting for.

"Thanks," was Michael's reply. "I'll be able to find it on my own."

That was a putdown if ever there was one. When he returned Tom was staring at the floor. He didn't bother to look up. Michael sat beside him on the settee and said very gently, "I really did want a pee. I didn't want to start in a lavatory. Not with you."

The plot for a romantic novel? Almost! But then the best fiction has to be based on fact. Michael sat beside Tom on the settee. They introduced themselves. They knew each other's names so there was no need for words. Lips, mouths and tongues can silently say so much.

A little later Ash came to see who the caller was. He looked into the sitting room.

"It might be better," he said very quietly, "if you two went upstairs."

And that was what they did.

Just before opening time, in the evening, Gareth arrived. The first thing he wanted to know was where was Tom, and had Michael arrived? Ash beckoned him well out of hearing of the customers in the bar and told him of the uncalculated hiccup in their planning. Reluctantly, but with a reasonable amount of good grace Gareth spent the Saturday night helping Ash behind the bar instead of helping himself to Tom.

113

As a boyfriend swapping evening it was a non-event. But since neither Tom nor Michael knew they had cocked-up their mentor's plans, they were blissfully unaware of any frustration they had caused. (Cock-up may be the wrong phrase to use.)

Over the next two weeks Tom and Michael met every day, usually away from the pub.

One evening was spent in a wood well screened from prying eyes. On an early summer's evening under trees cloaked deep in the beauty of the Cheshire countryside the two young men made love. Every move of their naked bodies and warm lips told the wonder of love to God's creation. A stream ran through the wood, quietly gurgling its pleasure, as if to accompany and counter balance the music of flesh on flesh.

No one disturbed them. The birds were too busy mating to bother. Tom and Michael had chosen the Duke of Westminster's land and had the gamekeeper happened upon them he would have wondered what game they were up to, or were they doing a bit of illicit poaching!

That night, each in his own bed, they were forced to face the facts of nature. They may have hidden themselves from humans but bare bums had to be a banquet to a multitude of uninvited mosquitoes.

But youth, virility and desire are not to be put off by a few bumps. Boots the Chemist provided, at a price, protection for the next occasion and the next. They even fell into each other's arms and kissed on the riverbank by the towpath, ignored by passers-by.

Gareth made only one comment on the loss of his boyfriend; "That's the way it goes."

Ash, on the other hand was much more magnanimous. "That was what I hoped would happen," Whether his remark contained any truth neither of the two young lovers ever knew, but it was at his suggestion Tom borrowed Betsy to make the travelling easier.

The last night of Tom's holiday came, as it had to. Tom knew they were to part. Holidays and holiday romances cannot go on forever. He had always wanted to meet a 'Michael'. The name conjured up everything that wasn't of his daily life. One

114

thing he did know, he was not as infatuated as he had been when he met Ash. He could say 'goodbye' and also say sincerely that he hoped they would meet again.

Tom and Michael faced each other. They were standing in the bus station waiting to be taken in opposite directions: Tom back to the pub for his final night and Michael to his parents. In a few minutes the buses would be leaving. There was nothing to be done but to say goodbye and promise to keep in touch. They did hold hands, but it was far too public a place to kiss.

"We will keep in touch," Tom said, "You have my address."

"Yes. Yes I have it." Michael was smiling. Tom thought it hardly the time for smiling.

"Good bye." Tom's bus was waiting. He spoke quickly. "Bye."

"I'll see you in a couple of weeks." Tom couldn't believe what he had heard.

"A couple of weeks?" Tom questioned.

"Yes. A couple of weeks. I've given in my notice. I'm coming to live with you in Dorset."

"My bus. I'll miss it." Tom was in a panic.

"Run." Michael pushed his lover towards the bus. "There will be a letter for you on Monday," he called as Tom ran.

Neither missed their buses, and there was a letter lying on the mat inside the door of Tuckers at Lower Budleigh when Tom returned after his first day back at work the following Monday. Michael had given in his notice and was coming to live with him.

The following Saturday week Michael stepped off the train at the old GWR station. Tom was waiting for him.

Before Michael could come to live with Tom at 'Tuckers' he had to give his family a very convincing reason for leaving home so soon after being demobbed. His mother could see no reason whatsoever why he should. He had a good job in the County Architect's Department which a bit of family influence had helped secure. There was a nice girl, connected with the church youth club, who would make him a very good wife. Both families were agreed it would be an excellent match. All

115

that was needed was for Michael to ask. The engagement ring had a reserved notice on it. What more could any young man want? Michael's father had little to say in the matter. Tom knew nothing of this. Michael must have lied very convincingly to his family. His actions were never questioned. For their consumption he had been offered a transfer to Dorset. It had all happened very quickly. The job on offer would lead to promotion. It was too good to miss. In fact no job existed. He had packed in his job with no idea what he was going to do other than live with the man he wanted. He would find something; it was the era when there was no shortage of work. He had to lie. He couldn't tell his mother why he was leaving home and moving to Dorset. Tom was not mentioned. Introducing Tom was to come later when the ground had been prepared, the seeds sown and a perennial relationship flowered.

Tom would often remind Michael that he wasn't even consulted if they should live together, to which Michael would always reply, "I wasn't going to risk being turned down!"

To make the move convincing he told his mother accommodation had been found for him with a Mrs Jones who had a beautiful old house right in the country. Jones was a half-truth. Ash would have been horrified at the implication of being a plain, unhyphenated Mrs.

Michael's fabrication worked. Regularly in letters from home Michael was asked to thank Mrs Jones for looking after him! Within a week of arriving in Dorset he got a job with the Government Land Agency dealing with property ownership sufficiently allied to architecture to save any more invention. He would, dearly, have liked to be able to tell his mother the truth. He had found the relationship that was right for him. He wanted nothing more than his mother to give her blessing. She, in her turn, wanted her only son to be happy but this blessing was too much to ask. Michael knew that had his mother been told the truth she would never be able to face her world again. The lovers knew, only too well, she had to be shielded from such destructive truth.

Michael was very close to his family but his orthodox Anglican upbringing had been stricter and was more deeply

116

ingrained than Tom's West Country version of Methodism. Michael had been a server at church before going into the RAF and his mother was one of the mainstays of that church. Michael hated lying, but he had no choice. He could not tell his parents he was leaving home to live with a man called Tom whom he had met while Tom was on holiday, and they had had sex almost every day for those two weeks.

Had he met a girl under similar circumstances, and believed he had fallen in love, the idea of going to live with her would have been totally unacceptable. His mother would have expected to meet and approve the girl. The approval would have been followed by a courtship and an engagement. What Michael did was to break all the rules of decency. To uproot oneself to live with a holiday pick-up was, totally, unacceptable to any decent family. Irrespective of convention it was taking one hell of a risk no matter what the sexes. To say his mother would have had a fit would be a cliché but Michael knew he would never be able to face her after. To even hint at the truth was more than Michael was prepared to do. There was nothing in the thinking of his parents' generation to even begin to prepare them for such a break with the established order as all right thinking people knew it. Michael's sister had married. Michael would do the same in God's good time and produce children.

The couple never spoke of the implications of Michael leaving home. They were doing what they believed to be right. The fact that they were flouting convention and adopting a lifestyle well ahead of the time did not enter their thinking. They were in love. They had found happiness. Why should they not live together?

Neither of the youngsters thought to ask Ashley if they could live together in his house. The presumption of youth!

In the period before meeting Michael, Tom had been able to leave farm work and obtained an interesting job in the Planning Department of the County Council. He was making his own decisions, but he could hardly claim to have had any part in the decision that Michael should come and live with him, though it hardly needs stating he was not adverse to that decision being made for him. Was it luck they met? Whatever the answer to that question Tom knew he had been, unbelievably, lucky that someone so beautiful, and able, had walked into his life when he heard the knocking and opened the pub door.

Michael had no idea of the world he was moving into. He had been brought up in a 1930s semi with a bathroom. Living in the cottage at Lower Budleigh was a risk neither he nor Tom considered. In the event, the lack of a bathroom and the basic sanitary arrangements did not bother Michael nor did the effort of having to carry water from the well a hundred yards away, or dispose of material that one pull of a chain, in any civilised house, would flush away, or light the fire when he got home from work, or not having a mother to clean and cook.

He was living with the man he loved and that offset any such minor inconveniencies.

When he went home the following Christmas he learned he had missed out! It was after church they broke the news. The girl chosen for him had given up waiting and was getting engaged to another.

"I am sure she will be happy," was Michael's heartfelt comment.

"I hope she will," was the reply from his mother. The word 'hope' was charged with irony. Then she added with feeling, "She could have done better." The implication being, had the girl tried harder Michael would have stayed and married her. It was to be a year before Tom met Michael's family. There was no problem. The two young men were friends and that was acceptable.

In Dorset things were different, Mrs Adamson had no problem taking her son's new friend into the family. She did their washing. This involved a weekly visit cycling over the hill which they enjoyed. Tom and Michael, two males in their early twenties, living together was simply accepted, and Tom hardly stopped to think how lucky he was. He had a brother and sister both married with children, and that must have helped keep the pressure off him to reproduce. As far as his parents were concerned their son was happy. What more could be asked? Were they simply human or were they almost half a century

118

ahead of the rest of society? Whatever the answer, the result was the same; two young men could live and love in peace.

Michael got on well with Tom's mother. They chatted and laughed together. It was several weeks after the first meeting that Michael admitted he couldn't understand much of what she said. Her broad Dorset accent, almost dialect, was a foreign language to him but he did know when to laugh. All her seventeen stones shook with pleasure and that was the cue he needed.

Tom and Michael made no promises to each other. Theirs was a whirlwind courtship that, against all the odds, survived and grew.

One winter's evening when they were sitting by the open log fire in the cottage Tom said to Michael, "I didn't fall in love with you."

Michael frowned in disbelief.

"No," Tom smiled and waited for what seemed forever. "No. That first day when I opened the door of the pub I saw something wonderful standing there. I wanted you. I was sure I'd been given the brush off when you said you'd go to the loo alone. This gorgeous thing doesn't want me."

"You were wrong."

"I know that now." Tom seemed to find the next sentence difficult. "I didn't fall in love with you. You made me love you."

They spent a year together in Ashley's cottage at Lower Budleigh before moving to London. It was a simple domestic period where they learned to live together. Other than that brief admission by Tom, they never tried to analyse their feelings or their relationship. Tom changed sex roles. With Ashley he always had to be the passive partner, now he was active. He was happy with either role. They instinctively felt they needed each other not simply for sex, that was important, but an emotional bond developed that would to have to stand a great deal of testing.

Tom and Michael were within a few months of being the same age and unlike Tom's relationship with Ashley, the two young men became interdependent. They met at lunch times, shared the housework, though Tom did the cooking. Two men living together? Nothing was more natural. Ash rarely came down to the cottage. He spent no more than a couple of weeks with them.

Most of the winter weekends were spent photographing each other. Portraits that could be developed by Boots the Chemist without a blush.

After that first Christmas, the idea of marriage for Michael was never mentioned again and any question as to the identity of this Mrs Jones was also somehow avoided. Michael and his friend Tom were '*Confirmed Bachelors*'.

Michael's family were never aware of the sleeping arrangements in the cottage at Lower Budleigh. The double bed would have been difficult to explain away, but they had been down London and visited the couple in their bedsitter. There the two single beds said everything. It seemed their relationship had nothing to fear - then one short letter and a garbled telephone message from Dorset changed everything. Michael was haunted by the spectre of his family getting any hint of his sexuality and the inevitable publicity that had to come from his involvement with Ashley. They lived within twenty miles of Ashley's family home making the danger a terrifying possibility. The damage the press reporting would do to him hardly mattered compared with the destruction of his family who were innocent. Even a hint of scandal would destroy his mother and he had no idea how he would be able to live with the consequences. Neither mentioned their fears. There was no point. Each day they looked for another letter from Dorset.

RID ENGLAND OF THIS PLAGUE

Chapter 11

The telephone call from Dorset was a week ago. There had been no follow up or explanation and more than three weeks had passed since Ash was arrested. Tom and Michael were beginning to feel safe lying naked on the bed, the prelude to the first love making since the letter from Tom's mother.

The telephone in the entrance hall rang. It was just after seven in the evening. Tom swore and said, "Let somebody else answer it." They weren't expecting a call and they were fed up with taking messages for tenants on the upper floors.

The phone stopped ringing.

Sex between the two young men had always been spontaneous and passionate; so it was that evening. They had eaten their evening meal and Michael was at the sink preparing to wash up. Tom took the tea towel to wipe the dishes. This meant he had to stand behind his boy friend. He put his hand down and felt the buttocks that had held their magnetism from the day Michael walked through the door of the pub near Chester. Michael almost resisted. Fear had not completely gone, but his hands were wet so all he could do was half-heartedly say "no" and hold his hands up. Tom undid his lover's belt, pulled down his trousers and pushed him onto the bed. Tom adored his lover's slim hairy chest and would often asked him to stand naked, then turn around so he could luxuriate in his firm round arse.

The phone rang again. The lovers ignored it. Tom rolled Michael over onto his face. The phone continued ringing.

"Let it ring. It will be for the girls upstairs as it was last night and the night before. They can hear it. They can come down," Tom said as he stripped.

The pay telephone, the only one in the building, was for the use of all the tenants but being in the hallway on the ground floor it usually meant Tom or Michael had to answer it. There was one old doorbell on each of the upper floors and it was a question of ringing the correct bell, then waiting for someone on the upper floors to answer. In nineteen fifty-four telephoning was still a bit of a luxury.

The phone would not stop ringing.

"Ready?" Tom whispered in Michael's ear as he lay on top of him.

The insistent ringing gave them no peace. "Better answer it." And Michael rolled Tom away. "It's got to be something ringing like that."

"I'll go," Tom stood up, "and I hope it is something."

He quickly pulled on a pair of trousers and went out into the hall. The phone stopped ringing. He swore and came back into room. He had hardly closed the door when it rang again. He shrugged his shoulders, grimaced at Michael lying naked on the bed and went back into the hall and picked up the phone.

"Gulliver 2708."

"Is that Tom?"

"Yes. Who's that?"

"Ashley."

"Ash!"

"I have to be quick. I thought you weren't going to answer. I'm in a phone box. I may be being watched. I have been arrested."

Tom tried to speak but all he could do was make a sound like a muffled cough. The worst had happened and he couldn't even ask.

Ash did not wait for Tom to speak. He spoke quickly, "I'm on bail. I will come up to London tomorrow. That's if I can. I get to Waterloo at six. Will phone you from there. Do not phone me at the cottage. The police. . . ."

The line went dead.

Tom put the receiver down and stared at it not knowing what to do. The silence made Michael curious. He peered round the door.

"What's up?" he asked.

Tom motioned him back into the room, followed, shut the

122

door deliberately and firmly so that no one could overhear what was said.

"That was Ashley. He has been arrested. It has to be serious trouble."

Michael was stunned. He picked up his clothes. The speed with which he pulled on his trousers was, in itself, a statement of fear. Fear of a law that showed no mercy.

A matter of minutes ago living had been fun. Now life itself had stopped.

Decently clothed he sat on the bed. "What did he say?"

"He is coming up to London tomorrow. He will phone us at six. I'll be able to get home from work by then."

They both sat looking at each other not knowing what to do.

"There's the washing up to finish."

That prosaic domestic task seemed to break the tension.

"You always do so well with the our meals, and I know it isn't easy." Michael said.

Tom smiled but for the rest of the evening they hardly spoke. There was nothing to say.

"Ten o'clock." Who said it hardly matters. It was the signal to go to bed. Tom undressed quickly and got into bed. Michael took his clothes off very slowly. They slept naked. Tom watched wondering what his lover was thinking. Michael hesitated. He stood still with his hands clasped across his chest, then slowly walked to the side of his bed and knelt and with his elbows resting on the side of his bed he prayed silently. Tom followed suit. Each recited every word of the Lords' prayer with great care. That night they did not even kiss before putting out the light.

Both, in their different ways, had been brought up to conform. Even so, both had expressed their sexuality when they had chosen to live together. Michael was faced with a far greater problem than Tom. The influence of his Anglican mother's fundamentalist beliefs was powerful. The fear of her reaction to the discovery that her son had - the act was beyond description - was more frightening than the vengeance of the law. But neither would have been able to analyse whether the act of praying was fear of retribution or a cry for help in a world that would not listen.

As there was only one bathroom in the Camden Square house they washed at the kitchen sink. It was no problem. A kettle on the gas cooker provided hot water and a small mirror made shaving possible. The mirror was screwed to the wall by the window and that gave all the light needed. The morning after the call from Ashley, Tom was at the sink. Michael was dressed and ready to leave. He had to get to Blackfriars by nine. Tom had only to get to Kentish Town. He wiped the shaving soap from his mouth and gave his lover a parting kiss. They looked at each other then Michael said, "They've got our addresses at least twice."

Tom nodded. They assumed the police were efficient at coordinating information. All night the knowledge that they were trapped had taunted him like some dervish dancer whirling and mocking with every twist of its body and grinning face.

Michael left, closing the door silently behind him. Tom had just turned the collar of his shirt up ready to put on his tie - going to work without a jacket and tie was inconceivable - when Michael came back into the room. Tom turned from the mirror in surprise and started to say, "Forgotten something?"

Michael made certain the door was shut before he spoke. "I think we will stick to what we agreed and not tell anybody about this. James no. Certainly not Denzil."

Tom gave an ironic half laugh, "No. Not Denzil. He would have too much advice to give. Remember what he keeps saying prominent queers should do? Why not tell James?"

"It wouldn't be fair on him." Michael's voice rose as if he was making the most obvious of statements. "He's finished college. He's got to find the right job. He doesn't need to be lumbered with our troubles."

Tom nodded, "They may well find out soon enough." Tom finished the knot on his tie and pulled it tight up to his throat.

They stood facing each other. They were alone. They couldn't even tell their closest friends. This wasn't a nightmare. It was the sword of Damocles hanging by a single hair that, with the self-assurance of youth, they never thought would break. Now it had broken. There would be no mercy from the law. They had lived by evading the law. Never questioning it. It was as though their thinking had been primed to accept the legal system as being divinely inspired.

The local London papers left no doubt how such cases were handled. The pillory still existed. They would have to stand, trapped, while anything from rotten fruit to shit was thrown at them. The penalty exacted by the law was nothing compared to that imposed by the media/society. Names and addresses and even family details would be given. The pillory was so effective that a teacher convicted of importuning for immoral purposes i.e. 'cottaging' committed suicide. The publicity, though only in the local paper, destroyed him.

Another man, alone, in an otherwise empty gentlemen's toilet was convicted of importuning for immoral purposes. As the magistrate said, "For what other purpose would you have gone into such a place at eleven o'clock at night?"

Then the magistrate added the prophetic words, "Decent men will lie easier in their beds when such places of temptation and iniquity are closed forever." Half a century later most have been closed on grounds of economy, though one had a notice on the door explaining the closure was due to anti-social behaviour!

That entire day Tom's mind was only half on his work. As the afternoon wore on Tom's work colleague asked, "What's wrong?"

"Nothing. Why?"

"You're not in any trouble?"

"No."

"You are not yourself these days."

"Your imagination."

"If you say so."

It wasn't imagination. Tom could think of nothing. If he tried, each thought was the almost impenetrable stinking darkness of the smog that stifled the city earlier that year. But through that dense swirling smog he could see, clearly, the Giant and the bars.

The past would not go away.

Both Tom and Michael left work early to be sure of getting back to South Villas in good time. By a quarter past six there had been no call from Ashley.

"He's late." Tom had to say something.

Michael looked out of the window at the garden. Tension tight he snapped, "I can tell the time."

"What if. . . .?"

"Wait."

Words they spat at each other. Words that filled the waiting. But words that could not hide their fears or lessen the anxiety. Eventually the telephone did ring. Ash was at Waterloo Station. He would get the Northern Line to Camden Town and meet them in a bar. Would Tom name a pub? It had to be an ordinary pub, certainly not one of the queer bars; somewhere quiet where they could talk and not be conspicuous. The pub Tom named was across the road from the station. It was one Tom and Michael never used. They were not known to the bar staff or customers. Ash had to be reassured. No one would know them there. Tom and Michael would wait in the public bar. There was very little chance of anyone recognising them. Ash would speak to them only when he was certain he had not been followed.

Tom and Michael walked to Camden Town not bothering to take a trolley bus. They walked in silence. Ash was not in the pub. There were only half a dozen customers. The imitation leather covered benches gave the public bar a feeling of bleakness. The dark floor covering combined with the black painted cast iron tables and the dark wood panelling, up to window height, on the walls served to emphasise that drinking beer was the sole function of that bar. In contrast to the drinking area, the bar counter was bright. Polished wood and brass and glittering glass drew the customer's attention to the source of pleasure or escape, and income for the landlord.

The two young men rarely visited any bars other than the queer ones. They ordered their drinks, the usual two halves of bitter. Again there was nothing they could do but wait. The quarter of an hour before Ash walked in seemed an eternity.

126

His entrance was not what Tom expected. There was nothing furtive about his walk. Nothing to suggest he was evading the police. He appeared the self-assured man whom Tom had followed into the GENTS nearly seven years earlier. Tom watched him carefully. The self-assurance was overdone; it was an act. His walk had lost much of its bounce. His face was drawn. This was no longer the handsome confident ex-officer. Tom studied every move of his first great love carefully. He felt no emotion. As so often, his theatrical training came into play and he felt he was in a theatre watching the opening act of an Agatha Christie play.

Ash chatted to the barman who was exactly his type. Old habits die hard. In spite of what he knew he had to face, he still had an eye for a handsome twenty year old. After a few moments Ash looked around the bar. Any observer would have thought that the last people he expected to see were Tom and Michael.

"Hello!" he called and brought his drink to join the couple at their table. It had every appearance of a chance encounter; three old friends meeting without a care in the world. Ash sat down, glancing round the bar to be sure he was out of earshot of the other customers, and as soon as the pleasantry act was over his mood changed.

"No one must ever know I've been here." He looked at each in turn. "You understand?" He was deadly serious. Michael and Tom nodded their agreement.

"What's going to happen?" Michael asked.

"It doesn't look good." Ash moved his head slowly from side to side. What he had said was obviously an understatement. The two young men wanted to ask more but lacked the courage to face the frightening truth. Ash swallowed another mouthful of beer before speaking again.

"There is one charge against me."

"One!" That one word from Michael was neither a question nor a statement. What he was thinking was, 'Thank God its only one.'

Then Ash added very slowly almost as if afraid to mouth the words. "The case has been deferred pending further investigations. There will be others."

There was no need for either to ask what it meant. Ash had been arrested and charged with one offence. That was not to be the end of the case. The police had been granted time to make more enquiries. That initial hearing would have only merited a few lines in the local paper, which explained why Tom's mother was only able to say, 'Ashley seems to be in a bit of trouble.'

The two young men held their glasses with both hands and stared into the beer as if gazing into crystal balls, hoping to see the future. Where would it end? How would it end? Their glasses clouded. They could see nothing.

"The police will be coming to see you. That is certain, and they have threatened to throw the book at me if I contact any potential witness. The police are out to get me. Have no doubt about that. They've as good as said so. They will involve anyone; anyone who will say enough to incriminate me." His voice was matter of fact. There was no emotion, no anger no self-pity.

There was a pause. Then Ash smiled and said, "You both look well." An incongruous thing to say but it broke the tension.

"What do the police know?" Michael asked.

"I've told them nothing about you two." Who else was likely to be involved he did not say. He had returned from North Wales to live at the cottage not long after Tom and Michael came to London. What had happened to his father's business was not explained. More importantly, Ash said nothing of his life in Lower Budleigh over the past three years.

"They took everything from the cottage: letters, addresses, photographs; everything. They ransacked the place. They've asked a lot of questions. They've dragged in everybody I've ever known. They must have been through my address book a dozen times, but all they know about you two is what they've guessed. When they come, and they will come, say nothing. Don't be tricked. They are very good at that. They will say I have told them. Well I haven't." He seemed to be saying, 'I can't do much for myself but I will do everything I can for you.' and his sole reason for taking the enormous risk of coming to

London was to keep the two of them out of trouble.

"Thanks." Michael touched Ash's hand and repeated, "Thanks."

"How did it all come out?" Tom asked, "How did it all?"

"Do you remember Rhys?"

"Rhys?" Tom was confused.

"The Welsh soldier. The slim blonde one. The one you picked up in the Town Hall cottage."

"He picked me up." Tom corrected.

"It doesn't matter," said Ash.

"Oh yes it does," said Michael. "If he's saying things against you it does matter."

"Maybe, but who are the police going to believe?" was Ashley's comment.

Tom butted in, "Yes, I remember. You were with me when we met him later in the Volunteer. What's the connection?"

"After you left and came to London he came over to the cottage and then when he was demobbed he came to stay a couple of times."

"And?" Tom wanted to know more.

"I introduced him to some of my friends."

"I imagine he was very popular." There was a slight edge in Tom's voice. He was obviously thinking back to his Pygmalionisation.

"He was very pretty." There was a pause.

"Shall I get another drink?" Michael asked.

"Yes, thanks." Ash and Tom spoke together.

While Michael was at the bar, Ash filled in the details of his journey up from Dorset. "I'm certain the police have been watching my every move. So I drove up to Wool. Poor old Betsy is on her last legs. She's been good. I'd hate to part with her. I drove through Weymouth once with two matelots kissing in the open dickey seat at the back. It was a great joke then." He stopped himself. Those days were gone. "I don't know." He said and shook his head desperately trying to put his thinking back where it belonged. "I parked well away from the station at Wool, waited until the last minute before jumping on the Bournemouth train. Changed trains there and got a later one.

At Waterloo I got a bus, then the tube to Camden Town.

"You weren't followed?"

"No."

Michael came back from the bar and put the drinks on the table. There were now only two other customers in the bar. "How did they catch Rhys?"

"They didn't catch him." Ash took a long drink. Then slowly put his glass back on the table, leaned back in his chair took out a packet of cigarettes and handed them round. Michael took one. Tom shook his head.

"You're still on the pipe," said Ash with his characteristic laugh.

"Yep," said Tom filling his pipe as the other two lit their cigarettes.

Ash drew a deep lung full of smoke and blew it up towards the ceiling. "When the business with the Darnley set broke, Rhys's mother read it in the papers. It was in all the papers. It couldn't be missed. You must have read it." He paused. "Rhys was living at home. He adored his mother. He always said she was his friend, not his mother. He wouldn't buy clothes without her. Whatever she said went. He was the only child. She smothered him. To cut a long story short, he told her about the people he'd met with me. He'd met the gentry. We had drinks together and . . . . well you knew Rhys. He wouldn't miss as chance." Ash took a mouthful of beer.

"He must have wanted to impress his mother." Michael added trying to help Ash tell a very difficult story.

"Possibly. Anyway," and he sat up, then leaned his elbows on the table and stared at his glass of beer. "Anyway, his mother remembered names. When he first told her, she told her friends, 'My son regularly meets with the gentry, the upper class.' You can imagine her loving every minute of it. The long and short of it was she made him tell her all. That wasn't difficult. Rhys would not have dared cross his mother in anything. His confession about himself and me must have shocked her. He couldn't have lied to her." Ash paused and shook his head in disbelief at what he had said and took another swig at his beer.

"What happened?" Michael asked.

"She marched him down to the Police Station. Between his mother and the police he didn't have a chance. From what the police have said to me he told them everything, but I'm not sure that he mentioned you." and Ash turned to Tom. "I imagine Rhys had never told his mother about you."

"I was just one more bit of trade along with all the others he couldn't remember." Tom added.

"Something like that," said Ash with a wry smile. He stubbed his cigarette out and held up his glass and gazed into it looking at the past. "He has turned Queen's Evidence. He will be a witness for the prosecution."

"He will be in the clear." was Michael's reaction.

"Yes. . . . yes. Rhys will be in the clear." Ash slowly lowered his glass. Then put it firmly on the table to emphasise the point. He had seen his future.

There was nothing to add. It was time for another fag. That a mother could deliberately implicate her son in such a scandal was something they could not understand. None of the other customers, nor the barman, in that Camden Town pub would have seen anything unusual, certainly nothing queer, in the behaviour of the three ordinary looking chaps quietly drinking and smoking in the far corner. No one even noticed that now they were smoking in silence, each preoccupied with his own thoughts. Tom and Michael were thinking of their own families and the devastation facing them.

It is doubtful if it would have done any good, or even helped, had they been able to hear Rhys's mother explaining her actions.

"I had to do it for his own good. Rhys has always been easily led. Ever since he was a child. If he ever did anything wrong I would say to him 'Why did you do that?' and, I tell you the truth, it was always the other boys who led him on. His father said going in the army would make a man of him. Now you can see what it did. Conscription - bah! All it has ever done is to make decent boys mix with the dregs. I have prayed, and the minister at chapel has prayed with me, that this will shock my poor boy and bring him to his senses. We are going to find

131

him a nice decent girl and he will settle down and put all this perversion behind him. That's what I say. That's where those men belong: right behind him!" She paused for breath.

"And you couldn't have spoken a truer word." interjected her confidant.

"You can see what happened," his mother continued "These people with money and such like turned the poor boy's head. In a way I'm glad it's out in the open. Though how I shall ever live down the shame of it I'll never know. Chapel has been a great comfort. No one is beyond redemption. I know he has been led astray, but the gate to the fold is always open. In a way I blame myself. I did tell him about camp followers, but it never occurred to me men could. . . . I tell you. . . . I cannot even mouth the words. I met this man, Ashley, once. He seemed such a nice man too and so charming but then, how else would the Devil work?"

And her confidant agreed, adding "Men! That's the bit about marriage I did not like. Being pulled and pushed around and things. I am glad we are past it now. My man's got the choir now and that keeps his mind off. . . . if you know what I mean."

And they both knew.

Ash finished his drink and without a word went to the bar for replacements.

"How bad do you think it is?" Tom asked his partner.

"No idea. There's not a lot we can do, is there?" was all Michael could say.

In silence they watched Ash get the drinks and bring them back to the table.

"What do you suggest we do?" asked Michael.

"Don't do what Kenneth did." Ash said with obvious bitterness.

"Kenneth?" The name meant nothing to Michael.

"He lives in Bournemouth. You never met him." Tom explained.

"He always was a bit dizzy, but he answered every question the police asked him."

"And he's turned Queen's Evidence?" was Michael's half-question half-statement.

"No. They are not working it like that. I think they are going to charge him with indecency and he will plead guilty. He will probably get a year at the most, but it's all going to count against me." Ash put his glass down, leaned forward and indicated that Tom and Michael should do the same. This had to be the crux of the visit. "If you do what Kenneth has done I shall be in even more trouble. It's going to be bad enough as it is."

The reasons for Ash's journey to London were more complex than Tom and Michael at first thought. Self-preservation played a part. He knew what was lined up against him and the last thing he wanted was for Tom and Michael to fall into whatever trap the police might bait for them. He went on, "Remember I've said nothing about either of you. I've done everything I can to keep you out. I do take some comfort in knowing you two are happy together."

"We'll do what we can." was all Michael could say and Tom nodded his agreement.

The bar was now beginning to fill. There were people within earshot. Ash was, obviously, uncomfortable.

"I think it's time we went," he said. They drank up and left the pub. Outside they shook hands. It was a very formal parting. Men embracing in the street would have been frowned upon. Kissing would have outraged public decency and possibly risked arrest. There was little the three could say. Tom and Michael thanked Ash for coming up to London. They promised whatever help they could.

"Don't come down to Dorset and don't contact me. That will be exactly what they want. Whatever else, do not say you've seen me." was Ash's parting.

They promised, and watched him cross the road to the underground station. Ashley disappeared without turning back. Both Tom and Michael knew they would not see him again until . . . . until? They thought it might be eighteen months, or possibly two years but they had yet to learn that even-handedness under the law was a fiction. Had they been able to look up at the statue of justice above the Old Bailey they would have seen the scales of justice were weighted against

133

them.

They knew the law. They knew that by, simply, being homosexual they were breaking the law and they knew there was nothing they could do. In common with many of their friends they saw the law as an enemy, an enemy to be outwitted in order that they might be able to live as they were meant to live. More, devastatingly, they saw the law as an enemy that could not be destroyed.

It was on that walk up the Camden Road that Tom and Michael made the decision to seek help or solace in the church, if there was a church that would even allow them through the doors. Fear of retribution had dumped such a weight on them they were being crushed. They had no doubt that when the case became public knowledge the shit would be spread so thickly over the papers making them sell like hot cakes. Then every cum flavoured crumb would be lapped up with relish by a populace so shocked that queers could dare enjoy their sexuality.

Chapter 12

The next day and the next brought neither the police nor any news to end their fears. Tom wasn't going to write his usual letter home but Michael persuaded him.

"You must let them know you are alright. If you don't write your Mother will think something has happened and that wouldn't be fair."

It was a totally noncommittal note:- 'We haven't done much this week. Michael sends his love etc.'. Tom found the letter difficult to write. He knew his parents would be worried, to say the least. His mother was a very strong woman. She was more than capable of holding her own and had weathered many a village storm, but this was not just a passing storm. This was a whirlwind that would destroy all in its path. What was being said in the village? Would his mother be damned for producing such a son? Everyone would have known by now of his involvement and that he had lived at Lower Budleigh. What they didn't know they would guess. It was better not to think about it. There was nothing he could do, but he could not stop thinking.

Would there ever be another letter from home? What was his father thinking and feeling? Tom had once found a risqué French magazine hidden at home, and his father had said that if his sister got pregnant by a soldier, during the war, the baby would be brought up as theirs, but that didn't mean he could accept this. Both the magazine and an illegitimate child spelled straightforward normal sex. This wasn't straightforward or normal. Not by the standards of what had to be his father's world. Tom admired his father. Would this destroy him? Would Tom, ever again, be able to go home? And what of the village? Would he dare show his face there again?

The plague had been diagnosed in the Hardy Country. Would this need a twentieth century Judge Jeffrey (the Hanging

135

Judge) and a cure as ruthless as that for foot and mouth - shooting and burning?

Tom was certain the relaxed world of his teens had disappeared.

Since Ashley's visit, Tom and Michael had not gone out. Even going to the pictures, as a means of escape, held no attraction. Tom cooked the evening meals then they sat and listened to the wireless until time to go to bed. There was little conversation. What was there to say? They couldn't run away. They couldn't hide. Since there could be no escape, there was nothing to plan. They sat and waited, like prisoners, for a sentence from an unseen judge.

It was nearly midnight on the fifth night after Ash's visit when the phone rang. They were both in bed. The ringing persisted. Both too scared to move. Michael eventually forced himself out of bed. Neither spoke. Obviously no one else was going to answer the ringing. Michael went out into the hall, leaving the door open.

Tom heard him say, "Hello. Gulliver 2708." Then a pause. When Michael spoke again he was angry. "Will I go and do what? Do you realise what time it is? Is it important? None of my business? It is my business. You've got me out of bed. I'll tell you what I'm going to do. I am going to put the receiver down on the table and you can shout up the stairs and attract her attention. Good night."

Michael came back into the room. He was furious.

"It was that bloody bloke who's living with one of the girls up on the top floor."

"Bet he's drunk again."

"Told me to go up and tell her he'll be late. It wasn't a request it was a bloody order."

"It's not the first time he's done it."

"I bet it'll be the last," and Michael got back into bed.

"Is the phone still off the hook?" Tom asked.

"I suppose so," and Michael pulled the bedclothes over his head.

Without a word Tom went and replaced the receiver. As he got back into his bed he said, "I was afraid it was Ashley again

136

or. . . . But they would not have telephoned at this hour." He did not need to explain the sentence.

"Well, it wasn't," was Michael's muffled reply.

"Good night."

"Go to sleep. I've got to go to work in the morning." At any other time midnight would not have been considered late. What Michael was really saying was, "Leave me alone. I want to cut myself off from the whole bloody world."

Tom lay willing himself into a sleep that would not come.

The next day passed, as the previous ones, with nothing from the police. That evening the two young men were sitting in their room when they heard the bloke from the third floor calling down the stairwell to the landlady.

"Mrs Urbano."

"Yes?"

"That phone is for the use of us all, isn't it?"

"Yes. Why?"

He launched into the tale of grievance about the refusal of those in room two to pass on a message. Then came the ultimate damning. "They are queer. They are a couple of queers. Do you expect people like me to live in a house with perverts?"

After a moments thought, Mrs Urbano said very quietly, "No, I don't."

"I can't hear you."

Mrs Urbano raised her voice, "I do not like shouting. If you want to speak to me, come down."

There was a pause. Then footsteps were heard on the stairs. Michael opened their door, a fraction, to be able to hear what was said.

"What are you going to do about it then?"

"Ask your girl friend to leave. She is the tenant, not you." Michael frowned in disbelief. Mrs Urbano was so matter of fact.

"Do what?" That was a shout.

"Ask her to leave and I assume you will go too. Tom and Michael are excellent tenants. Today is Friday and your rent would be due tomorrow. However, I would ask you to vacate the room by eleven in the morning." Mrs Urbano had assumed a very authorative voice which neither Tom nor Michael had heard before. She would accept no argument.

"If you want to let your house to poofs we'll go. We'll go tonight," the man from the top floor bluffed self-righteously.

"Fine." said Mrs Urbano. The condescension in her voice flowed like treacle laced with vinegar. "And I will put seven and six refund for your rent on the table here by the telephone."

"Don't bother."

"Oh, it will be no bother, I assure you."

Footsteps on the stairs indicated the altercation was over and he was returning to the third floor. Mrs Urbano opened the front door to go back to her basement flat when the voice called down, "On second thoughts we'll go in the morning."

"That will be perfectly alright if you feel able to suffer another night here." With that she closed the front door very firmly.

"Well I'll be. . . ." Tom and Michael laughed in unison and they fell on the bed into each other's arms.

When Tom got home from work on the following Tuesday there was a letter on the hall table for him. The handwriting was unmistakable. His mother's. Tom held the letter. Whatever he felt, there was nothing for it but to open the envelope and read what she had to say.

The letter must have been written in a hurry. His mother never put the full address. She simply headed her letters '*Home*' and under it the date. On this letter there was nothing. That was ominous.

Dear Tom,

The weather here is a lot better and your father can get on with the garden.

This morning three policemen came to the door and they said they wanted you, so I said you were not here. Then the one that did all the talking asked me where you were.

What odds is that of yours where he is? I said to him.

Then he went on about you being mixed up with Ashley-Jones so I wanted to know how he knew you was mixed up in it.

We have our ways of finding out he said.

I think they were going to come into the house. One of them try to push

138

*past me. He is not here. I said, and they looked at me as if I were telling a
lie. Well I were not having none of that. The one standing behind him took
out a pad and pencil all ready to write. I looked at him.*

*Go on and he said it again. Go on he said. Well nobody says go on to
me. Not the way he said it.*

*Tell us his address. He talked to me as if I were a kid. I said not a word.
We have our ways of finding out he said. Well that was it so I said. You go
on and you use your ways to find out where he be. Good morning to thee.
An I shut the door in their face.*

Your Mum.

Tom could hear his mother. She must have written the
letter immediately the police had gone. He bent his head and
kissed the letter mistakes and all. She must have been in a real
temper to misspell or misuse any word in a letter. That letter
told him everything he wanted to know. He did not have to fear
for his mother. She was protecting her family as fiercely as any
tigress would. He had hardly time to put the letter back in the
envelope when Mrs Urbano tapped on the door. It was the
news he was waiting for, and dreading. The police had called
that afternoon and would be back at seven. She asked no
questions. She simply delivered the message and turned to go.
Before she closed the heavy front door to go down to her
basement flat she looked back and very gently said, "I hope it's
nothing serious."

"I shouldn't think so," was Tom's reply.

Mrs Urbano half closed her eyes, half smiled and nodded.
A simple gesture but one that gave Tom a great deal of
comfort.

It was a quarter to seven before Michael got home. There
was no time to eat. Neither of them wanted to. Whatever
happened they would admit nothing. Accept established facts
i.e. they knew Ashley and had lived at Lower Budleigh but deny
everything else and stick to it. No matter what. That was the
agreement.

They did not kiss or hold each other. They nodded with
pursed lips and closed eyes. A silent assent.

At exactly seven the front door bell rang.

The timing had to be all part of police tactics. They would have calculated that the two potential prisoners would anxiously watch the clock. Fear plus precision would give them control. The police must have sat in their car, outside the house, and waited until the precise minute. Tom and Michael went to the door together. There were four men outside. They were not ordinary coppers. These were wearing peaked caps. One was at the door; the others had, deliberately, arranged themselves on the steps so that the whole street could see them. In Dorset they would have attracted a lot of attention but Camden Square was very different. In bedsitter land who would bother to look? Who would know or care what happened next door?

In a loud voice the senior of the four coppers asked, "Mr Thomas Adamson and Mr Michael Cliffe?"

Tom and Michael acknowledged their names. Two of the policemen stepped forward. "Mr Cliffe, will you come with us?" Michael said nothing. He followed the two officers down the steps to their waiting car. Was Michael to be taken away? Tom panicked.

"Mr Cliffe will be questioned in the police car." They were to be questioned separately. Tom hadn't time to work out why. The other two officers almost pushed Tom back as they blocked the doorway.

"May we come in?" It was not a request. It was an order.

Tom stepped back. They came in and closed the door.

"Which is your room?"

Tom silently ushered them into the bedsitter.

The officers looked around inspecting the room. One went to the window and looked out. The other looked at the sink as he took off his cap. Then he walked across the room taking note of the furniture. It was very disconcerting. It was a while before Tom realised it was a deliberate act. The inspection over, the officer asked, as he put his cap under his arm, "How do you think this compares with the cottage at Lower Budleigh?"

Tom wasn't sure if he was expected to answer.

"Depends what you want to do in it," observed the other.

140

"Single beds!"

"You can always get two in. One on top of the other."

"As I said, it depends what you want to do."

The allusion was so unsubtle Tom thought it had to be a line from a badly written play. Though it is doubtful if such a direct allusion to sex would have got past the Lord Chamberlain who censored all plays at that period. The feeling that their lines were scripted was to occur to Tom several times over the next hour.

"Do you have your own beds - you and Mr Cliffe?"

"Of course."

"Which one is yours?"

"This one." Tom pointed to his bed.

The officers appeared to make a mental note. Then the one who had removed his hat said, "Right. Shall we get down to business? If you will sit here." It was indicated Tom should sit in one of the armchairs facing the big marble fireplace and near the foot of Michael's bed.

The officer who had made the remark about the single beds was carrying a brief case which he put on the table. He then took off his cap and laid it by the brief case. He seated himself on one of the dining chairs and spread his papers on the table. This was done with great precision.

The other officer stood with his back to the fireplace. With his cap under his arm and one hand behind his back; he was dominating and slightly threatening. The policeman, who was using the table as a desk deliberately and officiously opened one folder, raised his eyebrows, glanced at Tom, and extracted several photographs. He looked at them, then with a display of great care and precision looked at his colleague for approval. He was given a nod. Then the evidence was laid face down on the table.

Tom was being softened up and he knew it.

"Relax. Sit and make yourself comfortable," the fireplace policeman said. "We are not here to harass you."

Tom sat in the armchair. It was quite low. The copper took a couple of steps from the fireplace and towered over Tom who made a mental note that the man looking down on him had to be No.1. The other sitting at the table was No.2.

"Well, where shall we start?" No. 1 said as he put his cap down and perched himself on the edge of Michael's bed where he was higher than Tom and could lean forward as he put his questions, still in a position of dominance. However, that was only partly effective as the mattress was soft and tended to rock, so he put his hands on his out-spread knees to steady himself. A miscalculation since it made him bob, almost imperceptibly, up and down. In spite of the seriousness of the situation, Tom found it slightly comic.

When he had stabilised himself, No.1 introduced himself. "I'm Detective Inspector Long, and this is Inspector Page. Now you have nothing to worry about. All you have to do is simply answer my questions. I'll be quite honest with you. We are not here to get you into trouble. You have a very nice room here. It's very comfortable. We spoke to your landlady this afternoon. She seems to think a lot of you. We want it to stay that way. Do you know why we are here?"

"No." Tom lied.

Inspector Page who was obviously No.2 said, "He knows alright." he said this almost to himself as he pretended to sort through his briefcase. Then he turned and looked at Tom. "I suggest you save yourself, and us, a lot of trouble by simply telling the truth." He would have said more if No.1 had not raised his hand and indicated he should stay quiet. No.2 picked up a sheaf of papers and again said, this time to himself, but obviously meant for Tom to hear, "I think he'd find these statements interesting, and I bet he could add a few spicy details."

"Why do you think we are here?" No.1 asked. His voice was gentle and fatherly.

"I have no idea."

"Pull the other one," No.2 said into the brief case. He then turned his head and said directly to Tom, "We are not stupid."

"Mr Ashley-Jones. You know him? Well, we know you do so don't bother to deny it." No.1 had taken over.

"Yes. I know, or rather I knew him."

"Now we are getting somewhere. I wonder if he knows

how much trouble Mr Ashley-Jones is in?" No.2 carried on making his comments into the brief case.

No.1 copper looked at his sidekick and shook his head and said very quietly, "Let me."

No.2 remained silent but watched Tom's every move. The almost imperceptible curl on his lip and the sideways glance designed to create a menacing atmosphere seemed, to Tom, to be straight out of a British B Cops and Robbers movie. No.1 spoke gently as if he desperately wanted to set Tom at his ease. "As my colleague said just now, it will save a lot of time if you simply tell the truth. Now let me start at the beginning. Mr Jones has been charged with a serious sexual offence. Do I make myself clear?"

Tom said nothing but he must have indicated he understood.

"How did you meet him?"

"In the Milk Bar in South Street." Tom lied.

"I asked how. Not where."

"We just started talking." Tom surprised himself. Ashley did use the Milk Bar. He was friendly with the woman who owned it.

"They probably do a good milk shake there." That was No.2. If it was meant to be a crude joke it did not register.

"What happened?"

"We. . . . We got to know each other?"

"How well?"

"How do you mean?" Tom was being deliberately slow to answer. He was trying to think. He knew full well what the questioner was getting at. He knew he had to be careful. He must make no mistakes.

"We are not in any hurry." No.1 smiled and gave a questioning frown. "I am sure you remember what happened when you went back to the cottage at Lower Budleigh."

"Nothing." Then a pause.

No.1 shook his head. "That's not good enough."

"I think we drank home made wine." Both policemen laughed. Even to Tom that sounded pathetic.

"Oh yes, we did find bottles of home made wine in the

143

cottage but I suggest that was just for starters. Do you want me to spell out what we know happened?"

"Nothing." was all Tom could say.

"We are not getting very far, are we? I came here to help you, and I do not like having my time wasted." No.1 sounded paternalistic and not in the least aggressive.

No.2 moved his chair. He said nothing, but Tom could feel the move was intended to be threatening. A pause, then No.2 noticed Tom's pipe on the table. "Yours?"

"Yes."

"You smoke it?"

"That's why I've got it." Tom was becoming irritated.

"Not cigarettes?"

"No." Tom was indignant. "I've always smoked a pipe."

No.2's tone changed. "What tobacco do you smoke?"

"Erinmore Mixture. It's there." He pointed to the pouch on the table by the side of his mother's letter. Tom was thrown by the sudden change of tone. There had to be a reason but he couldn't follow the tactics, unaware he was being softened up and his attention distracted.

No.2 leaned across and picked up the tobacco pouch, smelt it, then handed it to Tom. "Have a smoke. It will help you relax."

Tom did as he was told believing it would help him relax. It did not occur to him that No.2 wanted to see if he could actually do something as manly as smoke a pipe.

He had just struck the match when No.1 said, "We have been to see your mother." No.2 cut in, "Give him time to light up." No.1 paused. When smoke curled from Tom's pipe No.1 smiled and in the most fatherly manner repeated, with the emphasis on the word have, "We have been to see your mother."

This time, Tom was thrown by the change in questioning tactics. He had expected it to continue on his relationship with Ashley. He swallowed to stop himself reacting. He thought of the letter lying on the coffee table by his side. He dare not turn his head in case either of the policemen guessed where the letter came from. He was amazed how controlled he felt. The letter gave him strength. Both coppers watched him but did not think of looking on the table.

"Your mother is very worried. You must consider what you are doing to her. Believe me, you are making her very ill. You need to know what this is doing to her."

"She wants you to. . . . " No.2 spoke very quietly.

"We assured her, we would tell you." No.1 cut in very quickly. His subordinate was, possibly, going a lie too far.

No.2 was not to be silenced. "She's on the verge of a nervous breakdown."

You lying bastards, Tom thought. Far from softening him up this fatherly approach with its appeal to his love for his mother had misfired. It stiffened his resolve not to admit anything.

The fatherly line from No.1 continued, "Take a few minutes to think about it. She would want you to do the right thing. I'm right aren't I?"

Tom took the pipe from his mouth and blew smoke up to the ceiling.

Then No.2 said to himself but for all to hear, "I know what I'd do to my son if he ever hurt his mother."

"Any decent father would back you on that." The police were in agreement. "I'll say it again. We have been to see your mother, yesterday. She was very helpful. If she was here, I know what she would say."

'*Snidey sarcastic jibes and lies are not going to get you anywhere*' was Tom's reaction and he kept his mind firmly fixed on the letter.

"You were no more than a boy when you met Ashley-Jones. I am right in that, aren't I?" No.1 had dropped his fatherly attitude. This was direct questioning.

"No, but I have known him for several years." Tom tried desperately not to be precise.

"When did he first behave improperly towards you?" No.1's voice was formal but not aggressive.

"I don't understand," said Tom.

"Oh, I think you do." No.1 began to sound impatient. "Look at that pile of information. You are not helping yourself. We know what went on in that cottage at Lower Budleigh. You

145

didn't spend the odd night there. You lived there. You lived there with him. We know the man. He wouldn't have let you stay if you hadn't. . . ." He pointed to the papers on the table. "When this lot comes out in court he's for the high jump and I am not joking. Do you want to be with him?"

No.2 pulled a photograph out of the case and showed it to his superior with the comment. "D'you think he'll recognise that?"

No.1 nodded, smiled, the picture was waved in front of Tom who could only see the back. It was replaced face down on the table. Tom had no doubt they expected a reaction from him. He did his best to show nothing. He must not let them think he recognised the photograph, though he knew only too well what the picture showed. It had to be the one of Ashley standing by the outdoor swimming pool at one of the well-known Stately Homes, stark bollock naked, holding out his cock as a prize display, which it was.

The photograph trick was obvious. He knew he had to think each answer carefully and try to be aware of the tactics used to throw him. What should he say if he was asked about Rhys or Kenneth from Bournemouth? How much did they know?

His pipe had gone out. He was unsure what to do. He felt himself begin to panic. What was Michael saying?

RID ENGLAND OF THIS PLAGUE

Chapter 13

"Do we need to tell you that Ashley-Jones has been arrested?" Tom did not answer.

"Do you know?"

Tom nodded. "Who told you?"

"I had a letter."

"From Ashley-Jones?"

"No." Tom's reply was vehement.

"And you know why he was arrested?"

Tom looked down at the floor instead of answering.

"Has he contacted you?"

It was such a friendly throw away question that Tom almost said 'yes'. He was startled, caught himself, looked straight at No.1 and said, "No he has not."

"No?"

"No," and Tom jerked his head to emphasise his answer.

"You are sure?"

"Of course I'm sure."

"When did you last speak to him?"

"A couple of years ago."

There was a pause before No.1 spoke again. "I think I had better tell you. If he has contacted you and you do not tell us, we will find out. Be sure of that. As I say, if he has been in touch with you the consequences will be very serious. We haven't come all this way for nothing. I think you are a decent young man. Your landlady thinks so too." He looked at Tom as a caring father would look at a wilful son. "Think before you speak. It's in your interests to tell the truth, and you can be sure we will get the truth. There's all the time in the world. Believe me, and I'm being honest with you now, I don't want to see you in trouble. It seems to us, and talking to your landlady, we get the impression you are living a decent life now. Why ruin it all? I'll say it again; we are not here to get you into trouble. We are here to help you. You are away from all that now. Tell us what we need to know and I will give you my word that you won't be in trouble. Do you understand what I'm saying?"

"I think you will find your friend, Mr Cliffe, is being more sensible," No.2 interjected. "He will be telling the truth."

What was Michael saying? The coppers had him worried.

"Co-operate and you will be safe from prosecution."

Tom was losing control. He couldn't listen.

"Did you hear what my colleague said?" No.1 put his face very close to Tom.

"No." Tom gripped the pipe and banged it down on his knee.

"Co-operate. Tell us what we need to know and you will be safe from prosecution."

Tom was given time to think but before he could take in what No.1 had said, No.2 became aware of a magazine lying on the coffee table beside the letter from Tom's mother. Tom was scared. He breathed a, partial, sigh of relief when No.2 pushed the letter aside. The policeman's attention was focused on the magazine. It was a Health and Efficiency naturist magazine. Nude photographs! Mostly female but with some male nudes, and that was the danger. Were they legal? Michael had been given the magazine and they were planning to get rid of it so as not to offend Mrs Urbano. The picture on the cover was of a nude female, in an Isadore Duncan statuesque tit-stretching pose, with her arms above her head preparing to throw a large beach ball nowhere. As the law demanded, all erotic parts were carefully airbrushed out to obscure any suggestion of sexuality. No.2 was bothered. This Tom mistook for puritan shock. No.2 nodded to No.1 who looked and frowned. There was no way Tom could know their thinking. Why hadn't the magazine been hidden? To Tom's twisted puritan thinking it had to be obscene and exactly what the coppers wanted to find. Here was proof, if proof were needed, of his and Michael's degeneracy. Terror was stifling logic in a morass of orthodox gunge. Tom didn't, or couldn't, see that what was indecent to one is a turn on to another. He also could not know how puzzled the police were. They had a problem. How could any one totally corrupted by

Ashley-Jones have pictures that appealed to real men like themselves? If No.2 had opened the magazine he would have seen why Michael acquired it. On the centre page were two nude males, carefully posed with the indecent parts decently covered, but it did not take a lot of imagination to visualise what the left leg was hiding. But the cover girl held the law enforcers' attention. Neither policemen looked for more.

Had Tom been concentrating he might have noticed that as No.2 put the magazine, he had been holding, back on the coffee table he made a slight adjustment to his trousers. Both coppers frowned and looked at Tom. There was a pause that seemed to go on forever before No 1 continued the interrogation. He was still in fatherly mode though a slightly threatening note was detectable. "You don't need me to tell you how serious this is. You are young with a future. Are you going to let this man destroy it all? I don't need to spell it out. Young men do grow out of it and we think you may have. That is why we want to help you. You help us and we will help you." Tom said nothing.

Then No.2 chipped in again. His manner was distinctly aggressive. No fatherly tone. His words carried a threat; "You do understand. You do understand what we are saying. You do understand how serious. . . . very serious charges are being laid against your friend Ashley-Jones. You know where he'll be going, and for a very long time. Do you want to go with him? You will if you carry on lying."

No.1 frowned at his colleague telling him to lay off. "You enjoy smoking a pipe." It wasn't a question. It was an attempt to cool the atmosphere.

"Yes," nodded Tom.

No.1 then turned to No.2 "The photograph." No.2 picked up the Ashley nude picture. "Not that one. The one of the two young men. See if he recognises them."

Tom was handed a picture of two blokes both about his age. There could be no mistaking the location. It was taken outside the cottage. He shook his head. He lied. He did recognise them. They came from a village a couple of miles from Lower Budleigh. Obviously, the police had not been able

149

to track them down and Tom was not going to help.

No.2 again looked at the nude females on the magazine. No.1 brought him back to the business in hand with; "The other picture."

No.2 jerked his attention back, "Oh yes," and he handed Tom another picture. It was of a rather smart thirty year old. A full length carefully posed picture. This time Tom was honest. He did not recognise the man.

No.2's attention went back to the magazine nude. It then occurred to Tom that the copper might be getting a kick out of it.

Then almost as an after thought No.1 said, "Oh yes. Do you know the White Horse?"

"Which one?" Tom knew at least three pubs by that name, one in the Market Town and two out in the villages.

"The one at the bottom of High East Street. The one just over the bridge as you come into the town. You've been there?" the copper asked.

"Maybe once."

"Maybe? You've been there to a party?" No.2's question was an accusation.

"No." Tom was telling the truth. He did not understand the questioning so he asked, "Why?"

"We are asking the questions." No.2 was abrupt. "You just answer."

"I don't understand." Tom had no idea what they were talking about.

"What happened at the party?" No.2 demanded.

"What party?"

"We know you were there. It's time you talked." No.1 was putting on the pressure.

"I don't know what you are talking about."

"I'm getting annoyed. . . ."

Tom cut in, "Honestly, I have never been there to a party. I don't know anything about the place. I don't know what you are getting at." Tom was getting rattled.

"We were told you were there by a reliable witness." No.2 was playing the schoolmaster reprimanding a naughty

150

untruthful boy.

"Then you were told wrong." Tom had recovered his control and was now dismissive. "I tell you, I have never been to a party at the White Horse." Then almost vehemently, "I've probably only ever been there once in my life." He was telling the truth.

No.1 held out his hand palm down. "Calm down," and he repeated, "Take it calmly. Now let's go back to Lower Budleigh. I want to be clear about this. You lived there?"

Tom nodded agreement.

"With Ashley-Jones." That was only a half question. Tom knew he was not expected to answer. "What were the sleeping arrangements?"

That question was so casual he could have been asking about the weather but it didn't need a flashing light to tell Tom that this was the crunch question.

"I slept in the caravan." Tom tried to sound matter of fact. That was true. He had slept in the caravan that was parked at the side of the cottage. There was a period when Ashley wanted to sleep on his own. The caravan was old and had belonged to Ashley's father. Ash had towed it down from North Wales to use as an extra bedroom. The implication that he always slept there could have been easily disproved. In the early days of their relationship the caravan wasn't there, but the relationship was such that Tom slept where Ashley decided he should.

"The bedroom in the cottage has a very large double bed. Did you ever use it?"

"When he wasn't there, yes." Tom was desperately trying to keep his thoughts one jump ahead of his questioner.

"Tell us what went on when you and Ashley-Jones were in that bed together?"

"I told you."

"You did not."

"I said I slept in the caravan."

"We know how long the caravan has been there."

Tom gulped. He'd been trapped. Then he looked straight at his interrogator. "Originally there were two bedrooms. I had the one just big enough to put a single bed in. Then Ashley

151

made it into a sort of office work room."

"You. . . ." No.2 was losing patience.

No.1 interrupted by shaking his head and saying, "Try again."

"We know what went on in that bedroom." No.2 was playing the hard man.

"Nothing went on." Tom lied, but he was afraid he was losing his control.

"Don't expect us to believe that." No.2 was mocking Tom.

"Nothing." Tom repeated firmly.

"You are lying." The hard man banged the table.

Then No.1 suddenly became aggressive; "Are you trying to tell us nothing improper happened all the time you stayed at the cottage in Lower Budleigh?"

"Nothing ever happened." was all Tom could say.

"It must have." No.2 held up the sheaf of papers that had to be statements and he looked straight at Tom. "I think we know enough."

Then No.1 took over again. He was back in the fatherly mode. "Let me tell you we are quite prepared to accept that none of that sort of thing went on in your village, but the same is not true of Lower Budleigh." No.1 paused.

Tom looked at his accusers and thought; you can't be very bright to say something like that. You don't have to be queer to be aware of what young men do. What was the reason for saying it? Were they trying to say that without Ashley young men would have thought only of women? Then, for a second, the thought crossed his mind that these two up-holders of the law were saying and thinking what they had been trained to do. The two policemen turned and spoke in whispers to each other. This was the break Tom needed.

Again it was like watching a second-rate movie. It occurred to Tom that those dreadful supporting films he found so boring (he had played bits parts in three) were based on fact after all. There was the kind fatherly cop who did most of the questioning and the hard man whose job it was to scare the prisoner. The questioning punctuated with abrupt changes of attitude was all part of a stock plot. Whether the films copied life, or the reverse, he hadn't time to work out.

No.1 then spoke again in his fatherly tone. "Well, we aren't getting very far are we? Let's go on and see if we can do better."

No.2 handed his superior the photograph, the one he had already seen and had not recognised. Tom looked at it again and again said, honestly that he did not recognise the man.

"You don't know who it is?" No.2's tone was a mixture of disbelief and sarcasm.

"No, I don't."

"Sure?"

"I honestly don't." That photograph was put down and the first photograph again shown, but not to Tom.

"He'd recognise that," said No.2 and No.1 smiled his assent. It had to be the picture of Ash's cock. They both watched Tom intently to see if there was any reaction.

There was a half muttered throw away line, "They do say that queers go by size."

Without warning No.1 changed the mood and became much more aggressive. "What happened when you lived at the cottage? We will have the truth."

No.2 snorted his disbelief at Tom's claim that nothing happened. "Living in the same house as Ashley-Jones. We know the man."

"I lived there. I knew him." Tom was surprising himself at his ability to lie with so much conviction.

"We know what he does. He wouldn't have let you stay the night without trying something on. Don't treat us as though we're stupid."

Again the photograph of Ashley in the nude was waved. "He's seen that more than once." No.2 said almost laughing as he put the picture away.

No.1 paused, "As I said, we don't seem to be getting very far." Then, apparently, as an after thought he added. "Oh by the way, do you know any of the men in the Montagu case?"

Tom shook his head.

No.1 went on, "No?"

Tom again shook his head. He was afraid of saying an outright 'No'. They may well have found both his and

153

Michael's name in Michael Pitt-Rivers' address book. That line of questioning was finished and No.1 went back to his old line. "As I said just now we don't want to get you into trouble. I'm thinking of your mother. Let me give you a bit of advice. If you keep on telling me lies, you'll find yourself in the same position as Ashley-Jones. And let me repeat what my colleague has already told you. Things are serious. I'm not just saying this as a policeman. I am also a father. You co-operate and we can put an end to it. All you have to do is tell us the truth. If you do that, and I'll say again, it is the right thing to do. If you tell us the truth, you won't be charged. You will simply have to stand up in court and say what happened. We will help you say the right things. We can understand that you were young when you got mixed up with this man. It won't be held against you. Give yourself a couple of minutes to think. Don't ever forget, if your friend is telling the truth and you don't, you are heading for real trouble."

Tom's head was beginning to reel. He had heard phrases over and over. "Tell us the truth and we will see you're alright." What they were saying was "Shop Ashley. Turn Queen's Evidence. Shop Ashley. Turn Queen's Evidence." They were naming the price of keeping out of jail. But it wasn't as simple as that. If he shopped Ash, he would shop Michael. Michael would not drop him in the shit, Tom was sure of that. He had to keep lying and hoping.

Who spoke next Tom did not know. He was looking at the fireplace. He wasn't thinking clearly. He heard a voice say, "I will ask you just once more. Do you know any of the three in the Montagu case?"

Tom remained silent.

"I asked a simple question." No.1 said very quietly.

"No. I do not." Tom lied as positively as he could.

The photograph of the lone man was again shown to Tom. He still didn't recognise who it was.

"You don't know who it is?" No.2 sneered.

"No." Tom shook his head.

"Oh, you know him. We do do our homework."

"Who is it?" Tom asked.

154

"It's Michael Pitt-Rivers."

"It doesn't look a bit like him."

The words were out. It was then Tom realised he had trapped himself. The worst had happened. They had cross-checked. The questioning had gone on so long he had lost control of his thoughts.

"And you said you didn't know him. Well. . . . well." No.2 put the picture away.

"His photograph has been in the papers. He didn't look a bit like that picture." Tom knew it was a feeble excuse. He knew, too, that he had demolished his claims of innocence.

"I think he has told us enough." No.2 sounded smug.

"I think so," and No.1 shook his head. "On his head be it. He wouldn't listen."

They started to pack up. Then No.1 again looked at the magazine, picked it up and flicked it open. He passed it to his subordinate. Tom closed his eyes. He was afraid. What had they found? The men?

"Not bad. You wouldn't say 'no' to that would you?" No.1 said to the other policeman. The formality had gone. The two coppers were mates together. The magazine was handed to Tom. "What do you think?"

Tom took the magazine but said nothing. No.1 had turned up a page showing four nude women. He couldn't believe it. They hadn't found the page of nude men. What could he say?

"You could do worse." No.2 sounded almost friendly as he collected up the papers spread out on the table. "Think about it." he said as he closed his brief case.

By now they were both ready to go. No.1 moved to the door, "I'll go and see how they are getting on in the car." and out he went.

After he had gone No.2 looked at Tom. His expression changed completely. His cynicism had gone. He was into No.1's fatherly role even though he could only be ten or fifteen years older than Tom.

"I'd say you were a very intelligent young man. You've got a future ahead. It's still not too late. You know where our police station is." He pointed to the magazine. "Not bad. Not bad at

155

all. Oh, and smoking a pipe suits you."

No.1 came back into the room. "They were waiting on the doorstep." He looked at Tom. His face was set. He was now the dominating copper. He looked as though he was going to hit Tom. "You've made a big mistake. A very big mistake. I gave you a chance. We don't like being messed around. We'll be back. You can be sure of that."

The police left. Michael was standing in the hallway. They looked at each other not daring to speak.

"What did you tell them?" It hardly matters who asked the question.

"Nothing."

Though they had admitted nothing the words, "We'll be back, we'll be back," echoed round the room.

They sat side by side on one of the beds not daring to comfort each other. They did not discuss the questioning. All Michael said was that he sat in the front passenger seat with one of the coppers and admitted nothing. The other sat in the back prompting or making sarcastic remarks. It had to be a carefully rehearsed routine.

Tom was incoherent when he tried to tell Michael how he'd become trapped by the photograph. Michael needed to go to the bathroom.

"You alright?" Tom asked.

"I just need to go upstairs."

"You are sure you're alright?" Tom was concerned. He felt sick himself. While Michael was up in the bathroom Tom picked up the Health and Efficiency magazine and hid it. Next day it was destroyed. Had either of them been asked only a few days later how they spent the rest of that evening neither would have remembered. Before going to sleep they knelt by their beds to pray, as they had knelt every night since the first letter arrived from Dorset, but that night Tom could say nothing. Words - *'forgive us'* - were just words. He could not sound them. He stood up when he saw Michael stand. They did not kiss. A touch of the hand was all.

As they lay in their separate beds Tom asked of himself, "Who else will they question?"

Michael heard and asked. "Are there many?"

"Of course there are. I can think of three or four who could drop me right in it. They knew I was lying. They are not going to leave us alone." His words were mixed with tears of fear. They lay on their beds, silent, waiting for morning.

Mrs Urbano never enquired the reason for the police visit. The next day she asked, "Everything going alright?"

To which Michael said, "Yes."

"That's what I like to hear," was her response.

The police visit was never referred to again. This was an enormous help to Tom and Michael. It meant that one part of their lives could be lived with some semblance of normality. The fortnightly letter arrived from Tom's mother. Ash was not mentioned. Nor was he mentioned by Tom in his letters to her. Michael never breathed a word to his family.

Fear had reduced their sex urge to virtually nothing. They made no preparations or plans. They lived in limbo, fearing what each day may bring. They could only wait.

RID ENGLAND OF THIS PLAGUE

Chapter 14

There appeared to be no one to whom they could turn. They worked with people; they talked and ate in company but they were alone. Their sexuality isolated them. They had no intention of burdening their friends, and legal advice was out of the question. If they were arrested and charged it would be difficult to find a lawyer who would be sympathetic. It was certain they would be advised to plead guilty and throw themselves on the mercy of the court. They had broken the law and lied to the police. Tom's concentration had lapsed when he fell into the Pitt-Rivers photograph trap. The interrogation was over but that was only the beginning. After comparing notes the police were going to come back, there could be no doubt about it. Tom and Michael did not dare speculate what the next step might be. That was not in the lap of the Gods. Arrest was a certainty. Tom was actively conditioning himself to think in terms of prison. Prison, itself, might be bearable but what would face him when he came out? He dare not think that far ahead.

Michael did not have such a rough time as Tom. He stuck resolutely to the line, 'Nothing had happened at Lower Budleigh'. He was not a person to get rattled, unlike Tom. Now they waited for the inevitable. Tom was only too well aware that there were others in Dorset who could drop him right in the shit. Though they refused to turn Queen's Evidence who would believe they knew nothing of Ashley's sexual predilections?

Being faced with the reality of going to jail was very different from watching films or reading juicy court cases in the paper. Some lawbreakers were glamorised, but they were the honest-to-God straightforward villains! They might rob or swindle or even kill but they didn't corrupt anyone, or so filmmakers and thriller writers would have us believe, but sex between two males was corruption.

Most religious bodies would have been horrified at any admission of homosexuality. As repentant sinners they might be accepted but only on condition they kept absolutely silent about their sins. A reformed alcoholic, a blasphemer or even an adulterer could be accommodated but a (the word no decent lips could speak) came in a very different category.

Tom could see no point in thinking further ahead than each day. Michael was different. He had read that some defendants in homosexual cases were to receive treatment. Apparently, a cure was available. A very up to date medic advised aversion therapy, involving an electric shock every time you were shown a picture of a naked male. Treatment designed to put you off wanting to look at men, or that bit of the male body you found most attractive. Then to assist the cure you were given something you really liked, maybe a sweet, when you were shown a picture of a naked female. Sometime later an acquaintance of theirs did opt for such treatment and ended up an alcoholic.

With Michael's strong Anglican background, silent prayer offered hope. The plea each night, kneeling by their beds, was for forgiveness and absolution. Again it was Michael who took the initiative and they went to a church in Camden Town a couple of times, but sat at the back without any contact being made with either the clergy or members of the congregation. Tom was lost in a maze of conflicting ideas and emotions. Then, apparently out of the blue, Michael began to talk of a High Anglican church off Oxford Street and insisted they should go. Tom had no idea what High Anglicanism meant but was receptive to any idea. He never asked how Michael had learned of this particular church or how he discovered the Reverend Father would welcome them knowing the trouble they were in.

The concept of a deity controlling every aspect of life was very firmly rooted in their thinking. It was a fundamental part of their upbringing. In Sunday School, Tom had sung, a thousand times, the hymn with the line '*He sees the meanest sparrow fall unnoticed in the street*'.

That the Almighty was what his title claimed, Tom had put

to the test when he was at school and faced with an important exam. Each morning he would stop at the village chapel and say a prayer. He could then face the exam knowing the Lord was with him, and he did not wank for an entire week. When the exam results were published he came from nowhere to be second. However, he never managed to be top boy. That had to prove something.

Michael explained a little about All Saints, and if what he discovered was true the church and the vicar were straws to clutch at. High Anglicanism seemed to offer real solace with its structured ritualised services. The theatricality offered escape into a realm, high up in the bright blue yonder, where there were no prison bars. In face of the impending disaster, Tom's father's pragmatic Methodism seemed so totally inadequate. Tom had no difficulty in rationalising that when worshipping the great creator of the universe the informality of the village chapel was almost irreverent. If one would bow to an earthly monarch what then should one do to '*Him*' who is above all? In the village chapel there was no bowing the head or bending the knee. When you were in village chapel you were in the house of a friend, but he, nevertheless, could see everything.

Michael wrote and told his mother that they now attended All Saints, Margaret Street and she, with great pride, told her vicar. His comment said as much, or as little, as one wants to read into it: "We all know what goes on in that place!" Mrs Cliffe never asked for any further explanation.

"Incense!!!! Whatever next and in the Church of England!" exclaimed the curate and the vicar agreed.

Michael had chosen the High Road to Paradise whereas his mother's church travelled the more humble Middle Road.

The heavy Victorian Gothic church of All Saints was approached through a solidly constructed brick archway and across a small courtyard that never seemed to be a place to linger for a chat. It was a space created to separate the spiritual from the secular world of business and shops methodically laying the foundations of the consumer society.

The interior was a riot of colour. The altar, the tiles, the wall pictures and the windows combined with the all-pervading

160

incense to create an overpowering holiness so different from the sunlight-flooded chapel of Tom's childhood. Here in central London, in a man-made landscape far removed from the natural world, colour, aroma and music at high mass or choral evensong combined to give a sense of profound sanctity. The music was of utmost importance. The choir, men and boys only, singing in the traditional tradition of church music was of a remarkably high standard and contributed to a feeling of calm where the two young men could escape from the realities of a world in which they had no place.

That act of worship was charged with emotion. It was exactly what they needed. The litany gave absolution and the anthem soared above the gothic arches to where the ultimate judgement lay. Here was hope, but that word was confined to the world of the spirit. It did not necessarily extend all the way down to Lower Budleigh.

Michael had been baptised and confirmed into the Church of England. Tom, on the other hand, had been given a Methodist christening. He could only be blessed whilst his partner could partake of the bread and wine. Tom was excluded. The Reverend Father wasted no time in urging Tom to join the Anglican Communion. His christening was acceptable, he now needed to be confirmed, and so after the required preparation Thomas Adamson presented himself for confirmation. This had to be done properly, only the best would do. His confirmation took place in the crypt of Saint Paul's Cathedral.

It was during the sermons at All Saints that Tom's attention began to wander. Those sermons were usually cloaked in heavy theology that had little relevance to his world. He sat comparing the service with his rural Methodism. His father could not stand the bowing and scraping that took place in the village church and he certainly would not have countenanced anything like this.

"I do try and live a good life. You don't need all that other," was Mr Adamson's assessment of ritual.

Most of the sermons of his childhood had long since been put into the recycling bin but one did come back. It echoed across the years, though at the time of its delivery, the content of this particular diatribe puzzled rather than enlightened the young Tommy Adamson.

It was the performance of the lay preacher that stuck in his mind. Tom could still picture it after all those years. There was a thespian of talent. At that time, Tom had never been to a real theatre. He had only seen local shows in the village hall but he knew that up there, in the pulpit, was an actor. He was watching a man who could make you laugh or weep at will; a man who could enrapture a whole congregation; a man who could shake hands at the chapel door after the service and be told he had delivered a powerful message even if most of his listeners hadn't a clue what the message was.

What the villagers heard was jargon they could repeat with conviction.

To the boy, the preacher appeared as ancient as Moses in the picture of the prophet bringing the tablets down from the mountain, with the same wild white hair which he would comb back with both hands and shake it, as a horse would its mane, to emphasise a point. Moses claimed to have seen God on the mountain. This latter day Old Testementor claimed to have met the infamous Oscar Wilde not long before the sinner's death.

To the West Country Methodist puritan preacher, the sodomite's Roman Catholic repentance on his deathbed was further evidence of his degeneracy. But to the village boy the term Oscar Wilde meant nothing. He had never heard the word Oscar, not even the Hollywood version, and Wilde simply meant 'wild'.

"There, for all to see, was written on that haggard face the horrifying price of the wages of sin," ranted the prophet's successor.

The wages his rural listeners were paid would not have even covered the cost of a rent boy undoing his flies let alone dropping his trousers.

Tears rolled down the orator's cheeks. He wiped them away as he surveyed his flock. "Let no one shed such tears for you," he implored. "I beg of you, if you are tempted, or if the devil rears himself to anyone you know, guide them away. For it is written in fire that eternal damnation awaits he who strays from the paths of rectitude."

One wonders how many of the congregation would have known where Rectitude was even if they had seen the signposts along the path. It is certain that none of the worshippers had heard the contemporary wit who said, "Sodomy is when the paths of rectitude lead up the rectum tube."

"Lying one man with another is an abomination."

To the ten-year-old Tom that was simply stating the obvious. For one man to lie was bad enough but when two did it together, well, they deserved to get into trouble. No wonder this man went wild.

"Man's duty is to go forth and multiply."

Tom was quite good at sums so that was all right. Then the preacher man added a complication; "To waste your seed on the ground was a sin." Tom's dad always put his seeds in the ground.

Such mixed metaphors were confusing to the lad. What sums and gardening had to do with being paid, and being paid to sin, was more than he could figure out; and if all this sinning made you so miserable, as he heard with boring regularity, why not do something to make you happy? Then he looked around at the assembled congregation and wondered what category most of them fitted in. Some of them didn't look that happy, but then most of them never did.

Even when still a boy of some ten summers Tom was pretty sure most of the village congregation was thinking; "How long is this bloke going on for. There's Sunday dinner to see to when we get home, and there's still another hymn to get through when he's done."

It did not enter Tom's head that what the older boy had shown him in Lovers Walk Wood had anything to do with the tears being shed in the pulpit. Why should it? Neither of them felt miserable after, and he had learned a lot, and it couldn't be sin since neither he nor Derrick was old enough to be paid any wages.

The sun was shining when the congregation left the chapel. The preacher shook hands with each member of the congregation. One or two thanked him for the sermon. Whatever it was this wild man had done, such things could never happen in the village! It was all a long time ago and since they were never likely to meet anyone like that, there wasn't a lot of point in getting very bothered about it. But there were things to get bothered about. Snippets of conversation; "And they tell me Nelly Hawkett's got to get married."

"I bain't a bit surprised," a voice added. "Lovers Walk be not called that for nothin', and that's where Nelly goes, so I'm told."

"It be safe enough in Lovers Walk, that's if you keep walking," said another and the words were emphasised with at least two nods. Oh dear, thought the young Tom. He and the older boy had stopped walking.

The All Saints sermon ended and the choir rose, jolting Tom back into the present. This was 1954. It was not the village chapel. The congregation rose to sing the final hymn and receive the blessing and remain standing as the choir and clergy made their exit.

Here, sin was not overtly emphasised but the burden of sin and the need for repentance was a refrain to be chanted at each and every service. Repentance there was, and Tom and Michael knew that whatever they might have to face from the law they would be able to face their maker. Confession washed it all away. But, and the word rang like a tolling bell, the final trumpet call was a long way off, whereas arrest was an immediate fear. The thought of eternity in Paradise did little to alter the fact that prison would be still prison. The porno fantasy of being locked in with men deprived of female company and desperate for a shag was not a lot of comfort either.

Equally, the idea that the Establishment would ever change it's thinking was unthinkable. In fact it was revolutionary and it did not need a Lady Bracknell to tell you what that might lead to! The queer world was in the main (and thank god there were exceptions) very closeted. Most had learned to live with the status quo. There was too much to be lost by putting one's head above the parapet.

Tom and Michael had grown up into a world within a world. It had seemed safe but now the protective wall, kept up only by appearances, had collapsed and who would care if their families were hurt? The two young men could claim to be victims, to have been corrupted, but they would be forever contaminated; and most would say it was their own faults for taking up such a revolting way of life.

The Establishment trumpeted the truth. Who would doubt it? Had Tom stopped and remembered his old history teacher he would have realised that though the answers to every question were thundered out in the black clouds of prejudice, the fundamental questions had never been asked. With the history teacher it was not a question of sexuality but the basic principle was the same. At the height of World War Two he asked the class of fourteen-year-old boys who was responsible for the war. The answer had to be simple 'Hitler'. The class had been programmed to make the correct response. The teacher shook his head. "No! That is wrong, very wrong." and took the class through the history of the twenties and thirties. That was virtual treason. He had dared to tell impressionable boys, within a couple of years of being called up to fight, to question accepted truth.

Fear had closed both Tom and Michael's minds. They were being swept along not daring to stop and ask questions about their sexuality. That fear was making them accept as fact the Establishment's unquestioning doctrines.

It was again Michael who made the next move. He approached the vicar. Tom followed willingly even though his experience did not cover confiding in vicars. The first meeting with the Reverend Father was a getting to know you exercise. He came over as a very sincere man who wanted to help. He also had a sense of humour, saying he often felt his church was a welfare centre on weekdays but on Sunday it became a concert hall. The subject of their relationship was only briefly touched on. They were assured there would be no condemnation, but being a homosexual living a Christian life required a great deal of thought and commitment. This would take time but they were left in no doubt that the basis of the church's teaching had to rest on the doctrine that the marriage-bed was the only one on which to be laid. Fear had driven sex out of their lives so it wasn't difficult to accept the idea of chastity. Fear had also driven out logic.

Choral evensong gave them both comfort. They would leave feeling at peace with themselves and able to come to terms with the world. Could the euphoria last? That depended on many factors. They were young with healthy sexual appetites. How long could that be suppressed was a question not to be asked.

It was all in marked contrast to the preaching Tom had heard in the West Country market town on a visit home only the previous autumn. It was an open-air meeting by the Town Pump that he happened to be passing. What surprised him was not so much the oration as the orator. He was an old school mate of Tom's who was known by the nickname Bumper - why Tom never knew. It may have been because he was so short sighted that he knocked into things. On the occasion of the exams when Tom prayed for help and came second Bumper came third, lagging two marks behind. As a schoolboy Bumper had never mentioned religion but somewhere along the road to adulthood he had seen the light. What light had blinded him the Lord alone knew. He had obviously found more demons to slay in the market town than Tom had seen in all his subterranean visits at the back of the Town Hall. Bumper's oration had to be a paraphrase of the sermon in '*Cold Comfort Farm*'.

"Torments too horrifying to be spoken! Frying in the fiery pit of hell! Demons dancing! Have you ever burned yourself in the kitchen or lighting those godless pipes?" he said looking straight at Tom who, embarrassed, took his pipe out of his mouth and held it behind his back. "Well I tell you, Hell is like that only you burn all over, and forever." You had to mark his words. "There will be no cold cream down there to ease the pain and no water neither. Turn back; the slope is slippery and steep. Once you are on your backside there's no stopping the slide into the inferno."

Tom listened transfixed. He was drawn forward until he found himself standing by the side of his old classmate. The evangelist turned, this time he recognised who was by his side, clasped his forehead in horror and pointed. "You!" Words were failing him, but only for a moment. "You! Turn, my friend. Your feet are on that slope. Yours will be the pit of fire and brimstone."

Tom turned and walked away. "Brimstone and treacle more like."

But try as he would to dismiss the absurdity of it all, the concept of eventual judgement and the certainty that heaven, or hell, awaits us is a basic part of the psyche. Most think it a good idea to hedge their bets to avoid being sent in the wrong direction.

The slippery slope did feature, if indirectly, in a later preparation meeting for confirmation. Tom and Michael had been honest in their reasons for seeking help from the church and there was no doubt that the Reverend Father understood their fears, but he did emphasise a commitment to chastity. There was no escaping the fact that the two words S I N and SEX were interchangeable. The church had to be right. Once that was accepted there was no alternative to chastity. When the question, "Why was I made this way?" was asked, the answer came back, "It is your cross, my son. In this life we all have our crosses to bear. Bear it as the Lord bore his. His passion ended with an empty tomb. The gateway to heaven. Bear your cross and the gate will be opened unto you."

Tom and Michael took up the weight and tried not to stumble.

The police did not come back. Days passed, then a week. A letter from Dorset mentioned nothing. Mrs Urbano made one simple reference, "Those gentlemen never came back." It was not a question. It was a simple statement of fact, and she added, "I am glad." Then went back to her basement flat.

Michael turned to Tom and said, "She's O.K." Two letters that said everything.

The question, 'Could he ever go back to the village?' kept thudding through Tom's brain until he was forced to write asking his mother if it would be alright for him to come down to Dorset the following weekend. She replied by return of post.

Dear son,
Of course it will be alright. Your Dad and I will be pleased to see you.
Will Michael be coming with you?
Your loving Mum.

Michael decided not to go. They agreed it would be better if Tom went on his own. He travelled down by the early morning mail train. There was no bus from the station to the village until eleven in the morning so he walked out of the town along the Lynscombe road with the intention of thumbing any car that came along. The first car he thumbed stopped. Tom recognised the driver. This had to be the first hurdle. The driver was the man who delivered newspapers up through the valley and he had been to the station to collect the papers from the London train. Tom need not have worried. The journey covered safe, familiar, ground, geographically and gossip-wise. Ashley-Jones might not exist.

His mother was waiting. She cooked him breakfast. His father was at work. Everything was fine. Vic wagged a welcome. The cocker spaniel was born on the day victory was declared in Europe so what other name could the dog have? Vic jumped and barked insisting he would take Tom for a walk. How could the young man refuse to follow the dog up the hill, through a gap in the hedge into the wood, along a half overgrown path to the ruined dovecote where Vic had his first chance of the day to sniff out any rats or rabbits, and Tom to think of his second lesson on what men did to women. The first lesson was in Lovers Walk just across the valley.

Every part of that strip of the woodland, running along the crest of the hill and crowned with cawing rooks, held a fragment of Tom's adolescence from watching a hurdle maker weaving fencing in the hazel coppice or in the autumn, with his father, collecting hazel nuts for Christmas. There he had watched, in springtime, the men shooting young rooks to control their numbers and provide tender birds for rook pie. There, too, the leafy canopy had cloaked a number of his episodes.

"Let's just call them episodes and leave it at that," Tom said to the dog. Vic wagged his tail in agreement and hurried off into the undergrowth in search of game. The dog never caught a rabbit in his life, but it was fun trying. By mid morning both Tom and Vic felt it was time to go home so they turned, and wandered back to the village. Physically, little in the village had changed since his childhood, but new people were moving in and youngsters were commuting into the town to work. The closed environment was being broken open.

The village pub was just across the lane from his parents' cottage. Going there would be the acid test. Tom had to know; to know if he would be accepted. He made a couple of attempts to cross the lane but each time found himself wandering back down to the stream. He knew it was cowardice. A neighbour was hanging out washing. She waved a welcome. It was midday and there would possibly be no one in the pub. The landlord or his wife would have to talk to him. On the third attempt he made it. He walked in. The landlady had her back to the bar. Tom closed his eyes. Hearing a customer she turned.

"It's Tommy Adamson! Come to see your Mum?" And she clapped her hands. What the conversation was after that is irrelevant. Tommy Adamson could show his face in the village.

His father came home for midday dinner and suggested Tom should cycle down to see his Aunt and Uncle who lived in a village some five miles further along the valley. Tom could use his dad's bike. The tyres might need pumping up. The bike wasn't used much now. His dad had a car but it was easier to walk through the village to the butcher's shop than either drive or cycle. Tom's uncle, his father's brother, was very ill. It was cancer, lung cancer. He wasn't expected to live. It might be Tom's last chance to see him. Tom readily agreed to go. He had done the journey hundreds of times.

169

RID ENGLAND OF THIS PLAGUE

Chapter 15

It was just after two in the afternoon when Tom set off to visit his sick Uncle. The five-mile cycle ride to his Aunt's was no problem. He had done it hundreds of times as a boy since it was the only practical way to get to his secondary school. He was fit and, because there were no direct buses, cycling was the only method of travelling between the two villages. He would do the five miles to his Aunt's, leave his bike at her house, and catch the Wilts and Dorset double-decker bus the thirteen miles to Weymouth. It may appear a long journey to school but attending an establishment almost adjacent to a naval base did provide him with a first class, all round, education. The various passes with which he was accredited are explained later in this volume.

It was an easy ride as the road followed the level valley floor avoiding any steep hills. As a schoolboy, the countryside was of only minor interest to him, but now after four years in the big city he was much more aware of surroundings. It was a beautiful afternoon and Tom enjoyed being alone. There was little traffic. He had left the noise, and hassle, of the city behind. People who knew him waved. Cycling along he noted things that had changed in the years since he rode to school, but much remained as it was.

He knew he was going to see a sick man but the reality of death was not part of Tom's thinking. He was young. Life was ahead. His uncle was old. It wasn't heartlessness. Tom's world was centred on survival.

He didn't hurry; peddling leisurely allowed him to forget his reasons for being there. A couple of miles along the road to his Aunt's he passed the army camp. To his surprise it was half deserted. A couple of soldiers lounged by the entrance gate; all very different to the war years when, in the build up to the invasion of France in 1944, the camp was seething with military personnel. It was now quiet. There were no lorries, no jeeps or tanks. A soldier strolled from one hut to another. His lack of purpose seemed to be in tune with Tom's mood. When he started secondary school the camp was home to thousands of British soldiers, by the time he left school the Americans had taken over, but that was a long time ago.

That stretch of road brought back memories. Memories far from consistent with his newly found religious convictions. Memories, of cycling past soldiers on cross-country runs, Tom tried to suppress. Innocent enough activities for both schoolboy and military except that the youth was observing privates on parade, the pendulum swing inside the loose baggy blue shorts, and speculating that though all are created brothers, the share out of goodies is far from equal. Those thoughts had to be rapidly dismissed.

As a schoolboy the weather was not, usually, a deterrent to the daily cycle ride but the threat of snow just after the Christmas holidays, one year, did put Tom off. It was beginning to snow when Tom called at his Aunt's, after school, to collect his bike to cycle home. The possibility of cycling five miles in a blizzard raised real fears in his Aunt's mind and, egged on by Tom, she suggested he should spend the night with her rather than take any risks cycling along icy roads.

His Aunt and Uncle had no children. They had respected their bodies! That is how she explained the lack of children to Tom. One of his Aunt's sisters had married well, the phrase married well being used to indicate the sister was now financially better off than the rest of the family, which was not difficult. As it happened her youngest son, Niall, was staying with Tom's Aunt. Niall was a year older than Tom and in order to give him the best possible start in life, and cost being of secondary importance, he was at a boarding school on the outskirts of London. Keeping him at boarding school did mean his father having to work, in addition to his reasonably well paid daytime job, as a theatre sceneshifter at a Variety Theatre six nights a week and matinees on Saturday. Niall had two elder

171

brothers who were working and, also, expected to contribute. Boarding school did not come cheap.

It also meant Niall had an extra week's holiday at Christmas. This he was spending in the country.

However, in addition to the snow making Tom spend the night at his Aunt's, and not going home, it did mean having to sleep with Niall. If Tom had been able to be honest he would have admitted the attraction of sharing a bed with his handsome second cousin influenced his thinking far more than the fear of cycling a few miles through the snow. On other occasions the weather would have been no deterrent. There was no way of letting Tom's parents know he wouldn't be coming home that night. It was simply assumed they would know where he was.

Niall had never disguised the fact that his school was far superior to that which Tom attended. Rather than feeling put down Tom was envious. Niall's situation was the reverse of his. Though the youngest in the family he was the clever son and he did not live in the shadow of a brilliant elder brother. He was what Tom wanted to be, wearing good clothes and exuding an air of confidence. He looked as though he had come straight out of a schoolboy adventure book.

By 9 o'clock their Aunt decided it was time for the youngsters to go to bed. Tom had to get up for school and Niall was returning to London the next day so they both needed their sleep.

The boys had to share a double bed; an old-fashioned iron bedstead with brass knobs and enamelled medallions set in brass rings. The bed had been his Aunt and Uncle's until they acquired a much better modern wooden bed. The feather mattress, too, was old but it was wonderfully soft and cosy.

Niall undressed slowly, hanging up each garment with great care. Tom, on the other hand, was not so particular. He was more interested in getting into bed. He had no pyjamas so he kept his shirt on to give the appearance of respectability.

The bedroom was unheated as bedrooms were. In those war years fuel was scarce and, as everyone knew, a warm bedroom was an unhealthy bedroom. Tom was only too glad to get into bed even though it would take a few minutes for his body heat to warm the bedclothes. Niall, on the other hand, appeared to be in no hurry. He seemed insensitive to the cold. After having satisfied himself that his clothes were correctly folded he stood naked facing Tom.

Niall was beautiful, dark brown hair and eyes, a slim waist supported on firm muscular legs. But the body, no matter how perfect, was nothing more than a frame for the centrepiece.

Tom moved his pillow to be able to see this work of art more clearly. Perfect in every detail. Then, as if to brush invisible dust from his legs, Niall smoothed his hands down his legs and as a reflex action, Tom put both his hands deep under the bedclothes and gripped his own cock.

The second cousin made no attempt to get into bed. Then, with both hands, he brushed his hair back and as he very slowly lowered his hands he spoke. "You sleep with your hands down like that?" and he nodded his head at Tom's crotch.

Embarrassed, Tom mumbled, "I don't know."

"At school we have to sleep with our hands above the bedclothes." Niall informed him.

"Why?"

"I would have thought that was obvious."

It was not at all obvious to Tom. Niall, naked, gently lifted the bedclothes on his side of the bed, slid between the sheets and lay with his hands behind his head. This had to be an invitation but there was something in Niall's voice and manner that held Tom rigid, gripping his cock, unable to move.

"You were looking at me."

"Was I?"

"Why?" Niall asked.

"You are very good looking," Tom blurted out.

"Yes. I know." Niall's tone was recognition of a simple fact. He was good looking. Then he added, "I hope that was all."

Tom was thrown. All he could mutter was, "What else?"

Niall took his hands from behind his head and placed them above the sheets. Then he said, "Would you put out the light. The switch is on your side."

173

That wasn't a request it was a statement.

"Oh yes," said a very confused Tom who rolled over got out of bed and walked the few paces to the light switch that was by the door. He kept his back to Niall until the light was off and was grateful for the darkness to get back into bed. Instinct told him his second cousin must not see his hard cock. Once in bed he pulled the sheets up to his chin and lay still trying to decide if any move was to be made. He was about to turn away on his side when Niall spoke quietly but with the assurance of one who knows he is right.

"I think it better my Aunt and Uncle can't hear."

Tom was silent. He could still see this perfect naked body that was lying next to him in the darkness.

"From my first night at Delhurst. That's the name of my school." Tom knew this only too well. He must have been told a dozen times. "From my first night I learned we had to sleep with our hands above the sheets. This last term one boy was caned four times for repeated disobedience. If it happens again he will be expelled."

Tom had no idea what his superior second cousin was talking about.

"Don't go to sleep. You ought to hear what I am going to tell you. Masturbation, self abuse, they're the same thing." Tom had never heard the word masturbation nor the term self abuse but he accurately guessed they meant tossing or rubbing off. Niall continued in the most confidential tone. "Have you never been told? Doing that sort of thing is wrong. Humiliation in front of the whole dormitory is the punishment. I would never touch myself. Have you?" Tom pretended to be asleep. "Two boys were expelled for doing it together."

He was cut short. The bedroom door opened and their Aunt poked her head round, "Are you both asleep?" she asked. There was silence. Tom pulled the bedclothes over his head.

"Goodnight. Sweet dreams. God bless," she said and closed the door.

The next morning their Aunt woke the boys and brought a jug of hot water, for washing, which she poured it into the basin on the washstand. They both had to use the same water, but that was accepted. There was no bathroom. She told the boys the snow had come to nothing and that it was a clear frosty morning.

Except for the odd word they dressed in silence and went downstairs. Tom hurriedly ate a boiled egg. Chicken kept in the garden meant a regular supply of otherwise rationed eggs. Breakfast ended with a slice of bread barely covered by a very thin scraping of butter and a little homemade jam. He then ran for the bus to school after saying a very quick 'cheerio' to his second cousin, hardly bothering to think that Niall would be going back to London that day.

To Tom's surprise Niall was waiting at the bus stop that evening. The return to London had been put off for another day. Why the postponement? That was not explained.

It was only a few minutes walk from the bus stop to their Aunt's house but Niall, again without explanation, started to walk through the village.

"It's quicker to walk straight down," Tom said indicating the direct path.

"We are going to walk through the village." And Niall began to move off. Tom followed wondering why on a cold dark winter's evening they should walk twice as far as they need. By the time they reached the warmth of their Aunt's house he knew. Mr Dickin, Niall's House Master had done a very successful job of indoctrination. Like most masters he acquired a nickname. This particularly master was known as Ivah, the reason was lost in generations of boys.

The impressionable boys in his care knew of the dangers of indulging one's baser instincts. Niall knew that whatever his hero, Ivah Dickin, said or did had to be absolutely right. He was an older man. All the young teachers were in the services. He had authority and when he looked at you, you knew he could see right into your thoughts. Niall obviously adored him. He often took the older boys for P.T. (later known as P.E. Physical Education) and made a point of supervising them in the showers. This could take a considerable time in spite of the fact that water and heat had to be conserved for the war effort. Bath water was strictly limited to a depth only four inches. Whether

175

Ivah and his naked pupils exceeded those limits history does not record.

Developing a healthy mind in a healthy body was of equal importance, in a young man's education, to any of his classroom studies. Masturbation was the major destroyer of both mind and body. Such an act may be wrong but there was no mention of sin in anything Niall said.

Niall finished his lecture to Tom by making the important point that when the war was won and the evils of Nazism defeated, the new world would need men who were men. Tom was asked several times if he. . . .? The actual word was never used in the question. Tom admitted nothing. He was feeling cold. He had heard enough, so in order to escape any more interrogation he said, "What do you think I am?"

It seemed to satisfy Niall who went on to explain, as Tom was getting his bike ready, how a boy should use his energy. He was a good all round athlete. The sport he liked best was cricket and his school prided itself in a tradition of producing sportsmen. Cricket was a British sport. When the war was over the countryside would echo again to the sound of willow on leather. It may need to be pointed out this does not refer to a willow cane on leather trousers: rather cricket bats on leather balls!

It was a pity Tom did not have the benefits of such a good education.

Tom wasted no time in getting on his bike. By the time he was ready to leave it had begun to snow again, but there was no thought of spending another night at his Aunt's.

The boys never met again. After leaving school Niall did his two years National Service and eventually became a successful lawyer.

A few weeks after the visit to Dorset, Tom was to recall and tell this episode to the Reverend Father at All Saints, Margaret Street. The Reverend Gentleman listened patiently. When Tom had finished he sat back clasping his hands across his chest in a prayerful, contemplative gesture.

Then he said, "Well, I imagine you expect me to fully endorse the regime of that particular school but I have a

176

problem with it. Such authoritarian attitudes are not always the best examples to set to young people. In recent years we have seen that sort of thing carried to extremes. You have no contact with your cousin?"

"None," Tom confirmed.

"One wonders what sort of person he has grown into." The Reverend Father was not wondering. He was making a judgement.

"I believe he is successful," Tom said.

"Ah, yes success. I know many very good people who, by those standards, would not be classed successful." Tom had not sufficient experience to understand the wisdom of the Reverend Father's observation.

But none of that was part of Tom's thinking that day in Dorset. He found his uncle a very sick man. He was now old and gaunt. He was no longer the man who with his Aunt, had created their own jazz duo playing at village socials and dances, he on the drums and his wife at the piano. In the corner of their sitting room lay a pile of thirties and forties sheet music. It was to lie undisturbed until thrown out, as rubbish, when they had both died.

As he was leaving his Aunt asked, "They said he smoked too much and that's why he is coughing so badly. Do you think so? He did like his cigarettes. Do you think I ought to have stopped him?"

"I shouldn't think so," was Tom's reply. He liked his pipe too much to admit any danger.

He cycled back to his parents but could remember very little of the visit.

He wanted to remember only the peace of the quiet country road.

RID ENGLAND OF THIS PLAGUE

Chapter 16

On the Sunday morning after his visit to his dying uncle, Tom offered to cook the Sunday dinner. This meant both his parents could go to Chapel for the morning service. He had several reasons for offering. It gave his mother a break, and was a way of saying thanks for their support. It also avoided the inevitable gossip outside the chapel after the service; and having launched himself into High Anglicanism he had doubts about joining the village nonconformist congregation.

The offer could not have pleased his parents more. Sunday roast at twelve thirty sharp was an institution, which meant his mother had to stay at home and cook. His father was a chapel steward and had to attend both morning and evening services. More to the point, they liked Tom's cooking. He often cooked when he came home. His gravy was so tasty and his rhubarb crumble with really thick custard was something special.

Just as they were leaving for Chapel his father said, "Your mother has shelled the peas. They be in the pantry. I think I've dug enough spuds. If you do want a cabbage you'll have to go up top of the garden and cut one."

Vegetables were straight from the garden and fresh. Cutting a cabbage was no problem.

The cottage garden was long and the top end was opposite Mrs Parker's house. Mrs Parker, Mrs Rose Parker (known as Rosy), had two sons and a daughter. Tom grew up with them. It was her eldest son Derrick who, not to put too fine a point, had a hand in Tom's education. Now widowed, the lady had attempted to move herself a notch or two up the social ladder, or as Tom's father put it, "She cracks her jaw when she tries to talk posh."

Mrs Parker considered she lived in a house not a cottage. For one thing it had a slate roof, that meant you did not have that awful messy business of thatching every ten years, and the front door had a knocker with a letterbox, and as her late husband had been a basket maker she was a cut above a farm labourer.

Tom heard her voice as he approached the cabbage patch. He stopped, walked to the hedge and looked over. Mrs Parker was standing, arms folded, by her front door busily gossiping with a woman Tom did not recognise.

Then he heard the woman say, "It has been nice talking to you, but I'd better be going or I'll be late for Chapel."

"I am giving it a miss this morning. I don't go much on that preacher; a bit too much come and repent for me."

When Tom's head rose above the hedge Derrick's mother was looking directly across the road and she must have seen him though she gave no hint of recognition. She had been about to go back indoors but she stopped and unfolded her arms, raised the index finger of her right hand and pointed it at her gossip companion. When she spoke the volume was raised several decibels and each word became clearly audible.

"If you remember rightly, I said some time ago what were going on over the hill there in Lower Budleigh." A lapse into the vernacular but said with the best intonation. "My sister-in-law lives that way and she puts two and two together with what she's heard. Oh, and I keep reminding some folk that I was told to mind my own business, but now its everybody's business. Bain't it?"

Tom stood up so that he could be clearly seen but Mrs Parker had made her point.

"Well, I'd better go in and get the dinner, and you'd better get on to Chapel." she said as she shut the door.

Standing up and putting his head above the hedge was not an act of bravado on Tom's part. He wanted to call out, "You've got a lot of room to talk. It was your son who showed me what to do in Lovers Walk all those years ago, and we've

179

been doing it together ever since."

When he bent down to cut the cabbage he stabbed it. "You wouldn't have said anything about Derrick. You wouldn't have been that stupid," he said to the cabbage as he stabbed it a second time. Whatever the irony, his anger did not alter reality. In spite of the welcome he got from his parents, and the reaction of the landlady in the pub, it was obvious that people talked. The events at Lower Budleigh were a subject for gossip.

Tom's parents were home from chapel by ten past twelve, earlier than Tom expected.

"He kept the sermon short," said his father.

"And that's the way I like it," added his mother.

Sunday dinner was spot on time and a success. His parents now had an electric cooker, which made the task so much easier than in the days of the old coal fired kitchen range. Then it was almost impossible to control the oven temperature. Tom took real pleasure in being able to cook for his parents.

"That were alright," was the verdict on the meal from his father, and that said it all.

After the meal the dirty plates were piled up in the bowl. Washing up would be left until later. Tom's mother had gone into the sitting room for her nap and he expected his father to follow, as was the ritual after Sunday dinner, but that Sunday was to be different. Father and son stayed together in the living room.

"I be glad you've come down. I'd like to have a bit of a talk. I've bin worried. You see I only know what I read in the paper, and that don't tell me anything."

Tom was desperately trying to find some way of stopping his father. There was a pause that seemed to go on forever then his father spoke again. "I want to try and understand."

This simple plea was so unexpected that Tom could only look at his father. For a moment he thought it would have been easier to handle had he been faced with the conventional horrified, 'How could you do this and never darken my door again,' approach, but he should have known better. This was his father. This was the man he had worked with during the War, digging the garden, growing potatoes, cutting logs to warm the house in winter, and travelling round the local villages with the butcher's van. This was the mate who told him mummy rabbit said to daddy rabbit she would like some babies and daddy rabbit replied, "That won't take long. Did it!"

His father's voice was gentle, "Do you want to tell me?" he asked. There was no pressure, and there was no way Tom could refuse. The problem was how to tell him. He could think of nothing to quote, as far as he knew, no one had analysed a homosexual life style, and there were no role models. What could he say? He started very badly trying to excuse and justify his life. "We are not wicked. They say. . . They make it seem. . . ." etc. It all sounded so false. Then the problem resolved itself. He heard his mother move in the next room. "You and Mum are happy together. You made us three children. I can't marry. It wouldn't work. I can't have children. It isn't that I don't want to. It isn't like that at all. It's the way I'm made. You had children because that's the way you are made. I am sure you loved doing it. I never could. They say I chose the way I feel. That's not true. I didn't. I cannot go to bed with a woman. I don't know why but I couldn't. I live the only way I can. Michael means everything to me. We live like you and mum do. Does that make any sense to you? I hope you can understand."

Tom had exhausted his thoughts and fell silent. Father and son looked at each other.

"It might take me a bit of time but I will. You wouldn't stay away from us. Would you?"

"No, dad," Tom said. It was difficult for him to understand what was happening.

"I'll try and think things out."

"I know you will," Tom said, "I think of Michael as you think of Mum. I don't know why they say it is wrong."

His father gave a half nod, which said more than any words. There was a pause. Tom felt uncomfortable. He knew he should say something. He felt he had made a hash of trying to explain his sexuality but he was spared any embarrassment when his father asked, "You and Michael are happy together?"

"Yes, very."

181

"Then I wouldn't bother to get ~~married~~ if I ~~were you~~."
With that he stood up, gave a jerk of his head indicating Tom should do the same. Then his tone changed completely. "Now, young Tom, I think it's about time we made a cup of tea for your mother. She'll wonder what we've been doing."

The tea was made and the two men went into the sitting room. Tom's mother was awake.

"Brought your tea, mother," Tom's father said.

"I wondered how long you would be. I thought you two were going to stay out there nattering all the afternoon." That was so typical of his mother and he knew his relationship with his parents would come through the present storm undamaged.

Tom's father drove him to the station. His car had been bought for a few pounds. It was a real old banger but it did all that was asked of it.

The train back to Waterloo was unusually quiet. From Bournemouth there was only one other passenger in the compartment. Tom was too wrapped up in his thoughts to start a conversation; thoughts he could not share so he sat looking out of the window hoping the passing countryside would prove a distraction. His silent companion got out at Southampton, and was replaced by a heavily built man in his late thirties who sat in the window seat opposite. He was dressed in a well-worn brown striped suit that could have dated from when he was demobbed from the services. All servicemen were given a 'demob suit'. Those suits had a distinctive cut and a limited range of colours simply because thousands needed to be made quickly. Regular wear produced a shine on the seats and elbows that any sergeant major would have been proud to see on a squaddy's parade boots.

From habit Tom assessed his new travelling companion. He had put on weight since the first fitting. His thighs were exerting an almost intolerable strain on the seams and it would have been safer to leave the jacket unbuttoned. Tom was not attracted and the cap, which was, certainly, kept on to disguise baldness, made him even less attractive. The Errol Flynn pencil-line moustache did not help the overall effect either. The man made himself comfortable and nodded a greeting in Tom's

182

direction. Tom replied in the same manner and looked out of the carriage window. His companion unfolded the day's newspaper and began to read. The train moved off. Tom took little comfort from the fact that there was still an hour and a half of the journey to go. For no definable reason he felt uncomfortable.

A minute or two later the compartment door opened and a slim man, below average height, came in carrying a small suitcase and a briefcase. He carefully shut the door, took off his trilby and deftly flicked it up onto the luggage rack. The suitcase was put in the rack beside this hat though the man was barely tall enough to reach. Tom thought of helping him but decided against it. The case was stowed and its owner looked at it twice to ensure it was square and safe. Then he turned and sat down with the briefcase by his side. His suit was in direct contrast to Shiny's attire. Single breasted with a waistcoat and very neatly pressed. It fitted him very well though in all probability it came from The Fifty Shilling Tailors. When seated, to his satisfaction, he brushed invisible dust from his trousers and, from habit, ensured his creases were straight before he sat back resting his arm on his briefcase then gazed directly ahead deep in thought. He had to be some sort of commercial traveller.

Tom looked at the pair opposite and came to the conclusion he would try and sleep away the journey to Waterloo. He did look across the compartment at the man sitting opposite and could just see, over the top of the newspaper, the cap moving to the rhythm of the reading. After a few minutes the cap jerked upwards.

"I don't bloody believe it. Excuse my language but I don't sodding well believe it. Do you know what it says here?" and he crunched the paper down on his lap. "It says here: 'The sin and shame of one man in twenty'. "

Tom did not react. The commercial traveller put his arm more securely onto his brief case and thought more deeply.

Whatever he was reading in the paper was bringing Shiny to the boil. Tom decided it was time he really slept. He closed his eyes and put his head back. It was a position he was to hold for over half an hour. There was nothing else he could do. He was not prepared for the tirade about to be unleashed. After a few moments he lost track of who was speaking. It became a monologue for different voices.

"It says here this bloke, Kine-say, has been around asking about your sex life. Sex life? There's only one way to have sex, if you ask me."

"I think you mean Kinsey."

"Is that how you say it. Well he didn't bloody ask me. . . ."

"He's an American." was the next correction.

"Well that says it all. He should have asked blokes like me then he wouldn't have come up with anything as daft as this. I ask you! One in twenty men is a nancy boy. Think of how many there would be on this train. It doesn't bear thinking about. You would have to keep your hand on your arse all day."

Tom was more certain than ever he should stay fast asleep. Verbal abuse was one thing but he felt there was a real risk of physical violence had he dared admit he was one of the five percent.

"You say he's an American?"

"Yes. He's an American. The survey was carried out in America."

"My paper says it's the same over here. The sin and shame of one man in twenty. We fought the war for a better decent life and look what we are getting. There was this Monty thing not so long ago. Boy scouts and young airmen. In my day we'd have poked 'em straight on the nose. Should never have had the bleedin' Yanks over here. We'd have done better winning the war on our own. A lot of bloody shirt lifters. I mean, where's it going to end? It's no good sending 'em to prison. Locking 'em up! It's only going to infect the blokes locked up with 'em. I did read somewhere it's a sort of sickness. A good dose of arsenic is what they should have."

"While I don't altogether approve of your language though, I do have a great deal of sympathy with your sentiments. I have two sons and I have no doubt this is a matter that should be dealt with and not allowed to become rampant. It is a curse that must be stamped out."

The two very different travelling companions were in

184

agreement.

"That's what I mean."

Tom thought the debate was finished but he was wrong.

"As I said I have two sons. . . ."

"I'm lucky, I got girls and this sort of thing doesn't affect them."

"I have done everything in my power to bring the boys up aright. The youngest is still at grammar school. I carefully selected the school. It is an establishment with a heavy emphasis on sport and teamwork."

"I go and watch Millwall play, every home game."

"My wife and I disagree on a number of points. She feels the boys should be allowed to develop their own way. I was caned at school and I do not believe it did me any harm. I would not be the man I am today if I'd been namby pambied."

"That's what I say. It's the way you bring 'em up."

"My eldest, David, we hope and believe, will soon be courting the daughter of a very good friend of mine. There is no question that a match between the two would set them up for life. We get them together whenever we can."

It was as if only one person was talking.

"People poo poo the idea that it affects your eyesight. But I am not so sure. A boy I knew at school had serious problems."

Then there was a sharp, "Oh!"

Tom opened one eye far enough to peep in the hope of seeing what prompted the "Oh!"

Shiny had taken off his glasses. He was holding and pretending to clean them but in reality was telling his companion he was talking rubbish. Tom closed his eyes.

"I need them for reading."

"Yes, well. . . ."

Pause.

"What station was that we have just passed through?"

"Do you want to borrow my glasses?"

Another pause.

"Surrey are doing very well."

"Surrey?"

"Cricket."

"Na. I'm football. That's what I call a man's game."

"I did not mean to imply. . . ."

Mercifully they assumed Tom was really asleep. In fact, he was beginning to doze. The voices were drifting further and further away. When he awoke the two men were silent and the train was coming into Waterloo Station. Not a single word passed between the two travellers as they left the train. As they stepped onto the platform Tom considered asking if they had had a pleasant journey but thought better of it.

On the Underground journey from Waterloo to Camden Town Tom found a newspaper that had been left on a seat. He picked it up, intending to read anything that might distract his thoughts, but it was no use. He put the paper down. The one thought that had run through his head for days kept pounding away.

How would it all end?

RID ENGLAND OF THIS PLAGUE

Chapter 17

A letter from Tom's mother stated, just as briefly as the *'Ash is in a bit of trouble'* letter had, that the trial was coming up at Winchester. No details were given. Tom assumed it referred to Ashley and that he would be tried at the next assizes, though the letter specified nothing. Tom could never understand why his mother gave such meagre information, since she had given a vivid description of the visit by the police. He never asked, and could only guess at the reasons. His mother was, most probably, hoping to shield him from the lurid details that must have been common gossip. Maybe she did not want to repeat, or believe, what must have been deeply shocking. She liked Ashley and what was being said must have been well beyond her experience or understanding. Whatever the reasons, he knew only too well that there was an anxious time ahead for himself, his parents and Michael, before the case finally came to court. Then what? He closed his mind.

What neither he nor Michael knew was whether the police had completed their investigations, and there was no way of finding out. Logic told them the police must have brought all the charges they needed but they could not be sure. It was like being in purgatory. The final judgment was out of their hands.

The one great comfort from Sunday morning church going was, as always, beautiful music combined with a very positive message of ultimate forgiveness helping to dispel the fear of eternal damnation. The 'Cold Comfort Farm' sermon, *'Have you ever burned yourself in the kitchen? Well, hell is like that only you burn all over and forever!'* interpretation of divine judgment was never on the pre-Sunday lunch menu at All Saints.

Both Tom and Michael tried to give the appearance of life carrying on as usual. They would see their friends, if invited, but avoided the queer world as much as possible.

It was a Wednesday evening in early summer. Tom was on his own wandering aimlessly through the West End. He wanted his old life back but that was impossible. He had committed himself to a new life. Out of habit he went into the White Bear. Picking anyone up was the last thing he had in mind. He bought half a pint of bitter, drank only a couple of mouthfuls then decided to go. There was no point in staying. As he was leaving he was amused to see half way up the steps leading to the road, the doorman refuse entry to a potential customer.

"I am very sorry sir, but you are not wearing a tie," the doorman said in the most sarcastically deferential manner he could muster.

"And?" asked the Inadequately Attired in as grandly camp a manner as he could muster.

"I am sorry, sir." the doorman repeated. This time deference was replaced with aggression. "You are not wearing a tie, therefore, you cannot go in."

"Well really!" The young incompletely dressed man hesitated before starting to make one more attempt to enter, but as the doorman was of a considerably larger build than himself he thought better of it and turned. Before he left he delivered his parting shot, "Next time I will wear a tie but no trousers. Would that satisfy you? But then, perhaps you wouldn't even notice."

"Rules are rules, sir, and we have to maintain standards."

As Tieless swept off, the doorman muttered, "Get you!"

Tom passed and was given a nod. He looked back down the steps to the bar below and thought, 'What a difference a tie makes.' Everyone down there had to be queer but it was essential that an air of respectability was maintained. The bar was certainly a place of assignation but there was never a hand or a fly button out of place. One look from the formidable lady in black behind the bar ensured correct behaviour.

He decided to wander down the Haymarket to the coffee bar that would now be described as gay friendly. It was very spacious. The great attraction was the fountain that exemplified the spirit of the 1951 Festival of Britain. A huge creation where water bubbled out of the top into metal scoops which when full, tipped to fill the tier below and so on down to the pool at the bottom. It was modern - a defiant break with the conventional classical fountain. It is possible that this was why it appealed to the young homosexuals who gathered around it. At the entrance to the coffee bar he met Denzil. He was resting - out of work. The revue he appeared in only lasted three weeks, but as he explained he was able to get by. He was doing bits of film work that paid well, but it was all a bit frustrating. Then he added, "I've got something I must tell you. There's a table right over there in the corner where we can talk without being overheard."

Tom was about to ask what, but Denzil forestalled any questions, "We'll get a coffee and then I'll tell you."

When seated in the corner Denzil told his story.

The previous day he had met the most gorgeous youngster. Very shy but with the cutest smile. Not tall. His head came to about Denzil's shoulder, just the right size to cuddle. He said his name was John, eighteen years old, and had no idea he was attractive. That diffidence made him even more desirable. Where did they meet? Of all unlikely places it was at the top of the Monument in the city. As Denzil pointed out, the huge erection could so easily be mistaken for a phallus but it marks the spot where the Great Fire of London started. His enthusiasm for the eighteen-year old made Tom want to comment that a fire had been lit somewhere if only in Denzil's imagination.

The reason for being in the city was simple. He'd been an extra in a crowd scene near the Monument. By lunchtime, shooting had finished and he was at a loose end. He had never been to the top of the Monument so he paid the few pence admission and climbed to the top where, from the viewing platform, you could look out over the city. The only other person up there was John. He had been for an interview with a

189

Shipping Company and had got the job.

"You said he's eighteen?" was what Tom asked.

"Yes, just." Denzil's answer said plainly that he thought Tom's question odd to say the least. There was a pause. Then the reason for the question dawned on him. "Oh, I see what you are getting at. Why was he going for a job and not doing his National Service? He failed his medical. His eyesight is very bad. He always carries two pairs of glasses."

Denzil then went on to say that John explained he lived in Gravesend and had finally achieved his objective, working in the city.

"It is something I have been wanting to do ever since I left school. It's been my one aim," he told Denzil. Now he was looking out over that city where he was to work.

They picked out buildings and the new office blocks going up on the many bombsites.

It was John who said, "Up here you get some idea of how much bomb damage there was. But it will soon be put right. It won't be long before they have rebuilt it all."

Even to him the war was slipping into history.

It would be very wrong to say the lad was full of confidence. He seemed shy and vulnerable. He could hardly believe he had got the job. He was certain all the other candidates must be cleverer than he.

"But you got the job. That has to prove something," Denzil said. Then with an almost involuntary gesture Denzil put his arm round the youngster's shoulders and congratulated him, "You'll do alright."

"I hope so," said John as he looked up and smiled. Denzil wanted to kiss him but even being alone high above London was far too public. Another couple joined them landmark spotting, so they decided it was time to go. It was the middle of the afternoon, too late to go to a pub for a drink so Denzil suggested they wandered down to London Bridge and look at the traffic on the river.

Sex was not mentioned. John appeared shy and unsure of himself though Denzil had no doubt what the youngster wanted. They leaned on the bridge and gazed downstream toward Tower Bridge and almost as if it was an omen, the bridge began to open. The two arms of the road bridge began to rise. Neither had seen it before. It was then that Denzil felt it safe to invite John back to his room. It was in a basement in Pimlico. Denzil explained there were two bedsits in the basement with a shared kitchen and bathroom between. Denzil's room was at the back and opened onto a small garden. The room in the front looked out on an area well below street level and all you could see from the window were legs passing on the pavement above. The basement rooms were converted from the kitchens and servants' quarter when it was a family house in the old days.

John found this all rather romantic. He lived in a very ordinary nineteen thirties semi in Gravesend. In spite of Denzil's correction that it was only one room and he was only doing bit parts in films, going to a flat in Pimlico with someone who actually worked in films was really something. John readily accepted the invite telling Denzil he lived with his parents but was not expected home until the evening.

After leaving the Underground at Victoria there was still a ten-minute walk back to Denzil's place. They had to pass a GENTS, one of the old cast iron stand-up urinals. This particular erection had only three stalls. It was Denzil's idea they went in. However, there were three men at the stalls and one other waiting. After a few minutes the pair decided there was no point hanging around so they left together. Outside Denzil, involuntarily, put his arm round the shoulder of his companion and pointed the way they should go, unaware that they were being watched. A uniformed police officer had observed them leaving a well-known place of assignation. The officer also noted the questionable gesture of familiarity and the passing of information as to the direction the younger person should go.

If you put two and two together, in any well trained mind, it had to add up to sex.

The zealous lawman might well have had in mind a recent case in Kentish Town.

On that occasion the magistrate had commended a police constable for his perspicacity. He was obviously an example to

191

the force and should be held up as such. The diligent officer, whilst on his beat, had observed two male persons leaving a gentleman's convenience and having no good reason, other than intuition, he assumed the male persons in the dock had been in the afore-mentioned premises for the specific purpose of soliciting for an immoral purpose, and since they had remained together, he reasoned, they intended to commit a further illegal act on some other, so far, unspecified premises. This paragon of public propriety deemed it his duty to follow the miscreants and when sufficient evidence had come to hand he would apprehend them.

He proceeded at a safe distance. The suspects were so engrossed in planning their felony that they failed to notice they were under observation. They were seen to enter premises in a nearby street. A light appeared at a window on the ground floor of the dwelling, indicating to the observant officer that this was the place chosen for the act of indecency. The curtains were drawn but a gap was left sufficient for their activities to be scrutinized. The presiding magistrate allowed the officer to be spared giving a full detailed description of what took place but sufficient to say the accused disrobed displaying full evidence of sexual arousal. One of the accused was seen to take out his false teeth. Why he did this was not explained. He appeared to be going to bend down in front of the other pervert when the officer decided it was time to intervene. It took a considerable amount of door knocking and window banging before he was able to make an arrest.

The two men pleaded guilty as charged and were sentenced.

The uncorroborated evidence was accepted unchallenged, and his commendation would not have done his promotion prospects any harm either.

Tom had read of the case but did not make any link between it and what Denzil was telling him. Whatever the point of Denzil's tale was going to be, it was pretty certain not to be a graphic description of sex. That would have been true of most of Tom and Michael's friends. They would admit to having had sex with different men, but pornographic detail was never on the agenda.

Denzil and John did not hurry back to the basement apartment. John was fascinated to hear of Denzil's life in the theatre. He asked so many questions that by the time they reached the steps leading down to the basement apartment Denzil had been raised very nearly to star status. Once inside Denzil was in no hurry to seduce his admirer. It was a sort of getting to know you interlude. John was shown photographs and programmes of shows Denzil had been in. They were sitting on the bed and just as Denzil thought it the right moment to put his hand on John's thigh there was a God Almighty banging on the door accompanied by shouting. They looked at each other.

Denzil jumped up, "What the hell is going on?" and he rushed to open the door of his room.

The guy who lived in the front room was out in the passage. He was naked with only a towel round his waist.

"What the. . . .?"

"No idea," was all Denzil could say.

The banging started again. Then a shout. "Open the door. This is the police."

"It's got to be a sick joke," the front room man shook his head in disbelief.

"This is the police." The call was repeated, and again, "Open."

Denzil shrugged his shoulders as he moved down the passage, "I'll go. You are not dressed to meet the police."

The front room man went back into his room. Denzil opened the door. A uniformed policeman faced him.

"I am arresting you."

"You are what?"

"You have been committing an indecent act with a male person," said the policeman with all the authority he could muster. He must have been carefully rehearsing his lines.

"I beg your pardon."

"You may have pulled the curtains, but not well enough. You made a mistake when you put on the light. I have been able to see all I needed to through a gap in the curtains. I have followed you from the urinal where you made contact with a young man. I have followed you here. I have all the evidence I need. This is an arrest. You need say nothing. . . ."

The front room man came out of his room pulling on a pair of trousers and ordered, "Come off it, officer. Come in and shut the door, unless you want the whole street to know what an idiot you are."

"I beg your pardon, sir. You are not the young man he was with."

"No I am not, and you did not see anything he was doing. His room is at the back. You were looking through my window. Come here," he beckoned to the policeman, "Come here, you peeping Tom."

Dignity was having to be pulled up to its full height. The copper must have felt his braces had given way. "You will find yourself in trouble using abusive language to a police officer."

The situation was becoming a little difficult to handle.

"That's fine by me. Go on, arrest me. Arrest me for calling you a git."

The truth was beginning to filter through to the officer. "You are saying he lives. . . ."

"I live in the front with my girlfriend. That's true isn't it?" and he turned to Denzil for confirmation.

Denzil nodded, and the front room man went on, "Is there a law against that? Since when is making love in the afternoon illegal?"

He looked into his room. "Come in and see for yourself. She's respectable now."

The Officer peeped round the door, and then stepped back into the passage. "I must apologise, Sir."

The front room man continued to vent his fury. All the copper could have seen was him standing naked. His girl friend had been lying on the bed in the corner. John remained in the doorway of the back room.

Eventually Denzil intervened to calm the situation by saying, "Let's forget it." but that did not help. In fact it made matters worse. It gave the copper a chance to recover some sort of authority.

194

"Do I need to point out, Sir, that homosexual acts are not only illegal but they are abhorrent, and I had good reason to suspect you had made contact with another male person with the intention. . . ."

Denzil had now no intention of letting anything be forgotten. He did not let the copper finish. "The young man and myself have been together most of the day. Certainly we went into the Gents. It was full and there was a man waiting so we left. You have let your imagination run away with you."

The front room man had also heard enough. "I think its time you went back on duty. There must be some real criminals you need to watch."

And he held the door open for the police officer; but not to be totally beaten the copper looked at Denzil, "I will be watching."

The door was slammed behind him.

The front room man stayed in the passage but closed the door of his room, "Can I ask you a favour?"

"Sure, anything." It was the least Denzil could offer. Had he lived in the front room and had he made a pass at John, which the police officer could have seen, then he would have been in one hell of a lot of trouble.

"That's not my girl friend in there."

"No?" Denzil was not sure what question he was asking. The word boy friend slipped into his head.

"It's a girl I work with. Keep it to yourself."

"I promise." The front room man gave Denzil a hefty punch on the shoulder. They were mates.

"Go back and you two enjoy yourselves. It's alright by me. We'll keep it to ourselves."

They parted and went back to their respective lovers.

Tom drew the obvious conclusion from Denzil's punch line, but he was not at all sure how to react. He could hear the aggressive copper muttering about young men and here was Denzil meeting an eighteen year old. Only a month ago he would have seen no harm in it, but his world had turned over. He was only too aware that the world for Denzil had not changed.

He gave a half-hearted smile. He wanted to tell his tale. The police, the interrogation, the threats, but that would not have ended with a 'mates-together' line.

Tom sipped his coffee.

It was Denzil who broke the silence, "That bastard copper just wanted to get us. He'd have stood in court and beamed. A pervert enticing a mere eighteen year old back to his lodging and seducing him. The plot of a perfect melodrama. The villain would be expected to commit suicide. I almost felt sorry for him. What he thought he saw in the front room was depravity. What he actually saw was a hot-blooded young man doing what young men should do. Oh, and the girl was eighteen, the perfect age for a virgin to be deflowered, though it can legally be done two years younger. And John? He was too scared to do anything. I didn't try. He stayed for a while, but he refused to go out until I had made absolutely certain the place wasn't being watched. I think I convinced him the copper had no way of identifying him. I gave him my address. He folded it up very carefully and hid it in case he was stopped.

Both you and I knew what it was all about when we were fourteen or fifteen. He still doesn't. Oh, he knows what he wants but a mixture of family and Gravesend has left him in a no man's land. He wanted to tell me so much but found he couldn't. I don't know if he'll contact me again. I hope he does. He was lovely. I could have fallen for your Michael, but from the beginning I knew you were there. Don't get me wrong, Michael made it clear from our first meeting." He paused then asked, "O.K.?"

Tom nodded. They understood each other. Then Denzil went on, "I have fallen for John. If that copper has wrecked it I'll. . . ." he paused, "With the world as it is, what can I do? But what's the use of wishing?"

They finished their coffee. Tom made an excuse and they parted. He needed to be able to think so he wandered down the Haymarket and across to the Duke of York's steps where he sat and looked out over Horse Guards towards St. James' Park. On State occasions The Mall would be thronged with people but on that pleasant summer's evening few people passed. Piccadilly was only a stone's throw away but here, in peace, he tried to sort out his thoughts. He was not going to be successful; there was too much conflict. The past, the present, sex and the Church.

He recalled that a week after he met Ashley, he stood on the hill looking down on his home village and cried into the unhearing wind how unfair it all was. His sister could have a party when she got engaged. Everyone wished her happiness but he could tell no one that, like her, he loved a man. Smoke curled from the chimneys of the cottages tucked deep in the valley but no one heard his cry. There was no one to listen.

Denzil had been harassed like a common criminal.

Who would listen now?

How many more cries have to go unheard?

Will no one ever listen?

Tom sat silent on the steps. If he walked back to the vibrant busy city he would still be alone.

He would sit and hope the pain would ease.

RID ENGLAND OF THIS PLAGUE

Chapter 18

On two occasions, Tom put off going to confession. He was now sitting on the top deck of a number 629 trolley bus going towards Tottenham Court Road and eventually All Saints Vicarage. He saw it as an ordeal and found it almost too difficult to face. Where did it all - his sinning - begin? What should he say? If he deliberately left things out would that be a sin of omission? What words should he use? Should he use News of the World language like, '*They were intimate*?' He tried to organise his remembrance of past transgressions. Put them into some sort of intelligible order. What would the priest want? He went through the filing cabinet in his brain, but either chronologically or alphabetically the items made little sense. The cloud he was living under made sin and sex synonymous. Everything else paled into insignificance.

He was all too conscious of his life with Ashley, and what the police must have discovered. He knew exactly how it would read, but he did not put himself in the miserable sinner category. However, what could be termed the groundwork, going back to his school days, was buried at the back of his mind and to all appearances forgotten. Understandable. At twenty-six, what happened in his teens belonged to another age. Could it be forgotten? What was the age of responsibility? He felt sure the Lovers Walk incident could be left out. He was too young to know right from wrong. Boys playing with boys in the woods had to be childish innocence.

Responsibility started with that sailor. He may have been still at school but he wasn't too young. He may not have known what was going to happen but he was determined to find out. That he had to admit.

Two girls sitting behind him on the trolley bus broke his reverie. They were discussing something very important. Which of two dairies made the best milk? They assumed milk was manufactured like a fizzy drink and had no idea it came from cows. Tom wanted to turn and thank them for making him laugh but it did make him realise the difference between his rural and their urban upbringing. Then he envied them, if that was the worst they had to think about they were lucky. He tried to forget why he was on the bus, but even the quality of milk was no diversion.

In his mind's eye Tom could quite clearly see the sailor. He thought for a moment before saying to himself; 'Whose fault was it?' That episode was the climax. It was a bad pun and that didn't help. He was on that bus because he was going to confession and had to sort his thinking out. Would he have to include the incidents that led up to crawling under the barbed wire? And after! He was beginning to wish he had never begun raking up the past. He was now, for the first time in his life, becoming aware of the appalling risks he had taken in his adolescent years. An English soldier summed up those risks whilst he and Tom were lying half dressed and satiated under a hedge in a field on the aptly named Exhibition Hill. The soldier gazed up at the sky and said something Tom did not catch. It sounded like "dunno". The soldier then sat up, lit a cigarette, and looking out over the peaceful countryside said, "Do you realize that if we were caught I would end up in the glasshouse (the military prison) and you would be sent to a reform school?"

There was not only the risk of being caught by the law; there was also the very real risk of venereal disease. During the war, newspapers carried large adverts warning of the dangers, pointing out the symptoms and what to do if those symptoms appeared. Tom read them carefully. The notion of safe sex was not current. Condoms were only used to prevent pregnancy. He had been told sexually transmitted diseases could only be caught from a dirty woman - a very dangerous idea to put around - but logic told him that had to be wrong. Luck had been on his side. He made a mental note that the local hospital did have a clinic and hoped, if the worst happened, he could keep the secret to himself. The worst did not happen. Tom did not join the army and could not get a V.C. and he always thanked his lucky stars he did not get a V.D. either. He stayed free of disease and trouble, with two exceptions. He caught crabs, which an army sergeant spotted and prescribed metal polish as a cure.

When Tom said, "Metal polish?" The sergeant replied, "That's what we use in the army."

And he was once forced into parting with the enormous sum of seven shillings and six pence. It was blackmail. Even in a quiet market town such things happened. Tom made a pass at a man who seemed to be leading him on, in fact the man had unbuttoned his flies when his attitude suddenly changed and he demanded money or he would find a policeman. That incident aside, with the cocky assurance of youth it did not occur to Tom that he would be caught, and the idea of being corrupted was equally unreal.

Was he doing anything different than his sister with her soldier boyfriends? Though, to be fair to her, he was undoubtedly having more variety and just simply *more* than she was able to get.

A dozen incidents from his adolescent years flashed through his head making him realise, that strung together, they made a trailer advertising the big picture 'The Revenge of the Giant's Tool'. A film he did not want to watch but knew only too well it was one he might have to sit through with judge and jury as adjudicators.

His secondary school days were spent in the south coast town of Weymouth but that wasn't until the war was more than halfway through. Britain declared war on Germany in September 1939. The summer season was almost at an end and though the holidaymakers feared the worst, they knew the war would be over by Christmas. They picked up their towels and left the beach certain they would be returning with the sun the following year. They were wrong. No one was to paddle in the sea or lie in the sun on English beaches for many a summer.

When Belgium, Holland and France succumbed to the German onslaught and invasion became a reality the beaches were barbed-wired off. The beach huts were empty and Punch and Judy was silenced. The populace were exhorted to take their holidays at home, but though there were no holidaymakers the town did not die. Across the bay and round the headland in the harbour the Royal Navy anchored aircraft carriers, frigates and battleships. Ships that had been at sea for weeks on end, each with a complement of several hundred young lusty, very able-bodied, seamen.

It was a question of supply and demand. The ladies of the town could not meet the demand, or to be more precise they were not always supplying what was demanded. That was where the Toms of this world came, so gallantly, to the aid of the nation in its struggle against oppression.

When Tom won his scholarship and left the village school to move on to higher things, his only thoughts were on his education. Academically he did well and in that much belittled university of life he claimed, with a great deal of truth, he had an education second to none.

Events preceding the fateful sailor came into his consciousness.

He was in the sixth form and on that particular day was out of school early. There was a football match. He was useless at the game and wasn't even pressurised into watching. The school had no great tradition of sport, and there was a war on. The young P.E. teachers were in the services, so if you wanted to play football you did, if not there were other ways of spending your time. His school life was coming to its end and Tom's mother had accepted that her second son was not going to be a repeat of his elder brother, playing centre forward in the school's football team and captain of the rugby eleven.

Tom got down to the bus stop to begin his journey home to find there was a quarter of an hour to wait. There were only four buses a day. He wanted a pee and since there was a

GENTS on the other side of the road he did the obvious. He crossed the road and went down the steps into the underground loo. There was only one person at the long row of stalls, a civilian. A man, who for some reason, was not in the services. The man looked at the newcomer. The look was returned. Tom could see his penis. It was hard. The teenager was hypnotised. He stared. The man gently massaged his tool. Magnetism made Tom walk towards him. It must have been then that the man realised who, or what, his admirer was. He quickly, buttoned up, and left. Tom waited in the GENTS wondering if another man would come in, but the bus departure time approached and he had to abandon his vigil.

He was tempted to try again the next day, and the day after, but the other boys who travelled on the same bus were always with him. However, one evening after the Easter Holidays, in his last term at school, he was alone on the promenade. He had, again skipped the games afternoon and, instead, had been to the pictures to see one of the lush Hollywood musicals. The glamour, the romance captivated him. His two favourite stars were Alice Fay and Don Ameche. On this occasion he had played truant to see 'Hello Frisco Hello' and missed the bus. It meant an hour's wait before he could start the long journey home.

To fill in time he wandered over to the promenade and was innocently looking out over the sandy beach to the chalk hills across the bay. The beach had been barbed-wired off when the danger of invasion was very real, but the promenade was open. A sailor was leaning against the railings smoking. Tom looked as he walked past. The sailor said, "Hello." Tom stopped. The mechanics of eye contact were being learned.

If innocence is defined as not having performed a certain act then he was innocent, but this youngster was far from completely ignorant. His actions were instinctive, or it could even be said his brain was pre-programmed. He was attracted. It seemed that the whole of his body was being pulled toward this man in blue and he was not unaware of the bulge at the top of the left leg of the skin-tight serge trousers.

The sailor offered him a cigarette. He took it although he

never normally smoked.

"What's up that end of the beach?"

"Not a lot," Tom replied with all honesty.

"I thought I saw some beach huts up there."

"Yea, there are, but they're the other side of the wire."

What Tom said was quite true. After the fall of France in 1940 the danger of invasion was very real and all the beaches along the south coast were barricaded off to prevent the Germans from jumping out of their boats and rushing inland unimpeded. Those defences were impressive. Metal scaffolding formed a frame ten feet wide by fifteen feet high and this was draped with coils of barbed wire. But now the danger of invasion had passed and the salt laden sea air had, over the years, reduced the vicious barbs into rusting irritants.

"Can't you get through?" the sailor asked.

"I think you can if you crawl."

"Like to show us?"

"It's easy enough."

And they strolled along the prom to a gap in the defences, crawled through and went into one of the huts. The sailor shut the door.

Tom stopped himself thinking of those events a decade ago. Even the act of remembering had in itself to be wrong. He had the guilty feeling that he was enjoying reliving that evening. What word or words could he use to describe what happened? Would his confessor want to know in detail? Though he tried, Tom found he could not stop himself remembering every sequence. He could, with the bare minimum of concentration, visualise and even feel the whole episode.

The sailor, only a few years older than the teenager, took Tom's hand and pulled it towards his crotch. It was the first adult cock Tom had ever felt. The slight coarseness of the cloth seemed to be charged with an electric current that tingled through his fingers. The matelot undid the four buttons across the top of his bell-bottoms and pulled the fall front of his trousers down. Tom's hand was static. It was frozen inches away from the sailor's cock. It was the most magnificent thing he had ever seen. He stood motionless and felt nothing as the sailor undid his trousers. They dropped round his ankles. The sailor smoothed his hands round the boy's hips. Hands alive, transmitting expectation. Hands moving backwards encircling the young body that was too electrified to even tremble with excitement. Then with one quick practised movement Tom's underpants were down to his knees. The youngster found himself gently stroking the matelot's rock hard cock.

"What do I do?" There was no other question Tom could ask.

"Turn round and look at the ships out at sea."

The boy turned. There were no ships. The bay was empty but it hardly seemed the time to quibble over a mere detail.

Tom felt his arse being fingered. It made him quiver. The top of his cock seemed to be bursting. He knew that if he touched it he would spunk. A strong pair of arms wrapped themselves round his chest. Again the uniform material made the skin of his arse and legs tingle.

Then he knew why they had crawled under the wire and why he was looking at nonexistent ships. There was no pain. It was as if his whole body was being filled. The rhythmic movement lasted for only a few moments that were forever. Tom felt the warm pulsation of the sailor's movements. It was as if two large firm gentle hands were beating a hitherto undiscovered rhythm on the cheeks of his bum. Then the matelot's whole body stiffened, tensed, convulsed and relaxed. Tom did not move. He could only see the level blue horizon. A hand touched his cock and three violent contractions said it was all over.

The matelot smiled and thanked him. Tom smiled. As with an earthquake, aftershocks caused his body to quiver.

How he and the sailor dressed or crawled back under the wire along the beach is lost in the sands of time.

It was after this episode, whilst sitting on the bus travelling home and feeling more than a bit sore - bear in mind it was a very basic spit and push entry - that he vowed it would never happen to him again.

Tom shook his head. Should all those details be added to his confession? He could find no answer to that question. Had he kept that vow he made on the bus he would not now be waiting for the main film. But what made him make such a vow in the first place? Physical discomfort had something to do with it but, in spite of his liberal rural upbringing, the 'Thou shalt not' motto was never really out of sight. Every jolt of the bus reminded him of his vow and the five-mile cycle ride home, after he left the bus, pressed home the message.

However, it is surprising what a good night's sleep can do. By morning the soreness had gone and even though he did try not to, he had to admit he enjoyed the experience. Added to this, his history homework got an 'A'. The schoolboy knew his education had really begun. Tom had cultivated a superstitious streak. Simple events he interpreted as signs. If his history mark had been bad he would have known it was a signal telling him something. But it was good, therefore. . . . Such logic can justify anything.

A week later he deliberately did not catch the usual bus from school. He hung around. The matelot might . . . . Tom did not finish the sentence. There was no one in the GENTS. With all the virility of a teenager he was firing on all cylinders. But of Jolly Jack Tar there was no sighting. One of the schoolmasters did come along and Tom got out of sight as quickly as he could. Superstition again wormed its way into his consciousness but the next day it was all sorted out.

This time he had to catch a later bus. The master he had dodged the previous day wanted three boys to stay behind after school to help move some old books. Tom felt it his duty to volunteer. After having done his good deed he had plenty of time to spare before the next bus, so he took a detour along the prom. He stood innocently looking out to sea (this time there was a warship in the bay) when a sailor with his hat pushed jauntily and fashionably to the back of his head asked the simple question, "Where can a bloke get a piss in this town?"

"Just down the street over there," and Tom pointed.

"I didn't see it."

As the matelot turned to look in the direction indicated he faced Tom full on. From the knees up, his bellbottoms could have been painted on. The lad (who was also a Boy Scout) had

205

no choice but to be public spirited.

"I'll show you," he said.

The stirring in the sailor's crotch had to be a clear sign, from whatever shapes our destiny, that this offer to navigate the senior service and even help with docking, was preordained. The possibility that it was the devil at the helm did not enter the youngster's reckoning. He was at that particular spot only because he had been helping at school. The sailor was duly grateful and showed his appreciation. He shot his load as soon as Tom touched him.

The encounter that has to say it all was with a Petty Officer who was anything but petty.

It was the last week of his school life; Adamson (first names were never used in school) had left the primary level way behind since the sailor told him to look out to sea. He was now ready to take a Degree in Cottaging. Tom was in the usual convenient place for making contact and attracted the attention of a Petty Officer. Previous encounters had been below decks. On this occasion there was not even the attraction of fall-front bell-bottoms; instead he was faced with a tall, very handsome, bearded naval person, cap under his left arm and jacket open. He was about to button up when the youngster caught his eye. The buttoning was delayed. Then abandoned. Nothing was said until they were acquainted.

"Know anywhere quiet to go?" the usual question.

They left the meeting place and crossed the road.

The boy never wore his school cap in the town. It was always screwed up and put into his mac pocket. On this occasion it was sticking out. The Petty Officer saw it, pulled it from its hiding place, unrolled it, and looked at the name inside.

He gave a wry smile and said, "I've heard of you!"

How, or why, had this naval personnel, one of hundreds aboard the ships in the harbour, heard of a particular schoolboy Tom Adamson did not ask.

Tom paused in his meditation of what and how much he should tell his confessor of his schooldays sinning. The full implication of the Petty Officer's comment came suddenly home to him. Would he dare, or should he, tell his confessor that there must have been gossip in a certain section of the fleet that, when on shore, it was worth keeping a weather eye open for. . . . .? The exact phrase used is best left to the reader's imagination.

The realisation of such infamy made him gulp. If he were to detail his transgressions the confession session would make the confessor late for supper or he might, quite possibly, cancel sustenance fearing any loss of minutiae might endanger the validity of the exercise.

Tom was told that at a different religious establishment a young male sinner, in order to be granted absolution, had to describe down to the last detail how he and his friend had partaken of the forbidden apple right down to the core. His friend was certain he heard the holy man say, "Cor!" after listening to a very specific oral explanation. Tom stopped. It had to be the devil entering his head. There did not seem to be any logical sequence to his thoughts, but out of sight, and almost out of sound, someone or something kept hinting, 'Do the police know? Can they find out?'

By the time the trolley bus reached Warren Street and after much soul searching Tom, again, wanted to opt out of confessing. Under the present stress, admitting how he had spent his adolescent years was more than he could bring himself to do, but he knew returning to Michael without having fulfilled his religious commitment was not an option. Michael would not understand and Tom could not explain.

The Reverend Father, quickly, became aware of the penitents dilemma and gave an assurance there was nothing to worry about. He assumed, wrongly, that Tom's Methodist background was the difficulty. However, the repentant was eventually reassured. The Reverend Father would guide him through the ordeal.

Tom knelt. It was raining on that summer evening. The colours of the stained glass windows were dimmed concentrating Tom's attention on the dark curtained confessional. This was something outside his religious experience. His upbringing had included the regulation forgive us our trespasses, though a local farmer had caused some confusion with a notice that read 'Trespassers will be prosecuted'. But this was very different. There was no joking. Tom was faced with having to confront his transgressions. Where did he begin and what should he say?

The enormity of the event overwhelmed him. Incense hung heavily in the church. He was lost for words. The disembodied voice of the priest from the other side of the grill assured the new convert to High Anglicanism that, since this was his first unburdening, a general confession would suffice. He simply had to ask for forgiveness for all his past misdemeanours. This presupposed the penitent was sincere in not repeating the errors of his past. He was given absolution. Was the past now the past? To his maker it was.

To Tom's surprise Michael was waiting in the church. Whether he was there to give support or make sure that Tom did, this time, make his confession Tom never asked. They left together. Outside the conversation was brief.

"O.K.?"

"Yes."

And that summed up the event. The theology had been carefully explained in the preconfessional instruction. The father who guided them knew their problems. The weight of sin may have been lifted from their souls but the Almighty and the Law were two totally different institutions. They had no choice but to accept that though their eternal future was assured there was nothing to prevent the secular past from catching up on them. Hope and pray. Hope and pray. There was one other potential difficulty. 'Go and sin no more.' A lifetime of keeping one's penis soft was going to be hard.

Cracks were appearing in Tom and Michael's relationship. Fear and the lack of any understanding support was a major factor and early religious teaching was making it increasingly difficult to bridge the gap. They were unable to sit down and tell each other their fears and worries. Michael knew, because of his upbringing, that the teaching of the Church was unquestionable, whereas Tom's was very different.

An incident that occurred when Tom was in his early teens is a perfect illustration of the different attitudes. A soldier

208

stationed at the nearby army camp was a lay preacher who wanted to preach in the village chapel on a Sunday. On the previous Friday Tom's mother invited him to a Dance she helped organise in the village hall. Without explanation the soldier left early. From the pulpit on Sunday they learned the reason.

"I have seen Sodom and Gomorrah. Before my very eyes men were lasciviously holding females to whom they were not married," and he gave a vivid description of the sin and degradation he had witnessed.

The young preacher was due to have Sunday dinner with Tom's family but that was not to be. After the service Mrs Adamson pointed out to the evangelist the error of his ways. "Young man, your brand of religion may be what you want to preach about on Sundays but tiddint what we wan'ta hear. Now let I tell you, we don't want none of your town ways here. What we do in the week is what we do in the week, and we do very well, thank you. There's nothing in our dances to make thee get up there," and she indicated the pulpit, "and tell us we be whatever you said. I went to a fancy dress social dressed up as Lot's wife so I know what I be talkin' about. I hope you get back to camp in time for your dinner. Good day."

The evangelical soldier went off without his Sunday roast.

It was claimed that, from a safe distance, he exclaimed, "Sodom!"

RID ENGLAND OF THIS PLAGUE

Chapter 19

Michael's beliefs were straightforward. He and Tom had committed themselves to a particular course and they had to stick to it. Tom, on the other hand, was beginning to be far from convinced that sex was of itself sin. He and Michael had been happy. Now they were not. Fear of the law turned them to the church. Now they were also afraid of falling below the standards demanded by that institution.

Tom was preparing himself for his second confession. The session wouldn't take long. He had done very little to endanger his immortal soul but he had seen a film about a G.I. Bride at the Gaumont Cinema in Parkway, Camden Town. Not that there was anything reprehensible about going to the cinema or seeing a film about an American soldier who married a girl whilst serving overseas. What was causing Tom serious concerns were the thoughts the film triggered, and that was where the dichotomy lay. He more than half agreed with Michael, but he could not bring himself to believe that in the past he had been so wicked.

In 1941 the Japanese attacked Pearl Harbour. The whole world was then at war. Japan and Germany were allies. America had been pitched into the conflict in Europe as well as the Far East. The vast industrial might of the U.S.A. was marshalled to provide armaments, ships, tanks and guns. But of much more immediate interest to Tom, and more than a few others, was the fact that the New World was pouring into Britain shipload after shipload of men raring to use their weapons.

Winston Churchill had pleaded, "Give us the tools and we will finish the job." Which was exactly what they did. Churchill was, in fact, asking for weapons but what's in a word? Tools or weapons did the same job.

'Over-paid, over-sexed and over-here.' Tom could never decide if that was meant as an insult. The Yanks were certainly better paid than the British forces but they were generous. Over sexed? That was debateable. A lot of girls and boys managed to keep up with them. It is doubtful if many Yanks wanked out of frustration. Of course they were over here. We needed them.

The army camp he used to cycle past as a schoolboy was taken over by the Americans. To say they were welcomed with open arms would be very near the truth. They had a lot going for them. Simply being American gave them a 'certain' glamour. Hollywood had made sure of that. There can have been very few villagers of copulating age who had not been to the cinema and Hollywood had shown them what America and Americans were like, and the Yanks did their utmost to live up to that image.

To Tom an important factor was the uniform. It fitted and was made of far better material than the coarse serge in which our troops were enveloped.

The thing that influenced Tom far more than money or uniform was body odour. Call it what you will, the Yanks smelt different. To him this was an indefinable quality. Personal hygiene was not high on the agenda of the rural West Country. Baths were an infrequent affair. In the village a shower meant rain and a bath meant work. For Tom's family, it involved pumping water from the well at the end of the cottage, carrying it in pails, heating it on an open fire and manhandling the tin bath. Once a week was more than often enough. A good wash usually meant a damp flannel round under the armpits, between the cheeks of the arse, round the balls, and hopefully a quick rinse out of the foreskin. Circumcision removed the cheesy foreskin, which could be off-putting, and most Yanks were cut and that cut out the problem.

The rousing hit song *'The Yanks are coming'* meant exactly what it said.

His first encounter with one of Uncle Sam's boys sounds

like a script for a porno film. These were the disgusting thoughts roused by the film about a G.I. Bride.

The village was essentially one long road with cottages built wherever the valley widened sufficiently to provide space for a house and garden. Tom had been on an errand for his mother to the chapel caretaker at the far end of the village. It was a warm summer's evening and he was in no hurry. On his way to the chapel he passed a Yank chatting up one of the village girls. Nothing unusual in that, and as usual he subconsciously wished he was in her place but he knew he did not have a chance. That particular girl was known as a bit of a tart. The errand was completed and on his way back Tom looked to see how things were going.

The street appeared deserted. He reasoned the Yank must have clicked but a couple of hundred yards further along around a slight bend in the road Tom saw him. He was alone. For whatever reason he had not made it with the girl and since establishing good relations with our allies was the duty of every patriotic Britisher, Tom spoke to him. The girl was not mentioned. The Yank was looking at the Manor House through the heavy iron gates. The square, solid, undistinguished building disappointed the American. Hollywood had shown him what olde English houses looked like and this looked nothing like it, but it provided as good a starting point as any for their meeting.

The conversation continued on this level for a while but quickly deviated, or degenerated, into an ad hoc lesson on the confusing facts of British currency. The dollar was simply divided into one hundred cents. The pound made no sense at all. Tom carefully explained that it did. All you had to learn was that twelve pennies made a shilling and twenty shillings made a pound. Oh, and the penny is divided into two halfpennies (know as ha'pennies) or four farthings; not forgetting the all-important half-crown, the florin and the ten bob note; the bob, the tanner and the thruppenny bit. Trying to understand such essential Englishness brought forth the historical fact, "Hell man! I know now why we signed the Declaration of Independence."

By now the seventeen year old and Uncle Sam's nephew

212

were firm friends, though cementing that friendship was to come a little later. He said his name was Joe. They walked on through the village until they came to the pub, the New Inn that was far from new. The logic defeated the American. The name, in fact, dates back to the dissolution of the monasteries in Henry VIII's time. Inns were established to replace the hospitality previously provided by the Abbeys. Hence the name New Inn.

Opposite the pub a couple of cottages had been pulled down creating a small parking space but Tom could not remember them. The hillside had been cut away to provide a level site for the cottages, and part of the back wall of the buildings still stood acting as a retainer supporting the hillside. The G.I. Joe noticed a hole that had been cut at ground level into the wall, and the material excavated piled up in front of the entrance to what appeared to be a tunnel. He was curious and wanted to know what it was and where it led.

Tom was able to provide the information since he had helped with the digging. It was an air raid shelter. It had never been used and had been dug in the panic days of September 1939. A shaft had been cut into the side of the hill and a small room created, in the chalk, to form a dugout.

Joe's interest was aroused. "Was it possible to get into this shelter?" he asked.

Tom assured him it was but there was no lighting inside. Did that matter? Matches were produced and they should provide the necessary illumination. So in they went. Joe lit the way but when they reached the end of the shaft the match went out. The pair were in total darkness groping their way around, and groping was the operative word.

It would not be accurate to say what happened next came as a complete surprise to Tom. Striking another match was not even suggested. He put out his hand to check where Uncle Sam's nephew was. He was right there, unbuttoned, hard and ready for action and though it was the time it was certainly not the place.

Tom knew a place. Not far away. The fact that it was half a mile mattered not. They were both young and fit. It only

213

meant scaling the wall above the shelter, scrambling through bushes, crossing two fields, over a hedge and through a gate until they reached a barn. There they climbed up into the loft and bedded in the hay. The evening sunlight flooded in through the unshuttered loft opening and it would be too easy to link the sun shining with making hay, but it would be a pretty safe bet that the barn loft had witnessed many similar acts in all kinds of weather over the century or so of its existence.

What Joe and Tom did had less to do with war and nationality than the simple basic interaction of one male with another, though war and nationality had doubtless played a part in dismantling inhibitions.

The soldier pulled the boy down onto the hay and kissed him. It was the first long kiss that the boy had ever experienced. Tom lay back. This wasn't the sex he had become used to; two males with only one thought, that of getting their rocks off. For the first time he found he was being made love to. As they kissed the G.I. carefully pulled Tom's shirt out of his trousers and his hand explored the young body. Then without a word he lifted Tom into a sitting position and pulled his shirt over his head. Tom moved to play his part. He put his hand on the G.I.'s crotch but the soldier smiled and moved the hand away.

Tom was again laid on his back. He closed his eyes as he felt the warmth of the soldier's tongue across his chest, his armpits and his nipples. All the while an experienced hand had loosened his belt and undone his fly buttons. He did not attempt to move when the soldier knelt up. He lay still as he was stripped naked.

This was a totally new dimension; a new experience. Simply being with an American added glamour but this was not sex as he had known it. This man in uniform had taken him into a world the youngster had not even dreamed existed. Had he tried he would not have been able to explain his feelings. It is doubtful if he had ever heard the word sensuality. Each gentle touch, each kiss, was as though he was being bathed in warmth; warmth that had to come from lips and fingers wanting to give and take pleasure handling something of great value.

Hollywood had shown him romance but this wasn't

romance. This wasn't moonlight and music. This was two bodies creating an exquisite pleasure in an old hayloft. The loft may have been old, but the hay was new. A new world. Its sweet clean smell lingered. Tom could smell it as he lay in his bed that night and for years after the scent of hay carried with it a sensuous eroticism he so rarely experienced again.

Tom often thought of his G.I. He met others who were more handsome, more manly but it was never quite the same. His G.I. was not in the hunky male class. His body was light and delicate. He was special. Tom often wondered if he survived the war.

A couple of nights later Tom was again going down to the chapel and again he saw the same G.I. chatting up the same girl. Neither Tom nor the G.I. showed any sign of recognition. Both knew the rules of the game.

The chapel errand was completed in double quick time but both soldier and girl had disappeared. Tom's luck was out, and though he looked, he never saw the Yank again.

The summer passed into autumn and autumn into winter; month following month in nature's inevitable cycle until the swelling of the girl's belly could not be hidden. In the fullness of time she displayed a healthy baby boy.

The child learned to talk with no trace of an American accent but in spite of gossip his parentage was never proven, though Tom always felt a certain relationship with the boy named Joey.

When another girl, who had been consorting with a Captain did acknowledge the parentage of her baby, it drew this comment from one of the village matrons, "That is what comes of playing around with officers."

To which Tom interjected, "I always thought it was the privates that caused the trouble."

A 'Tut Tut,' left nothing more to be said.

One assumed that all American G.I.s were white, after all the camp was full of them, but as the build up to D.Day mounted certainty gave way to reality. On the hill away from the village army camp, tents began to appear. This canvas town was erected for black American soldiers. The white Americans remained in their huts with a gym and showers and recreation rooms. Up on the hill, surrounded by blackberry bushes, the tented black G.I.s had no such luxuries.

Tom regretted not getting to know any of the men put out of the way on the hill. A separate canteen was set up for them in the village. It did not occur to him to ask why all the soldiers could not use the same canteen. He was aware of the indoctrinated hatred of the Germans but it was to take time to throw away the racist baggage that was all part of Empire and white superiority that had been a fundamental part of his village primary school education. He was now; a decade later, wondering if the contents of the same sort of baggage was being used against him.

It was a very confused Tom Adamson who sat in the Reverend Father's study. He was feeling lost. He had actually enjoyed remembering the encounter with G.I. Joe. Time had most probably glamorised the incident but he did realise it was the point where his attitude to sex changed. Simple animal sex can be great fun. It can satisfy a very real need and get rid of a mass of frustrations but something more than that is needed. The G.I. showed him that two men can give each other warmth and affection and it was this Tom's whole being was screaming for. That contact and warmth was now denied him. It had been replaced with fear and guilt, generated by unjust attitudes and laws. He was penalised because he wasn't made the way society said he should have been and that was his fault and his hard luck!

Though Tom had asked for the meeting it was Michael who had instigated the idea. It was he who had persuaded Tom that this church offered the only hope. The Reverend Father did, to some extent, help. Here was someone in authority who did not brand him a sinner or a criminal. The following year the Rev Father published a 'Letter to a Homosexual' in which he set out his views. The 'Letter' was virtually a transcript of that interview.

"You cannot help being homosexual nor can you help it if your sexual feelings are very strong. That is a matter of natural endowment."

A sickness was the only let-out Tom had heard.

"It is not much good hoping that by a miracle you can change your temperament. . . . So it is much better to reconcile yourself to the fact that you are homosexual. . . . I would go further; I say that your homosexual bias can be used for the glory of God."

The Reverend Father then guided the interview onto a positive path by saying, "Contrary to much one reads, homosexuals can play a constructive role within the family. Many are very caring. Forget what you read in some of the papers. I often think the press is guilty of inciting crime by constantly putting ideas into people's heads. Uncles, far from being a threat, can add a great deal to family life. Youngsters often need someone to turn to. Someone disinterested. Someone who is part of the family but detached from it. You and Michael can find fulfilment. You both have families, you have told me, and you have nephews. You have a lot to give and you will find it rewarding."

Then came the sting, "Perhaps you are beginning to think, here is a very broad-minded priest who really understands my case and has shaken himself free of the sexual taboos of his church. I am afraid you are wrong. . . . Because you are homosexual you are not, therefore, entitled to seek physical satisfaction with whom you please, for you, as for every unmarried man there can be no legitimate sexual activity. You are called upon to live a life of continence and chastity. . . .

You may say, indeed, that much of this you agree with, and that you desire liberty not to live a promiscuous homosexual life, but to live one based on fidelity to one particular friend of whom you are fond. But the same principle, which rules out other kinds of unnatural sexual behaviour, rules out this. Under no circumstances can it subserve the continuance of the race. . . . And there can, in any case, be no guarantee of the permanence of such a relationship with another man; experience goes to show that such a relationship is usually of comparatively brief duration."

The Rev Father did add a final very progressive view, "I have stated what I take the Christian point of view to be, but I am not upholding the attitude of English law on the subject. It seems to me absurd that it should take cognisance of, and punish conduct between, two adult men, which is undoubtedly a sin in the eyes of God, when it does not take cognisance of or punish similar conduct between two adult women, or promiscuous behaviour between members of the opposite sex, though these two kinds of behaviour constitute equally grave sins against God."

Tom remembered his childhood problem and mentioned adultery. The Reverend Father nodded slowly and very deliberately. "That is taken care of in the Ten Commandments. Such doings may provide salacious historical reading from royalty downwards but that alters nothing. "

Finally he added, "Like most people, you need advice and encouragement, and you need forgiveness. I strongly recommend sacramental confession and absolution."

Tom and Michael never discussed the guidance handed down to them. There appeared nothing to discuss though there was a fundamental difference in their reactions. Michael knew the Reverend Gentleman had to be right. Tom wanted to believe he was right. That difference was to widen the gap beginning to cut deep into their relationship. They did not dare analyse its implications. The word love had not been used though they knew the bond between them had been far stronger than words like attraction or friendship could cover.

Who in any position of authority would dare say it was right for two men to have sex together? That would be incitement to commit a crime and the law of the land had to be upheld.

How could Tom or his spiritual guide have any inkling that the harshness of the law and the handing down of fines and prison sentences was building to a crescendo, like the banging of a thousand drums forcing awake our rulers who had dozed for centuries in the warmth of their self assurance and certainty? They would have to shake their dulled brains clear of all that baggage and look at the reality of the human condition, or were they people who repeated the law because it was the law?

The War was still only a few years behind them and

everyone knew the evils of Nazi indoctrination, but who would have dared describe the current attitudes to homosexuality as the result of indoctrination?

Tom paused as he wandered through the side streets towards Tottenham Court Road. If what the Reverend Father said was the word of God then it was absolute truth, and how can absolute truth ever be changed?

He stood in the narrow street hemmed in and overwhelmed by buildings, some still bearing the scars of war, and he thought of his adolescent days where there was space and sky and the miserableness of sin was blown away in the fresh clean air.

He felt he was caught between hell and high water.

"It's time you learned to swim," he almost said to himself. Almost! He dared not complete the thought. The fear of prison appeared to have passed only to be replaced by a greater fear.

A very good looking young man passed. Tom looked at the pavement. He knew himself. He was afraid of what he had undertaken.

The water was rising.

Lying each night next to Michael was going to be hell.

He walked on and shook away his thoughts. A member of the establishment had told him he was of value.

Well, well!

There may be a tomorrow but what was the point of thinking that far ahead?

RID ENGLAND OF THIS PLAGUE

Chapter 20

On 27th June 1954, Mrs Urbano took several letters from the box behind the heavy front door of 13, South Villas. One was from Tom's mother. She knew the distinctive handwriting and the postmark had that strange name which she could never read. The letter was placed on the table for Tom to find when he came in. She felt she knew them, Tom and Michael. They had been with her longer than any of her other tenants, and the reason for the police visit was in the past and was no business of hers.

Tom was apprehensive every time he opened a letter from home. He would scan the page hoping not to see the name Ashley, but one day he knew he would. There had been five letters full of gossip. His Dad's crop of peas had been very good this year and they are putting mains drainage through the village. Now they wouldn't have to go down to the bottom of the garden, in all weathers, to go to the loo, and they could have a proper bathroom. His mother was thinking of giving up being secretary of the village Women's Institute, she thought she had done her share.

He counted to ten before he opened this letter. Would it say the case was over? He wasn't sure what he wanted to read. There was only one sheet of letter paper, less than half a page was used.

> *Dear Tom and Michael,*
> *Hope you are both well. We are. Ashley has been sent*
> *to prison for seven years.*
> *Love*
> *Your Mum.*

> *P.S. You Dad wants to be remembered to you.*

He read the words time and time again until he could not even see the paper. Seven years! Seven years! Would he have got seven years for manslaughter?

Tom handed Michael the letter who read it and in stunned silence, then put it down. There was no way they could have followed the trial since Ashley had told them not to go down to Dorset. They had not been charged and it would have seemed almost like gloating to have watched the man who had brought them together being torn apart in open court. They did not need to be told the kind of language used by the prosecuting lawyers and the judge. Who else had been involved, Tom did not dare think. The unspoken question each asked himself was; 'How had they escaped?' Even wanting to read an account in the local papers would have been tantamount to treachery. Whatever their feelings, they both realised there could have been no other verdict than guilty, but the length of the sentence was beyond belief.

A journalist friend commented, when told that Tom and Michael knew of someone who had been given seven years, "Didn't they realise, though no one dare admit it, the prosecution service would arrange for particular cases to go before judges known to hand out heavy sentences for certain crimes?"

This was something the two young men were not prepared for and certainly not ready to accept. In spite of what they had experienced the idea that the British legal system was not way, way, way above reproach was so totally alien to their mental conditioning they did not even try to believe it could be otherwise.

Tom realised fate played cruel tricks. The handsome well-endowed young man who had pleased the rich was now, like some faded star of yesteryear, forgotten and unable to afford a team of lawyers who, though unlikely to get him off, would have been able to obtain a greatly reduced sentence. None of his old patrons came forward with help. Possibly they did not know the trouble he was in. It was a dozen years ago he performed and, presumably, been well recompensed for his performances. His show was over. The audience had left the theatre. What happened to the actors was not their responsibility.

O.K. Ashley had an eye for a good-looking youngster but he would not have done anything so dreadful as to deserve seven years in jail. For Tom and Michael it was over. For Ash it was only just beginning. They had embraced the church. What did the next few years hold for them? The strains of chastity were already telling. What Tom feared most was that his love for Michael could turn to a kind of hatred. He could feel it happening. He knew if he made any show of affection towards the man he loved it would be rejected. Nothing would be said but it seemed the hand of God would be ready to slap him down.

By mid July Tom had a week's holiday to come. He would take it and go down to Dorset. He needed to be on his own, to wander in the woods of his youth and hear again the skylark's song or hear the rooks cawing at the end of day. He felt he could cope with the village, even deal with Mrs Parker if need be.

No one in the family ever knew of the conversation between Tom and his father and a bond grew up between father and son. As Tom grew older he realised how rare, and wise, a father he had. He was a simple countryman. He left school at thirteen and had been called out of school to kill his first cow, for the village butcher, at the ripe old age of twelve. The bond had nothing in it to catch the headlines, nothing to feed great drama. It might have made this a highly charged story had his father rejected this apparently deviant son and held up the sportsman brother as the example he should have followed. But his father was not interested in competitive sport. He didn't even play darts. He enjoyed two events at the village sports day. The men's three legged race - one left leg is tied to the other's right - that usually finished with the competitors in a laughing heap, and the slow bicycle race where the last to cross the line is the winner. Had he been the heavy handed father he would have provided the material for popular drama but here was a man who did not fit the stock mould. His obituary should have been one simple sentence: 'He was a man who sought to understand such things.'

As before, Tom travelled down by the Mail/Newspaper Train. This time it had been arranged for the paperman to be waiting to give him a lift out to the village. Dawn was just breaking when the train left Poole but it would be another hour before the sun rose above the horizon. There was only one other man in the compartment. They were half way to Wareham before his companion spoke. Tom was only too well aware of the tirades delivered on the train the last time he travelled and had no intention of getting involved in any conversation.

"Have you travelled on this train before?" the man asked.

"No," was the short reply. It was a lie intended to stop further questions. The ploy failed.

"I do it several times a week. I'm a commercial traveller." Tom feigned interest. "Sometimes the train stops along here, and if we are lucky we might hear the nightingale."

Tom looked at his companion. This was not what he expected to hear from a commercial traveller, or anyone, in the early hours of the morning.

The train did stop. "Do you mind if I open the window?" the commercial traveller asked.

"No. Go ahead. I've never heard a nightingale," Tom said and added, "I've listened to the skylark."

"Now, I haven't done that. One day I might be lucky." He stood at the carriage window listening. "Hark! We are going to hear it. I think you will agree the nightingale's song is one of nature's most beautiful sounds." He sat down and together they listened.

The train moved off. "Can't think of a better way to start the day."

The rest of the conversation was the usual mundane, 'Do you live in Dorset etc.'

The newspaperman was waiting at the station. The trial was not mentioned on the journey. Tom was relieved. He certainly did not want to know how much gossip there had been. That part of his life was now over, he hoped. It never even crossed his mind to find out what was going to happen to the cottage at Lower Budleigh whilst Ashley was in jail. In any case, Ash had told them not to get involved.

On this visit Tom did not cook the Sunday dinner. His father thought he would want to go to Chapel and meet the lay preacher who had been one of Tom's old school masters. In fact, he was the teacher who questioned the responsibility for the war. He had given Tom a lifelong interest in history, but as a pupil Tom had serious doubts about him as a teacher because of another point he made to the class. Exams were coming up and the pupils in the class wanted to do well. So much depended on exam results that it came as a shock to the boy to hear his teacher say. "Exam results are not a priority with me. If I have taught you to think then I will have done my job."

It took many years and a lot of experience for Thomas Adamson to appreciate the truth of that remark.

The morning service in the chapel was unremarkable. Buck, for that was the teacher's nickname, was now a very old man, and he repeated a sermon Tom had heard in his youth. Worship over and, as on every fine Sunday morning, most of the congregation gathered in the street outside the chapel. One worshipper remarked how badly behaved children were these days to which Buck replied simply, "Well, we are their parents."

A good gossip in the roadway outside the Chapel was a tradition; there being virtually no traffic to disrupt what had become an obligatory conclusion to the service. Ever since the chapel had been built the more radical elements of the village, who did not subscribe to Anglican orthodoxy, praised the Lord for a full hour inside and then got down to the serious business of village and family affairs outside.

Tom had a brief chat with his old teacher in the chapel porch before going out into the street. He did not hear the beginning of the conversation. Whether or not he was intended to, he never discovered; but from a small group he heard the phrase, "Thinking is changing. What doctors, and those who understand these things are beginning to realise, it is an illness and not a crime. Let us hope that one day we will see a cure. I think we should try to have more understanding and be less ready to judge. Isn't it said that we who live in glass houses should not throw stones?"

Mrs Parker threw her head up and her bust out, and for the second time in Tom's experience, muttered something about the Sunday dinner and hurried off up the village street saying to herself, "I know what I think and you can put that in your pipe and smoke it."

The group turned their attention back to the speaker, a prominent farmer's son, a confirmed bachelor, who smoked neither pipe nor cigarettes. He had joined the navy as a rating but rapidly donned an officer's cap. He was now virtually running the farm and taking an active part in chapel affairs. It must have required a lot of courage to take the stand he did. It should be noted that Tom never had any reason to link him with an active sex life.

His views were radical, and even more so in a West Country village. Back in the 1890s Havelock Ellis had dared claim homosexuality was neither a crime nor an illness but he didn't pay the piper and he most certainly did not call the tune. The Establishment, hell bent on avoiding eternal damnation, had the bulk of the population singing their chorus.

Ash was the subject of the conversation and Tom was inevitably linked by implication though it did not seem that way as he stood on the edge of the circle. He felt, rather, that he was viewing it all from a distance. The half dozen or so in the group did not appear to be getting at him. It was more that they wanted to bring him into the discussion.

The sickness and cure theory brought one response, "It'll be nice when they do."

And, "Yes. He always seemed such a nice man."

And again, "That's what I say. It'll be nice."

The group was about to break up when a young woman who had said nothing made a remark that, like most profound statements, have few hearers or rather few who actually get the full implication of the words. Norma had grown up with Tom and was just a year older than he. She was the youngest of five sisters. Her mother was convinced when pregnant for the fifth time the baby would have to be a boy. He would be named

Norman after his dad. When the infant proved to be another female it only required a slight adjustment for the baby to end up with most of her Dad's name. Norma did grow up to be almost a sister to Tom. They regularly danced together in the village hall inventing their own version of the tango. Dancing was one thing, but they knew each other too well to think of taking things further. Norma did marry a regular soldier who had served with the 8th Army under Montgomery in the North African Campaign.

He had been an army truck driver and had driven from Tobruk to Tunisia.

One could never be sure whether Norma said things without thinking or whether her more cutting remarks were carefully calculated. She looked around the group, shrugged her shoulders and said, in the best tradition of throwaway lines, "Dave (her husband) says if all the soldiers who had done a bit of that were put in jail there wouldn't be much of an army, and not many left, to fight."

As she spoke Tom could not resist a wry smile. Dave met Norma when he was stationed in the nearby army camp and his twenty-four hour leaves were spent in the village. There was no room in Norma's house, and as Norma and Tom's families were good friends and as Tom had a bedroom to himself, with a double bed, the solution was obvious. Dave had no objection to sharing Tom's bed. Neither had Tom any objection to Dave's company.

Sharing his bed was an arrangement that dated from the beginning of the war when an evacuee lad from Whitechapel had been billeted on them. This lad also had a hand in Tom's sexual development though he, like thousands of others, eventually married and had children. For them the chapter marked 'What boys do together' was consigned to the back volumes of 'Boy's Own Bi-Annuals.'

But to return to Dave.

On the first occasion of providing a bed for Norma's suitor nothing happened, but the second time when both should have been sound asleep Tom, who was lying on his back, felt a hand sliding over his thighs. Very gently the fingers inched their way over his leg and onto his crotch. Tom did not move. His entire body went rigid with excitement. Slowly and gently the index fingers moved down between his tightly closed legs and started fingering. This was Norma's fiancé. They were engaged. Suddenly Tom's body jerked as he realised what was happening. His bedmate was asleep and dreaming; dreaming of Norma, but he couldn't be dreaming of Norma, he had his hand on Tom's crotch. The excitement the movement of Dave's hand made Tom's head spin. What could he do? What should he do? Even in the deepest sleep the difference between him and Norma had to. . . . Tom's reasoning collapsed. Dave had to realise his mistake. What then? Tom rolled over onto his side away from danger and the invasive hand had to slide back over the teenager's hip. The ultimate rebuff! That was what was intended. Sound asleep or not, a different message was conveyed to Dave.

The invasive hand slid back over the teenager's thighs and onto the firm, well-rounded cheeks. The hand came to rest. It had found what it was searching for. Tom held his pillow. Did he dare say, 'Dave you've got it wrong'?

Tom gulped for breath. The hand was removed. That seemed to be that. But 'seems' is rarely fact, and it wasn't this time either. Dave had not got it wrong. His army training was going to stand him in good stead. The hand was needed to take aim He had always claimed to be a good shot and this time he aimed for the bull and got it in one. It didn't take him long to fire, withdraw, retreat, roll back and relax.

Tom lay still; satisfied he quickly drifted off to sleep like a cat stuffed with cream.

Next morning the conversation was so mundane!

Dave was the first to speak, "Sleep well?"

"Yea. You?" was Tom's reply and question.

"Don't remember a thing after my head touched the pillow."

To that there was no reply. Dave wasn't that well endowed, but he did a good job. The next twenty-four hour pass detailed Tom's head under the bedclothes, and all the while they were both so sound asleep! For whatever reason, there were never any remarks about stains on the bedclothes. In due course Dave and Norma married and no reference was ever made to past sleeping arrangements. Dave never mentioned Ash. It was as if the case had never happened.

Years later whilst watching a performance of Madame Butterfly Tom had a mental image of the bronzed 8th Army sleeping soundly throughout the hot, sweaty, North African nights after Tunisian Arab boys had helped keep up the morale of our troops in the same way as he had done at home. Madame Butterfly may have been way out in the Far East, and scored to become great art but was there an Arab boy's tale to be sung to much the same tune? Pink-erton! The colour would be right.

Dave and Tom always remained on the friendliest of terms.

After the Sunday roast, when his parents were having the traditional forty winks, Tom thought he might find, somewhere about the house, a copy of the local paper giving a report of Ashley's trial. He didn't, and he knew it would be wrong to ask; also, he wasn't at all sure he wanted to read the details. Newspapers were not hoarded. They were recycled, lining the shelves of cupboards, lighting fires, given to the local shop for wrapping food or cut into neat squares and hung in the lavatory to be used for wiping your backside which is probably what happened to the trial reports.

RID ENGLAND OF THIS PLAGUE

Chapter 21

It was on the Tuesday, two days after the post-service discussion outside the chapel, that Tom went to the village shop on an errand for his mother. The shop was also the Post Office. 'Oh God!' he said to himself as he went in and saw Mrs Parker at the Post Office counter. He had been in the shop the previous day with no problem; in fact, he had a long chat with the postmistress about living in London. She had been there once but she wouldn't want to go back. "All them people!"

It was all about to be ruined now. Tom braced himself, trying to decide what to do but Mrs Parker didn't give him a chance. She turned and looked at Tom and exclaimed, "Tom Adamson." There was a note of surprise in her voice as though she had not seen him in the chapel the previous Sunday. "Tom," she repeated, "It was only last night we were talking about you. Derrick was telling me he had seen you. He's a bus driver now. He hasn't got any family yet but I'm sure there will be. I know he'd like to meet you. If you go into town on the bus you will. Time does fly! It only seems like yesterday you two were playing together as boys."

What Derrick said can only be surmised. Whatever it was had profoundly changed his mother's attitude. Tom said a silent, 'Thank you' to his boyhood tutor, and he smiled a smile that was seen as one of greeting but was, in reality, one of relief and gratitude.

Then he said, "It does seem like yesterday, doesn't it," but thought, 'Playing? Was that what happened in Lovers Walk?'

On his way home from the shop he passed Lovers Walk. He stopped and looked at the, now, broken gates and wandered in, just for old times sake. There was little water in the stream.

229

Time and animals had worn away the artificial bank that was a vital part of the perfect landscape design. There was no gurgling, no music as the clear water fell between the rocks, only a sluggish brown liquid seeping away into the earth. A branch from a beech tree had fallen across the path marking the spot where the boys had lain. Tom sat for a while astride the bough thinking of everything and nothing.

The next day was spent helping Dave, Norma's husband, lay linoleum in the sitting room of their cottage. The physical effort moving furniture and moving rolls of linoleum was exactly what Tom needed. Ash did not figure in any conversation, though Norma did say she had heard Tom's brother quip, 'He had never pushed shit in his life.' Tom and Dave worked well together. The past was not mentioned. In the evening they went to the pub for a pint.

Dave and Norma had two young sons. Though no relation, Tom was their favourite uncle. A role that proved perfect casting.

Tom slept soundly that night in the double bed he and Dave had shared. The occasional squeak of a spring as he rolled over could well have been an echo from the past, but he heard nothing until the dawn chorus of birds accompanied by the mooing of cows told him everything about the peace of the countryside.

The day before he returned to London Tom met Ron who reminded him of the day he won the six-penny bet when he pissed over the electric fence.

"I reckon I did win it. Got a bit of a shock, but they bloody paid up!" A wink, a side ways flick of the head and laughter left nothing more to be said.

Ron was now married with a daughter. He still worked on the farm but things were changing fast.

"It be different than it were when we were youngsters. Dunno if I like it so well or no, but there you be. We had some good times. I godda say that. You ain't changed nar bit. Thee dussent sound like somebody from London."

Tom suddenly realised he had ditched his R.A.D.A. voice and reverted, unconsciously, to the vernacular.

Ash was not mentioned for the rest of his stay. There was no further conversation between father and son. The warmth of his father's welcome, and the pride Mr Adamson showed when the chapel service was over simply being with his son, especially when talking to his old teacher, said everything.

Possibly, the most telling point was when Tom's father asked after Michael, "You must bring him down next time. He's good for you."

The return journey to London was uneventful. The compartment was full and in the best British tradition no one spoke. Tom had a window corner seat where, for the first part of the journey, he could watch the familiar country side fly past. At Southampton the seat opposite was taken by a man not unlike the man in the shiny suit on the last return journey from Dorset. There the similarity ended. This man settled to read a, well thumbed, copy of a D.H Lawrence novel and he did not need glasses.

The silence was comforting.

Left to his thoughts, Tom drifted from Ron and the electric fence and then across the compartment to Shiny and back to Ron who had reminded him of dances they used to cycle to in nearby villages when they were teenagers. Then Shiny figured again. What would his reaction have been to the night out for the returning P.O.W.? Ron was there that night and he had laughed with the rest. Tom smiled to himself. Would he dare remind any of the village lads of the P.O.W. tale? Would they remember? He thought not. They had probably cleared it completely from their memories.

It was summer 1945. The boys were being demobbed and returning to civilian life and a semblance of normality was returning. Women were being encouraged to return to their place in the kitchen and reject the abnormality of bus driving, or welding and other work rightly done by men.

One serviceman's homecoming was very special. Eddie Laycock had joined the army the day after war was declared. His basic training completed, he came home on embarkation leave and patriotic romanticism almost demanded that he should marry his village sweetheart. His wedding day was a wet

October Saturday but no one cared about the weather. When the honeymoon, spent in Torquay, was over Eddie left the village to rejoin his army to the euphoric strains of: -

'We're goin' to hang out the washing on the Siegfried Line.
Have you any dirty washing mother dear?
We're goin' to hang out the washing on the Siegfried Line,
If the Siegfried Line's still there.'

The Siegfried Line, which ran along the French border, was an up to the minute fortification designed to protect Germany and menace France, but everybody knew it didn't stand a chance against our boys. Facing it was the Maginot Line. An impregnable defence built by the French. No washing was ever hung out on the Siegfried Line. The Germans didn't play fair. Instead of facing up to the might of the combined armies of France and Great Britain they rained down troops from the sky and skirted the armies by invading Holland and Belgium.

By this time Eddie's wife was heavily pregnant.

Our boys stopped singing and headed for the coast and home but Eddie's battalion did not make it up to the beaches of Dunkirk. There were no small boats waiting to bring him home. Instead he was forced, at gunpoint, to board a train heading south well out of the war. Private Eddie Laycock spent the war in a Prisoner of War camp.

His story was told returning home from a village dance. During the later War years youngsters would cycle to neighbouring villages, dance until midnight then cycle home and be on the farm ready for work by seven the following morning. Tom was a regular. He almost always cycled with his particular mate but except for one unsuccessful and never repeated attempt, their nights out were platonic. What the standard of their ballroom technique was has to be left to the imagination but they enjoyed themselves. They didn't get drunk. They didn't have the money. They danced with the girls but didn't screw them. They didn't have the inclination. Getting a girl in the family way was a real fear. French letters (condoms) were not freely available even in the village Post Office!

On one occasion not long after the American soldiers arrived in the U.K. Tom was chatting to the local Scoutmaster/Sunday School Superintendent when a truck, loaded with Yanks, passed them in the village street. Tom closed his eyes. Half a dozen inflated French letters decorated the back of the vehicle.

"Look!" said the respected gentleman.

Tom tried not to.

"They're just what we want for our Christmas Sunday School party. Do you think if I went down to the army camp they would let me have some?"

He, obviously, thought the condoms were balloons.

Tom's response came as a surprise, even to himself, "Wouldn't it be better to wait until we can get some coloured ones?"

"You may well be right."

Embarrassment was saved but the subject of sex was never far away, and so it was with Eddie Laycock and the return journey from the dance.

An enterprising ex-serviceman, who had been wounded and demobbed early, bought a large limousine that had been laid up for the War years. It cost only a few pounds but it meant he could start up a taxi business. It was one way of getting petrol in those tightly rationed days and somebody had the bright idea of hiring it to take Eddie, and as many others who could be piled into the car, to a specially big dance being held in a village over the hill.

The overloaded vehicle slowly chugged its way up the steep hill out of the village and then to save petrol careered, out of gear, down the other side to where the dance was being held. Eddie had been welcomed home but this was an extra rehabilitation. A night out boozing with the lads, with a dash of dancing added to make up for the years in a German Prisoner of War Camp. Eddie left his wife pregnant when he went to France at the outbreak of war so she had to stay home to look after the five-year-old son.

The evening went well. They had plenty to drink but no one was drunk. The dance ended at midnight and the revellers piled into the ancient limousine and it grumbled its way back up over the hill. When it reached the top of the hill the engine settled to a quiet purr along the flat mile, or so, before descending into their home village. It was then that one of the lads, emboldened by beer, asked how Eddie had got on for a bit of ugh ugh. He clenched his fist and pumped his arm up and down a couple of times to illustrate his question.

"It wasn't any great bother," was the reply.

"You didn't have German girls did you?" the questioner was puzzled.

"No," Eddie was deliberately teasing. Then he added, "Though I did hear of a camp in Bavaria, or some such place, where they were allowed out, and some of our fellers had German girl friends. But they were so far away from anywhere. It wouldn't have made any sense to try and escape."

"Did you try?"

"Thought of it but that's as far as it got."

"How did you get on for best part of five years without having a bit."

"Who said I didn't?"

"What did you do then?"

"You want to know?"

"Yes."

Eddie then explained. "There was this bloke. He were a Cockney. A Londoner; you've heard them on the wireless. He was a real comedian. Put on some bloody good camp shows. Dressed up as Mae West. Didn't give a bugger."

"How do you mean? Didn't give a bugger."

"He'd take it up the back. He was as good as any woman. There were one or two others who'd do it too, but Mae was the one I liked best. Never knew what happened to him after the Americans came and we were all released."

Tom wanted to hear more, but guffaws stopped any further explanation. It was a great joke. Did it matter if it was true or not? It was a laugh, though the two who laughed loudest, one of whom was Ron, had regular wanking sessions with Tom, but never took it up the back. An attempt had been made a couple of years earlier with one but since their sex

234

technology was not lubricatingly advanced, the experiment was doomed to failure. One of the group had asked Tom, several months earlier, if he knew what a soldier meant when he said he fancied a bit of brown. Tom did see him talking to a soldier a few days later. Whether it was the same guy or what happened he never knew.

The laughter in the limousine did ring a little hollow.

By now the overloaded vehicle had reached the top of the hill and as it gathered speed to rush down into the village and home sheep were roused from their sleep by a raucous rendering of '*We'll meet again.*'

It all ended as if Eddie had simply told a dirty story and nobody ever thought he was a nancy boy, even if he'd had it off with one. The Cockney? Nobody knew him. It was a good story and war was war. The yarn had been told to the lads. No female could hear. They weren't laughing at Eddie, but somebody who'd take it up the arse could be laughed at.

Tom never heard the confession mentioned again. It was apparently forgotten. That is, except for himself. He pondered the tale. He looked at Eddie, but something told him not to try his luck. Would he get the same treatment as Mae West? Would he be a joke? Tom was learning fast. Bum and nancy boys and shirt lifters all had their uses but they were, in the end, figures of fun. The lads in the limousine would have said it was the beer talking when Eddie Laycock admitted to pushing his prick up another man's arse. If he did, so what? It was war.

There was a sequel to the Mae West tale, which Tom did not witness.

A couple of weeks later Eddie called a bloke out of a pub and beat hell out of him. It had been hinted to Eddie, and the Gossip was never identified, that this bloke, who being a farm worker was in a reserved occupation and never called up to fight, had been paying visits to Eddie's wife. Just visiting was grounds for revenge.

To quote Mrs Parker, a lady of considerable rectitude, "Whilst I cannot approve of brawling, particularly outside a public house, I be bound to say I have considerable sympathy for Mr Laycock. He had been serving his King and Country. He were defending our right to live our own lives in peace and then to be incastrated in a camp prison. Laid night after night in his lonely bed thinking only of his wife. Then to return home to find his wife had, for the want of a decent word, a comforter. If she were cold, she could have had a warming man. I am sorry I am getting confused. I meant pan."

She could say no more. Eddie had every right to punish his wife's seducer. Tom was, probably, the only person to see the irony of it all. The marriage did not break up. The whole affair was quickly forgotten.

Taking it up the back was put where it belonged, wherever that was. Different sets of rules applied to different applications of sex.

The only comment Tom ever heard on the Mae West/Cockney affair was, "Bugger that for a game of soldiers."

RID ENGLAND OF THIS PLAGUE

Chapter 22

Tom's visit to Dorset had given him hope. The only overt reference to Ashley's trial was made at the 'After Chapel Chat'. He could go down to Dorset again and wander in the woods he loved with Vic, without fear. For whatever reason, the village was not linking him with Ashley. Maybe he would ride on the bus driven by Derek and be able to quietly say thanks.

Life was getting back to normal.

About a month after the visit to Dorset, Tom and Michael made a tenuous attempt at having sex. Michael was lying, undressed, on his bed ready to turn in for the night. Tom sat on the edge of his bed looking, longingly, at his love. He could not be sure if the invitation from Michael was real or imagined but he took the short step between the beds and lay with his Michael. They simply hugged each other, pressing their bodies together. Michael was even able to convince himself that it was not an act forbidden by his spiritual pastors and masters. Neither attempted to do more, but they were young and the closeness of their bodies proved to be more than they could control. They simultaneously ejaculated.

Michael was shocked. He said nothing. He had done wrong. He pushed Tom away, got out of bed, cleaned himself and then went back to his bed.

Tom touched Michael's arm wanting to say they had done nothing wrong, but Michael shook his head. Instead of marking a new beginning for their relationship it marked the point where Michael withdrew more and more into himself.

As each day passed the relationship became increasingly formal. Tom knew there was nothing he could say that would influence Michael's thinking since the doctrine of celibacy had been accepted as absolute truth. They had been absolved of their past sins which meant there could be no going back. Indoctrination rooted in fear was changing their lives. Tom was lost in a maze of contradictions whereas Michael could see the path he had chosen. Tom accepted the church's ruling on the sex act but what could be wrong in seeking the warmth of holding the person you loved? Each night they would recite their prayers and bid each other 'goodnight' but there was no physical contact. Most nights, the words were spoken after they had put their heads on their pillows and closed their eyes. Neither could see he to whom they had wished peaceful sleep.

Early evening a week later, Tom had finished work and was back in Camden Square, Michael was doing overtime and would probably go for a drink with his work mates after but Tom was not sure what he wanted to do. There was no point in going out alone. As always, he looked on the hall table for any letters. There were two. Both addressed to him. One was from his mother. In spite of the fact that the trouble was behind them, Tom still opened his mother's letters with some trepidation. He need not have worried. The worst news was that the pub across the lane was changing hands. He looked at the second letter. The smudged postmark was impossible to read. His name and the address were printed in capital letters, deliberately it seemed, to make it almost impossible to recognise the writing. He took the letter into the room before opening it. There was something not quite right about it. There was no message inside, only four neatly folded newspaper cuttings from the local Dorset papers with no indication as to the sender.

Before him were detailed reports of the arrest and committal of Ashley in May and the trial at the Winchester Assizes in July. The cuttings had been carefully saved from the first account that his father must have seen '*Lower Budleigh Man Arrested*' to the trial and sentencing. Tom carefully examined the envelope in the hope of finding some clue as to the sender, but there was nothing. Who had sent the cuttings? Why had they waited so long? Questions to which he could see no answer. He looked at them only briefly but long enough to see that Ash had pleaded guilty. Tom felt he was holding poison.

He couldn't bring himself to read all the details but he did see that seven young men gave evidence. Police pressure must have been such as to force them to choose the only way out. He realised how fortunate he was in having Michael. They were able to support each other. Had he been alone. . . . .? Tom closed his eyes; he dared not think what damage he would have done.

Two others were charged with Ashley. Names jumped out at him from the printing. Tom knew two of them and they could have confessed enough to put him in jail with Ashley. What had they said? How much was in those statements Copper No.2 had laid out on the table. For three months Ashley's fate had hung over Tom and Michael. Presumably it was over now and those statements would not be used. Why? Why had the police not returned?

Holding the cuttings Tom asked himself aloud, "Who has sent them and why?" That was a question he asked himself repeatedly. There had to be some well-wisher who felt Tom needed to be reminded of the company he used to keep, but he couldn't think of anyone who knew his address. Did the police. . . .? No, he reasoned. They would not be so vindictive.

Ashley was in jail for seven years. The headlines screamed:-

'SEVEN YEARS FOR PEST TO SOCIETY
BROUGHT YOUNG MEN TO HIS FILTHY PRACTICES'

One young man was nineteen, the others in their twenties.

That case was over but Tom and Michael were still afraid. It was still possible that the police could bring charges against them and Tom felt particularly vulnerable. The police knew he had lived in the cottage at Lower Budleigh with Ashley and no matter how many times he said that nothing ever happened between them no one was going to believe him. He must have relived the police questioning a thousand times. The coppers knew he was lying. His reasoning was numbed. Now, he could only believe the police were waiting and would get him. He threw the paper cuttings on the table. He was going to destroy them but that would not have been fair to Michael. He had to be given the opportunity to read them.

Tom made himself a cup of tea. He longed for peace, for peace of mind. He remembered the day of the late King's funeral two years ago when the traffic stopped and all the noise of the city ceased for the two minutes silence. Then he could hear the birds as he stood in their Camden room looking out over the garden. They were two precious minutes of peace, celebrating death, in a world rushing headlong God knows where.

The phone out in the hall rang. He put the cup down. He'd have to answer it. It was most probably for someone upstairs. It wasn't. It was Denzil. He was phoning from a call box in the nearby Caledonian Market. Could he come round?

"What are you doing there?" Tom asked.

"Can I come round?" Denzil was insistent.

"Of course you can. But where have you been. Haven't seen anything of you for weeks," and Tom added, "What's up?"

"Tell you when I see you. Is Michael there?"

"No. He won't be home till later."

"Never mind." Denzil was very excited. "See you in a few minutes. I know the way."

Ten minutes later Denzil rang the doorbell and it wasn't until they were in the room that Denzil spoke, "I'm sorry. It's been quite wrong of me. I should have been in touch, but John's been. . . . "

"John? Oh yes, you met him on top of the monument." Tom was trying to help. "And the policeman banging on the door."

"Yes. It's all been a bit of a farce. I'm very fond of him; but there are so many problems - mental - emotional. I feel more than a bit responsible." Denzil was having difficulty in finding words.

"You weren't to know you were being followed when you came out of that toilet in Victoria. Fancy a cup of tea?"

"Thanks," Denzil said as he plonked himself down on a chair by the table.

"It's not been made long. It should be still O.K." Tom took a cup and saucer from the dresser.

"As I said, it's all been a bit of a farce." Denzil was

240

explaining himself very badly. He wasn't sure what he was thinking. "His, John's family are a bit, well more than a bit, suburban, but that's being unfair. Let's just say John is all mixed up."

"I know what you mean," Tom said with feeling as he started to pour the tea.

"I didn't have any of that to cope with when I was young. Growing up in the theatre isn't exactly the place to find people worrying about what the neighbours will say," Denzil added as Tom put the cup of tea on the table beside him.

It was then Denzil noticed the newspaper cuttings on the table. His arm was almost resting on them. He picked them up.

"What's this?" he almost shouted, "Seven Years for Pest to Society."

"Its nothing. Forget it," Tom said as he tried to snatch the cutting away, but Denzil held on to them. He wanted to read more.

"Seven years imprisonment. Defence pleaded homosexual tendencies had already been great punishment." Denzil stopped reading, looked at Tom and almost spat his words, "What a lot of bloody rubbish. Punishment for what? Seven years in jail. You are not involved in this, are you?" Tom again tried to retrieve the cuttings. Denzil was adamant, "No. Leave it, let me read them."

Then he read aloud, "In a search of the accused's home address books were found containing the addresses and telephone numbers of a large number of male persons some of them very well-known people. There were also a few addresses of females. A quantity of photographs were also found, including some of nude men.

Passing sentence on Ashley Ashley-Jones of Lower Budleigh, Mr Justice Goodfellow told him, 'It is perfectly obvious you are a complete and absolute pervert whose one aim is to get young men and bring them to your filthy practices. You are one of those men whom society regards as a pest and whose interest is to spread filthy doctrines about society. There is one thing to be said in your favour: you have not interfered with children.' Does he mean children or seventeen year olds?"

Denzil asked.

It was a rhetorical question and he read on, "If you had interfered with children the sentence would have been 14 years," he paused. "I don't believe it!" Denzil stopped reading. He turned to Tom and asked, "You know this Ashley-Jones? Now I think of it, you have mentioned his name. I am right?"

"Yes. He was my first big love affair." Tom briefly explained the relationship, and he added, "We didn't tell anyone about the case, not even close friends like you. There was no point. There was nothing you could do."

"Have your parents said anything?" Denzil asked.

Tom told him of his visit to Dorset and his conversation with his father.

Then Denzil asked, "Who sent these cuttings? Your family?"

"No. I think they have destroyed their copies of the local papers. I couldn't find any when I was home. I have no idea who sent these or why they have waited so long. It has to be somebody telling me my past hasn't been forgotten."

"Do you mind if I read them?"

"No it's alright. Go on. You know now." There was nothing else Tom could say.

"Did you know the other two men in the dock with Ashley-Jones?"

"I knew one of them, Dave Whitley. I don't know whether he told the police that we'd had sex together."

"Did he object when you had sex?"

"You are joking! He asked for it, but what difference would that make?"

Denzil shrugged his shoulders in agreement then read aloud, "Of Whitely, the Judge said, 'You are a feeble character but that is not your fault. I think you have been led into this way of life that is not really what you would choose. A course of treatment will put you back on the right path.' I don't believe it." Denzil stopped reading and looked at Tom and asked, "Was he feeble?"

"No." was the very emphatic answer.

"The Judge: 'appalling nature of a case like this is the way this viciousness is spread among people who would otherwise be uncontaminated. It is my experience, over and over again, that youths and men who have been turned aside to these filthy practises behave like animals. Even young Rogers'. Who was Rogers?" Denzil asked.

"I didn't know him. I believe he'd been in a case at Somerset Assizes with fifteen or sixteen other men," Tom told him.

"How dreadful!" Denzil said with a heavy dose of theatrical shock and horror. "Sixteen men. Condemn him? I envy him." Then he carried on reading, "Even young Rogers was probably once a decent creature. He became an appalling pervert - no better than a common prostitute."

He put the paper down and said, "I don't believe it. And you could have been caught up in all this."

"Could have been?" Tom corrected him. "We were. You might as well read the rest."

"One point in favour of Ashley-Jones, his solicitor said, was that if any young man resisted, he was a gentleman and never persisted." Denzil laughed which seemed right out of place. "I'm sorry, but resisted and persisted sound like a cue for a song in the new review I'm rehearsing." Then he read on. "Ashley-Jones had been conscious since his schooldays of his homosexual tendencies and that in itself had been an enormous punishment through life, isolating him from his fellow creatures." Denzil shook his head. "We queers behave like animals and that separates us from our fellow creatures. I think I'll stay an animal rather than be reduced to being nothing more than a creature. Oh, what's this bit at the end?" He read on. "His defending solicitor said, 'When he has served the sentence you must pass, he intends to go straight into an institution in an endeavour that these tendencies which have dogged him his whole life may be cured.' I don't believe it!"

Tom shrugged his shoulders and paused before he spoke, "Ash could only afford a local solicitor. He couldn't afford the big boys who would have put up a fight."

Denzil could not take his eyes from the paper cuttings. He read silently for a few minutes but had to say aloud the comments regarding one of the accused, "Until a year ago he was living a perfectly normal life. It is unfortunate that he quarrelled with his fiancé just after he met Whitley." and he added his own comment, "Perhaps he realised what he wanted."

Tom tried to stop him, but it was no use. Denzil read on, "A doctor has said there is nothing abnormal about him. It is simply a matter of loss of confidence."

"Please." Tom put his hand out and took hold of the paper cuttings. "I don't want to hear any more. I can't. . . ." he could say no more.

"How long has this been hanging over you?" Denzil asked.

"Since last summer." Tom flicked his head and looked out of the window.

"Why didn't you tell your friends? It would have helped to have talked about it."

"Michael and I decided not to. I don't know why. It just seemed it was our problem." Tom was finding it difficult to explain. "Ashley was so much part of my life, but I've never wanted to go back. My affair with him was pretty well over even before I met Michael. It's all a bit complicated. When I came to London and Michael followed, we were starting a new life. Perhaps you can't run away from the past. Ashley has taken the blame. He broke bail to come to London to warn us. That was a hell of a risk. It was one of the conditions of bail that he contacted no one."

"Did the police know that?"

"No. We denied everything when they came here to question us." Tom filled in some of the background of his relationship with Ashley but Denzil wanted it in detail.

After Tom told of the police interrogation (the details were engraved on his memory). Denzil asked, "Why weren't you two arrested?"

"I don't know." was Tom's reply. He paused. "How do we know we won't be?" He spoke so quickly Denzil could hardly understand what he said.

"Sorry I didn't hear . . . ."

"How do we know they, the police, won't be back? If there

is ever a bang on the door I almost mess my pants."

"I'm sorry," Denzil said very quietly, "I'm sorry. I didn't mean to. . . . The case must be over. I am sure you are in the clear. Thank your lucky stars. Somebody is looking after both of us as far as the police are concerned. Come on, Tom, its over now. I am sure it would have helped if you had told me about it."

Tom was not so sure. He cut Denzil short, "Poor Ash, he had to stand in the dock and listen and be told he's a pervert; there was nothing he could do. He was always so confident, so assured. I can't take any more. I just want to try and forget it."

Denzil, very gently, put his arm round Tom's shoulder. They both looked at the floor. That act of understanding and comfort was exactly what Tom needed.

There was silence as Tom put all the cuttings together and laid them on the table. Denzil leaned forward and put his hands either side of the cuttings. He looked at them, thinking and half nodded his head as he said, "I can't help thinking your Ashley was playing with fire. In London it's one thing but not in the country. I'm not saying what he did was wrong, but in a small village . . . . . . What is there to say?"

Tom said nothing. Denzil was simply churning over old thoughts. It did cross Tom's mind there were two blokes who lived together in his village and had to be fairly well off since they owned a largish thatched house. He was invited there one night and did visit one of the pair on several subsequent occasions. He was pretty certain he was not the only young man to be offered hospitality by the couple but they were very discreet and, as far as Tom knew, the police never asked questions and there was never any village gossip. Was it all a bit like playing Russian Roulette?

There was silence for a few moments before Denzil, stood back, shook his head and spoke again. "My God! I don't believe it. What the hell! We have coppers following you through the streets hoping to catch two men having it off, but it was O.K. to shag a girl. Sorry Sir, I thought you were a pervert. I don't understand this excuse that he found being queer an enormous

245

punishment, or was it some crass solicitor trying to get round the judge. I don't find it an enormous punishment. I think it's a privilege, and I don't know any creatures. You said it was only a local solicitor. I can tell you who should be in bloody prison. The solicitor and the judge!"

"Drink your tea." Tom held out the cup.

Denzil gulped it down and then he said, "Let's go for a drink. I think you need it."

Tom agreed, "I'll get out of this suit if we are going for a drink."

"Do you mind if I read all the cuttings while you change?" Denzil asked.

"If you must," Tom said as he changed from his suit into a more casual sports jacket and grey flannel trousers. They were the very first trousers he possessed with a zip fly. Tom and Michael had bought a pair each and couldn't wait to get back to the bedsit to play. Sliding a zip down was a hell of a lot more erotic than fiddling with fly buttons but that was the past. The past. He couldn't see a future. He didn't bother to change his tie. Even though the temperature was in the seventies he would not have considered going out not wearing a jacket and tie. But things were changing; Denzil, the rebel, was wearing a pair of Lee Coopers jeans.

Tom watched his friend. He wished the cuttings in hell. Who had sent them, and why? The question went round and round in his brain. Who ever it was, were they trying to torture him? Were they telling him he should have been there in the dock? Was the sender labelling him 'A PEST TO SOCIETY' and should be in jail?

It seemed to take forever for Denzil to finish reading.

"I'm ready," Tom said as he combed his hair.

RID ENGLAND OF THIS PLAGUE

Chapter 23

As Tom and Denzil walked up to the pub at the end of the road Tom said, "You never explained what you were doing here. Why are you in this part of London today?"

"I've been with John."

"John? Your lovely John. You haven't been followed by another copper, have you?" Just meeting John did not explain why Denzil was in Camden Square.

"No. It's much more interesting than that."

"And?" Tom's curiosity was aroused.

"John has taken today off work. Claimed he was sick." Denzil seemed to be deliberately confusing.

"I thought you said he lives in Gravesend." Tom was confused.

"He does. I took him to Charing Cross and put him on a train to go Gravesend. That's the station you go from."

"You don't say!"

"I do, but that wasn't what you wanted me to say," and he looked at Tom and laughed. "O.K. When I tell you it's going to sound like a joke. We have spent the afternoon in bed together, but he had to get home at the usual time. That's not the joke. The poor lad was conscience-stricken. He hates lying, particularly to his parents, but he had no choice. He couldn't tell his mother."

"Tell his mother what?"

"Where he'd been," Denzil said as though stating the obvious.

"Of course he couldn't tell his mother he'd been in bed with you. Talk sense."

"He couldn't tell her why he had lied and taken the day off

work."

"I do not understand." To emphasise his frustration Tom stopped walking and said, very carefully and slowly, "We cross the road here. The pub is just round the bend, which is where I'm going if you do not explain yourself." They crossed the road. "Charing Cross Station is not exactly Camden Town. If my London geography is correct they are three or four miles apart. Are you being deliberately misleading?"

"Yes," replied Denzil, then he added as though the thought had just jumped into his head, "There's one thing I must tell you."

Tom was getting more than a little impatient. "What?"

"John has settled into his new job with the shipping company. He really feels he has achieved something."

By this time they were outside the pub. "Is this the pub?" Denzil asked.

"Yes."

"I'll finish telling you this bit before we go in."

Tom stood still. He turned to Denzil and said with a resigned sigh, "I'm all ears."

Denzil ignored the sarcasm. "Apparently they were discussing poofs and pansies in the office. Poor John was so embarrassed. He was afraid it was a subtle conspiracy to get at him. He wished he could crawl under his desk when they started asking if any of the group knew one of those. No one did. John breathed a sigh of relief. 'There's one in Romford.' A very prim senior lady, who had said nothing previously, made the claim. 'How do you know that?' An obvious question to ask. 'My husband knows him.' That finished the discussion and the lady carried on with her work and it also finishes the anecdote."

Denzil pushed the pub door open. "Now let's go in and have a pint. I will explain what's been happening today when we are sat down with a drink."

And they went into the pub.

"Reading your paper cuttings has completely thrown me. Now, what are you going to have to drink? Whose beer is this?" Denzil asked looking around the bar to see what brewery owned the pub.

"Trumans."

"Their bitter's O.K. You having bitter as well?"

Tom nodded. Denzil got the drinks and they moved to a table away from the bar, as it was still early in the evening there were only two or three other customers.

"Start talking." This was a real reversal of roles. Denzil always led and dominated the conversation, but now Tom was telling him to stop prevaricating.

"Your Ashley-Jones. Was that his real name?" Denzil still seemed to be deliberately stalling.

"Yes. Now go on. Why are you in Camden when you'd seen your boyfriend off at Charing Cross?"

"Because, my dear Tom, I had to tell someone what's happened," and Denzil took a mouthful of beer.

"Oh! More trouble?" Tom's brain was programmed to expect the worst.

"No. Anything but, and because it's so funny I got the Underground to this god forsaken place."

Tom's face lit up. Camden Town may not rank with Pimlico socially but good news was something he desperately needed. It was obvious that the Romford story was intended to set the tone for what was to follow. Tom half laughed as he said; "Remind me not to speak to you when we meet again. But do tell. I can do with a laugh."

Denzil folded his arms and leaned on the table. What he was going to say had to be confidential though it was possible he might be over-playing the part.

"John has been aware of his homosexuality for several years. He's never done much about it. He had read about Soho in one of the Sunday papers and had spent a whole hour walking round in the hope of meeting someone, but nothing happened. He simply didn't know where to look. He swears I was the first person to pick him up. When he was much younger he played around with a school friend but felt it had to be wrong and never did it again. Comparing his adolescence to mine it's difficult to believe two queer boys can grow up so differently. I didn't have any problems at home. John did. Only

249

child, etc. Mum wanting to see him with a steady girl friend with a big chunk of chapel, 'If you are enjoying it, it has to be wicked' thrown in."

"My chapel going wasn't like that," chipped in Tom.

"It appears his was. The upshot was he'd convinced himself there was something wrong with him." Denzil paused.

"I don't imagine the copper incident helped," Tom commented.

"No, it did not. I have met him a couple of times since. Once in a café and once in the park. The poor boy was getting so screwed up, and I have to admit my sympathy was running out. Being queer has never bothered me. Well, to cut a long story short," and Denzil leaned back in his seat; "John read in some trashy newspaper that it was a sickness which could be cured. I do know the Guardian equated us with Lepers."

"It? Us?" Tom queried.

"Being queer! According to your Ashley-Jones reports they were lining up for a cure. I can only imagine it's an injection with a very large thing-a-me-jig up the back passage. My reaction was predictable. If you want to be cured, get cured, but don't bother me. I could see he was hurt. What else could I say? I had to be honest. I wished I'd kept my mouth shut. He seemed so vulnerable. Anyway, we parted. I felt so awful I had to run after him and tell him to think again and telephone me. He nodded a sort of promise but he didn't think again, not then. He set off to find some Witch Doctor who could cast a spell and cure him."

"Ashley is supposed to be going for a cure when he comes out of jail," was Tom's comment.

"And another of the accused, I read, had put himself in the hands of a minister of religion, and if I remember correctly he was bound over. The mind boggles!"

Tom's only reaction was to turn his head away. He looked at the clock, not to see the time. He did not even want to know what day it was. Denzil might joke. The mock horror in his voice only served to emphasise the awful reality of that young man's position. Tom knew, only too well, had he and Michael been standing in that court they would have done the same.

They would have begged the Reverend Father to enter a plea on their behalf. Being bound over would have been infinitely preferable to prison. The bound over joke, the double entendrè had not registered.

Denzil was so absorbed in his own thinking he was not aware Tom was on a very different tack.

"Bound over by a minister of religion," Denzil scoffed. "I ask you! I believe some people would enjoy it. I had a one-night stand, a euphemism if ever there was one, with a chap who wanted me to bind him over. He got the rope. I thought it was a joke but it wasn't. He put his hands behind his back for me to tie them together, and I did. It was then I remembered I had promised to meet my maiden aunt and said I had to leave." Denzil laughed at his admission. "Oh, I did untie him. He was, obviously, enjoying himself but what pleases one doesn't please us all, anyway, good luck to him but I am not sticking to the point and not really telling the truth either. John was put in touch with a psychiatrist in Harley Street, by whom I did not ask. It had to be Harley Street because only the very finest medical brains would be capable of dispensing such advanced psychiatry; any lesser brain might have passed on the advice of Confucius, 'If rape is inevitable, lie back and enjoy it.' But again I digress." Denzil was enjoying telling the story. "John made an appointment and went along for this miracle cure. I had no idea he was going. He guessed what my reaction would be. As far as I know he didn't tell anyone he was going. I like him so much, but he had got himself in a bit of a state and I couldn't see where we were going. I know it's not like me but I just couldn't tell him how wrong he was. I am not sure why he kept in touch with me, but he did. Anyway, as I said, he went along to Harley Street." Denzil raised his glass: "Bottoms up," and drank the beer in one go. He put his glass down. Tom picked it up, went to the bar, and had it refilled.

"And?" Tom said as he put down the glasses giving Denzil the cue to resume his tale. "This nut doctor looked at John over his rimless spectacles and asked the problem. Poor John stammered so badly there were ten Os and six Xs in homosexual. I am certain the quack put on his most kindly

251

fatherly voice as he explained to the very nervous patient, one could almost say penitent, things had moved on. We were no longer living in the Middle Ages. You don't have to live forever with this affliction and then asked very tactfully, 'Do you masturbate?' 'Yes,' confessed the patient. And to set him at ease the specialist then said, 'Now, there's no need to be embarrassed, but tell me, what you do think about when you masturbate?' John did not know what to say. What was this man expecting to hear? He'd be shocked at some of the things John thought. 'What I mean is. Do you think about men?' The psychiatrist was working in the paternal mode. John had to admit he did think about men. I think he must have felt like a naughty boy caught with a stolen lollipop in his mouth. The paternalism then went into overdrive. 'Now that is where you go wrong. You should think about women. You think about men in trousers don't you?' Poor John had to confess he did. 'Now that is, again, where you go wrong.' And a look of infinite wisdom must have flowed over the top of his spectacles as he went on, 'A lot of women wear trousers these days. You have a lot to choose from. I remember land girls in the war in breeches, and ladies on horses do nowadays. Lots of very fine ladies in the country go around in slacks. Take a look in any good book shop and you will find lots of magazines. Lots of pictures to help you. In high society, I believe it is fashionable to wear tight fitting silk trousers. So you see, there is no problem.' With that incontrovertible advice the consultation ended."

"You're serious?" Tom was laughing. "You've made this up."

"I have not. I told you you'd think I was joking. What I've said is exactly what John told me and I have no reason to doubt his honesty. I don't think he could tell a lie even if he tried. Thinking about it on the bus I wondered if the psychiatrist doesn't get a kick out of looking at fashion magazines himself. But that is not the end of the story. 'How much do you earn?' John was asked. 'Five pounds a week.' 'Oh! Well my fees are usually eight guineas but I will only charge you four.' That cleared John out for the week. He left the consulting room

252

totally at a loss, financially and mentally. Magazines! He couldn't afford them and what would his mother say? My lovely John went down the stairs and out of the door into the street, not knowing which way to turn. He stood on the top of the steps and there in front of him were two very good-looking men in expensive suits carrying tennis rackets, obviously, on their way to the park. They were so handsome; he couldn't take his eyes off them. One of the men looked at John who was sure the man half smiled. They passed and walked on. John looked back at the brass nameplate on the door and then at the backs of the men. He made a very quick calculation and decided he could not afford to be cured. Then he came round to my place hoping I would be in. I was and I will get you another drink."

"Thanks."

Tom's head was swimming. Trying to take in the newspaper reports of the trial was bad enough now; on top of that, he had to listen to this crazy tale about Denzil's new boyfriend. He watched Denzil as the drinks were pulled up. No matter how improbable the psychiatrist's advice sounded, Denzil wasn't the person to pass on something untrue.

The drinks were placed on the table. They each lifted their glasses: "Cheers."

There was a pause before Denzil spoke. "What do you think about it?"

"About what?"

"The prison sentence." Denzil waited for a reply. "You must think something."

"I'm not thinking. We've been through enough as it is," was all Tom could say.

That gave Denzil the cue he had been waiting for. "Had this Ashley been the chap in the front room bedsit the law couldn't have touched him and I am damned sure the copper was envious of my front room man."

Tom didn't get the point. "But in Ashley's case they weren't girls."

Denzil now felt free. "That's the point. The girl on the bed in the front room was no more than eighteen. John's age."

Tom shrugged his shoulders.

"She's female. That made it O.K. Why? He wasn't going to marry her. What's the difference between her and what your Ashley did? Did that judge have any idea what he was talking about? I can't believe he did, any more than John's psychiatrist. What that stupid judge said was if you touch another man's cock he'll never want a woman again. Once you've caught the bug you are hooked for life. All I can say is women can't be that good if you can be turned off them that easily, and as for cures, I don't believe it. What happened today has to be proof enough. I'm not sick and I resent anybody saying I am."

Tom didn't argue.

Denzil went on. "Are these people so blinkered, or do they think what they've been told to think. If that's the case then a lot of 'them that know' haven't had an original thought in their heads for centuries. Can't they just look and see what's going on around them." He then appeared to change the subject. "I see in the paper that Parliament has set up a committee to look at homosexuality, the Law and that sort of thing. Whether it will do any good, God knows. I hope it does. I can't believe I'm the only one who thinks this way. There must be others, but do you think they are ever going to say it's O.K. for me to love an eighteen-year-old John? I hope I live to see the day," he said and half sighed, "But I don't know. The chairman is a John Wolfenden. Vice Chancellor of some university, but I've no idea who he is or what his qualifications for the job are."

Then he returned to the Ashley case.

"As for the solicitor going on about tendencies that dogged Ashley all his life. He wasn't telling the truth. He was just trying to get a lighter sentence. Dogged! I don't feel I'm dogged. Did Ashley when you were in bed with him?"

In spite of himself Tom had to smile. He took a drink and said, "Now you are asking. Some dogs can be very randy."

"I'll drink to that," and he raised his glass. "Come to think of it there are times when I do feel doggy. On second thoughts I don't. Dogs are, usually, told when and what they can shag and that is not for me." Denzil put his glass down. Then he asked, "This chap Whitely, that was his name? Was he one of the ones you knew?"

Tom agreed he was.

"Was he emotionally and intellectually immature? I think it said he was twenty nine." Denzil waited for an answer.

"He was a bit camp. . . ."

"That doesn't make him immature," Denzil cut in. "Sounds to me like kids making excuses. 'It wasn't my fault teacher, I'm easily led.' And what about the 'abominable' things found in Ashley's house? Letters from men! Address books with only a few women's names and photographs of men, two of whom were nude. Seven different men in four years! That's nearly two a year. What is the world coming to! Pity I won't pass any cottages on the way home."

Denzil looked at the clock. "I could go on for hours but, anyway, I'd better be going."

With that he finished his drink and they strolled up to Camden Town Underground Station.

Denzil bought his ticket for the Underground and they were about to part when he suddenly remembered, "Oh, I nearly forgot. I've brought this magazine article for you. Thought it might amuse you. Fifteen ways to spot a queer."

He handed Tom the cutting. Tom hid it in his pocket. He felt almost guilty carrying it on the trolley bus back to Camden Square.

When he was safely indoors Tom looked at the heading:- *'Fifteen ways to spot a Queer.'* and did not bother to read the list properly. He was not on Denzil's wavelength. He could not believe there was hope. The law was a fact. Anything else was wishful thinking. Tom stared out of the window. His reasoning was swirling in a cannibal's cauldron.

'Fifteen Ways to spot a Queer'

(1) It is not difficult to pick out queers they invariably walk with mincing steps. Their walk is the reverse of a manly stride and causes the characteristic wobble of the buttocks.

255

(2) They often flick their eyes up to the right to emphasise a point.

(3) At the beginning of a conversation a man who is one of those will keep his hands still, but as he talks his gestures become more and more exaggerated.

(4) They wear suede shoes.

(5) A detailed survey produced two interesting points: a/ Men of a homosexual disposition are often colour-blind, and b/ They can rarely sing in unison.

(6) They often remain bachelors.

(7) They look effeminate and have high-pitched voices.

(8) Homosexuals are mummy's boys and later in life are good to their mothers.

(9) Such men rarely drink pints of beer in mugs. They prefer half pints in glasses.

(10) They smoke cigarettes in holders. They never smoke pipes.

(11) They adore operatic sopranos, and like the theatre in general.

(12) A man who is a lady's hairdresser is invariably one.

(13) Boys allowed to play with dolls often develop female tendencies in adulthood.

(14) They cannot whistle.

(15) The index finger and the fourth finger are, invariably, the same length.

Tom was about to tear the paper up. Then he stopped and read it carefully and wondered if there was any connection between his smoking a pipe, possessing the naturist magazine and not being arrested. He was thankful the police did not ask him to whistle because that was something he was never able to do, and would not have thought to deny that he was also colour-blind! Denzil had also included a paper cutting, that had nothing to do with homosexuality, dating from the late 1940s, quoting an American science journal claiming sterility to be hereditary!

Later, for some inexplicable reason Tom carefully folded

the sheet of paper and hid it in a glossy publication giving details of the Queen's coronation. Where else should it reside except with the institution that had solemnly sworn to uphold our heritage and traditions?

That evening Michael picked up the newspaper cuttings from Dorset. He made no comment. The couple sat in silence. The cuttings rested on Michael's lap.

"What do we do?" Tom asked.

"There's nothing we can do."

"No, there's nothing." Tom saw no point in repeating Denzil's comments and Michael was in no mood to hear the psychiatrist tale. It would achieve nothing.

"Do we keep these?" Michael asked holding up the paper cuttings.

"Don't think so."

Michael stood up. "The wrong people might read them."

He took the cuttings over to the gas cooker and set fire to them. He dropped the flaming paper into the sink and watched them burn. Then he turned on the tap and washed the ashes down the drain. Tom watched. It was as if Michael were performing some symbolic cremation.

"Poor Ashley. Whatever else, he brought us together," he said to the sink as if trying to convince himself the water was washing away the past?

It was still only nine thirty, but they went to bed.

Alone.

RID ENGLAND OF THIS PLAGUE

Chapter 24

The old queer haunts were now no go areas for Tom and Michael. This meant conditioning themselves to a whole new way of life whether they liked it or not. Occasionally, they would have a drink in a normal bar but that gave them an increased sense of isolation. Michael did spend evenings with a couple of work colleagues; they were about the same age with sufficient common interests to keep conversation going for a couple of hours. On a pleasant summer's evening Tom would wander over to Regents Park, but the couple were spending more and more time in the bedsitter listening to the wireless to help pass the time. It wasn't that they deliberately cut themselves off from their friends, except Denzil who kept up regular contact; it was more that they tried to hide from themselves.

Making excuses, or lying, was alien to both of them, but they could not be open with their friends. James would have condoned keeping their heads down but would have said they were crazy trying to deny their sexuality in religious terms. Denzil had made no secret of his views. They lived hoping, one day, they would find that the past year had not happened or, by some miracle, it had been consigned to a forgotten past.

One Saturday Michael was in Oxford Street and to avoid coming face to face with Denzil he slipped into a shop and was more than a little embarrassed to find it was one selling ladies lingerie.

Television existed but such luxury was not for bedsitter land. Tom's brother who lived over in Dulwich bought a set in

1953. He and his family had to be able to watch the coronation. The pictures were in black and white and so small you could pretty well cover the screen with your hand. It was no competition for the cinema. There the screens were big. If you sat in the front row you were faced with a screen five or six metres high that overwhelmed you. The back row was reserved for couples necking - young heterosexual unmarrieds who wanted somewhere dark and comfortable to kiss and cuddle. In the cinema you could forget reality and allow yourself to be absorbed into the film almost as a participant. The world of glamour and kitsch became reality for a few hours.

It was not only the film. The cinemas were often designed to offer a sense of luxury and escape. The favourite cinema for the two young men was the Odeon Astoria, at Finsbury Park. Simply going there was an experience. On a Saturday it meant queuing for at least half an hour if the film was a success, but it was worth it. The magic began as you passed the pay desk. Walk through the swing doors and you were transported into another world. The foyer was a Moorish courtyard complete with fountain, but that was only a beginning. When you walked into the auditorium you did not need to imagine you were out of doors in another land, the architect had done it for you. The proscenium was the arch over a huge Moorish gate. On either side hills stretched away into distant mountains, and dotted up the sides of the hills were houses with lights shining through their windows; lights than went on and off as different rooms came into use. You may have paid to watch the film but even the biggest stars did not always hold your attention. When that happened escape was at hand. You simply leaned back in your seat and gazed up at the ceiling, or rather the sky for there above your head were stars that twinkled, as distinct from the heavenly bodies shining on the screen. The magic did not end there. Clouds would drift across the night sky. They were never thunderclouds nor did they threaten rain.

The films Tom and Michael watched are now part of the Hollywood legend: 'From here to Eternity', 'High Noon', 'On the Waterfront', 'Rear Window' and their favourite 'Seven

259

Brides for Seven Brothers' (the plot may be very politically incorrect but the dancing was sensational. It was men dancing - not pretty chorus boys). They may now be seen on video or television but even the best living room is not the Odeon Astoria.

Entertainment reached new heights with 3D. The two young men went for any form of escape. Wearing a pair of cardboard spectacles with one eye looking through a red filter and the other through a green one you could see the action in three dimensions - width, height and depth.

Watching Howard Keel in 'Kiss Me Kate' was an experience. In tights and with a codpiece the imagination was extended, though neither Tom nor Michael would admit to enjoying anything other than the music. That was escapism. Reality was very different, both were only too well aware that they were living in an unscripted world with no guarantee of a happy ending.

Tom was home later than usual from work one night. Michael had arrived back at South Villas before him, and Tom was expecting the evening meal to be ready. The front door was not properly shut. He pushed it open and walked in smoking his pipe as he always did. A voice yelled, "Get outside and put that bloody pipe out. Do you want to blow the place up?"

He was facing a policeman. Tom stumbled back through the door and almost fell down the steps, the policeman was so threatening. Michael had arrived home an hour earlier and as soon as he got inside the front door he smelt gas. It was coming from under the door of the other ground floor bedsitter. He banged on the door but got no reply. The only thing to do was to call Mrs Urbano. She opened the door with her passkey. The room was full of gas. All the taps on the gas cooker were fully on. A lot of money must have been put in the gas meter deliberately to keep the gas flowing. On the bed were the nude bodies of a man and a woman.

Michael turned the gas taps off, opened the windows and called the police.

The couple had been tenants for only two weeks. They had gassed themselves. There was a hand written note by their side.

It was a suicide pact. They were both married, not to each other, and lived out of London. The note briefly said they were in love and could not face the scandal and asked their respective families to forgive them.

Michael and Mrs Urbano had to attend the inquest. After it was over, Michael made the apt comment, "It's not only us queers who have to suffer if our love breaks the rules."

The bedsitter was relet. The tragedy was not mentioned. What would have been the point? Tom and Michael were not callous. They had their own problems to contend with.

Michael's sister, brother-in-law and their young son were planning to visit London. It was to be part of their annual holiday. A weekend sightseeing with Michael and Tom then onto Eastbourne to stay with a cousin. Accommodation proved no problem. Mrs Urbano found them bed and breakfast only a few minutes walk from Camden Square. Saturday was devoted to the sights, Buckingham Palace, Westminster, St.Pauls etc.. Sunday was likely to be difficult. Which church to attend? In view of their local vicar's scathing remark All Saints was not thought to be appropriate. St Martins-in-the-Field was a real possibility. It was Low Church and services were regularly broadcast from there.

The question was carefully phrased, "What would you like to do tomorrow? We had thought. . . . ."

Michael was not given time to finish before the answer came. "If it's alright by you, we'd thought of going to Petticoat Lane." The famous East End street market.

The irony was not lost on Tom. Chester could offer churches but it had nothing to compare with this market.

It was only a few days later, without thinking Michael made a statement that would not have been out of place a decade later. He had been transferred to the Personnel Department working with new recruits to the company. They were reviewing the progress of a particular young man, and it was suggested he might be one of those. What was to be done? It was Michael, still very much a junior himself, who waded in over the ums and errs.

He asked a simple question. "Is his progress rating good?"

"Well, yes. Yes, it's pretty. . . . well, actually very good."

"His behaviour?"

"Behaviour? How d'you mean?"

"You said you think he is one of those. What has he done?"

"Oh, I see what you mean. No, nothing like that. It's more the feeling . . . . It's the way he moves. His manner."

"Does it affect the business?"

"No. I suppose not."

"Suppose?"

"In fact he's very good with the customers."

"Well then?"

The question was not answered and the young man continued his training.

A line from a contemporary translation of the Greek play *Lysistrata* by Aristophanes could be taken as the theme for the next part of this chapter. Tom and Michael had seen a production of the play and thought it immensely funny, but that was before. . . . The women of Troy were on strike. They refused to have sex until the men stopped the war. In the version the two young men saw, a herald comes running on stage panting. When asked how things were in Troy he gave the only possible answer, "Hard, very hard."

Tom noted that the male members of the audience, who were accompanied by a female, would glance at their companion to see if they dare laugh. Had he been asked the same question now he was chaste, his answer would have been exactly the same, but he would not have laughed. He had to face his Armageddon on the London Underground. To be more specific the Central Line coming into Queensway. Where else? Whether he won or lost the battle has to be a matter of opinion.

He had to act as a herald carrying some important information to a client. Information needed that day. Delivery by hand was the only option and the task fell to Tom to go by public transport from Kentish Town to Queensway. It was no problem. He enjoyed travelling around London. In the 1950s

262

traffic jams were newsworthy.

Since it was mid morning he was surprised to find the Underground train had no empty seats when he boarded it at Tottenham Court Road. That was most unusual since it was not even the rush hour. By the time the train left Marble Arch it was packed. Bodies squeezed tightly together was, at first, a mild irritant but quickly became something very different. He had started standing in the space between the doors but with the sheer weight of numbers he was pushed back into the far corner, away from the platform side of the carriage. He had to admit that the young man who had done most of the pushing, was very good looking, or at least he was in profile. He was side on with his shoulder against Tom's chest. Their faces were only inches apart. The smell of Brylcream was very disturbing. Memories. . . . Ashley - memories. Fortunately the man proved to be most considerate; he realised it might be uncomfortable for Tom and moved slightly so as not to be actually leaning against him.

The doors clanged shut and the train gave its usual jerk. The standing passengers were involuntarily rearranged. Tom felt a slight pressure on his crotch, obviously due to the swaying of the train. The swaying and the pressure increased though not in time with each other. Tom closed his eyes. There was no way he could back off since his arse was firmly wedged into the corner of the carriage. He opened his eyes and looked at the profile in front. It was absolutely passive. This man was oblivious of any moral problems the back of his hand was creating. Fear of the Law, aggravated and abetted by the dread of eternal damnation, had put a stop to any physical sexual activity by Tom but here was a classic case of a lack of communication between mind and body. His physical functions had not been consulted when his mind went into the chastity mode. The major problem was the pumping system. He could hear the blood thumping in his ears. His brain seemed to have totally lost control of the timing and the amount of blood being forced into his penis. He was willing it not to happen. 'I must not get the jack (a hard-on),' he said to himself, but his will was weak and his orders were ignored. All he hoped was that the profile would not be aware of what was happening.

The hand stopped moving. Tom breathed a sigh of relief. He was not to be tempted. His little prayer had been answered. He tried to move but that only served to stir the devil. The hand made a full hundred and eighty degree turn. The train swayed and the hand sought for support. It found a firm anchor. By now Tom's pump had been primed. His cock was rock hard. The profile still betrayed no emotion.

Tom could, and possibly should, have whispered, "Excuse me." But he reasoned otherwise. The London Underground could be likened to the wilderness and, if so, even though he was not planning to spend forty days on the Central Line, was this not his time of testing? Come what may, he would stand the test, and cumming was exactly what he feared. The hand relaxed its hold. Tom had been tried and not found wanting, though that may be a misuse of the word wanting. He felt the hand brush against his thigh. For the first time in his life he was aware of just how much a train swayed and jerked. The impassive face looked in his direction. Tom knew he should have scowled but the face was so deceptively angelic that Tom's lips moved to betray what could have been mistaken for the faintest of smiles.

Then his reasoning clicked into place. This had to be one of the disguises of the Devil. Tom did not think it was the devil tempting him. He knew it was. The whole panoply of indoctrination so completely enveloped him that he could almost smell incense as he fought to adopt a holier than thou attitude; but the handsome Devil in front of him did not let up though his slight movement away to one side made it appear that he might do so. This had to be his time of testing. His forty days in the wilderness. He wanted to raise his hands in prayer but fear made his arms rigid; fear that his right hand would not obey the instructions from his brain. Tom knew only too well what his hand had been trained, over the years, to do in such a situation.

Hope as Tom may, the Devil's hand was not stilled. Thank God for the modern zip that defeated even this Devil's handy work. He would rise above it. The problem was his cock had risen as if it were trying to hoist his white underpants as a signal of surrender.

The train slowed. He had reached Queensway, his destination. He pushed his way off the train without daring to look back to see if he was being followed, which is exactly what he would have done before.. . . . As he left the station he did glance over his shoulder. He was not being followed. He said a silent 'Thank you' and decided to return on the bus. It would take longer than the Underground but it would mean he did not have to risk another such encounter with a molester.

Again there was a problem. His cock was still hard. He painstakingly lit his pipe in the hope that sucking and blowing might do the job but to no avail.

He was able to distract himself, to some extent, by seeking out his destination, a tall building ten minutes walk from the station. When he got there he found the lift was not in use. The operator had gone, either for a cup of tea or to the loo. Without the operator riding up and down working the old-fashioned machinery the lift could not function. It meant climbing four flights of stairs, which was no problem to the young, fit, Tom. He was relieved that by this time his erection was fading. His trousers were well cut and fitted snugly round the buttocks, as was the fashion, and the last thing he wanted was to face an office full of people, he had never seen before, with a raging hard-on. Climbing the stairs would use up a considerable amount of energy and quickly put things right. The incident on the train was being consigned to the past. Tom grasped the firm wooden knob at the beginning of the balustrade and decided, since he'd overcome the temptation, it was something to remember. With that in mind he started the ascent. A shaft of sunlight shone down the stair well and though the thing in his underpants had not fully resumed a recumbent posture the sunlight had to be a symbol of hope.

There was no problem in getting to the first bend in the stairs, but the next flight to the first floor did indicate there might be trouble ahead. The regular rhythm of his knees as he lifted his feet up to each step caused just the slightest massaging action on his loose underpants, which was in turn transferred to

265

what poor Tom had hoped would become a sleeping dog, and allowed to lie. But no such hope.

The shaft of sunlight disappeared. A cloud must have gone over the sun. By now the new, but sorely tried, convert to purity felt he was being deserted. It was so easy while singing hymns to keep one's thoughts above one's navel, but the Devil on the Underground had cocked things up. However, there was nothing to do but to press on.

Each step was an agony of ecstasy. Though he held the banister firmly each step was one step nearer masturbation. He had to get to the top whatever happened.

To relieve the pressure Tom put his free hand down to undo his flies. That was his fatal error. The slight movement of his hand against the top of his knob was all that was needed to trigger the gun. It fired wildly and uncontrollably. He stood still and gripped the banister with one hand and held his thigh with the other. His stomach muscles convulsed as each contraction pumped more and more semen. It seemed it would never stop.

Chastity by the gallon saturated his under pants and he could feel the warm fluid running down his leg. Suddenly the sun came out again and the stairwell glowed with light.

He heard footsteps on the stairs above him. He did his best to take up a normal climbing stance as a middle-aged man came down the steps towards him.

When he passed he said, "Your flies are half open."

"Thanks," Tom muttered and pulled up his sticky zip. He was thankful his suit was brown striped and did not show the stain too obviously. His cock went soft but it was too late. He had lost the fight.

Facing him at the top of the stairs was the office. He hesitated, then his eye saw the sign he needed: 'TOILETS', however, it was too late to mop up all the seed he had spilled in defiance of the biblical injunction. He put his hand in his flies and felt pubic hair stiffening, pricking his hand as though he had secreted a stiff brush in his trousers. He felt his sticky underpants and was almost overcome with the guilty feeling that he had enjoyed the experience, as he adjusted his tie, he tried to dismiss the notion.

Had he then been asked, "How are things in Troy?" an honest answer would not have been as in the script!

"Not at all hard now, thank you," would have been nearer the truth.

When he left the office he became only too aware that going down the stairs was a very different experience from coming up. With each downward step he realised he was now wearing protein-starched underwear, something that should be avoided whenever possible.

True to his word he returned by bus. He did draw a parallel with his first encounter with the Royal Navy and his vow, after that incident, as he cycled home in some discomfort. Then, a mere schoolboy, he kept his vow of chastity for a full week! He agonised over the current situation and had to admit that, this time, the odds were against such an extended period.

The word trauma existed, but the concept of being traumatised did not. Tom did, however, reflect on the cost of the experience. To dry clean trousers = 2/6 (12.5% of £1) plus the cost of lying when he took the trousers to be cleaned was incalculable. Saying he had dropped rice pudding in his lap was not going to sound convincing. To that, had to be added nearly a day's discomfort. A wet dream was one thing but having one while you were awake was something very different.

All this forced him to the conclusion that the price of chastity was too high. He smiled to himself when he saw the parallel with Denzil's boyfriend John. He found the cost of a cure too high.

Whatever conclusion he may have come to privately, remained private. He did not dare tell Michael how he fell from grace climbing the stairs, and how he had to endure cardboard hard underpants for the rest of the day, or how he managed to slip them unnoticed into the laundry bag. Nor dare he admit, even to himself, that he was questioning the whole concept of his conversion and the vows he had made. The deceit added to his other problems. He could not bear the thought of losing Michael but he knew the commitment of the man he loved to his Anglican upbringing and the iron will that would not allow any deviation from a path so seriously undertaken.

"You must keep trying," would have been the maxim. Their relationship remained platonic and they were still regular churchgoers.

A couple of Sundays later Choral Evensong was in full flood. Sacred music, like water from a holy fountain, deluged the congregation. The choirboys' unbroken voices sent jets of the purest sound soaring high into the Gothic arches, striking the carved stonework and scattering like stars from an exploding, heavenly, firework. The organ would vibrate like the rumbling of the Almighty's voice and the bass male voices heralded another flash of divine inspiration. As the music ebbed away and the flood subsided, the wonder-filled worshippers knew they had bathed in the waters of Galilee.

For a few moments there was silence and in that silence the choirboys, angelically attired in lace and linen, sat and remained thus throughout the sermon without twitching even an eyelid. There was no sound except the voice of the Reverend Father. That particular sermon was based on a text Tom had never heard. It became a learned dissertation on some obscure but important point of theology. He had no idea how many words of impenetrable wisdom had come down from the pulpit before he was aware that Michael was trying to attract his attention. It took a firm pinch on the thigh to bring Tom back from his reverie. Michael wanted to whisper something. Tom turned his head and frowned. Michael beckoned him closer.

"Look at the choir boys," Michael whispered.

Tom looked. They were as neat and tidy and well behaved as ever so he raised his eyebrows to say, "So?"

"Look at them."

Tom looked. They were still as much choir boys as they always were. Michael even daring to whisper, no matter how quietly, in the middle of a sermon was beyond belief.

"They look like a row of little Queen Victorias. Just like grandma's photo."

Tom looked. Michael had a photograph of his grandmother dressed as Victoria. She had played the Queen Empress in a pageant staged for the 1935 Silver Jubilee. A copy of the picture had been sent to Her Majesty Queen Mary who, through her lady-in-waiting, graciously replied accepting this act of loyalty to the crown. Tom closed his eyes. He could see the photograph. The only difference between that and the boys was a piece of lace curtaining pinned to grandma's grey hair.

Michael had hit the button. There, side-by-side in neat rows, were miniature replicas of the well-known portrait of the lace-bedecked Queen upon whose empire the sun never set. It needs to be remembered that in the fifties reverence for anything Victorian was at an all-time low. A guidebook published around that time stated simply. 'This church is nineteenth century and therefore of no interest.'

Tom could not contain himself. The strain of chastity and piety had been too great. He looked again. The act of looking at those boys was like releasing a safety value. The pressure that had built up was more than his tightly clenched teeth and lips could contain. He exploded. Faked a fit of coughing. In disgrace the pair left the church.

Tom felt sure he could now be honest but any such idea was soon dispelled. Michael deeply regretted making the joke. Disturbing a service was unforgivable.

Where were they heading? Ashley had brought them together. Was he going to tear them apart?

RID ENGLAND OF THIS PLAGUE

Chapter 25

1954 passed into history. Tom and Michael were still together but it was fast becoming a non-relationship. They were now friends sharing living accommodation.

The winter was coming to an end, days were getting longer. From the window of their bedsitter Tom and Michael could look out onto the garden and see daffodils in full bud waiting to bloom, but even that did little to brighten things. Their life together was far from miserable but it had lost its purpose.

A post card arrived addressed to Michael and Tom. It read:-

> *Dear Both,*
> *Above is my new address and telephone number.*
> *So much to tell. I can barely keep up with my life.*
> *Ring me before seven on Friday and come round.*
> *Yours as ever*
> *James.*

James must want to tell them something important so Michael telephoned James.

"Michael, my dear, how are you?" It was a rhetorical question. Without waiting for an answer James went on, "Wonderful to hear you. I will tell you one piece of news and the rest of the gossip can wait until you come over. I have taken this flat with an Australian. I'm still in Earls Court. There are worse places to live. And before you start getting ideas, this is a purely business arrangement. Nothing between us - nothing at all. I know how your dirty little mind works. I assure you there is nothing. After the first fumble we decided it wouldn't work and now we are the best of friends. There are two bedrooms. But you'll be able to see it for yourself and I won't keep you, I'm sure there's a queue behind you waiting to use the telephone. Far be it for me to waste time with tittle-tattle. Now this is how you get to the flat. . . ." and James detailed the route from Earls Court Underground Station. It was only a few minutes walk. He would expect Tom and Michael as soon as they could make it.

James in a two bed-roomed flat! That was really something. He was obviously coming up in the world.

Tom and Michael left for Earls Court almost immediately, and had no problem finding the flat. As instructed they rang the bell marked flat C. James was waiting for them.

The flat was spacious. It was also furnished. The armchairs and settee were thirties comfortable with shawls thrown over, either to protect the original coverings or hide the worn patches; whatever the reason, they gave the room a slightly down at heel exceedingly smart, camp feel. It was the perfect setting for James. Both Tom and Michael immediately thought, "How much is this costing?"

"I know what you are thinking," James said, "And it is. It is costing the absolute earth. Without Gordon I could not have thought of taking a place like this, but then, a professional lady has to keep up appearances. Gordon he's the Australian I share it with. His family are something to do with wool and those hefty great outback sheep farmers shearing away to keep us girls busy knitting, but then you, Tom with your rural experience, would know all about what is supposed to be done with sheep! Now don't tell me, I don't want to know, it is too disgusting. You'll meet Gordon if he's back before you go."

James produced a bottle of good French wine. Tom and Michael were impressed.

"I brought it back from Paris. I take it you will join me in a glass. In Paris they drink wine as we drink beer," James said as he put three wine glasses on the table. In their bedsit, Tom and Michael had to make do with a couple of tumblers.

It would be so easy to misinterpret this as 'camp show off' but that would have been unfair. James wanted nothing more than to share his good fortune, and his sense of fun, with his friends.

"I am going to have to go to night-school. My schoolboy French is utterly useless."

He handed a glass of wine to each of his guests. "Cheers."

They touched glasses and drank the toast proposed by James, "To us and the future."

The irony was not lost on either Tom or Michael. James could never be accused of bragging. He simply replied honestly to Michael's question, "What have you been doing since we last met?"

He had been to Paris photographing a fashion show and his pictures were being used in at least two magazines, and as he said, "Who am I to complain? I'm being paid to do things and go places I couldn't even dream of." Then he added the real bit of news. "My dears, Paris is unbelievable! Cocks flashing in every direction. It makes this city look like a nunnery. I was going to say monastery but one can never be sure of some of those monks' habits. Glad to be back for a rest, believe you me."

Each time they met James, Tom became more aware that their worlds were spinning into very different orbits. While he was toiling away in Kentish Town worrying about leather handbags, wallets and soles for shoes and boots, James was swanning off to Paris, something far beyond the wildest aspirations of most people in 1955.

In spite of the fear of the law and all the rest of the problems that went with his sexuality Tom did admit, but only to himself, that he was more than a little envious. The Cross he had tried to bear should have made him stronger but somehow it kept slipping; pulling him down as it dragged on the rough ground. He would not have dreamt of admitting to Michael but this constant battle with himself was dominating his life.

James was not religious. His family were barely nominal Anglicans. There is no doubt he would have reacted very differently had he been faced with a vindictive law. It almost seemed he had a charmed life but his was a world where being artistic covered a multitude of activities.

"Do you like the wine?" James asked.

They both agreed it was excellent. "I thought of you two when I bought it. So glad you like it. How's your mother, Michael?" He had stayed with Michael's parents when they were in the Services together.

"She has heart trouble. She can't get upstairs now."

"Poor darling. Give her my best when you write," James said and meant it.

"I will," Michael promised.

"I think she preferred you to me," Tom put in.

"I don't believe it, ducky." James laughed.

"It's true," Tom insisted. "She said you were a very nice young man. Just the sort of friend for Michael; and your parents lived in a detached house."

"Get you!" camped James.

"Not a thatched cottage."

"No need to ask why you are so at home in a cottage." A round of laughter finished that exchange.

They sipped the wine and then he went into a confidential mode and said very quietly, "I envy you two. You have each other. Gordon is good company but that's all. For me it's one-night stands."

In an attempt to change the subject, Michael hinted that James should show some of his photographs. This was dismissed with; "They are so boring, darling." But it did provide the cue to a confession. "Oh and by the way, and this is my great secret, I try to photograph all the cocks I have. Close ups. There is no way of identifying who they belonged to, of course! I develop and print the pictures myself."

This time there was no hint from Michael they should be shown the photographs.

James refilled their glasses. "I met that friend of yours, Denzil. He's very attractive and great fun. I thought it best not to refer to the nonsense he was going on with in the Salisbury. Do you remember? The night we went to see *The Boy Friend*."

Neither Tom nor Michael remembered. So much had happened since. James noted the blank looks and reminded them of the nonsense.

"Oh he was saying that if you were hauled up before the Law you should name everybody you've had, especially anyone prominent or well known. Balderdash! I have no idea why someone like Denzil should have said it. We have to live in the

273

world as it is. Not in a load of airy-fairy nonsense. What good is it going to do us if we have camp little badges saying 'I'm queer'? I am sure it's a lot more fun as it is. We are all in the big Club together with, of course, a few hon. members. And I deliberately said 'on' because there are a lot who are members only when they are off wifey at home. Need I say more? But seriously though, I can't see there is any need to get into trouble. I know I keep saying this because it's true."

Then he turned to Michael, "I know it is so much easier for me to be myself in my job than for you working in the head office of such a respectable food retailing company. What would happen to you if they even thought?" There was no need to finish the sentence.

Michael shrugged his shoulders. He knew only too well what would happen. There would be very little future for him. Only a week or so before the Ashley trouble blew up, on a particular Monday morning, a half dozen senior staff from the Meat Department were discussing their previous Friday night out in the West End.

It turned out to be quite an evening and was such a great joke that the whole office had to be told. The group walked through Soho, and everybody knows what happens in Soho. Several prostitutes accosted them. One or two were well built, if you knew what they meant. A meaningful nod and a wink and a nudge of the shoulder said exactly what they meant. Then the emphatic heterosexuals crossed Piccadilly and found, by the side of the Criterion Theatre, a flight of stairs leading down to a bar. At first sight it looked like any other ordinary West End bar. It was obvious to Michael they were talking about the White Bear. He guessed what was coming next but the rest of the office hung on every word wondering what sordid scene their superiors discovered. Michael closed his eyes and wished he was a hundred miles away.

"You are not going to believe it," the upper management said in unison. They paused and one, up and coming, member of the pig buying team flicked his wrist and wobbled his shoulders as everyone knew poofs did. He then announced the bar was full of queers, and when he said full he meant full, and when he said queers he meant queers. And it was only nine o'clock! Would you credit it? Only nine o'clock. Michael had left the bar, no more than ten minutes earlier! Had he waited those few minutes more. . . ? He thanked his lucky stars he had promised to be in the Salisbury at nine o'clock.

The prostitutes in Soho were O.K. but down in that bar surrounded by that lot was different. As one of the respected senior staff, the Quality Controller for Sausages, said, "I dropped a half a crown (more than the price of a drink) on the floor of that bar but I wasn't going to bend over and pick it up. I'd rather lose the money than take the risk."

Roars of laughter from most of the males in the office. Michael was too engrossed in his work to join in the hilarity or make any comment on the boys' night out. He and Tom had enjoyed the irony of it all, but that was before. . . . . It did not occur to Michael to relate the incident to James. It was so out of line with his mood.

A slightly embarrassed pause was quickly broken by James.

"Oh yes, and talking of your friend Denzil, which we weren't. He told me that John Gielgud is to keep his knighthood after all. All those silly rumours that it was to be taken away from him! There was no truth in them at all. Though I'm sure there were those who would have liked to have seen the poor man made to pay and pay dearly. I believe Frederick Ashton, the choreographer you know, said, 'He's ruined it for us all.' My god! If we'd all been caught there'd have be a queue from the palace right down the Mall and back again ten times over."

Neither Tom nor Michael reacted.

In October 1953 John Gielgud the famous Shakespearean actor, was arrested for homosexual importuning in Chelsea. He gave his name as Arthur Gielgud and said he was a clerk. He pleaded guilty and hoped the false name would provide anonymity. The morning desk sergeant tried to keep the story out of the papers by getting a duty magistrate to come in early but a journalist from the *Evening Standard* was in court. Scandal was predictable. **HOMOSEXUAL MENACE** was trotted out to reinforce public homophobia. Gielgud was appearing in *A*

Day by the Sea at the Haymarket theatre.

"You do know I was in the theatre on that night. I must have told you." James was hoping he had not told them as he was dying to repeat his description of the event. They both shook their heads. "My dears, I can't tell you!" But, of course he was going to. "As you know I always go to the theatre with my friend Julian. You've never met him. Going to the theatre is the only thing we do together, in case you think otherwise. We planned to go that night and why should we change just because he, of all people, got himself caught with his dick out? I was going to say with his trousers down but that would be carrying things too far. As I said, before I wasn't interrupted, we planned to go. Well, that was the problem. We always go in the gallery but because of what had happened, we thought twice about it. We reasoned that the gods would be full of louts who were there for one purpose, and one purpose only, to disrupt the performance and hurl abuse at Gielgud. They would be like a load of chimpanzees except that chimpanzees would have more intelligence. So we decided to spend another whole five shillings and sit in the upper circle.

This never got in the papers but, and my dears I do not lie, all around the back of the circle, I have no idea what it was like above or below but, as I said, the back of the upper circle was lined with policemen, in uniform, with truncheons at their sides. What they were planning to do with them I dread to think! Trouble was, obviously, expected. You can imagine what I felt like. As much as I wanted to support a sister in distress I was beginning to wish I had stayed at home. What could a poor girl, like me, do if that lot ran amok and with those weapons?

Anyway we sat there. Then the moment came for the disgraced star to make his entrance. I could not believe it. The audience erupted. I clutched my seat wondering what the hell was going to happen.

My dears, I could not believe it. He got a standing ovation. The entire audience stood up and applauded. It was unbelievable. It has to be the most thrilling, wonderful thing I have ever experienced. Gielgud must have been near messing his pants waiting to come on and them to be met with such a reception was beyond belief. It was wonderful and one in the eye for the *Evening Standard*.

When the applause died down I looked around and the police had gone. Julian said they had their tails between their legs but I think it was just their truncheons."

At that point James' flat mate, Gordon, came in.

He was well built, self-assured, in his late twenties. His personality filled the room without overpowering. James had found the right man. He was introduced to Tom and Michael.

"Pleased to meet you. I've heard a lot about you from James."

Gordon had barely a trace of an Australian accent. He noticed the wine and picked up the bottle. "A farmer I know is trying to produce wine back home in Australia. It isn't very good, but he's convinced he'll get it right."

James commented, "France is the only place that can produce good wine. It's a simple fact. Something to do with the soil and the climate."

"Some home-made wines can be pretty powerful," Tom added.

"But who's talking about country wines, ducky!" and with that James finished any further discussion on wine.

Gordon poured himself a glass. "Are you going to invite your friends to your party?"

"My party?" James queried.

"It is your idea," Gordon corrected.

"He's so modest this one," and James turned his attention to Tom and Michael. "Gordon is a pianist with a brilliant future."

"Oh, really," interjected Gordon.

"If I say you have, you have," James said with absolute authority. "We are going to have a party to celebrate his first public concert, as a professional, and it's going to be broadcast on the *Third Programme*."

"Congratulations," Tom and Michael said in unison. "When?"

"Three weeks on Saturday."

"Where?"

"The party is going to be here."

"What will you be playing?" Michael asked.

"Liszt."

Whilst Michael was asking about the music Gordon would be playing, James noticed Tom looking around the room.

"Are you looking for the piano?"

Tom nodded.

"My dear Tom, if you put a grand piano in here there wouldn't be room to swing a cat, as they say, and Gordon couldn't manage with less. I mean a grand piano – not a cat. Even a baby grand would be an insult. No darling, there is a studio, not far from here, where he can go and practice to his hearts content and one has to think of the neighbours."

The couple were so impressed they could think of nothing more to say. Gordon came to the rescue by changing the subject. "I know what James will have told you about Paris, but for me London is the place. It has opened up opportunities I'd only dreamed about, and as for meeting, how do you say it, 'like minded men' nothing could be easier. Last night I discovered Speakers Corner - Hyde Park - Marble Arch. I know, I've been told today the entire queer world knows Speakers Corner, but I only discovered it last night. I saw this crowd in the park so I went to see what was going on."

"The home of free speech." interjected James.

"You can say that again. Free something." Gordon nodded agreement. "Speakers holding forth from *'Come the revolution'* to *'The hour is at hand'*. It didn't take me long to learn that something was at hand. This old man, with enough charisma for six, was ranting on about the sins of the flesh and warning of the final judgement while half the men in the crowd were busy groping each other."

"Including you?" James chipped in.

"Only half-heartedly. The one next to me suggested we crossed the park where there were bushes, but I prefer the comfort of a bed."

"How boring." James said as he poured more wine.

"Then it started to rain so I went on my way empty handed if you must know!"

"Boring." James repeated as he put the wine bottle down.

"Oh, I shall go there again. A little later I did venture into the Welsh Harp, the pub not far from the Coliseum."

"Ducky, that's where you go if you want a guardsman." was James' retort.

"I had been told, and I thought I'd made it. He was holding an empty glass so I bought him a pint. He said I was a gentleman. Very flattering! Not bad looking, and he even detailed his physical attributes, size wise, which was probably a gross exaggeration. Then to my surprise he named his price. He obviously assumed I expected to pay. I pointed out to the guardian of Her Most Gracious Majesty that I was, in all probability, better equipped than he and undoubtedly better looking. So why should I be the one to pay? His reply was unprintable."

"And where did you spend last night? You most certainly did not come back here to the flat?"

"As I try to tell you, my dear James, though you will not believe me, London is an exciting city with endless possibilities. . . ."

Before Gordon could tell more, Michael looked at his watch and realised how late it was. He and Tom had to go.

It took almost an hour to get back to Camden Square. Nothing was said about Gordon's view of London. The question had to be, 'In future, how do we live with our friends?'

In an attempt to make conversation Tom said, "We didn't ask Gordon what time the broadcast will be?"

"I did think of it, but trolling was more important," Tom deliberately ignored Michael's icy tone.

RID ENGLAND OF THIS PLAGUE

Chapter 26

Day followed day as it always will, a boring fact, but for Tom and Michael the days and months that followed the trial were a constant struggle to find some kind of normality. Michael's transfer to the Personnel Department was offering him satisfaction and the possibility of a rewarding career, but Tom was still haunted by doubt. Was he wrong to abandon a career in the theatre for a sexless existence that was anything but fulfilling? As a young man in the village he had been able to put on shows and play in them but for some reason he could no longer find that kind of drive and confidence. He did get an interview with an agency looking for recruits, not just actors, to go up to Birmingham and work in television but he was so half hearted he got nowhere. Whatever talent had got him to R.A.D.A had gone. Several of his excolleagues were making a life for themselves in the theatre or television but he was lost.

Tom had told Michael little about his relationship with Ashley. Certainly nothing of their sex life nor that he had deliberately set out to free himself from Ashley's dominating personality. They came to London to have a future together. Now guilt from the past dominated their lives, and lying in their separate beds at night it became near unbearable.

They had lied to the police and kept themselves out of trouble and by doing so had not loaded more shit onto the head of Ashley. There had been no contact with him since the meeting in the Camden Town bar because he had specifically told them not to get in touch. Now the trial was over should they try and contact him, wherever he was? They had no idea which prison he was in. Would they incriminate themselves if they tried to find out? Would the police start asking more questions? But that was only part of the problem. They, or more precisely Michael, had rejected their sexual past and left platform sixty-nine and were now standing on platform one waiting for the fast train to heaven, but where was their relationship going? That was a question to which they were unable to find an answer.

Until the newspaper cuttings arrived they knew nothing of the trial - only the sentence. Michael had, deliberately, not read the paper cuttings before they were burned. He did not want to know what the judge had said of the man who had brought them together. He had glanced at them, but the details were more than he could bear, and he had not forgiven Tom for allowing Denzil to read them. They had made a promise that none of their friends were to know. Tom had broken that promise and Michael would not accept Tom's version of what happened. Denzil, of course, knew nothing of this and when the three met a couple of weeks later he felt free to air his views. Michael remained noticeably silent. Tom could not believe Ashley wished to be free of his homosexuality although he claimed it had dogged him all his life. Without prompting Denzil had given a credible explanation.

"Like being tortured, Ash must have been under tremendous pressure facing the certainty of prison. He was prepared to say anything to lighten the inevitable sentence. He pleaded guilty. The evidence against him was too strong and he did not want to subject those who had been his friends to more public humiliation.

'Take the line I am suggesting.' You can hear his solicitor saying it. 'Say you want to reform. I will add that you have never really liked the life you've led and even go so far as to say you are grateful for the opportunity that when you are released you will be able to seek a cure and start a knew life free from perversion. That will go down well with the judge.' On second thoughts the pressures could have made him believe it. Who would have said he was not wicked? I can understand anyone believing it in his position. You could say he was clutching at straws. What else could the man do? In the end it didn't help. The learnèd judge knew that such wickedness had to be punished, and an example had to be set to deter others who might feel they had the right to live their lives as their natures told them. Who makes the laws and why? That's the questions you have to ask. Learnèd judges, my foot! They administer laws and that is as far as their learning goes."

Denzil was intrigued by Ashley's double-barrelled name. Ashley had told Tom how it was acquired but Michael's short sentence, "Can't we talk about something else?" was all that was needed to make Tom stay silent.

To a large extent Tom understood Michael's feelings. They were much the same as his. Guilt, remorse and a feeling of being adrift in a world of uncertainty; but even in that world, one thing was certain, your sexuality had to be a secret if you were to survive.

Tom mused on the hyphenated name as he lay in bed that night. He had spent one Christmas with Ashley at his father's house in North Wales and noted that his father was simply Mr Jones and he, therefore, assumed the hyphen was an invention. However, when he checked Ash's ration book it did show, unmistakably, Ashley-Jones. He learned the whole story, on Boxing Night, after drinking some of Ashley's rather potent home-brewed liquor. The alcohol could be the blamed for Tom throwing discretion to the wind and asking why the double barrel, and also for Ashley admitting how it was acquired.

His mother, whom he adored, was an Ashley. The Ashleys were a prominent local family and they were not too happy when their daughter became plain Mrs Jones. His father stuck to the doctrine that a wife took her husband's name and as a sort of compromise their only son was given the Christian name Ashley. That had to suffice until the young man came of age.

As a very attractive young man he had ridden with the 'High Society hounds' and quickly proved his ability in the saddle. He rode well and could even have been likened to a stallion. It was whilst going over this in his mind that the thought struck Tom, Ashley had learned those hunting techniques so thoroughly, and applied them so well, that he now found himself in a prison cell because he had forgotten that the hounds he rode with, a decade and a half earlier, were themselves being hunted by a pack determined to taste blood.

In the thirties 'High Society' world a double-barrelled surname said 'Status', with a capital 'S', and it had to be the ultimate twenty-first birthday present that fitted Ashley's persona so perfectly.

The setting was a Ball at Grosvenor House, three years prior to the outbreak of the Second World War, when the hyphening took place. Ashley was three weeks short of coming of age. As he entered the ballroom he had to be introduced and the master of ceremonies, quite rightly, assumed no mere 'Jones' could be attending such a function so he bestowed upon the handsome young man a hyphen thus raising the Jones boy above the common herd and Mr Ashley-Jones was created.

This accolade was given legal status at a party in a house on Park Lane to mark the all-important twenty-first birthday. A gentleman of the upper crust, whose name Tom did not remember, but whom Ashley described as well placed and from the very best circles said, with the most fashionable clipped queenly campness, "Arise Ashley Ashley-Jones," A document was then produced to prove the legality of the name. As he said, "It gives a certain cachet to an otherwise plebeian nomenclature."

All through that summer of 1954, after Ashley's arrest, Tom dutifully went to church, but never again, to confession. The strains of his relationship with Michael had reached the point where anything as personal as sex was not mentioned and Tom had no more meetings with the Reverend Father. At times he felt he was being a hypocrite. There was no question of going to bed with anyone but he was making use of the cottages. In the privacy of a public convenience two or three minutes was enough. He never allowed himself to be touched. Logic should have told him exactly what he was doing, but logic didn't apply. He was in all probability only doing what numberless other males were doing to save a relationship either heterosexual or homosexual.

It was just before Easter 1955, almost a year after Ashley's arrest that Tom left the leather firm. It was largely Michael's idea. He felt Tom needed to make a new start. He was right. Tom was now certain he could not go back to the theatre. His thinking was in such turmoil that the concentration acting required would have been impossible, and Michael, who was making steady progress with the food company, was able to get Tom a job in the Meat Department. Michael had a week's holiday due and it was his suggestion they should travel up to his parents and have a complete break before Tom settled into a new life. They both needed it. They were only too well aware that things weren't right between them though they pretended nothing had changed. What else could they do? They were not willing, or able, to face the truth.

They would be back in time for Gordon's concert. Though it was mentioned so briefly it hardly seemed to matter. Tom thought it best to wait.

Michael's parents lived near Chester and within easy reach of the beautiful North Wales coast. Away from London they would be able to relax, and there would be no doubt about the warm welcome his family would give.

Tom was accepted as Michael's friend and he asked for nothing more. The week flew by. Unlike Tom's visits to Dorset, here no one knew anything of Ashley. The day before they were due to return to London Michael suggested a visit to Hawarden, the home of the Gladstone family. One of Michael's prized possessions was a mug given to the school children by the then Lord and Lady Gladstone on the occasion of George V jubilee. He wanted to show Tom the tomb of Mr Gladstone and the stained glass window in the Gladstone Memorial Chapel. The tomb completed in 1906 was designed by Sir William Richmond. The figures of Gladstone and his wife Catherine, carved in Carrara marble, lie in the boat of life beneath the angel-winged prow. With the window it is a mass of symbolism from Homer to the Cross and beyond. The visit was a welcome escape into the Arts and Crafts era. They both felt

284

they were beginning to live again.

It was late afternoon but still light as they walked the long straight road back to Michael's parents house. It was a couple or three miles but that didn't matter.

A car hooted and pulled up behind them. They took no notice. They knew no one with a car in that part of the world. The car hooted half a dozen times. They turned together to see who was making the noise. A well-dressed man was standing by the side of an expensive looking car. The driver's door was open and he was waving with one hand and pressing the horn with the other. They had no idea who was trying to attract their attention. Tom and Michael started to walk towards the stranger. They did not recognise him. He stopped pressing the horn and called their names.

"Hello, Michael and you Tom."

He obviously knew them but neither had any idea who this man in his late thirties and wearing a well-cut suit could be.

"Gareth," he said as he walked towards them holding out his hand. "You can't have forgotten me."

"Gareth?" Tom still wasn't sure.

"Gareth. We didn't expect to see you," and Michael took the outstretched hand.

It was then Tom realised it was Ashley's friend who had helped plan the boy friend swap that did not go to plan. But this person with whom he was now shaking hands was completely different from the one he had known five years previously. Gareth now gave every appearance of being a businessman with his purposeful walk and expensive Wolseley car. The bookshop business must be doing well.

"What are you doing in these parts?" Gareth asked.

"Visiting my parents for a few days," Michael said.

"Of course, you used to live near here. I only live a couple of miles away now. I've got a house in the village. I do this journey often. Been to see a client this afternoon. It's all been a bit of a waste of time, but never mind. As I drove up the road I said to myself, 'I know those two' but it wasn't until I got right up to you I realised who you are. Anyway, how are you?"

It was a meeting of old friends.

"We're fine. And you?"

"I'm fine." He looked at his watch. "Pity, we're too early for the pubs. It would be nice to sit and have a chat. Let's get in the car. We can talk there."

Michael sat in the front passenger seat.

"Nice car," said Tom as he got in the back.

"My father died last year. I've taken over the business. Branching out a bit."

The pleasantries over, Gareth eventually got around to talking about Ashley. Had Tom and Michael been involved? What had happened? Gareth listened intently as they related most of the events of the past year. The religious connection was carefully avoided.

Then Tom asked, "Were you involved?"

"No."

That simple word was followed by a long awkward pause. Obviously Gareth was trying to decide what and how much he should say.

"The police didn't come up here. Ashley would never have needed to write down my address. He would have known it by heart. The same with my telephone number. The police wouldn't have found anything to incriminate me when they searched the cottage. When he went back to Dorset after you two left for London we didn't have any real contact. Ashley got this Mrs Burton to take care of his father. She was an excellent housekeeper, I agree, but I have my own views on that. I looked after my own father - anyway we won't go into it. Ashley always did do what suited himself."

"What happened to the Estate Agency business? I take it his father wasn't able to run it."

"No, his health wasn't good enough. The Ashley family took it over. His mother was an Ashley. I don't know if you know the connection, the reason for his hyphenated name?"

Tom acknowledged that he did.

"Ash did contact me." Gareth went on. "Much as he did you. He telephoned twice, always from a call box. He didn't come up to North Wales. There was no reason why he should. I do have a contact who has kept me informed of the trial and everything. The whole thing was dreadful. It did not get into the local papers here. I have no idea what would have happened if it had. I went through hell. As you did."

Again there was a pause. The three were silent not knowing what to say.

"It was then I decided. . . . I reckoned I had run enough risks. There was the family. There was the business. . . . Do you know what I am trying to say?"

Tom and Michael nodded. Fear had made him rethink his way of life.

"Two people I know were caught in the GENTS in the riverbank where I met you, Michael. That's all in the past now. I do have a friend whom I see regularly. He's married so there isn't any problem."

Looking around the car Michael said, "Your business looks as though it's doing well."

"Can't complain. It's my main interest. I've two shops now."

It seemed that everything had been said. Tom looked at Michael trying to hint it was time they went. Michael took up the cue. He looked at his watch (the replacement timepiece) but before he could say anything Gareth interjected. "Did you know Ashley's father had died?"

"No," They said in unison.

"Five weeks ago."

"We have no contact. There was no way of knowing," Michael explained.

"Ashley was given leave from prison to attend the funeral. I must confess I wondered what might happen. I assume the two men with him were prison warders but they were in civilian suits and kept very much in the background. In fact they behaved very well. I was able to talk to Ash - privately. He told me quite a lot. I think he needed someone to talk to.

The prison sentence was devastating. Ashley's pre-war years were very different to mine. His mother encouraged him to live it up with the upper crust. Then suddenly the established order he had serviced so well had, viper like, turned and bitten him. I know that sounds a bit graphic but that's the only way I can describe what happened. It was difficult for Ashley not to feel some sort of bitterness. If he serves his full sentence he will be an old man, getting on for fifty, before he is released."

Gareth became silent, gazing through the windscreen, along the road and into the far distance. Then he spoke again in a very matter of fact tone, "Ashley always had a remarkable ability to adjust to the situation in which he found himself and he did discover one redeeming feature in his confinement. Prison life did not entirely stop men from doing what men have always done together.

Two things did weigh heavily on his conscience. Firstly his father. When he returned to Dorset, after you two left for London Mrs Burton, the housekeeper, was left to look after his father whose health was not good. From Ash's point of view it was an arrangement that worked since he and his father weren't getting on too well together. But, as I said, I have my own views on that. He'd been in jail for about six weeks when his father had a stroke. Ash said he could not escape the fear that he might have been responsible. Then there were the others who were dragged into the trial. Could they be blamed for giving way to pressure? Or was he responsible for the problems they now faced? They had all willingly had sex with him and enjoyed it, but would it have been better had they never met him?

He told me the whole business; the others who'd been dragged in churned though his brain as he walked round and round the prison exercise yard each day. Such monotony replaced the treadmill. His words. The sun only ever got down into one corner of the prison yard. Round and round he tramped with the other prisoners, in and out of the shadows. That was their daily exercise. Ash remembered being in the pool of sunlight and holding his head up to the sky enjoying the few moments' warmth. The prisoner behind him spoke, 'If you'd gone for girls instead of young men you'd have been a bit of a lad and you wouldn't be here.'

Two more steps and he was again in shadow. But back to the funeral; chatting together we had wandered away from the main group of mourners. It wasn't deliberate. I was just so interested hearing what he had to say. He was coming to terms with things. He reckoned he had every chance of getting full remission on his sentence. As I said, we were so engrossed we were unaware how far we'd gone. Quite suddenly we were confronted by his two guards. They couldn't have thought he was trying to escape - we were just strolling. One of the guards called his name and went to step in front of us. Ash reacted faster than I did. To be perfectly honest I didn't even see what was going to happen. Ash did. He grabbed the man. He was a big bloke. Ash got him with a rugby tackle that would have done credit to any one in the national team. It's funny now when I look back, but at the time, I was terrified.

This warder or guard, whatever he was, was about to step into a half dug grave. Ash had pulled him back and saved a very embarrassing situation. They fell together. What that bloke thought with a convicted homosexual lying on top of him is beyond belief. I helped them up. Neither were hurt, except for the guard's pride.

It all got a bit confusing after that. The guard was more concerned with making sure nobody saw what happened. I saw a reporter from the local paper not far away and thought, 'Oh dear!' As, I think, I said the case had not been reported up here. Thankfully it had been kept quiet. What would have happened to my business if it hadn't doesn't bear thinking about. And there was just a straightforward report on the funeral in the paper. It even said Mr Jones' son came up from the south of England to attend his father's funeral. That was true and it avoided telling the whole truth. Ashley's uncle, his father's brother-in-law has a lot of influence up here. That possibly had something to do with it. The Ashley family would not have been at all happy had any scandal even been hinted at.

And another thing, and I don't think I was meant to hear this, Ashley assured his guard the incident would not be mentioned. Without a word they shook hands on it. Ashley is no fool. The other guard said something about a grave mistake, which I thought was an unnecessary pun and not in very good taste. But there you are."

Tom wondered why they were being told all this. Was it that Gareth wanted to get it off his chest? He must have talked non-stop for a good ten minutes.

"I hope I'm not boring you?" Gareth asked. They assured him he wasn't and so he went on. "All in all it's been a difficult time. You have to be very careful in a small place like this. That's why, I say, I don't run any risks now. This chap I see, it suits him and it suits me. Being married nobody thinks anything. It's different for you in London. I don't suppose you know anyone in your street. You don't have gossip to contend with. You are lucky, from what I hear, you can get away with almost anything."

That's the picture the papers paint Tom thought, but he said nothing.

"Oh, don't get the idea I was the only person Ashley spoke to. He chatted to the mourners he knew, as if nothing had happened. He was his usual charming self and it worked with the guards which has to be all to the good. He did mention something about an open prison. What he did say, and I am certain this applies to you two, he would rather serve out his sentence without the risk of involving any one else, meaning us. The police aren't beyond raking up any muck they can if it suits them."

"What do you mean?" Tom asked.

"Don't contact him. It's safer. And, I think you had better forget everything I've told you."

Gareth then started the car and said he'd drive Tom and Michael home. He thought it more convenient to drop them on the corner a couple of hundred yards short of their destination. They understood and it suited them. It was easier to give the impression they had walked than explain their connection with a local businessman since it was certain Michael's mother would want to know all the details. High tea was waiting when they got in. Michael's sister was an excellent cook. Her cakes were always a treat. The whole scene was so homely that the episode with Gareth could be pushed aside. A family around a table having tea was reality.

That evening they went, with Michael's father, to the workingmen's club. Plenty of beer and matey chat. The union had negotiated a pretty hefty pay rise for the local factory and that meant another pint all round. Things weren't so bad. One man, as he swallowed his beer, calculated how big their pay packets would be in ten years time since they were certain to get the same rise every year.

The expletive, 'Bugger me, we'll be rich! This country is a bloody good place to live in,' summed it all up. Michael looked at Tom and they smiled to each other. A few more pounds in your pocket and everything will be fine. They joined in the laughter and raised their glasses to the future. No one noticed the hollow ring as their beer glasses touched. Who in that group would have understood? In spite of the fact that more than one must have played around, they would have seen no reason to change the status quo. After all there was another pay rise to look forward to next year.

Good conduct was rewarded. Ashley Ashley-Jones was transferred to an Open Prison and got full remission. How much his sealed lips covering up for the guard, who nearly put his foot in it, history does not record. But there is a touch of bitter irony. In the mid twentieth century, seemingly light years away from the hypocrisy of Victorian Values, Ashley spent more time in jail than the gay icon Oscar Wilde.

.

RID ENGLAND OF THIS PLAGUE

Chapter 27

The day of Gordon's concert arrived. Tom and Michael enjoyed the broadcast. Gordon was very talented, even through their poor quality wireless, the sensitivity of his playing was unmistakable. The Speaker's Corner and the Welsh Harp episodes were forgotten in Michael's admiration for Gordon's interpretation of Liszt, especially the Liebestraume and the Impromptu in F sharp major, but it wasn't until they were actually leaving that Tom was sure he and Michael would get to the party.

Michael had rejected the homosexual world. He was in limbo. Superficially his life with Tom had not changed. There was no suggestion that they should part; but the basis upon which their relationship was founded had been torn away. It was now locked up and hidden deep down, as if dead, in the catacomb below the confessional in Margaret Street. Tom was beginning to fear the key to the burial chamber had been thrown away and lost forever. They never kissed and only rarely touched. They did not confide in each other and never mentioned how they were trying to cope with the sexual side of their natures. Frustration. There was no escaping the signs; short tempers, irritations. Tom hoped against hope the party would ease the strain; there they would be amongst old friends drinking and laughing. Nothing else was likely to be suggested.

Only once since James and Gordon had given the invitation had Michael even mentioned the party, and then it was a simple short, "We will have to see."

Gordon's escapades were never referred to. Over the four years they had been together, Tom learned there was a sealed world into which his lover could retreat. It wasn't sulking. It was as if his mind and thinking became trapped in a cage where each bar had been carefully welded so closely, since childhood, that once inside it was almost impossible even to put a hand through to ask for help. Now, in their world of fear, Gordon finding it funny to be groped at Speakers Corner and saying he was more attractive than a guardsman added yet another bar to the cage.

Michael's world had stopped that spring morning when the dairyman's wife saw the two police cars pass her window before the sun had risen above the hills behind the village of Lower Budleigh. It now seemed there would never again be rays of sunlight to warm his love for Tom.

By late afternoon on the Saturday of the party Tom was exasperated. "Are we going, or aren't we?"

"You go," said Michael and after a pause he added. "If you want to."

"Not without you." There was silence. "We need to go out." Tom was speaking almost to himself. He turned to his lover, "Oh Michael. . . ." He wasn't able to finish the sentence for the simple reason he had no idea how to voice his feelings.

They looked at each other then Michael gazed out into the garden. Tom sat on his bed and looked at the floor. Michael turned, "Alright, we'll go."

They dressed. It had to be suits and ties for this party, it would not have occurred to them to wear anything less. All the guests would have to look their best. Tom thought back to the days when getting ready would have been almost as much fun as the party itself.

Tom looked at his love. If anything, he had been in greater danger than Michael. The police must have been told what he'd done. There must have been enough confessions signed and dated to fill half a dozen C.I.D. files. He looked again at his love and prayed silently that the trouble was over.

What in God's name was keeping them apart?

He would not dare admit he knew the answer. He touched Michael but there was no reaction.

They would go by trolley bus to Camden Town and then by Underground to Earls Court.

When they arrived, the party was in full swing. The flat was crowded. The best description of the revelry had to be 'Terribly respectable high camp'. Not a word, and most certainly not a hand, out of place.

It was a parade of models of the female fashion variety all longing to be admired by Gordon's music student friends, plus a number of more mundane Tom and Michael types. The upper echelons of either fashion or music were foreign territory to both Tom and Michael but they had sufficient social skills to be part of whatever conversation happened to be buzzing in their immediate vicinity.

It was a Martini-sipping cocktail party. What could have been smarter than delicately holding a glass in one hand and a cigarette in the other? It has to be said, that a great deal of expertise was required to flick, oh, so nonchalantly with the index finger, ash from the end of the cigarette into an ash tray at least two feet away; particularly if the cigarette was in a long elegant holder as many were. In fact, it could be quite dangerous in such a crowd. One had to avoid having one's eyes gouged out by burning fag ends. Tom's pipe was quite unacceptable. It was labelled a nasty smelly thing though, often, one couldn't see across the room for cigarette smoke.

James swept aside any reference to his work. This was Gordon's party and praise for his playing was euphoric.

Chatter about nothing and laughter at anything made for a marvellous party and they couldn't have liked it more! It was all very self-consciously High Anglaise Camp.

A willowy beauty, male, a friend of James surveyed his friends and enemies alike with disdain through half closed eyes. His ultra slim waist and rhythmic hip sway when even standing motionless screamed a performer of a talent yet to be discovered. In white tie and tails, with a tray in one hand, it was difficult to know whether to ask for a drink or pretend you were Ginger Rogers and ask him to dance. His talent for dancing was obvious with every step he took, and that for dispensing cocktails displayed itself in the delicate flicks of the wrist. The tray of glasses that swirled, terrifyingly, above the heads with never a drop slopped was an entertainment in itself.

Michael was smiling, chatting to a bevy of leggy beauties (female). His beautiful dark brown eyes were alight. He was so gorgeous. Tom emptied his glass and wanted to throw it up to the ceiling and shriek. Life had begun again. He felt so relieved. There was going to be fun again in their lives, and exactly on cue to his mood he heard, "Tom Adamson! How wonderful to see you."

It was Laurence, a fellow student from his R.A.D.A. days. Laurence had got himself into television. Television was the thing of the future. It was where the work was going to be. Tom carefully avoided saying what he was doing. Planning the butchery of pigs for pies and sausages was hardly the subject for such a piss elegant party.

Laurence reminisced, "I remember the first voice production lesson. We each had to read a short piece. Angela was terribly plummy and upper class. That had to be corrected. I had a common-as-muck flat 'A', but you launched into the Ancient Mariner sounding like the fruitiest farmer I'd ever heard. I loved it."

"You may have loved it," Tom tried to sound haughty, "but Hugh didn't. 'With an accent like that', the eminent elocution teacher said with great disdain, 'the only parts you will ever get are comic ones.' So I practised and practised."

"Now you sound like all the rest of us from that illustrious voice-production machine."

Then Laurence changed the conversation. "You were at that party where we aspiring stars were queuing up to let that old queen of an impresario get his hands on us?" It was a half statement and half question.

"I didn't get anywhere," was Tom's reply.

"Neither did I," Laurence laughed. "He didn't fancy me. He was after something of your build. Unlike Mae West he wanted the six-foot and the seven inches. I may have the inches wrong but you know what I mean. You would have been his type. I'm surprised you didn't try."

Tom shrugged his shoulders and sipped his martini. It wasn't the time or the place to explain. An invite to that particular party had been engineered on the assumption that Tom knew the ropes and was ambitious enough to exploit his good looks and virile enough to perform on the casting couch no matter how awful the other half of the double act. Sadly he let his sponsor down. Tom remembered the scene where the would-bees were clustered around the honey pot prepared to sting anyone who got in their way. The impresario queen bee regally accepted the homage as of right. Tom decided he couldn't be bothered. He left the party, went straight to the Queen's Head in Chelsea, picked up a very good looking out of work actor and finished up with a dose of the clap. A shot of penicillin put that right and there is no need to look for a moral in that twentieth century Aesop fable.

Most of their conversation was unmemorable but Laurence did pass on one interesting piece of gossip about the Gielgud arrest. Neither needed the background filled in. They both knew the great actor had been arrested for cottaging. James had given a graphic account of the actor's reception in the theatre.

Laurence was very friendly with the Drama Academy's stage director. It appears that shock waves from the great actor's exposure rippled all the way up Gower Street and almost caused a tremor in the voice-production classes. The stage director was called into the office to be questioned as to whether any of 'that sort of thing' went on among the male students at the R.A.D.A.

"Oh no, no, no, no. Heaven forbid! Even the thought is too too." There was not the slightest hint of campness or piss take in his voice.

"Glad to hear it." was the relieved reply. "You are in a better position to observe the students, being much closer to them, as it were, than the other tutors and lecturers which is why you can help. Such behaviour would destroy our reputation and one dare not contemplate such a situation."

How could the stage director possibly disagree?

"Keep a very close eye on the toilets on the first floor. That is where, if the information is correct, such activities start."

Since he had always kept a close eye on such activities it wasn't difficult to agree. He could also say with complete honesty that such things did not go on in the toilet. There were lots of far more comfortable places in which to have it off.

Tom was laughing so much he could hardly speak. "I hadn't heard that one before but I'm prepared to believe it. One of the cast of a production of *Twelfth Night* went on stage in tights but without a jockstrap! Forgetting his lines could not have been worse than giving the audience an eyeful." and almost as an afterthought Tom added; "Oh yes. You remember Evelyn White the very grande dame with so many theatrical connections?"

Laurence nodded.

"It was the day the news about Gielgud's misdemeanour broke. She was shocked. 'I can't believe it,' she said 'I thought that sort of thing had all been sorted out with Oscar Wilde!' "

"Didn't you win a R.A.D.A. Scholarship?" Laurence threw in as an afterthought.

"I couldn't have afforded the fees if I hadn't."

A friend of Laurence's joined then and the conversation, fortunately, moved onto television and careers. Tom listened politely for a while, made an excuse, then moved to another group.

By nine o'clock it seemed the candles had guttered. The party was ending; after all it was a cocktail party and the martinis were running out. The model girls and their escorts were saying their, "Good-bye darlings. So wonderful to have met you. Must fly. We shall be dancing till dawn. The Hammersmith Palais? How could you! Nothing less than Grosvenor House, if you please."

Carriages were not called as one might expect. It was Underground to Hyde Park and then the last couple of hundred yards by cab. After all, one had to arrive in style! Their escorts either giggled with the girls or looked too utterly bored. The London season was over and the Sloane Rangers had not yet saddled their horses, but it was fun pretending whatever you were pretending to be.

Soon only the host's intimate circle was left. It also appeared to be nearly time for pretty boys to hurry off to bed; theirs or some one else's. The old adage could apply, 'If you are not in bed by eleven, go home.'

"It's about time we went," Michael said and Tom agreed. They tried to find James to say goodbye but the dining room was a scene of great hilarity. A tray of empty glasses seeming to float through the air came out of the room and under it was White Tie and Tails.

Tom asked, "What's going on?"

"Come darlings," and he gestured they should follow him. "Your auntie will tell you, but let me get rid of this bloody tray before I crown someone with it. Mind you, some of these queens here tonight do need to be crowned. As I said to dear Norman, Norman Hartnell, you know, the Queen's dressmaker, as he was dressing this morning, and I am not a name dropper, darling I said, isn't it time you finished my frock. All I have to wear is this old thing. I know I look frightful but it does give a touch of class. Do agree!"

As W.S. Gilbert put it, many years earlier, 'The meaning doesn't matter if it's only idle chatter. . . .'

White Tie put the tray in the kitchen and gathered around him the remaining guests who were not in on the joke in the dining room.

Then he began to explain what the laughter was all about. Tom looked at him. This was a different person. The high camp had gone. That was an act. An act he could turn on and off as the situation demanded. There was no doubting the seriousness in his voice now but with it went a wry very individual sense of humour.

"Once upon a time, and this isn't a fairy's tail though by the time I've finished you might think it is. Once upon a time Gordon sat opposite a young man on the tube. Not any young man, I assure you. This was a blond blue-eyed Nordic god. Their eyes met, and I do not exaggerate, you could have heard the clanging the entire length of the District Line. Gordon should have got off at Earls Court but by just sitting still he seemed to be getting off O.K. if you get my meaning!" (Laughter from the group of guests and thanks from the speaker for an appreciative audience.) He continued. "After what to the uninitiated, would have appeared to be searching in one's trouser pockets for loose change, they did get off - and they also left the train and walked out, maybe not hand in hand but one could say 'Hand in glove'." (Groans, dismissed by White Tie with a flick of the hand.) "By now they were friends and in order to find out the lengths to which they could go, or how much they might be expected to take," (More groans and this time an apology) "Sorry, I'll put it another way; how intimate the friendship should become they decided to go onto a bomb site and, in the pitch darkness, see if they could handle the situation that had arisen." (Laughter this time. The speaker raised his hand and shook his head) "There, I am sorry to tell you, the fun ended. In less than five minutes they found themselves being marched off to the police station and charged with committing an indecent act."

Silence. He waited for the full impact of what he said to sink in. "Well, what can I say? Anyway, to cut out all the boring bits I went to court to give Gordon some support, and by sheer coincidence the press reporter was a friend of mine. We had a little chat, as old friends do, and he decided that a mere music student wasn't news. Oh he, my reporter friend, is so sick of listening to all this crap day after day. He'll have to pack it in before he goes out of his tiny mind. He left the court one day and couldn't remember where he lived. He even had difficulty, and I do not joke, remembering who he was. But to get back to the tail in hand." He tried to illustrate the pun by stroking where the tail would be, but the joke fell flat.

He shook his head seemingly at a loss for words. He moved over to a table. Sat on one corner, one foot on a chair, and leaned forward with both hands on his knee as he looked down at the floor. Then looking up he said very quietly, "The policeman said he saw these two males go into the bomb site, then the lying sod swore he shone a torch on them and saw what they were up to. Gordon says there was no torch, and I believe him. They had their arms around each other. They were kissing, but the copper could not have seen it. Not in a million years. And, I ask you, why should two men kissing be a crime? When challenged, the magistrate said bluntly that he knew whom to believe. He knew who would tell the truth."

White Tie straightened himself and stood up, collected the rest of the glasses scattered around the room, and more or less speaking to himself said, "British bloody justice! A liar believed just because he was wearing a copper's uniform. At worst they were guilty of trespass on a bombsite. Something has got to change. Something has got to happen. We defeated and destroyed a corrupt and unjust Nazi Germany." He snorted a kind of sardonic laugh. "Gordon's pick-up was German. I ask you; what message has Heinz taken back to Hamburg about the victors? A kiss and a twenty pound fine."

By this time he had finished clearing glasses. Guests were beginning to move from room to room as others were leaving. Tom and Michael found their hosts to say good night and thank them for the party. Rather than interrupt a conversation they listened. The topic was different from the previous one on British justice. It was on Australian weather! How did summer in Sydney compare with summer in London? Tom knew he was never likely to go to Sydney, but it was a relief to talk about it.

Suddenly White Tie reappeared from the kitchen. Camp was back in fashion.

"Ladies and, if by mistake, there are any gentlemen, I want to propose a toast to our hosts. Oh silly me. I've cleared all the glasses away, and there isn't any bloody martini left even if I hadn't cleared the glasses. But why should a mere detail like that stop us? Raise your imaginary glasses. I am told it was Doctor Spooner, who at Oxford, intended to say, 'Raise your glasses to the dear queen (and I am not implying that would be appropriate here) but actually said; 'Graze your arses to the queer Dean,' not that that would apply tonight. So do whichever takes your fancy but thanks to James and Gordon."

Invisible glasses were raised. "To James/Gordon and Gordon/James." The order was immaterial. Then came the surprise. "I propose we put money in a hat to help pay the fine. To show that we are with you, Gordon."

One of the guests Tom and Michael did not know and whose clothes were quite wrong for a cocktail party stepped forward to speak. He was wearing American jeans that made him look like a cowboy. This was not a fancy dress party. He simply shouted, "Shit!" as he disappeared into the bedroom.

Gordon and James both stepped forward to speak but they didn't get a chance. They were stopped with an imperious wave. "Hush the pair of you. I haven't finished. It seems wrong that all your tinkling of the keys, Gordon, should have to go to pay that rotten lot who ought to be in jail themselves."

Gordon then did get a word in, "I appreciate the thought."

That was all he was able to say.

The wearer of the Levis (purchased in New York and sailed across the Atlantic in one of the Queens) came back into the room.

"Sure as hell Gordon would not want us to turn him into a charity, but to show that we are one hundred and one per cent with him and that kissing a guy sure ain't wrong." There was no doubting the accent that fitted his clothes; "I may not have been in your country long but I've learned my way around and gotten to know one or two of your institutions so I have here the perfect receptacle." He flourished a chamber pot above his head. "Gordon had to explain what this thing was. Now, I invite you all to contribute one penny. It may not seem much but pennies have been known to open doors to all sort of things."

(One penny was the charge for opening a cubicle door in a public lavatory. Cubicles designed for the relief of one were large enough to accommodate two, and often did. It was the price of privacy.)

"I'll take the pennies," said Gordon laughing. For that he got a round of applause.

"Thank you. I am at a loss for words," he mumbled, then as an after thought said, "I feel I am keeping up the family tradition. My great great great grandfather had his passage paid out to Australia in the early nineteenth century but we don't talk about that. Nobody would, would they? But I am going to. Legend has it, and it's a good story not to be repeated in decent company, that it was for pissing against the wall of a bridge somewhere in the West of England. I don't believe it but you could say they've made me a convict for much the same thing."

Tom put two pennies in the jerry. One for himself and one for Michael. Michael nodded and forced a smile. When he could get near his host he told him he could confirm the possibility of his ancestor's conviction. On one of the bridges leading out of Tom's Market Town is a cast iron notice proclaiming:-

*'Any person injuring the bridge will be guilty of a felony
and liable to transportation for life.'*

Tom was sure he had the wording near enough right. He
had crossed the bridge hundreds of times. Gordon vowed he
would go down to the West Country and photograph the
plaque. The party began to break up. Getting something to
eat was next on the agenda before doing the rounds of the
queer bars.

A couple of the guests, acquaintances of Tom and Michael,
said they were going on to another very different party in a
mews in Maida Vale. It would certainly be O.K. for all four to
go together.

"What sort of a party?"

"Do you need to ask?"

The mews party would have been of great concern to those
charged with ridding, or simply, containing the plague. *The News
of the World* or *The People* would have revelled in the goings on
and, even more, in the cummings off within a discarded
underground ticket of Maida Vale Tube Station. It was hinted
that whilst most of the partygoers would be drinking and
chatting, odd, not to say queer, couples would sidle off into one
or other of the bedrooms.

It is doubtful if any judge would have been able to hear the
evidence, so thick would the disgustingness have been that it
would not have penetrated his wig but, no matter, the hosts
would have found themselves in jail.

Tom and Michael did not take up the invitation.

The irony of the evening was that after the glasses were
washed and the flat put more or less straight, Gordon left with
the Yank; White Tie had to return the full evening dress he had
borrowed as it was needed for a late night cabaret show. Poor
James, who had instigated the party, was left to get his own
supper and go to bed exhausted and alone.

The first part of the journey back to Camden Square was
made in virtual silence. While they were waiting for the trolley

bus at Camden Town Tom asked, "Enjoy the evening?"

"You did," was Michael's answer. Then, when they were on the bus Michael added, "I hope this doesn't affect Gordon's career."

"So do I," Tom agreed.

"He's a good pianist."

"I just hope everybody keeps their mouths shut," Tom commented.

Gordon's brush with the Law was a 'no go' subject and he had found, to his cost, London was not the city he eulogised when they first met.

Tom felt it was one of the most bizarre evenings he had ever spent. To keep talking he added; "You seemed to be enjoying yourself chatting to the models."

"I don't know about enjoying. Had to say something." It was said almost in a monotone. Maybe Michael was tired.

Tom hoped that at long last Michael was coming out of his shell. Tomorrow things would be O.K. again.

Chapter 28

Back in their room Tom asked, "Tired?"

"A bit."

They didn't kiss or touch.

As they undressed Tom said, "It was almost like old times."

"Almost." One terse word from Michael.

They went to bed.

"Good night."

"G'night."

Then there was silence. Lying on his side Tom could just make out the form of his lover in the other bed. His hopes that the party would clear the air were obviously wrong so he turned onto his back and gazed up at the ceiling.

The little light that came in through the windows turned the ceiling into a starless night sky. Did he have to face the fact that things would never be the same between them? He closed his eyes. Such a thought was unbearable. It would be a bitter irony if they had escaped prosecution only to see their love destroyed.

The establishment would have won and the future would be a blank. In that insect infested wood in North Wales he had not fallen in love. Michael had taught him the difference between sexual attraction and love as they grew together. Please God, the reverse was not happening. Eventually anxiety was lost in sleep.

Next morning was Sunday but there was no suggestion of going to church. That had to say something was very wrong and Tom needed, desperately, to know what it was. He needed some sign from Michael to make him believe the dark period of fear was over, and that the party marked a new beginning.

He stood looking out of the window at wind-rattled fencing. The weather had changed telling him the English summer, like his hopes, could be an illusion. Large drops of rain splashed, pebble like, against the glass in the flashes of sunshine. Clouds broke and closed. Sunlight and shadow zipped across the garden. The rain paused. Nothing was stable.

"What's up? What's wrong?"

"Nothing. I tell you nothing." Michael's flat tone belied his words.

"I'll make a cup of tea." Tom went over to the sink and picked up the kettle. There was no point in just standing looking out of the window at the forever-changing light on the static garden.

Tom desperately wanted to create a scene. He wanted to shout, to do something. The silence was stifling. He wanted to act out his emotions. The great writers, great minds, portrayed and illuminated the human condition with what were claimed to be real characters who all, bloody, talked. Lecturer after lecturer had analysed Shakespeare, Ibsen, Shaw - the list went on. Tom had studied them all. He had a degree to prove it. They all explained their emotions. O.K. they could shout, quarrel even be violent but you knew what they felt and thought. Such great minds, such great writers could not be wrong.

Then, what the sodding hell was wrong with the world he lived in? Two people who had loved now found their love suffocating in silence. Tom needed to clear the air. He opened the window but the wind shrieked. Nature made itself heard.

"Close it," demanded Michael.

The rattle of the sash window drowned Tom's frustration. He went back to the sink to finish making the tea. In desperation he broke a cup. "Bugger!"

"There's no need to swear," Michael said as he went towards the door. "I'm going for a paper."

Left alone Tom walked back to the window, to the ever changing sky and his own confusion.

It was to the Almighty God, whose word had shaped

their thinking from childhood, that they ran for shelter when the tornado swept across the landscape. It may not have spun their entire world into oblivion, but the debris was there for all to see. Tom had now to live in a world where the certainties were unanswered questions. In a world where he was labelled sick or sinful when all he asked was to live at peace with he whom he loved. It was little enough to ask but the wind still rattled the windows.

They had begged for shelter when the storm struck. Shelter had been given. Why? That was not for him to ask. Now that the storm had abated or even passed, he was beginning to realise they could not leave the shelter together.

There could be no doubt Michael still loved Tom. Tom also knew Michael could never express his thoughts. Michael had told him how he had grown up knowing little boys should be seen and not heard. When he was seven his grandmother shut him in a dark cellar for interrupting adults. That was lesson enough to make anyone stay silent.

Whatever Michael felt about his sexuality the serpent of sin still hissed in his face. Wanting to be free of it all was no help. Where was freedom to be found? Chanting our miserable sins did not cut out the forked tongue.

Could any ranting from Denzil change thousands of years of religious teaching? But why did they love as they did?

They had been together four years. Most, of which, had been a virtual honeymoon. The film script for an age yet to come. The cottage - a rural retreat - Tom's scholarship to the R.A.D.A. - sought after - handsome youngsters new to the London scene - now reality - awful reality. A reality rapidly becoming totally unreal.

Michael was so long getting back with the paper that Tom wondered where he had been.

"You've been a long time?" The question from Tom brought no reply.

"Where've you been?"

"In the square with the paper."

"It's trying to rain."

"That's why I came back," Michael said implying had the

306

weather been fine he would have stayed out. Then he pointed to the table. "You have spilled your tea."

"It was your tea. I made it for you, but you walked out. It's cold." Tom threw the tea in the sink.

"Don't break another cup." Michael's tone was ice, and Tom deliberately smashed the cup.

"What's the matter with you?" Michael asked, shocked at Tom's violence.

"Everything," was all Tom could say.

"There's nothing I can do about that," and Michael sat down with the paper.

As with so many rows the quarrelling had little to do with the cause, nor was there any logic in what they were saying. Then almost in tears Tom asked, "What's gone wrong?"

"Nothing has gone wrong with me." There was silence for a while.

Michael sat in one of the armchairs apparently reading the paper but had Tom watched him closely he would have seen his lover's eyes were glazed staring into nothing.

The silence was solid.

Ten, fifteen, twenty minutes may have passed. Then the silence was broken. Staring at the paper Michael seemed to be reading aloud, "You would have gone to that party at Maida Vale last night if you'd had half a chance."

Tom did not appear to even hear the accusation. He carefully cleaned up every scrap of broken crockery. Cleaned all traces of spilt tea. Put the kettle on. Waited for it to boil. Then made fresh tea and put a cup beside Michael.

"If you want to think that, then think it. Drink the tea. Don't let that cup get cold."

"I didn't ask for it." Michael said without moving his eyes from the paper.

"Drink it!" Tom raised his hand, thought better and let it drop. He walked away and sat at the table.

Michael picked up the cup. Then very slowly put it down. Again he could have been reading from the paper. "We turned to God when we were desperate. The Church gave us support. You can turn your back on it. I cannot." The next sentence was not spoken. He had mocked the choirboys. They had returned to mock him. "We made promises. Perhaps they mean nothing to you."

It was impossible to walk out from the shelter of the church. That needed no explanation. It could not be done. A few days earlier Tom had criticised a specific Anglican doctrine. Michael turned on him.

"Who are you to question the Archbishop of Canterbury?"

There was no answer Tom could give. Michael had to be right. Large drops of rain hit the windowpanes. The clouds thickened. Now there were no flashes of sunlight.

"Michael had to be right. Michael had to be right." No matter how many times Tom repeated it to himself nothing altered. When he climbed the stairs at Queensway he knew he could not live the life demanded of him. He was only human. He was almost ready to curse the power that had shaped his desires and his needs. Denzil also had to be right and so had White Tie.

For Tom, caught in the cross fire of so many certainties, there was only uncertainty. But of one thing there could be no doubt; he and Michael were no longer free to live the lives that had given them fulfilment.

"You wanted to go to the Maida Vale party." Michael folded the paper and put it down. Tom knew what he meant. He had no intention of giving any answer. The implication was that now the Law was off their backs, Tom wanted promiscuous sex. He wanted to go back to a world they had accepted as wrong. It was useless to say he would not have hurt Michael.

As if acting by impulse Tom crossed the room and lifted his suitcase from the top of the wardrobe. He put it on his bed then leaned on it thinking. He heard one of the tutors at R.A.D.A. say; "You will never make it in the theatre if you stay with Michael."

Leave him!

Leave him!!

Tom had never analysed the statement about his career. It was so easy to say 'Blame Michael' but that would have been less than a half-truth. What his tutor did not say was; if you are going to make it in the world of the theatre, you have to see yourself as the only person who matters. You have to put yourself and your career first. Others are there to support you. Their relationship had not developed that way. Tom was now agonising for in his heart he knew that life without Michael was the very last thing he wanted, but he could see only a meaningless future if he stayed.

Michael picked up the paper. He tried to read, Tom could see that, but he could only guess at Michael's thinking. Of one thing Tom was certain; the man he had loved was demanding more than he could give. Their abortive attempt at lovemaking said everything. The pressures of the past few months were turning Michael into an automaton. He seemed unable to think beyond the immediate. Tom watched as Michael stared at the paper. His eyes and his thoughts seemed locked, unable to move.

"I shouldn't have broken the cups. I'll pay for them," Tom said as if saying that was an explanation for getting his case.

"What are you doing?" Michael asked.

"What does it look like?"

"I have no idea. I am reading the paper," Michael said without making the slightest movement with his head.

"I'm going. I'm leaving. I've had enough." As soon as he began to speak Tom felt he was delivering lines in some hack play that would never make the West End. He was being forced to go on and give a good performance. God only knows what was forcing him. It was as though all the clichés ever written had to be spewed out, but no words came. He dried. The ultimate disaster for an actor. He'd forgotten his lines.

"What the hell has happened to us?" was all he could say.

"You should know." Michael continued to stare at the paper. "You didn't answer my question."

"What question?" Tom asked. His tone was deliberately antagonising.

"It doesn't matter now." Michael's words were not only a lie they were also a challenge.

"I am going."

"So you did hear!" Sarcasm was now Michael's weapon. "Where are you going?" he asked.

Tom had not thought that far ahead. How could he admit it? So he said, "That's my business."

Michael wanted desperately to say, "Stop. Don't go." It may have been pride that stopped him. He didn't know. He did know that fear was driving him, God alone knows where, and he did not even appear to be conscious of the fact that Tom was taking clothes from the wardrobe. "You would have gone." Tom stood still holding a pair of trousers. He was sure he had heard Michael accuse him again over the party, but Michael had not even moved his lips. The party had taken on a life and a meaning in line with any newspaper sensationalism. If that was Michael's thinking then Tom had no choice. Tom folded the pair of trousers. He touched the zip. The zip that had turned them on so much when bought new only a year ago. It will never happen again. He knew how strong Michael was. If he could not break a promise to a man, how could he break a promise to his God? But what of himself? Tom put the trousers in the case. He smoothed out the creases. Then impulsively screwed them into a ball and jammed them into the corner of the case. Temper and frustration was being taken out on his clothes as he pushed and twisted them into the case. He looked again at Michael. Fear of violence made him close his eyes as he punched the clothes.

Again he could hear Denzil and White Tie, but above them, the voices of learning told him they were wrong; yet through it all one camp and one rebel voice said, 'No. You neither are a sinner nor are you sick.'

Outside the wind had risen. Tom could hardly hear himself think. But did it matter? He knew he could not live with Michael any other way than as lovers. The physical attraction was too strong. Where he would go or what he would do hardly mattered. But he wasn't thinking. Lumps of half ideas pounded his consciousness. Lines for a slanging match wrote themselves. Minor wrongs, false accusations piled up like rocks to be thrown smashing one's love until it bled to death.

He looked at the man he had learned to love. Michael had

no molten rocks of burning hatred to throw.

He believed Michael's faith had to be a straight broad road that led to the sunlit uplands but now, even though the wind had dropped as suddenly as it had risen and the rain was easing off, he seemed to be in a maze built of solid high stone walls with no hint of any way out.

Tom spoke stopping that train of thought. What he was about to say was devastating. "I've known for several weeks that I cannot live this way. I cannot live with you. I cannot live with you just saying good night. What the hell does 'good night' mean? You can say it to anyone. I've been through hell and out the other side. If being queer is my cross then I have to admit I cannot carry it. Call me weak. Call me what you like, but I cannot live this way. It's no good, Michael; it's no good. We shall end up hating each other. You look at me as though you feel sorry for me. I don't want anyone to be sorry for me. If my father can try to understand me, then so can you, and so can everybody else."

He stopped the flow of anger. Thoughts piled up in his head. Disorganised thoughts that would be meaningless if spoken. For weeks he had been trying to understand and come to terms with what had happened.

He turned his back on Michael and sat on his bed with his head down and his eyes shut. He had believed that the man on the underground train had actually been the devil incarnate. The devil had been put there to temp him, to test his commitment.

He repeated to himself, "I believed it. I believed everything I was told. I believed that man had been placed there by some divine power to test me." Then he banged his fists on his knees. "I believed it until I saw him again in the men's department of Selfridges Store in Oxford Street."

He shook his head. What could he do? He wanted to tell Michael. He wanted to tell the man he loved he could not believe he was so wicked.

"I just want to live. I just want to be happy with you." his words were inaudible but he heard in his head, "Ask anybody in the street what should happen to queers." There was no need to wait for the answer. He banged his head again he had to stop

311

his brain spinning. He was abandoning logic. There were his parents. There was Mrs Urbano. They cared.

He closed his eyes and tried to reason. It was Denzil who had forced him to try and think for himself, and it didn't take much thinking to realise he lost all sense of reason in that crowded train. He had done the same thing as his imagined devil, more than once, when he had been pushed against someone he fancied. What was happening, and why couldn't he tell Michael?

He had to say something. He had to speak. He stood up, half turned to face Michael but, instead, turned back and banged the door. "Don't tell me that they are all chaste at that church. Chased! They deliberately stand still to be caught. I wouldn't have gone to that other party last night. I wouldn't have hurt you. Please believe me. What have we got? Nothing. You are not happy, neither am I. Being together is not making us happy any more. I thought James and Gordon's party, last night, would put an end to all this. I was wrong. There is no point in going on pretending. You barely speak to me. I might as well not exist. It will be better for both of us if I am not here."

Tom could only see Michael's silent staring at the newspaper as sulking, stubbornness, moodiness or a refusal to even try and accept what had happened to their relationship.

"Why is sex with each other a sin? If we hadn't wanted it, we wouldn't be together. I can't believe what happened in that pub four years ago was wrong. I want to believe we were meant to meet." Tom blurted. They were words he hadn't even thought. Words that came from gut feeling.

There was no reaction from Michael. The silence confirmed Tom's worst fears. He was wrong. He was so very wrong, but he was never to know Michael's thinking. Michael was never able to voice his inmost thoughts. Being shut in the cellar as a child had robed him of that ability. To understand what was destroying them it is necessary to try and look behind the wall of silence. Denzil would argue that all homosexuals should stand up and be counted, but for

Michael that was not an option. He valued his family too much to put them in the firing line of homophobic abuse. His mother, particularly in her present state of health, mattered more to him than any right to live his life as he would wish.

It was not simply a question of religion, though that had a direct bearing since it was a fundamental part of his upbringing. In order to be able to live with the man with whom he had fallen in love he had lied to his mother. Not just a simple lie, he had woven a web of deceit that at the time seemed clever and expedient, but now he was enmeshed in the lie that had become his life. The lie that he was not queer. The lie he was acting out at work was something he could have handled but the greater lie to his family was forcing his mind to close against any form of reasoning.

Michael adored his mother. He owed her so much. She ruled the household and set the standards. Honesty was fundamental. She made him return a penny when the local shopkeeper had made a mistake in giving change. He had been dishonest about his sexuality, but what choice did he have? He could not live the life his mother knew had to be the only right way to live. Tom was accepted but only as a friend. She could not have even begun to understand her only son. Was he at fault? He had enjoyed his late teenage years discovering his sexuality, but that life was in direct conflict with his love for his mother.

His parents had worked to pay the fees to enable him to attend the local grammar school. He knew his mother would have, dearly, liked him to stay at home until he married. He went to Dorset to escape marriage. Was he beginning to wish he wasn't queer?

He turned his head and looked at Tom who was gazing at the floor and biting his fingernails. He looked at the dark hair now tousled, not the neatly combed waves of the aspiring handsome actor, and he did not notice Tom close his half packed case and lean on it.

One doubt haunted Michael and it had nothing to do with sex. Had he undermined Tom's belief in himself as an actor? Michael knew he had not gone into raptures over any of Tom's performances but that was because the person on stage was always his Tom. It was too late to turn the clock back. Michael had had enough flings with budding stars, including one big name, to know he did not want his Love to develop an ego that demanded constant admiration to survive. He wanted the man who had made love to him in the insect infested wood. He did not want the world of artificial glamour. He had fallen in love with a warm West Country accent and wanted nothing more than that handsome sexy speaker.

Tom reopened his case and continued to pack. Michael suddenly became aware of what was happening. He had heard Tom say he was packing and he had heard him say he was leaving, but they were mere words. Now those words had taken on a meaning. The packing seemed to take ages. Michael tried but could not make his mouth form words, nor could he make his body move.

Eventually the packing was done. Tom held the lid and stood motionless and did not notice that Michael had found the will to fold the newspaper. Momentarily the rattle of the paper attracted Tom's attention but he saw nothing. He was deliberately cutting himself off, thinking only of what he should do next. He wanted to leave nothing behind. For days he had been afraid that the break was inevitable. He didn't want to contemplate the future. The whole world had turned over. It was time to begin again.

The two men seemed totally unaware of each other's existence. Tom shut his case. He could barely understand his own motives. Analysing and explaining them to Michael would have been impossible. He did know he had changed. Playing Hamlet was no longer a goal. Michael may have had something to do with it. He thought again. Michael had everything to do with it. How could he say anything? It would only sound as if he were blaming the one he loved for his failure. Had he failed as an actor? He lifted the case and banged it back down on the bed. Had he thrown away his training? Did it matter? He no longer wanted the constant moving that the acting profession demanded. He no longer wanted always being somewhere different. He no longer wanted always being someone different. He did not have whatever it takes to be an actor. It had taken him until now to learn he did not have the killer instinct to make it to the top.

He wanted nothing more than to be able, each night, to hold and love the gorgeous ex-airman who had faced him when he opened the pub door. The beautiful brown eyes who had slung in his job and travelled to the other end of the country to take on a new life with someone he had known for only a couple of weeks. Michael who had followed him on to London and, for the second time, made a new life.

He looked at that person before he picked up his case to leave.

Michael's case was open on the other bed. Tom had not even seen him take it from the top of the wardrobe. He could now only see his back, the shoulders, and the waist. For a while they were motionless. Then they moved and Tom suddenly became aware that Michael was looking in the wardrobe.

"What are you doing?" Tom asked.

The reply was muffled, absorbed by the hanging clothes.

"I said what are you doing." Tom repeated.

Michael turned but did not look up. "Packing." He almost whispered the word.

"Why are you packing?"

"I'm coming with you."

An echo from the bus station in Chester four years ago.

315

EPILOGUE

Ashley was transferred to an Open Prison and given full remission. Tuckers, the cottage at Lower Budleigh was taken care of and used for weekends and as a holiday home for the four years Ashley was in jail.

It was early 1959 when he returned.

He never could resume his old lifestyle, but he was not going to be beaten. An old contact helped him get a job with a firm of seed merchants that involved travelling around the county to various farms. He very quickly made contact with Tom's parents' who accepted him and asked no questions and never made any reference to the case or his life in prison.

Tom went down to Dorset and met Ash. They spent a day together calling on customers in the north of the county. Poor old Betsy had been laid to rest. Ash had a new car, but, as he said, it wasn't the same. To the best of Tom's knowledge Ash had no farming background but he did his homework and was able to earn a living as a seed salesman.

He gave no indication of bitterness. It was now over. He talked very little about prison life, except to say he became resigned and made the best of it until he got out. He was still able to give the appearance of self-confidence but the four and a half years had taken their toll.

As to his future? Ash shrugged his shoulders, "Something will come up."

Almost twelve years had passed since that meeting under the Town Hall. It was not an easy day for either of them. They carefully avoided any reference to the past. Their relationship had long since burned itself out. Tom was not invited back to Lower Budleigh. Ash was keeping a very low profile.

They kept in touch for a while but after telling Tom's mother his father's estate had all been settled he left Lower Budleigh.

However, that was far from the end of Ashley Ashley-Jones. Amongst the Christmas cards, a year later, was a specially printed card wishing them a happy Christmas and signed Ash. It was from Palma, Majorca. The wording simply said, `Recuerdos de Mallorca´ and an address. It gave no other details.

A month or so later a picture postcard arrived saying, very simply, that he had opened a small Guest House/Hotel; presumably with the money his father had left.

The postscript was the important part of the letter.

Getting started again. Wish me well.

It is also worth recording that, in later life, Denzil wished he could confront Mr Justice Goodfellow and Lord Kilmur with a very simple question, "The law has changed so are we still pests and creatures that need to be purged?"

Denzil also challenged the argument that it was the thinking of the day with another question. "Did they think?" He argued they were simply regurgitating and processing accepted dogma as the established way to rise into positions of power and influence. The judge would have, undoubtedly, claimed he was interpreting and administering the law, ignoring the pronouncements that brooked no question. The politician knew he had been elected to his position of power and it was his duty to protect the moral fibre of society. Both would claim to think, but what is the definition of the word?

Neither Tom nor Michael were in the least bit impressed when the Wolfenden Committee was set up. The committee lumped homosexuality and prostitution together. What was there to hope for?

The couple stayed together as lovers but the Establishment had done damage. Experience had told them that nothing could change. Attitudes set over centuries had hardened into a bombproof cover over a large chunk of society. As far as they could see this Parliamentary Committee had no big guns. The best they would be able to muster would be a couple of peashooters.

But with time the damage was repaired. Things did

change. Tom and Michael's relationship was accepted by their families. This was made very clear when Michael did not accompany Tom to Dorset to discuss the selling of the family cottage on the grounds that he was not family. Mrs Adamson was furious, "He is family and don't you ever do that again."

Michael steadily climbed the promotion ladder and was well on the way up when he was told by a colleague that his relationship with Tom had been the subject of a discussion at a coffee break in the office. The matter was emphatically closed by a member of staff, a mother of two, who surveyed the group and with a look that left no doubt to whom her remarks were addressed said, "They may be gay, or whatever word you care to use, but they've made a better job of living together than some."

Half a century after the setting up of the Wolfenden Committee Tom found himself walking across Piccadilly. The pavements were crowded. Thousands were watching. He was almost at the head of the Gay Pride march. The White Bear and Wards Irish House had long since passed into history. He stopped. This was a different world. He was helping to carry a banner for a gay outdoor group and within twenty paces of him marched the Gay Police.

Things had changed. In spite of his early misgivings the 'peashooters' had put one in the eye of the Old Established Order. A registered same sex relationship carries the same rights as a heterosexual marriage. Denzil could love an eighteen year old without fear of a knock on the door and a nude male photograph would not land you in jail but, do not forget that around the world there still echoes, "Gay. . Sex.. . Sin."

As the Pride March reached Trafalgar Square another member of the group took over the banner from Tom and he walked towards Whitehall, able to look around and become absorbed in his reflections. He looked at the people lining the route and said a silent 'thank you' for having lived long enough to be there.

Though he had given up smoking fifteen years ago he still possessed the pipe that may, possibly, have helped save him from arrest. Was the fact that he and Michael were spared facing a learnèd judge, who would have called them perverts or pests, simply because they did not fit a stereotype? Or did the police believe he had cured himself of the plague? Whatever the answer, did it equate with his knowing the groper on the underground was the devil incarnate? Brain washing! Tom smiled to himself as he thought; is manipulating attitudes a thing of the past?

He didn't need to be reminded just how regularly the media carried the views of powerful religious and political figures around the world who are far from gay friendly, but why spoil the day with such thoughts? He then realised there was still some way to go, and they had to pass Westminster before the Gay Pride March reached the Embankment and they could claim it was all over.

There is a future but as the young Tom learned; 'The past is only just over your shoulder'.

At a Campaign for Homosexuality Equality Conference in the seventies Glennis Perry said, "Freedom isn't just won then automatically kept. It is only kept by constant vigilance."

Printed in the United Kingdom by
Lightning Source UK Ltd., Milton Keynes
140375UK00001B/6/A

9 781904 585084